The Sav

Elizabeth Darrell

This novel is dedicated to all British flying cadets who trained in Florida between 1941 and 1945, to their hosts who offered Southern hospitality, and to the Rotary Club and the American Legion of Arcadia who every year hold a memorial service for twenty-three cadets who lost their lives during training and who are buried in the British Plot of the local cemetery.

I hope those men who were at Carlstrom Field between June and August 1941 will forgive me for putting fictional events and characters into what is really their story.

Table of Contents

Shot Down

Smith got the chop last night, I watched him go,
A fiery streak across the savage sky:
Burning and breaking up, a crimson glow,
A fearful, searing, bloody way to die.

He only joined our flight a week ago,
A timid little chap, devoid of fun,
And ill at ease deep down, quiet and slow,
No time to make a friend of anyone.

Last night a fighter jumped him, belching fire;
The Mossie shuddered, then blew up and spun.
Smith spiralled earthward in his funeral pyre,
Another grieving mother's only son.

Group Captain J R Goodman DFC and bar, AFC
A Flight Lieutenant with No 627 (Mosquito) Squadron,
Pathfinder Force, Bomber Command RAF 1943-44

Chapter One

It was a day of driving, icy rain when Robert Stallard was called to London to identify the bodies of his parents and grandmother killed in an air raid that had flattened two entire streets near the docks. Numbed by shock, Rob followed an elderly man wearing Red Cross armbands, who reverently pulled back the blanket covering each corpse and waited for a nod of recognition. The most terrible aspect of it was that some faces were virtually unrecognizable, and Rob shook his head without being absolutely certain of the denial.

They had reached the last row laid out in the hall of a working men's club where rain dripped through the roof damaged by a previous raid, when the man uncovered a face that was familiar. Rob stared at the stiff white features of his mother and waited for them to smile at him the way they had for eighteen years. He waited for her eyes to open and glow with warmth on seeing him.

'Son?' A gentle voice prompted him, and he nodded without taking his gaze from the grey curls thick with dust and splinters of brick. They should have brushed her hair. Someone should have done that.

Fred Stallard's body was separated from his wife's by those of two strangers. There was dried blood on his forehead, and dirt streaked his weatherworn cheeks. He did not look as serene as Mary Stallard, but then he had not in life. Rob said hoarsely, 'They should be together ... side by side.'

'I'll see to that, son, now that we know.'

They moved on. Gran was right at the end of the row. Rob could not take his gaze from a face that seemed to belong to someone twice her age. The pallid skin was heavily wrinkled across sunken, hollow cheeks, and her chin protruded as if in a caricature. From somewhere came the explanation that Gran would not have been wearing her teeth in bed. They would be lying somewhere in the rubble of Benedict Street. It bothered him that Gran was not complete.

A hand took his arm. 'Let's go into the office and have a cup of tea while we talk about the formalities, shall we?'

Rob resisted. 'I can't just leave them there.'

'That's what we're going to talk about.' The hand gently urged him forward. 'It won't take long, and you need something to warm you up. Come on, lad.'

As he stepped over the grey humps once more to reach a small room beside the entrance, Rob thought blindly that if only Gran had agreed to live with them all in Somerset when the raids began, his world would not have come to an end.

The effects of shock lasted throughout the funeral held at Thoresby village church, and while Rob dealt with the necessary legal matters, including a claim for compensation for Gran's house and possessions. He was helped with this by his employer, Sir Charles Guthrie, who had known the family for many years. It was while trudging home through the dark lane at the end of his working day, just a week before that sombre Christmas of 1940, that Rob's numbness melted. All at once, the icy chill of coming night seemed to slide in on his indrawn breath to enter his lungs. Aware of an unbearable sense of being the only person left in the world, Rob began to quake with an alien fear. Stopping beside a five-barred gate, he gripped it until his knuckles turned white. He and his father had walked home together so often, but he could not now remember what Fred Stallard had looked like. He could not picture that stern face. Nor could he visualize his mother's or Gran's.

Panic welled up inside him. All he could see were grey humps laid out in a freezing hall where rain came through the roof. None of them had a face. Racked by sobs, he bent forward across the gate moaning over and over, '*Why?*' Lost to time and place, Rob only knew that the terror rioting through him gradually changed to a burning desire for revenge.

When he eventually arrived at the stone, thatch-roofed cottage he was chilled to the bone and every part of his large frame ached, but he had allowed his grief full rein and had made an irrevocable decision during the expression of it. Leaving his muddy boots and waterproof in the stone-floored scullery, he walked through to the kitchen where a fire was burning in the large range and the smell of rabbit stew filled the small room. Rob stared at the empty chair his father used to occupy and sensed his disapproval of what he meant to do.

His sister entered from the parlour. '*There* you are, at last. Wherever have you been? Supper was ready an hour ago.' She looked at him closely. 'What's happened? You look terrible!'

'Do I?'

She took one of his hands. 'You're frozen! What've you been doing to keep you so late?'

He gripped her fingers with his icy ones. 'Jen, I need to talk to you very seriously.'

Jenny's green eyes grew wary, and she moved away, saying briskly, 'Eat your supper first. There's plenty of time to talk.'

'I'm not hungry.'

From the stove, she said with forced brightness, 'I never thought the day would come when you'd say that.'

'And I never thought the day would come when half our family was lost overnight.' He saw the pain in her expression as she swung to face him, and he went to her. 'Sorry, I didn't mean to hurt you. I did some thinking on the way home. I ... I suppose it all suddenly caught up with me.'

Jenny was immediately sympathetic. 'It had to sooner or later, Rob. You've been so splendid. I don't know what I'd have done without you to shoulder the burden and provide a prop for me to lean on. I've done so much crying over the last month, but you've coped with everything without once giving in. You're as human as anyone else. We all knew you couldn't go on much longer.'

He turned away, unable to confess even to his sister that he had sobbed like a child a short while ago. His father had ruled that men never gave way to emotion and Rob already felt ashamed of that moment of weakness. It was an additional reason why he avoided looking at Fred Stallard's chair when he said, 'I've decided to volunteer for active service.'

Jenny immediately protested. 'You can't make a decision like that now. You're too upset to think straight.'

He shook his head. 'I've made up my mind.'

'But you can't give up your job on the estate. Sir Charles needs you.'

'He simply needs a farm manager to replace Dad.'

'And *you* have. It's what Dad always wanted.'

'But not what *I* wanted. You know my heart has always been set on being an engineer. Dad and I had enough rows over it.'

Jenny sat on their mother's usual chair and gazed at him unhappily. 'Dad worked his way up from cowhand to farm manager. He was proud of his dairy herd and the way he ran the estate. I think he sometimes thought of it as his own ... something to leave to his son.'

'I know, I know,' Rob said heavily. 'And Mum worked her way up from parlourmaid to housekeeper, but you're as happy working at the manor as she was.'

'I have plans,' Jenny said with a touch of defiance. 'Mrs Brumby is firmly installed as the new housekeeper. That's not for me. I intend to be Lady Guthrie's secretary one day. My shorthand and typing lessons are for a purpose.'

Rob seized on that. 'Lady Guthrie told me at the funeral that you'll have a job at the Manor for as long as you wish, even after you marry Phil. I think she guessed I might leave. And I'm sure Sir Charles does, too.' He perched on the corner of the scrubbed table to add gently, 'There's just the two of us now, and you'll marry Phil when he comes home on leave. You'll have babies and start a new family. That leaves me out on my own to do whatever I want.' He sighed. 'Dad was pleased and proud when I became the first boy from Thoresby to win a scholarship to Darston Grammar, but he still expected me to follow in his footsteps on the farm.'

'A lot of fathers want that, Rob. It's not unusual.'

'And a lot of sons have different ideas about what they want to do. Dad only agreed to let me take a night-school course in engineering because he didn't believe I'd manage it, after working all day at the farm.'

'None of us thought you would,' she said frankly. 'I felt so sorry for you cycling to Darston Chase four nights a week, and spending so many hours in your room when the rest of us were out enjoying ourselves. Why did you?'

'To get some qualifications.'

'But you haven't yet,' she pointed out with a hint of pleading. 'Wait until you finish the course before making any decisions.'

Rob walked to the kitchen range and squatted before the red glow to warm his face and hands, knowing he must try to make her understand what had happened to him tonight. Gazing at the vivid coals, he said quietly, 'I can't forget those blanket-covered bodies. Some were children, Jen. Mere babies. I need to hit back. My two years of study can be put to good use in the forces. It might not be much in the full scheme of things, but I can't stay here doing nothing. You must see that.'

Jenny arrived beside him, and he stood up to find she had tears on her lashes. Drawing her close he murmured, 'It'll be a while before they call me. By then you'll be married, with Phil's parents to keep an eye on you.'

'I'm so sorry, Rob,' she said against his rough jacket. 'I do understand ... but I'll worry about you.'

He held her away and forced a smile. 'I won't be in the front line, silly, I'll be messing around with engines so that others can go out and be heroes.'

*

Five months later, after suffering the additional shocks of RAF discipline, communal living and frequent bombing of the airfield and nearby industrial towns, Aircraftman Robert Neil Stallard was stunned to find his name on a list of men selected for pilot training. He stood before the notice board certain someone had made a serious mistake.

'What's up? You look as if you've seen a ghost,' said a voice beside him.

Still staring at the selection lists, Rob said, 'I don't want to learn to fly. I'm halfway to being an engineer.'

'I'm halfway to being an accountant, but it's no use dropping a load of invoices on the Jerries, is it?' came the cheery response. 'Looks like we'll be taking off into the blue together. Name's Bradshaw.'

'I'm not having this,' Rob declared angrily. 'I was persuaded to volunteer for aircrew to become a flight engineer. I'll ask to see the Wingco.'

'Won't do you any good.'

Bradshaw was right. The request for an interview with the Wing Commander was refused, and Rob saw instead an ageing squadron leader in charge of selection who told him he was in the RAF to do as he was told, not what he fancied.

That evening he went to the NAAFI to drown his sorrows. Fred Stallard had believed in sobriety at all times, so his inexperienced young son became roaring drunk very quickly. He was helped back to his hut by his amused fellows, loudly vowing to punch all squadron leaders on the nose. He felt so ill in the morning that he was put on a charge for rendering himself unfit for duty. The experience put Rob off beer for ever, or so he thought at the time.

A week passed and those selected for pilot training were given leave before departure on a secret posting. Rob made a six-hour journey home in crowded trains, then trudged from Darston Chase with his heavy pack, conscious only of the familiar smells and sounds of home. As he walked he felt a sharp pang of revived grief, and a sense of culpability that put a lump in his throat and remained until he reached the door.

Jenny practically hurtled from the cottage to fling her arms around him. 'I've been watching since six o'clock,' she cried. 'What've you been doing?'

'Changing trains four times and getting held up by air raids for the last stage of the journey. How are you, Jen?'

'Very happy to see you. I've a rabbit pie with greens and carrots. I hope you're hungry.'

'I could eat a horse.'

'Rumour says some people already are. Isn't it terrible!'

As soon as he stepped into the kitchen Rob was once more stricken by a sharp sense of loss. He realized that the past months in different surroundings had held it at bay, but his sister had been here alone with all the painful memories. He dropped his kit, deeply affected by the emptiness of that room which had once been used by a complete family.

'I've grown used to it,' Jenny said quietly. 'It's hit you again, hasn't it?'

He slung an arm round her waist, his sense of guilt returning. 'I'd forgotten how it feels to see those vacant chairs, that's all.'

'Don't be sad. You've only a few days and we must make the most of them.' She looked him up and down. 'Fancy you being a pilot. I know you're disappointed about the engineering, but you never dreamed you'd fly an aeroplane, did you? It's set the whole village talking.'

'It's nothing special.'

'Of course it's special!' she said indignantly.

'I'll probably fail the course.'

'Don't you dare! I bragged about it to everyone after getting your letter. Go and wash while I put the vegetables on. I've had hot water ready all evening.'

As Rob ate a hearty meal, comfortable in shirt sleeves and braces, he broached the subject of Jenny's future. 'It was a blow when Phil's leave was cancelled. I was expecting you to be married by now.' He put down his knife and fork, bringing his feelings into the open. 'I shouldn't have gone off like I did without making sure you'd be taken care of. Admittedly, I never thought they'd call me so soon after my application, but I was confident that Phil's folks would keep a close eye on you for just a few weeks. It's turned into *months*. I feel bad about it, Jen.'

'Don't be silly!' She rose abruptly and crossed to the range. 'There's rhubarb and custard for pudding.'

'What does Phil say in his letters?'

'You know how it is. He can't tell me where he is, how long he'll be at sea, or when they're likely to get home.' She returned with a bowl of stewed rhubarb and a jug of custard. 'He's been away so long I've forgotten what he looks like.'

Rob frowned at his sister's tone. 'It's not his fault.'

'I know, but the wedding dress has been in the wardrobe for so long I'll never get rid of the smell of mothballs. I wish I'd waited before asking Mrs Tolworth to make it. I don't like it now.' Then she added, to Rob's dismay, 'I'm not even sure I still like Phil. His letters are so formal he doesn't sound the same person. And he never puts anything loving at the end.'

'They'll all be censored. I expect he finds that awkward.'

She glanced up from pouring custard. 'I think we shouldn't have got engaged so quickly. Everything's changed and I don't want to be married in a hurry.'

'But I only joined up because I thought that's what you were going to do. You can't go on living here on your own,' he cried.

'Why not? I've done it for five months. Lady Guthrie has asked me to do some secretarial work for her in the evenings. Just letters for various charity committees. I've got a typewriter in the parlour, and I go to the meetings to take down the proceedings in shorthand. It's ever so interesting, Rob. I really enjoy it.'

Rob ignored his rhubarb and custard. 'So poor Phil has had it, has he?'

'Of course not,' she cried, but without much conviction. 'I just think we should wait until the war's over and see how we feel then.' She pushed custard aimlessly around her dish with her spoon. 'You've made a new life for yourself. Why shouldn't I?'

'No reason at all. You seem to have it all worked out,' he said heavily.

'Rob, you mustn't feel responsible for me. You're not. Anyway, you're going to be too busy learning to fly.' She rose to fill the kettle. 'Let's have tea while you tell me a bit more about it.'

Rob felt weary and heavy-hearted. He could almost hear his father castigating him for abandoning Jenny and the Guthries. It was coming back to this cottage, of course. Everything in it was the same as it had always been. Why had Jenny not rearranged the furniture? That empty chair beside the range disturbed his peace of mind.

A hand waved back and forth between his eyes and the half-eaten pudding in his dish. 'Where are you? I hope you won't go off into another world when you're flying an aeroplane, Robert Stallard.'

He glanced up at Jenny's teasing words. 'I'm very tired. Do you mind if I go to bed? We'll have a good talk in the morning.'

'Yes, go on. Leave all your dirty washing outside your door. I'll put it in to soak tonight because I've got to go to the Manor first thing with a couple of typed reports. I'll be back by ten. Lady Guthrie's given me the rest of the day off. Sleep well, Rob.' She kissed his cheek. 'And don't worry about me. I'm a grown woman, and we Stallards know how to stand on our own two feet.'

*

The days flew as Rob slipped back into the old life again. He chopped a mountain of wood to store in the lean-to, secured hinges on doors, cleaned out drains prone to clog up, dug and planted out the vegetable garden, and dealt with a few outstanding matters concerning his parents' and grandmother's deaths. While his sister was at the Manor he changed the kitchen furniture around. She made no comment on her return.

On Rob's third morning he walked up with Jenny to pay a courtesy visit to his former employers. Mrs Brumby greeted him warmly and soon returned with a message from Lady Guthrie asking them both to go through to the morning room. She rose from her desk as they entered and offered Rob a well-manicured hand.

'How good of you to come, Robert. My husband will be in directly. He's on the telephone to the Ministry again.' She made a face. 'Villains, every one of them, if he's to be believed.' As they shook hands, she said, 'You look extremely smart in your uniform. How are you enjoying your new life?'

She waved a hand at a chair, and Rob waited until she was seated before he perched on the edge of it. He never felt at ease in what he thought of as the private area of the Manor. The office was fine, even Sir Charles's library, but huge chintz-covered armchairs and side tables with spindly legs worried him.

'I've been so busy I haven't had time to decide if I'm enjoying it or not, ma'am.'

'I suppose you've had to learn so much in a very short time,' she said with a smile. 'I think you are all so splendid leaving your homes and jobs to train as airmen in just a few weeks. Jenny says you're to become a pilot. Congratulations.'

'It's not certain. I may fail the course,' he said hurriedly.

'I shouldn't think so. You did so well with your engineering studies you're certain to grasp what's needed without any problems. Has Jenny told you of the invaluable work she's doing for me in her spare time?'

Before Rob could comment, Sir Charles entered and approached with a broad smile. 'Robert, how good to see you.' He shook Rob's hand very heartily. 'What splendid news. I'm delighted for you. Delighted.'

For the following half-hour Rob trudged the familiar fields with Sir Charles and Jack Morrison, the new farm manager, forgetting he was dressed in air force blue and no longer part of the farm he had known all his life, but when Jack went off leaving them to walk back to the house Sir Charles became warmly personal.

'You did the right thing, Robert. You always had your sights set higher than the pastures. I like to think that your father could have been persuaded to see it once you qualified. You'd have made an excellent farm manager, but your heart wasn't in it. A man has to follow his instincts to be truly happy. If I'd had a son ... well, it's no use thinking along those lines. I know flying isn't exactly what you wanted but it's no small skill you'll be undertaking, and when the war's over it'll stand you in very good stead finally to embark on your chosen profession. Keep that in mind, and take care of yourself when you get up there.' He

17

prodded his cane skywards. 'Call in before you go back. There'll always be a welcome here for you, lad.'

Rob walked back to the cottage pondering the fact that everyone but himself was thrilled about the notion of his being a pilot. It was not until later, as they sat outside after a meal of stew and apple pie, that Rob got around to confiding his news to Jenny. It was a perfect spring evening with stars just becoming visible in the milky sky, the only sounds being those of woodpeckers drilling in the nearby copse, tractors returning from the fields, and dogs barking to greet their masters at the end of a wearying day. Rob felt a sense of *déjà vu* rather than one of belonging. It was all so familiar, yet he had moved on from it. Birds flew overhead with wing flurries as they sought final titbits for their hatchlings before nightfall, and the cherry tree smothered with blossom, together with wild honeysuckle, filled the air with heavy perfume. Rob compared this against the nightly bombardment of factories in the town adjacent to his camp. The people of Thoresby should be grateful for their peaceful haven.

'You're quiet,' said Jenny from beside him on the old wooden seat.

'Remember when we all used to sit out here; Dad smoking his pipe, Mum darning, and us lying on our backs counting the birds as they flew to roost?'

'We had Rusty then.'

'Why don't you get another dog, Jen? He'd be company for you.'

'Yes, I might. You could teach him Rusty's old tricks when you're on leave.'

He turned away from the serenity of the pastoral scene he knew so well. 'I shan't be coming home for a while, I'm afraid. We haven't been told officially, but we're all pretty certain we're off to America as soon as we get back to camp.'

'*America*!' She stared in incomprehension. 'There's no fighting there. They're not even in the war.'

'We were told this is embarkation leave, and our destination is more fact than rumour.'

'It doesn't make sense,' Jenny declared. 'Why would you be sent there? Men have been learning to fly in England for years.'

'Yes, of course they have, but the Jerries made such a mess of our airfields by destroying planes on the ground there aren't any places for training left. With day and night raids still going on, and squadrons having to use makeshift bases so they can tackle bombers as they approach over the Channel, it's impossible to conduct a training programme undisturbed.' He sighed. 'I know our fighter boys stopped the invasion last autumn, but the Germans aren't going to give up. We lost so many aircrew, we need hundreds of replacements as soon as possible. In America, we can be trained under peaceful conditions. That's the theory going around, and it makes sense.'

She gave him a frank look. 'It would make more sense if the Americans came in and provided some of the hundreds of replacements.'

'I agree. We all do.'

Jenny gripped his hand impulsively. 'Dear Rob, who'd have guessed what would happen to you in such a short time, and whatever would Mum and Dad say if they knew?'

Rob gazed at the green vista before him. 'They'd say I should have stayed here. You know they would.'

*

Jim Benson had intended to dodge going home for Easter and instead join a party of friends at Palm Beach. Then he received a letter from his father which constituted a summons. James Theodore Benson II was the head of a pharmaceutical corporation; a man whose business flair had raised him to the echelons of greatness. His letter revealed that he was about to aim higher still by running for senator in the coming election. He had invited a number of influential guests for the holiday and his son's presence was vital. There was no way Jim could ignore this command, but he found it difficult to believe that his father could be unaware of the situation between his youthful second wife and his son whom he was going to throw together once more.

When Maybelle Benson contracted a wasting disease which killed her at the age of forty-two, Theo had appeared to be as grief-stricken as the sixteen-year-old Jim. Yet only two years later, with much frothy ceremonial and cupids among huge floral arrangements, the twenty-two-year-old daughter of a respected colonial family became the new Mrs James Theodore Benson. More than a few of the wedding guests commented in undertones that Shelley and her stepson looked so well together it was easy to forget who was the bridegroom.

Shelley had made it obvious from the day she returned from their honeymoon in Europe that marriage to a silver-haired, wealthy tycoon lacked the sexual kick she craved. It was then Jim found his resentment of her tinged with reluctant attraction. Blonde, green-eyed, perfectly formed, Shelley Benson was a severe challenge to a young athlete with a hearty sexual appetite. For four years he had been fighting desire for her. At Christmas she had turned up the heat to danger level, which was why Jim had planned to go elsewhere for Easter. Now he had been summoned home to add family gloss to a man already known as a hard-hitting negotiator and a staunch patriot. It would be strain enough trying to be the perfect accessory to a prospective senator, without fighting the urge to take the candidate's wife to bed.

Jim was uncharacteristically subdued during the drive to the Boston house which was one of four owned by the Bensons. Jim's favourite was the one on Palm Beach, because it allowed him to indulge in the athletic pursuits at which he excelled. A man always felt good when he was enjoying what he did best, and for J.T. Benson, renowned socialite and sportsman, that included dazzling the beach bunnies who abounded there. As he turned the car into the long driveway, Jim studied the house he regarded more as his home than any other. It had been left to his mother by an aunt, owner of several important galleries, and it still retained the stamp of artistic taste, despite the advent of Shelley. For the past four years, a sensation of bleakness had replaced the rush of warmth Jim used to feel on coming home. Today, to that bleakness was added a curious foreboding.

Handing over his sky-blue convertible to Henry, who greeted him with the warmth of an employee who had watched a lusty infant grow into an extrovert six-footer, Jim went first to his room to wash, run a comb through his thick, dark hair and study the cut of his new uniform. Would Flying Cadet J.T. Benson make the kind of impression to gain votes for his father? He sighed. He sure as hell had better. This nomination was really important to a man for whom challenges were designed to be triumphantly surmounted.

When Jim joined the guests, Shelley immediately excused herself to the group of men surrounding her and headed for him with hands outstretched. She looked stunning in a tailored dress of flame-coloured wool with a brooch of diamonds and opals high on the left shoulder. Jim was stirred despite his vow to hold out against her.

'Darling, how handsome you look in that well-fitting uniform,' she murmured, eyes glowing with invitation as she gazed up at him. 'What a good boy you are to do as Daddy ordered.' She kissed his cheek, whispering in his ear, 'But don't be too good. I'll be *so* disappointed.'

He was already fired up and said bitingly, 'This is important to the old man, Shelley. Keep that in mind. You've got one inside that beautiful head, so use it this weekend, for all our sakes.'

Their low exchange was interrupted by the sound of Theo's booming voice.

'Get on over here, you two! Plenty of time to catch up on all the news in the next seven days. Come on, son. People here I want you to meet.'

During the next fifteen minutes Jim was introduced to the guests, and he lost count of the number of times his father clapped him on the shoulder or said, 'That's my boy!' with a hearty laugh. Jim had seldom seen him so openly full of *joie de vivre*, yet the slightly twitching muscle at the corner of Theo's fleshy mouth told another story.

By the end of that long weekend, Theo had presented such a perfect picture of a loving family man that Jim thought he must have been coached in the role by a drama teacher. However, one good aspect of those unnatural three days was that Shelley had played the part of doting wife to the hilt.

After the guests had departed, Jim went down to dinner apprehensive about how soon Shelley might break from her self-imposed wifely devotion and seek some excitement. He was also depressed by the undeniable proof that his sporting achievements, his social success and, now, his military career were being used as mere embellishments of the glittering ascent of James Theodore Benson II.

The large, airy drawing room, which for the last few days had been seething with men and women who had an eye to the main chance, now only contained Thomas, the black butler.

'Good evening, Mr Jim,' he greeted him with a smile. 'How are you tonight?'

'Appreciative of a little peace and quiet, Thomas.'

'Yes, *sir*, it's good to hear the birds singing again out there on the old oaks,' he agreed, as he poured whisky and handed it to Jim, who crossed to the window.

'Mother used to sit here at dusk to catch the last of the birdsong when she could no longer walk out on the porch to hear it.'

'She's hearing all the angel songs now and there's nothing sweeter than that, so the preacher says.'

'I'm sure he's right,' sighed Jim, gazing at the sweep of lawn and visualizing his mother being carried to a cushioned chair by a husband who had sobbed unashamedly at her funeral, then replaced her within two short years with a taut-breasted New Yorker whose avid sexual appetite he could not satisfy. Marrying Shelley had widened the gap between an ambitious, self-centred father and a son in danger of losing any hope of rapport with him.

'You all right, Mr Jim?' asked Thomas, coming up beside him.

Jim turned. 'How long have you been with us — twenty-six years?'

'Your granddaddy was alive then. Mrs Maybelle came here as a bride just after old Mr Benson took me aside and said I would step into Jackson's shoes when he retired end of the month. Mrs Maybelle was a real lady. She treated us as gracious as she treated everyone she met.'

Jim was surprised to see moisture in Thomas's eyes. 'We all have to move on, old feller.'

'You've surely done that, sir. She'd be so proud to see you taking to the skies.'

'When do you get started?' asked Theo, entering the room with his accustomed briskness.

Jim turned to him. 'Once I report to the Riddle Aeronautical Institute.'

'Where's that?' Theo took a glass of whisky from the servant and took a swift pull at it. 'You can serve dinner as soon as Mrs Benson comes down, Thomas. I have work waiting for me.' As Thomas departed to warn the cook, Theo asked again, 'Where's that?'

'Arcadia, Florida.'

'That little two-bit cattle town?'

'You can't learn to fly in a big city, sir.'

Theo tossed back the rest of his drink and poured himself another. 'I'll get Jerry Warner up from Palm Beach to cover it.'

'Cover what?' asked Jim cautiously.

'Your training. He can get some pictures, do a regular write-up, arrange the necessary interviews. He knows how to handle it.'

'There's nothing to handle,' said Jim swiftly. 'The Institute's under military command now. Jerry Warner can't walk in and organize a press release. What we do there will be under wraps and I'll be just one of around fifty cadets on a primary training course.'

'You'll never be just one of around fifty of *anything*, boy. You're my son and that means something in this wonderful country of ours.'

'When I'm flying an armed military aircraft it won't matter who I am, so long as I can handle it the right way,' Jim protested. 'Sir, I did all I could for you over the last three days, but you can't use my military training to boost your electoral chances. No one's going to take pictures of me learning to fly. That's private and personal; it's my future career.'

'You're wrong,' Theo declared, finishing his whisky and moving forward to meet Shelley before she had come more than ten feet into the room. 'Your future career is Benson Pharmaceuticals. Once I'm established in the Senate I'll need you on the board learning the business. Have your flying lessons — it'll be a useful skill — and make the most of your spell in uniform. A man's reputation can be enhanced by his past military service — the ladies are invariably impressed.' In the doorway he turned, his arm around Shelley's waist. 'I'll give you a year, eighteen months at the most.'

'Just a minute, sir,' said Jim forcefully. 'We had an agreement four years ago that I'd go straight from Harvard into the army. It was understood that I'd make a career of it.'

Theo looked back over his shoulder. 'Understood by you, maybe, but never by me. It was merely my solution of how best to quieten you down, introduce you to discipline. You've run wild since you entered high school. Nothing wrong with that when you're finding your feet, but a company man has to take responsibility. The army will teach you to do that.'

'It'll teach me to be a *fighting* man,' he cried.

Theo released Shelley and turned back to face his son with implacable assurance. 'And who do you plan to fight, boy? If you've been fed notions that this country is going to enter the war in Europe, you can forget them. There's no way we're going to spill American blood in a political scramble that's no concern of ours. Once I'm elected, I'll add my corporate voice to those of the men who are true patriots. We're presently one of the great nations of the world. By the time this conflict has been settled we'll be the greatest. Losing an entire generation of young men would interfere with that.'

'A maniac called Adolf Hitler might interfere with it if we don't stop him,' Jim said pointedly. 'You hold the views of a man of commerce, but surely you can see the military angle.'

Theo narrowed his eyes. 'You're a babe in uniform, that's all, unqualified to pass judgement on *any* military angle. Leave that to the four-star generals.'

Conscious of Shelley's amused gaze, Jim hit out. 'I've been through two months of basic training. Babe or not, I believe I'm more qualified to speak on army involvement in the war than anyone who *hasn't* been through the military system. And of *course* this "political scramble" is our concern. Do you really want a massive German-dominated European state as the *second* greatest nation in the world when it's all over? As an army flier, my job will be to help prevent that ... and I think that's more vital than sitting in a boardroom discussing deals that may never come off while our allies are dying wholesale. If we continue to stand off there may not be anyone to cement deals with. We might well become the greatest nation in the world because we're the only one left,' he finished with great passion.

Theo came back into the room looking grim. Jim knew that expression well and braced himself. 'Now look here, I've been around in this world a damn sight longer than you and you've just given me a bushel of crap. When someone attempts to invade our shores, or makes a deliberate attack on any of our people, *that's* when this country will take up arms. Not before. The British and the French once had vast empires as a result of conquest. What happened, eh? They overstretched themselves and exhausted their resources on undeveloped parts of the world, instead of building up their own strength and preserving their young men to increase their national prosperity. The key to greatness is wealth, boy. Money creates power: guns create dead men. You're not going to be one of them. Forget the notion of becoming a posthumous hero and prepare yourself for stepping into my shoes.'

Flying high on anger, Jim cried, 'I won't do it.'

'You sure as hell will!'

'No! I'm Flying Cadet J.T. Benson. I'll *never* be James Theodore Benson the Third.'

His father jabbed a finger in his direction. 'Wrong! You have been from the moment you were born.' He turned back to his highly entertained young wife and led her from the room.

Shelley and Theo exchanged company and social gossip throughout the meal while Jim silently nursed his rage, telling himself he had been crazy to obey the summons to Boston when he wanted to go to Palm Beach. He was entitled to a life of his own and would fight to have it. However, his father was right about money creating power ... and Theo had an abundance of wealth. He had also ensured that he had friends in all the right places. It was formidable opposition for a twenty-two-year-old babe in uniform to take on.

As soon as his father left for his study after coffee, Jim got to his feet and headed for the door. Shelley challenged him. 'Only James Theodore Benson the Third would walk out on me right now.'

He turned on her, saying savagely, 'Whatever it is you're hoping for, you won't get it.'

She stood in one fluid movement and approached him, eyes glittering. 'You're more like Theo than you imagine. Isn't that what he's just told you?' She put her hand on his arm. 'We've been on our best behaviour for three days. Stop fighting me, Jim. I could help you if you'd relax a little.'

'Oh yeah?' He broke contact.

'I'm on your side, darling, I swear. You're going about this in quite the wrong way,' she continued in soothing tones. 'Theo has to be treated with subtlety. Facing him like a bull about to charge, roaring that you won't do his bidding, only makes him dig in his heels.'

'Aggression is the only reaction he recognizes. I've known him a lot longer than you have.'

'And seen very little of him. Small wonder you don't understand each other.'

'And you do?'

'Women are more intuitive.'

Jim's mouth twisted. 'That's not the first word I'd use to describe you.'

'I should hope not. I work hard to suggest other adjectives to the men I meet.' Her hand moved to rest on the lapel of his jacket as she closed on him. 'Go off and learn to be a pilot like a good boy. He gave you eighteen months of freedom. During that time I'll work on him in a manner not open to you.' Her smile was wicked. 'I'll expect some gratitude in return.'

Jim picked the elegant hand from his tuxedo and shook it. 'Thanks a million, pal.'

Her *eyes* widened. 'You're a very provocative man, J.T. Benson.'

'So all the girls tell me.'

Before he guessed her intention her arms slid around his neck as she melted against him. 'When we met before the wedding I wanted you. Each time we get together I want you more. Theo treats me like porcelain. I need someone more red-blooded.'

Jim responded instinctively to her passionate kiss, his wandering hands proving that she wore nothing beneath her clinging dress. Then he came to his senses, realizing how close to betrayal they were getting. Pulling Shelley's arms from his neck he held her wrists together in a bruising grip.

'I'll not do what you want any more than I'll do what he wants,' he breathed. 'You'll have to find your red blood elsewhere.'

Chapter Two

Carlstrom Field on the outskirts of Arcadia had been used for military training during 1914-18, but had gradually been phased out and fallen into neglect until farsighted men anticipated the need to train fliers in greater numbers than before. A massive aid programme to keep Britain free needed to be backed by preparations to defend their own shores, argued US defence chiefs. Accordingly, the civilian flying academy at Arcadia was one of several opened up and made ready to carry out training programmes within an amazingly short time.

Jim drove to Carlstrom from Palm Beach after spending the weekend at the Benson house with someone who had become a good friend. Buck Etwell had been called 'Bucket' by his contemporaries from an early age, and the name had stuck. His easy-going nature accepted the inevitable, and he even introduced himself thus. A tall, rangy man with ginger hair that refused to lie flat, Bucket was above average at basketball and a handy doubles partner on the tennis court. Above all, he loved jazz, and in the back of Jim's car, which was piled high with sports gear, was a set of drums on which Bucket was no mean performer. The friendship had led Jim to learn to play a saxophone, and the pair had been much in demand at Harvard.

It was soon apparent that life would be slightly more relaxed during the ten-week primary flying course than it had been during their initial military training, which had required them to be little more than automatons with faces carefully schooled to be expressionless. Aside from the Commanding Officer there were only two other military officers, and four enlisted men. All the remaining staff members were civilians, with a sprinkling of girls to soften the atmosphere. Along with two other friends from Harvard, Jim and Bucket were delighted to discover new air-conditioned classrooms, comfortable living quarters and excellent sports facilities on a campus they were the first to occupy.

During the first week the only cloud over Jim's pleasure was the advent of Jerry Warner, Theo's East Coast public relations man. Unfortunately for Jim, the Army Air Corps was happy to make capital from the presence in its ranks of a young athlete who had won every national tennis championship, who had been the star of the Harvard football team, and who was the son of a very distinguished family whose head was about to embark on a political career certain to be as successful as his rise in the business world. The handsome J.T. Benson was exactly the type of clean-cut, healthy and popular young man the army wanted in its service, so Warner was offered every facility. However much the subject of this PR attention might deplore it, his fellow cadets were delighted to have a tough but glamorous image rub off on them as gallant defenders of their country ready to obey the call whenever it came.

Jim soon had more than publicity to worry about. Learning to fly was not the simple business he had expected it to be. He found the technical details difficult to grasp. Although he had an astute brain, he had always been lazy about using it for serious study. Sitting bent over books for hours on end was not an occupation that had ever appealed to Jim, who was happiest during hard physical exercise, and he had only just scraped through his finals at Harvard. He was at his best when involved in something demanding co-ordination of eye and muscle.

Flying was such an activity, but he found the training restrictive. Once in the air, looking down on endless flat miles of orange groves and cattle ranches, he was filled with the urge to swoop and soar until his desire for mastery was satisfied.

After his third lesson his instructor, Biff Grogan, a civilian flier of wide experience, said, 'Listen here. I'm aware that you drive around in a highly expensive piece of engineering able to reach speeds well above the legal limits on any of our roads, but an airplane is not an automobile. If something goes wrong you can't park it and look under the goddam hood. If it stalls it's not a case of turning the ignition, because you'll be plunging earthwards. Stop trying to burn rubber when you're in that rear cockpit, and accept that you have to start from scratch in a machine you seem to know nothing about. You apply none of the theories and rules of aeronautics to your flying. You'll never become a pilot until you do.'

By the end of the second week there was still little improvement in Grogan's attitude towards his pupil, and Jim's longing for speed and thrills had in no way diminished. At the end of his lesson on a hot, sultry Friday, the older man summed up his list of criticisms by saying, 'I wonder I care to go up with you day after day. That landing you just made had my guts all shook up.'

It was nothing to how Jim's guts felt. He had thumped down, taken three great kangaroo hops, then zig-zagged with engine roaring towards the small group of cadets waiting to go up, scattering them in fright, before coming to a halt twenty-five yards from the CO, who stood his ground but looked paler than usual.

Back in his quarters to remove his flying suit and don swimming trunks, Jim relieved his feelings to Bucket. 'Old man Grogan comes down so hard on me he makes me real mad, then I forget what I've learned. In the middle of a tight manoeuvre he's telling me to check the altimeter, have a care to the fact that I'm losing speed, increase throttle, pull back on the stick, watch I don't stall.' He flung his leather helmet in the direction of his bunk. 'Heck, if he'd just leave me alone I'd be able to concentrate.'

'If he left you alone you'd soon be a pile of bones on the ground,' said Bucket, stooping to pick up the helmet and place it on the bunk beneath his. 'I guess he'd not worry too much about that if he didn't know he'd be the pile of bones next to yours.'

Jim ignored the joke. 'I mean it. Some men need to be talked through the whole darn lesson. I don't.'

Bucket turned, naked, at his own locker and studied his friend frankly. 'I suppose those hops along the field this afternoon were a sign of high spirits. I'll stretch a point and take your word you can fly, but you sure as hell can't land.' He advanced on Jim with his swimming trunks in his hand. 'You know your trouble? You like to be boss.' He thrust one leg in the black shorts. 'You shout orders at me on the tennis court — you're better at singles — and you do the same playing basketball. Okay, so you *are* the boss on the football field, but you've got to accept that you ain't when sitting behind Biff Grogan. He is, and he's been flying since you were in diapers.'

'Some pal you are!'

Wobbling precariously on one leg, Bucket twice tried to finish dressing before he was able to pull the brief garment up to his waist. 'Jeez, have you noticed how your balance goes haywire straight after flying?' At Jim's silence he added, 'You'd rather I told you go take up an airplane after lessons just to show what you can do when left alone?' When Jim headed towards the bathroom in his underwear, Bucket followed to lean on the door frame. 'Hey, just joking. Give it time. You'll get there.'

'Sure I will,' Jim told him above the noise of running water, 'but I'm the only cadet on this course with a PR man on his back waiting for him to outshine the rest.'

At that point, the two other occupants of the room entered in flying gear. Gus Buckhalter's father was an army general greatly disappointed in his son's decision to take to the air. Gus remained unrepentant. Peter Kelsey had been orphaned by a train crash, then adopted by a very wealthy maiden aunt who doted on him.

Gus dropped his helmet and goggles on Jim's bunk and imparted the astonishing news that a hundred cadets of the RAF would be arriving at Carlstrom on the following Monday week, to join the training programme.

'They're the first of a regular flow,' said Gus. 'The British have been granted a lease on the field and are set to take it over completely by Fall.'

'So what happens to us?' demanded Jim, unsure whether the invasion from across the Atlantic would make the situation better or worse for him.

'We complete our ten weeks here, but future courses will be held elsewhere. We're opening up fields all over now.'

Gus hooked a chair forward with his foot and sat heavily. 'The British have just shown the world the value of an air force against invasion so I guess *we're* being taken more seriously by our defence chiefs from now on.'

'Hey, is that right, RAF guys are coming here?' asked a cadet from the open doorway. 'Someone said a hundred. What the heck's the idea?'

'Don't you read anything but sexy magazines?' demanded Bucket. 'It's in the news how they've no place left to train pilots.'

'That's their tough luck. If they didn't get into wars, they'd have no problem.'

'It might soon be our problem,' warned Gus.

'So we need to train our own men. I don't see why they have to come to Carlstrom. We're doing okay as we are.'

Another head appeared at the doorway. 'We *were* doing okay. I don't get it. Seems we're expected to nursemaid them; show them how we do things here.'

The first man said, 'I'll soon show them how we do things. We'll be upperclass men soon as they arrive, and I know how to reduce rookies to size.'

'No,' said his friend, 'from what I understood, we have to treat them as guests in our country and make allowances for their situation.'

'Their situation is the same as for any rookies, pal.'

Impatient with this exchange, Gus continued with his theory that a worldwide conflict would not be avoided. Jim listened with mixed feelings. If America went to war Theo could not then force him to join the company, but operational flying demanded enormous skill. Would J.T. Benson be found wanting when called to defend his country?

The serious moment was broken by a commotion which drew them all to the window. A large number of cadets in flying suits were moving in a jostling, cheering mass with one of their colleagues held aloft.

'What's going on?' called Bucket to a man on the edge of the group.

He laughed with the exuberance of youth. 'Brad's just flown solo. The first to do it! We're going to give him a dunking.'

Although he shouted and cheered with the rest as Brad Halloran, son of a Kentucky horse breeder and an amateur racing driver with nerves of steel, was tossed fully clothed in the swimming-pool, Jim felt hollow inside. This early triumph served to highlight his dissatisfaction with his own progress.

During the next week six more cadets, including Gus and Bucket, were thrown in the pool after flying solo, but Grogan still refused to let Jim take up an aircraft alone. However, he listened to his pupil's protests and compromised on the Friday afternoon.

'You can give me a ride today, and I won't say a word. It'll be just like flying solo, and if I see everything's as good as you claim it'll be, I'll parachute down and leave you to it.'

Jim gave a grim smile in response to that wisecrack, but he knew this was his chance to prove himself. He took off confidently and completed his schedule with the kind of panache he gave everything he did, taking Grogan's silence as a sign that the man was deeply impressed by his ability. Landing was his *bête noire* so he had to make this one good enough to prove that he could conquer it.

Nearing Carlstrom the sky no longer belonged to Jim. As he had been taught, he fell into place within the circuit where the cadets prepared to land in correct order. Half the aircraft around him now had only one man controlling them, so he had to make this good in order to join the privileged ranks. He bit his lip and concentrated on the tricky business of returning to earth. Starting to throttle back, he alternately watched the ground, the altimeter and his speed. As he dropped lower and lower, he began to relax. His approach was near perfect. Watching the ground rise up to meet him he grew exultant. He had finally cracked it. Landing was a cinch!

'Increase throttle and climb!' came the sudden harsh instruction in his ear, making him jump nervously.

With the grass no more than seventy-five feet below, Jim played deaf. He knew he was spot-on this time, and he had no intention of risking the usual kangaroo hops on a second attempt when this was the best landing he had ever made.

'I have control!' roared Grogan, and the aircraft began to climb with laboured engine noise leaving Jim to sit helplessly as a mere passenger.

Grogan's face in the mirror was livid. 'Take a look down there, Mister! Take a damn good look at what you failed to see!'

As he glanced over the rim of the cockpit, Jim's fury melted, and he grew cold. He had been so concentrated on proving his ability that it had not occurred to him that the field would not be clear. Two hundred yards from the hangars an aircraft stood on its nose, one starboard wing smashed into pieces scattered over a large area. Jim swallowed, his throat suddenly dust-dry. The accident must have happened during his own slow descent; mere minutes ago. Had some poor devil been killed?

'Just you listen to me, Mister,' said Grogan's voice with a cold bite that completed Jim's sense of guilt. 'When we're in the airplane together you do whatever I tell you. I don't know who the hell you think you are, but you're just another goddam cadet so far as I'm concerned. Right from the start you've been a smart-ass. Well, I tell you, there's no room for them in this game. Any fool who thinks flying is kids' stuff sooner or later ends up like that guy down there. That's why you can find some other instructor from now on — if you don't get washed out right away. You can do as you damn well please with your own life, but I value my own too much to fly with a learner who thinks he knows it all and can teach me some.'

Brad Halloran was admitted to hospital with a broken arm and three smashed ribs. He was lucky to be alive after over-confidence had led him to forget one of the basic rules of landing. His crash considerably sobered the cadets. The Chief Instructor addressed them all that evening, ending with a caution.

'The successful pilot never believes he's infallible. If he doesn't feel a faint element of healthy apprehension each time he climbs into the cockpit, it's wiser for him to stay on the ground. Bear that in mind.'

Jim was given a blistering reprimand by his CO and was told his place on the course was now under review. 'I'm giving you a second chance, Benson, because you've shown enough skill to suggest you might make it if you knuckle down. I also feel it would be bad for morale if you were to go at the first fall. Halloran's crash has unsettled everyone as it is. I expect you to justify my decision and improve dramatically. Mr Grogan refuses to continue teaching you, and I think that's best for both of you. We have an influx of new instructors arriving to train the RAF men, so you'll be added to the list of one of them. Now just hear this, Benson. You'll get nowhere unless you learn to obey orders. If we go into any war, other men's lives may depend on their pilot's ability to do so without question. *No matter who he happens to be.* Do I make myself clear?'

Jim stood alone for some time in the afterglow of sunset, smarting from the interview. Thank God Jerry Warner had not been on hand today!

*

Rob stared from the window of the train in numbed silence. Laughter had petered out long, long ago. Now, none of them could even be bothered to talk. They had passed two days and nights sitting on hard seats in a train with no air-conditioning and a heating system which had not changed since leaving Canada, and they had all had enough. Those who could not wait to learn to be pilots had lost their enthusiasm. The man who had hoped to be an engineer was plunged into deepest dejection. His plan had misfired. Not only was he caught up in something which did not interest him, he was also full of guilt over leaving his sister to cope on her own. He was not even able to go to Thoresby on leave to see how she was faring because here he was on the other side of the Atlantic, heading for a town named Arcadia. It sounded like a place from a fantasy novel — somewhere where time stood still and everyone was happy and beautiful.

They had all left England two weeks ago when masses of scented roses bloomed in country gardens, and some had even managed to push up through the debris littering tiny front areas of houses in town streets which were now no more than rows of ruins. Rob had thought the sight almost obscene, until he had seen a child with its mother picking roses to carry off to their makeshift quarters in some school or church hall. He had not forgotten that little cameo, nor would he until he returned to his battered homeland.

On boarding the liner, which had been painted grey to serve as a troopship, Rob had realized the finality of what he had done. They had slipped out of Liverpool under cover of darkness and stood offshore waiting for their escorting fleet to assemble. It had been awesome to witness an air raid on the port from the chilly deck, the darkness of the blacked-out city slashed by vivid areas of fire as incendiaries preceded high-explosive bombs. They had all seen it as a tragic farewell, and could not help feeling that they were somehow running out on their country when they were most needed. They had turned in that night with their spirits considerably dampened and fear for their families uppermost in their minds.

Two days out on the heaving sea and their regrets at leaving England, and even their apprehension over encountering German submarines, had been forgotten in the misery of seasickness. After a whole day and night of wishing he could die, Rob had found his sea legs and stayed well for the rest of the voyage. All the same, he spent long, solitary hours leaning on the rail, haunted by all that had happened since the day Sir Charles had come across the rainswept fields to break the news of the deaths of Mum, Dad and Gran.

The one bright aspect of the transatlantic crossing had been his budding friendship with the man who had introduced himself on reading the list of those selected for pilot training. Johnny Bradshaw was a chirpy Londoner who told Rob, with a broad grin, that he could hardly tell a sheep from a cow. He had been working in the accounts department of a chocolate factory before he volunteered, and consequently had had so many free samples he no longer craved them.

Although Johnny told his new friend all about his family and his background, Rob's inborn reticence prevented him from saying much about his own former life, apart from impersonal details about farming. Of his triple loss he said nothing. Grief was still too raw, and he had been brought up to hide his emotions. Yet he found a curious rapport with the blond nineteen-year-old who was so different from himself, and was grateful for his company.

Now here they were after two weeks in Canada, dressed in thick grey suits, on the last leg of their journey down the Eastern Seaboard, across the border, and on to the southern American state of Florida. They were obliged to travel as civilians to the neutral United States, where they would receive the training given to members of the US Army Air Force. Opinions on this were divided. The cadets were proud of their connection with the young airmen who had held the Germans at bay across the English Channel last autumn, and they were also proud of being British. Did they really want to become part-time Americans?

As they sat in the train, staring listlessly at the sun rising over a flat landscape that continued as far as the horizon, the answer was an unequivocal *no*. They were exhausted, bleary-eyed, saturated with perspiration and aching all over. The air inside the carriage was by now so foul it had induced lethargy and mental stupor, so that when word was passed from the front of the train that they would reach their destination within ten minutes it had little effect on most of the men.

'We've been on this bloody train exactly forty-eight hours,' muttered the Welshman sitting opposite Rob, 'and all you can see out there is miles and miles of trees. What's there to get off for?'

Johnny stood up, stretched, and began hauling his kit from the overhead rack. 'I'm all for the great adventure, lads. Somewhere amid those palm trees we might find Dorothy Lamour.'

The man scowled. 'Doesn't anything ever wipe that grin off your face?'

'Yes. Glum chaps like you.' He nudged Rob 'On your feet *Mister* Stallard. The freedom of the air awaits you.'

'Pipe down.' 'Shut your bloody mouth!' 'Kick him in the teeth, someone,' chorused several others who were making no attempt to rouse themselves.

'Anyone who can be as cheerful as you in this flaming heat, after the journey we've had, ought to be shot,' declared the first speaker, still staring out of the window with red-rimmed eyes.

'If you were all as cheerful as me, we'd defeat the Jerries by laughing 'em to death,' returned the irrepressible Johnny. 'They couldn't take that. A very dour, earnest race, they are.'

Rob forced himself to his feet, easing his shirt from his back, and pulled his heavy pack down to the seat, together with the jacket of the suit he was wearing. There was no turning back now, but of course there never had been from the moment he had signed up.

The young RCAF officer who had been in overall charge of the cadets throughout the transfer from Canada, now came through the carriages to check that all was well. 'Sleeves down, ties and jackets on,' he ruled in a voice husky with tiredness. 'They've most likely never seen a Britisher before, but they've been reading that you RAF guys are some kind of supermen. So, although it's ninety plus outside, you got to look as though you don't give a damn. Come on, jump to it!'

He was greeted by a chorus of groans from men whose only desire was to down a long, cold drink, take a shower and throw themselves on a bunk in the path of an icy blizzard. None felt like a superman or had the least energy to pretend they were as they rolled down their damp sleeves, slipped on their ties, and donned their winter-weight civilian jackets.

Johnny cast Rob a sly glance. 'Well, we've arrived at your storybook place where everyone's happy and beautiful.'

'Someone should have drowned you at birth,' he grunted, then fell backwards as the train stopped with a jerk.

'If you wanted to sit on my lap, darling, you should've said earlier,' snarled the cadet beneath him. 'It's too late now. I'm about to leap out and prove I'm a superman.' He gave Rob a thump in the back. 'Get off me, you great erk. You stink.'

'So do you,' snapped Rob, struggling to his feet.

'We all stink,' said Johnny, then added as he bent to peer from window. 'Blimey, where did that lot spring from? The whole town's out there, by the looks of it.'

Rob glanced from the window as he tightened the knot of his tie and had the first sight of his storybook town. A wide area of grass dotted with palm trees was filled with people in summer clothes who were smiling and waving. He gazed back in dismay. He and the others aboard the train were in no fit state for such a reception. Hot, dull-witted and sweaty, they would present a pitiful impression to Americans expecting RAF supermen.

'How did they know when we were arriving?' he asked of no one in particular, his heart sinking at the prospect of being swamped with North American generosity feeling as he did at the moment.

'How did they know, boyo? Because news got around that they'll never have seen anything like us before,' said the Welshman, shrugging on his jacket. 'We're curiosities, see.'

'You can say that again,' put in Rob's neighbour heavily. 'We should've been allowed to freshen up and put on our uniforms before parading in front of the whole town.'

'Hey, there's girls out there,' enthused a known womanizer. 'This is supposed to be a cattle-ranch town. You can't tell me cowboys are all spick and span. The women here probably like their men smelling of BO.'

'Don't be disgusting,' said Johnny absently, still taking in the scene outside. 'This is most likely the only hero's welcome you'll ever get, lads, so forget how you look and try to be charming, for once.'

The crosstalk ceased as they were told to get out and form up beside the track, where they were hidden from the waiting crowd by the train. Heat hit Rob as he scrambled down with stiff limbs to stand beside Johnny before a long, low station building with a raised wooden platform on to which their heavy kit was already being stacked from the baggage car.

'Oh God,' breathed Johnny, eyeing the gathering of sun-tanned men in cool clothes to whom their accompanying RCAF officer was talking. 'I think we're going to get a speech from every one of them. We'll be here all day.'

He could not have been more wrong. After a brief but clearly sincere welcome, the cadets were told there were cold drinks and light refreshments for them at a hotel one block away.

'We guessed you boys would be badly in need of both after journeying so far, so make yourselves right at home and relax a while. We're real glad to have you with us.'

All thoughts of service formality or impressions of supermen flew, as they walked in ragged files no more than a hundred yards to a two-storey wooden building painted white and grandly named Arcadia House. The American and British flags flew side by side, but Rob hardly noticed that tribute as he headed, with the rest of his carriage companions, for the tables on the lawn which were piled with oranges and doughnuts, jugs of chilled orange juice and urns containing tea and coffee. As he guzzled glass after glass of ice-cold orange juice Rob thought it was the most wonderful drinking session he had known. Between great gulps of juice he made inroads into several doughnuts, and his concentration on satisfying thirst and hunger at first prevented his noticing much except the women serving this bounty.

Then, in the middle of taking a bite from yet another doughnut pressed on him by a smiling matron who insisted that a big lad like him must have a sizeable appetite, Rob's hand froze and his eyes opened as wide as his mouth as he was approached by a girl with long dark hair, intense brown eyes and the kind of bosom which usually had him frantically looking elsewhere. This time he was unable to tear his gaze from her, because she wore a large, stiff-brimmed hat secured beneath her chin with a plaited leather cord, a blouse with very full sleeves, a leather waistcoat decorated with studs and tassels, and edged with a deep fringe, a leather skirt also fringed at the hem, high boots with a tooled pattern on their sides, and silver spurs. Round her waist was a belt bearing two ivory-handled guns in decorated holsters. Rob goggled at these in disbelief.

'Hi,' she greeted him huskily. 'I'm Patsy May Grant, DeSoto County cowgirl. Who are you?'

Rob lowered the doughnut from his mouth. Did she actually fire those fancy weapons? Whatever kind of town was this where girls had to wear guns to protect themselves?

'You *have a* name, don't you?' she teased, sending colour to Rob's cheeks.

'Stallard,' he blurted out automatically, fascinated by this astonishing girl's clothes.

'Welcome to Arcadia, Stallard. Are you missing home?'

'I ... this is very different,' he stammered, trying without success to edge away through the press of cadets and Arcadians.

'We'll make you feel right at home just as soon as you've settled in. I live two blocks from here with my family. Y'all come on by any time.'

'I expect I'll be busy ... flying ... you know,' he hedged, then flushed a deeper red as she advanced on him and linked her arm through his, wafting perfume over him as she turned and urged him to smile at the camera. There was a flash. Rob jumped nervously, and a photographer approached, hand outstretched.

'Hi! That'll be something to remind you of your visit when you get back home. It'll be in tomorrow's edition.'

Rob remained in a state of bemusement as women calling him 'Rarb' in soft, beguiling accents kept his colour high by asking him very frank questions about himself, and men pumped his hand up and down telling him he must have a real American barbecue at their ranch some Sunday. He was given another doughnut and some very hot, sweet tea which he drank to ease a dry throat caused by embarrassment. He envied Johnny standing a short distance away, apparently charming a large group of women. Would he ever be as socially assured as his friend?

Time passed, and Rob's sensation of unreality increased. By now it was Madge, Betty or Mary Lou; Jed, Clay or Mait. The cadets were Geoff, Billy, George or Lionel. If there had been any barriers to break down, they had disintegrated at first sight of the laden tables and women in pretty dresses. Rob gazed at them through sore eyes. Their skin was golden from the sunshine and their faces showed none of the strain presently on those of the women in Britain. The men were hearty and assured, volubly proud of their womenfolk and their town, and bore little resemblance to the men at home who were overworked, worried about the safety of their families and wondering how long they could keep the invader at bay.

This *was* a storybook place, where everyone was happy and beautiful. It had appeared as if by magic as the sun rose. The buildings were white or pastel shades, palm trees abounded, there were flowers on bushes and trees, and the sky was the most incredible blue. Rob had never seen the heavens this colour before. Even on the brightest summer day the sky over Thoresby held a soft, dreamy quality in its hue; a gentleness to match the meadows and hedgerows beneath. The sun there was also more benign. In Arcadia in the middle of June it blazed down mercilessly.

Rob soon began to wish he had not been persuaded to eat a sixth doughnut. An unpleasant sensation was assailing his stomach. The voices around him seemed to be rising in volume, his brain refused to work, and either he was swaying or the lawns of Arcadia House were swinging from side to side. He accepted another cup of tea, hoping it would revive him, but it made him perspire more than ever and increased his sensation of imagining the scene before him.

At that point, the entire kaleidoscope broke up and Johnny appeared. 'We're moving off. There's a line of cars to take us off to the airfield. Stick with me so's we get in the same one.' They began crossing to the road where the vehicles stood. 'I heard we'll get showers and breakfast on arrival. I never want to see this bloody suit again once I take it off. The idiot who chose them for chaps coming to Florida ought to be pushed out without a parachute.'

Rob said nothing as he plodded beside Johnny. He longed for the coming shower, but the thought of breakfast reminded him too forcibly of what he had just consumed. The friends were allocated a car with a short, good-looking former stationery salesman named Bryce, and Cyril Shaw, a thickset man from Essex who had worked in a bank. Sandwiched in the back seat between Johnny and the salesman, Rob hoped it would be a short drive. He would gladly agree to fly *anything* if he could first be allowed to shower and sleep until his head stopped spinning.

Their driver was a large, hearty man who introduced himself as 'Dook' Foster and immediately invited all four to dinner on Saturday. 'My wife Peggy was giving out doughnuts — the pretty one in blue — and she told me to ask you boys over for a real American meal. Big juicy steaks, dishes of black-eyed peas, mashed potaters and hot biscuits. I bet you've seen nothing like that for a good long time, eh?'

Rob's stomach reacted violently to his description of rich food, and he realized he was going to throw up before long. Closing his eyes, he prayed it would not happen until he reached the airfield, but the well-sprung car bounced and swayed for a full twenty minutes in the motorcade before turning through some gates and pulling up with a jerk in front of a white porticoed structure labelled ADMINISTRATION. Waiting there were several uniformed officers who had already been joined by the cadets' escort from Canada, and it was obvious service

40

regimentation would now take over. Rob knew how long-winded that could be. He would never last out through that.

In the midst of the general mêlée as cadets spilled from cars, said goodbye to their host drivers, and wandered to form ranks in front of the reception committee, Rob slipped away and made for the cover of a nearby hut, already starting to heave. After violently ejecting the result of his inability to say no to generous strangers, he slowly raised his head to find two tall men watching from the other end of the hut. They wore lightweight khaki uniforms with unfamiliar insignia, but he knew officers when he saw them and cursed the fact that they should have been passing at that moment.

'Get that disgusting mess cleared up,' ordered one, 'and be quick about it.'

'Yes, sir,' mumbled Rob, forgetting he was in civilian clothes and almost saluting.

'We have a hundred British airmen arriving,' said the taller officer. 'They won't want some hick puking behind their quarters, giving the idea we're all morons over here.'

As they walked off Rob realized they had no idea he was one of the supposed 'supermen', yet they would surely recognize him later. What a way to start his reluctant career as a pilot!

Chapter Three

By late afternoon Rob and Johnny were well enough rested to explore their home for the next ten weeks. They were delighted with their comfortable quarters — four men to a room with its own bathroom, working desk and lockers — and they had slept throughout the hottest part of the day. They shared a double-bunked room with Patrick Bryce, and Cyril Shaw who had become engaged before leaving England and was unashamedly lovesick. As a result, he was not particularly talkative. Johnny and Patrick were, so it was as well that Rob was also a man of few words.

Leaving Patrick snoring and Cyril writing a letter to his beloved Norma, the friends showered, then put on the light khaki uniform issued to them on arrival and studied each other critically.

'I think the local girls will love us in this,' Johnny enthused. 'You look a typical American.'

'I don't feel like one. In fact, everything still seems unreal,' Rob told him heavily. 'I'm a farmer who wanted to be an engineer, so what am I doing here?'

'Fighting for king and country, lad.'

'Dressed like this? They haven't a king.'

Johnny grinned. 'You look so dashing you'll be fighting for your honour before long. I saw you with that Rodeo Queen, you sly dog.'

'Let's have a look around,' said Rob pointedly. 'I heard planes overhead earlier, when I was still half asleep. It's quiet now, so we'll probably be able to have a look at them on the ground.'

It was still sweltering outside and the brightness dazzled them for several moments as they looked around to get their bearings. The sounds of laughter and splashing drew them towards a vast, tiled swimming-pool with a stone-slabbed surround beside which ran a straw-roofed shelter to provide shade. The American cadets were cavorting in the water, sunning themselves on towels, or reclining in the shade to chat or read. Beside the pool were six tennis courts where sun-browned players in white slammed balls back and forth with great ferocity.

'Gosh, it's like a scene from a technicolour film,' breathed Johnny with delight.

Rob looked at it all and thought of the RAF camp where he had drilled, practised firing on the rifle range and sat in the patched-up huts to learn the basics of service life, all in freezing winter temperatures. Their quarters had been wooden huts housing twenty men. The two iron stoves had invariably belched smoke and the windows let in draughts. They had shared an ablutions hut with another twenty men whose hut was adjacent to it on the far side. The stone floor had been covered in puddles, the hot water only ever lukewarm, and the latrines were often inoperative because the sewage pipes had been ruptured by a bomb and inefficiently repaired. Recreation facilities had been darts, table tennis and billiards in the NAAFI, football on a three-quarter-sized makeshift pitch and the occasional film in the camp cinema, which doubled as a classroom because one had been flattened by a crashed German bomber.

'No wonder they won't come into the war,' Rob murmured. 'Who'd exchange this for what we've got at home?'

'We'll have to at the end of our training,' Johnny reminded him.

They stood for some moments on the fringe of the activity, which continued as if they were not there. 'Do you get a feeling that we're being given the cold shoulder?' murmured Johnny. 'After the terrific welcome this morning the atmosphere has turned decidedly cool.'

'Maybe they resent us invading their camp and dressing up like them.'

'It wasn't *our* idea. It came from one of their own generals.'

'Maybe they resent him,' suggested Rob briefly. 'Come on, let's find the aircraft.'

'Hang on a minute, one's looking this way and smiling. The natives might be friendly after all.'

'Hi there,' said a brown-haired American, rising and approaching despite the continued lack of interest from the group he was with. 'I'm Jordan, from Nashville. My mother's English. Comes from Cornwall. Welcome to Carlstrom.'

Johnny shook his hand. 'Thanks. I'm Bradshaw, from London. This is my chum Stallard.'

'Hi.' Jordan shook Rob's hand, saying, 'that's a town I'd like to see. All those old buildings. I mean, *real* old.'

In accordance with their instructions to say nothing about the war, Johnny did not mention the bombing of London's old buildings. Instead, he indicated the clothes he was wearing. 'This uniform is much cooler than the suits we arrived in, but we'll have to get used to wearing it. We spent half a year in RAF serge, a couple of weeks in Canadian khaki, then two days as civilians. Tell the truth, we're not sure what we are at the moment.'

Jordan laughed. 'You'll soon find out in the morning. The routine here is tough.'

'It looks like it.' Johnny nodded at the fun under way all around them.

'Ah, your arrival means we have a free afternoon.'

'Is that why your chums are so glad to see us?' asked Johnny dryly.

The American glossed over that. 'We've had the campus to ourselves for three weeks. Suddenly, we've become upperclass men to a whole lot of Britishers.'

'Is that bad?'

Jordan gave an uncomfortable smile. 'Only if you make it so. Look, why don't I dress and show you around?'

'That'd be jolly nice. Thanks.'

When Jordan left, Johnny turned on Rob. 'You didn't have much to say.'

'I didn't get a chance. You were rattling on all the time. Anyway, what's this "upperclass" business?'

'Search me. As he said, we'll find out in the morning.'

'I want to find out what I'll be expected to fly. That's the most important aspect of being here.'

'Jordan from Nashville will show us. Perhaps when you see them they'll arouse some enthusiasm in you.'

'Don't count on it.'

A voice spoke from behind them. 'Taking a look around?'

Rob turned to see a tall American in tennis clothes who was undoubtedly one of the officers who had caught him being sick behind the hut. He waited for recognition, but it did not come. He breathed a sigh of relief. Then relief turned into another emotion as the man introduced himself.

'I'm Buckhalter, Cadet Captain.' He did not offer his hand. 'If you need any advice in adjusting to our military discipline, we upperclass men will be ready to put you right. I've called a meeting after supper tonight to get you familiarized with the way we do things in the Army Air Corps. See you then.'

As the American walked away, having failed to associate a smartly dressed RAF cadet with the white-faced 'civilian' he had chastised, Rob began to burn with resentment. Who did Buckhalter think he was to throw his weight around like an officer? He was merely another cadet!

Jordan returned at that moment and, while Johnny questioned him about Buckhalter, Rob's attention was drawn to two men in the swimming-pool. As a non-swimmer he could not help envying someone who dived with graceful ease and swam a length underwater, turning at the far end to embark on an effortless backstroke, his powerful bronzed arms slicing the water with scarcely a splash. When the man hauled himself up to sit on the side and exchange banter with his friends, Rob's envy swiftly vanished. With his dark brown hair, deep blue eyes, dazzling smile and perfectly proportioned physique, the swimmer would stand out in any crowd. He was the man with Buckhalter, who had added the comment about puking like a moron. Rob's blood boiled. He was also merely another cadet!

Into a break in the conversation, Rob asked Jordan, 'Who's that chap over there?'

The American's expression brightened considerably. 'He's our star, known as J.T. nationwide. He has every reason to be bull-headed, but he's such a nice guy.'

'Why's he known nationwide?' demanded Rob, watching the 'star' turn somersaults in the water in company with another gifted swimmer.

Jordan was also watching the aquatic display. 'He's a brilliant all-round athlete. He played tailback for the Crimsons when he was at Harvard, and could easily have gone professional. Several teams were after him. It was out of the question, of course.'

'Why?' asked Rob, having no idea what Jordan was talking about, but with a perverse desire to know why this man should imagine he already held commissioned rank.

The American turned his attention back to Rob. 'Because of who he is. J.T's grandfather started a drug company from nothing and made it big. It's now one of the largest in the country, with interests in just about every associated line, making the family one of the wealthiest along the

Eastern Seaboard. J.T's father is certain to be elected senator later this year. J.T. himself has won every national tennis championship — you'll be able to watch him on the courts here. He has us all beat, but he doesn't mind spending time to help any man with his game. He's also a terrific basketball player, and a qualified lifeguard. A man has to be a top-class swimmer for that.' His smile deepened into a grin. 'It's not hard to guess he's a favourite with women, and he makes the most of that. There are always pictures in the society journals showing him with some glossy blonde or brunette out to catch him. He don't aim to be caught just yet, he says, but I guess it'll happen one day. After all, he's James Theodore Benson the Third, heir to a gigantic pharmaceutical corporation. Yet he's such a nice guy.'

Rob heard all this in silence, knowing already that he did not share Jordan's unashamed hero-worship. Fancy any man calling himself Benson 'the Third'. Did he consider himself on a par with royalty, like Henry the Fourth or Richard the First? Was that why he had thrown his weight about this morning?

Johnny took up the conversation. 'We have a couple of chaps who went to Eton and Oxford, and there's one whose father is a baronet, I heard, but we haven't anyone as famous as your J.T.'

'Would you like to meet him?'

'Yes,' said Johnny, as Rob breathed a silent 'no'.

'I'll introduce you. Let's go over.'

The 'star' was now standing up to his chin in water balancing a lanky ginger-haired man on his shoulders, and Rob hung back as Jordan hailed Benson. 'Hey, J.T., these boys want a tour of Carlstrom, and you're part of it.'

Benson gave his dazzling smile, heaved the man on his shoulders into the air, where he executed a perfect arched dive, then waded across. 'Hi. Welcome to Florida. Where are you from?'

'London,' put in Jordan.

'I guess you're glad to get away from England right now,' said J.T. Benson.

'It's certainly hotter here,' Johnny said non-committally.

Having seen his friend wince as he shook Benson's hand, Rob was prepared for a strong grip. He had one himself, and his hands were as big as the American's, so he put all his strength into the handshake. As human clamp met human clamp, then tightened to a point where bones might crack, the surprise in Benson's eyes changed to sudden recognition.

'I guess your feelings about being here are decidedly mixed.'

Rob stiffened at the hint of derision in the deep voice, and his resentment increased. 'Not in the least, Benson,' he said coldly. 'And they're unlikely to change.'

'Here's your chum,' put in Johnny, apparently unaware of the undercurrent of hostility. 'He's pretty nifty at diving.'

'Hi,' said the ginger-haired man, arriving beside Benson. 'You boys look hot enough to earn a session in this pool, but I warn you not to do that again. I figure he let you off because you just got here, but anyone who shakes hands with J.T. from the side finds himself flying through the air and into the water.' He grinned. 'It's his favourite trick.'

Benson laughed, then arched backwards in a skilled somersault to swim away underwater, a shimmering shape in the sun-sparkled pool.

'See you around,' cried his friend, and matched the display of swimming expertise.

'As I said, J.T.'s such a nice guy,' mused Jordan, smiling as he gazed after the two swimmers. 'And so's Bucket. They're kind of cool on drums and sax, too. You'll hear them play in the canteen sometimes.' He shook his head fondly. 'Great guys!'

As they left the recreation area and walked alongside a building from which came the smell of dinner cooking that had Rob's digestive juices gurgling, he told himself that here was one cadet who had no desire to hear them play in the canteen. Could the friend really be called 'Bucket'? Perhaps so in a country where men were named Duke, Clay or Chuck. All interest in the aircraft they were to fly had vanished after that encounter. Rob only wanted to eat a hearty meal to compensate for missing breakfast, then lie on his bunk and forget his unhappiness by starting the Edgar Wallace thriller he had bought on the boat. And if Benson *had* pulled him into the pool on shaking hands he would have received a punch on the nose, in return!

*

The British cadets tried to settle to their new life, knowing they could be failed, or 'washed out' as the term was, at any stage of their training. American military routine was vastly different from their own. They had to learn new terms for familiar orders; new movements when marching. They had to accept that they were being treated like cadets in a foreign air force, some members of which were deeply resentful at their intrusion. There were beetles, mosquitoes and snakes; and it was debilitatingly hot in the middle of June. It was not surprising that they found it difficult to come to terms with the demands made upon them during those first days.

The Cadet Captain, and the company and platoon commanders, could impose demerits on any RAF cadet who did not measure up in their eyes, and when these totalled more than five the transgressor was order to 'walk the ramp' for however long he was told to do so. This meant loss of free time in order to tramp back and forth along the wooden platform outside the administration block until the penance was paid. Demerits were mostly awarded for official faults such as dust on window-sills, beds improperly made, shirt buttons left undone, or not falling in the moment the order was given. Sometimes, however, they were given for failure to stop smiling when told, for leaving a single (invisible?) whisker on the chin after shaving, or breathing too noisily. These latter built up resentment in men from a country at war, who saw it as unnecessary and somewhat infantile. Yet it was an integral part of the harsh and exact training of Americans, so they had to accept it.

What they were not prepared to accept from the men on the senior course were their attempts at 'hazing'. Bullying designed to humiliate was rendered impotent if it instead created laughter, so the British cadets adopted that strategy. When someone was randomly pulled from his chair by an upperclass man and told to stand to attention and recite just how worthless he was, half a dozen of his colleagues did the same with hilarious exaggeration, until a hundred cadets were falling about with laughter. When upperclass men descended on the British quarters and attempted to force someone into degrading himself, either they were told to go and fly a kite or else the full complement of the hut gathered to explain that RAF personnel did not indulge in that kind of thing. With odds of two to one, the hazing soon ceased.

Yet there were compensations for the newcomers. There was no blackout, no air raids, no rationing. They ate steaks and fresh fruit bigger than any they had seen before. In the canteen they could buy the most delicious ice-cream sundaes ever devised, bars of chocolate and sweets;

and they all had invitations for the weekend from Arcadian families, who seemed more welcoming than some of the men with whom they shared their demanding days.

Rob wrote to Jenny telling her of part of his new life. He did not mention his acute homesickness, only aspects he thought she should hear, such as the food, sunshine and very comfortable living quarters. He ended with:

They gave us something called peanut butter today. It tastes quite nice spread on bread, but they put jam on top of it. They do eat some curious mixtures. I hope you are managing all right on your own. Maybe when Phil has leave you'll want to go ahead with the wedding after all. He's a nice chap and fond of you. We have our first flying lesson tomorrow. Can't say I'm looking forward to it, although I enjoy learning aeronautics as much as engineering. Take care of yourself, Jen. I'll write again next week.

Four days after their arrival the new cadets were marched out to the flight line. From his first sight of the sturdy Stearman PT 17 training biplanes Rob had felt uneasy about being several thousand feet above the ground in one, but if the famous J.T. Benson could do it, so could the unknown R.N. Stallard, especially as he had learned that flying did not appear to be one of the American's talents. He had not yet soloed, and was currently under review for careless flying.

Each instructor took a group of RAF cadets aside to cluster around one of the aircraft while he explained the contents of the cockpit. Rob found himself in a group with a man named Clint Lawson, who was around forty with shrewd eyes and an unhurried voice that inspired confidence. He spoke clearly, in an accent they could all understand, as he indicated the basic controls, outlining what pilots must and must not do with them. Then he disconcerted Rob by inviting him to climb aboard for his first adventure into flight.

'Don't look so scared. An airplane is only a machine. So long as you know what you're doing, so will the Stearman.' He smiled at Rob as the rest walked off to await their turn. 'You took in what I said just now about communication? I can talk to you, but you can't answer back.' His smile broadened. 'An instructor dreamed up that convenient arrangement. When we get airborne I'll take you through the basics before handing the controls to you. Now, don't look that way. I'll be there the whole time and we'll keep eyeball contact with the help of that mirror above my seat. Just one more thing. Do you drive an automobile?'

Rob shook his head, his stomach churning nervously.

'Pity, it would have aided your understanding of steering. What's your name?'

'Stallard, sir.'

Lawson nodded. 'Okay, climb aboard and let's fly.'

This is it, Rob thought. The last thing I want to do is learn to fly this great blundering machine — or any other — so the obvious solution is for me to fail the course and be sent home again. His decision was then blown to the four winds as a deep-throated roar heralded the start of the engine. The propeller created such a backdraught it was like a miniature cyclone hitting Rob's face, making him gasp. Then the machine began to trundle forward over the field, where a large number of similar blue and yellow aircraft were also starting up. The afternoon had burst into roaring life as the British cadets embarked on what they had travelled so far to do.

Rob's machine gathered speed. The engine noise increased further, and he was almost breathless in the stream of air rushing past his helmeted head. With his pulse racing, he realized the Stearman was off the ground and rising fast to join others resembling a flock of double-winged geese. His stomach appeared to have left its usual place to rise up to his throat, and an unknown force was pressing down on his head. He swallowed and clutched the padded rim of the cockpit to stop himself being blown away despite his restraining harness.

'How does it feel?' came a voice in his ear.

'Very strange,' he muttered, then remembered that he could not be heard and glanced up at the mirror. His instructor was smiling so he tried to smile back, though without much success.

'Relax and look around. We're now eight hundred feet up and going to cruise here awhile. Take a look and see what you can identify down there.'

Still clutching the side of his cockpit Rob gave a tentative glance at the ground. It was amazing! He saw Carlstrom as an open green area amidst orange groves. There was the circular perimeter, the accommodation blocks, the blue rectangle of the swimming-pool, the six tiny tennis courts. The hangars looked so small from here. Over to his left lay

Arcadia, its streets showing as a giant tree-dotted grid, lined with miniature buildings and containing cars no bigger than dinky toys. Swivelling his head, Rob realized he could see as far as the horizon over a flat green landscape cut by shining ribbons of water and large, glistening lakes. A sensation of amazing joy started to creep over him as he gazed up at the sky. Up here a person could be anything he chose to be. He was free; unbelievably free!

'If you've seen enough, shall we start learning to fly?' asked a crisp voice in Rob's ear.

'Yes, please,' he agreed fervently, then remembered and merely nodded at the mirror with a smile born of his excitement.

'Take a look at the wings in relation to the horizon. That's how you must keep them in order to fly straight and level. If the horizon drops, you'll know you're gaining height and you'll ease forward with the stick until it becomes level again. If the horizon appears to be rising, the reverse applies. Never make violent movements or you'll find yourself in trouble. She's like a woman; treat her gently with a light touch and she'll give you exactly what you want. Besides watching the horizon, keep glancing at that large centre dial. That's rather like a spirit level. If the ball's right in the centre you know you're flying level. You'll need that in the clouds, or when you're heading into the sun and can't see the horizon. Now, take hold of the stick with your right hand. Got it? Good. You have control.'

All nervousness had fled. Rob concentrated on the horizon and thrilled to the knowledge that he was in charge of this large, noisy, *wonderful* machine. He, Rob Stallard, was eight hundred feet above the ground in America, flying an aeroplane! Only six months ago he had been working on a farm and yearning to be an engineer. Like Toad of Toad Hall, Rob now knew that this was the *only* thing to do.

'You're doing fine,' came the voice down the speaking-tube. 'I want you to make a turn. Push the stick gently but firmly to the right. The right wing will dip and the left will rise. But watch the nose. Don't let it drop. Keep your eye on the altimeter, which now shows eight hundred. The needle must stay right there. Take your time and go into the turn when you're ready.'

Rob followed through, loving the sensation of the Stearman responding to his commands. With Lawson's voice warning him that he was losing height, and then telling him to pull out of the turn and fly level again, he completed the manoeuvre reasonably well. When told to make a left turn, he did so bearing in mind what he had done wrong before. After half a dozen more he was turning more easily and with confidence. Then came Lawson's voice to say he had taken control for landing. It was a blow. Rob was not willing to return to earth.

He listened to his instructor explaining all he was doing as they dropped lower and lower, and he saw the entire flock of Stearmans making their way homeward to where other cadets were awaiting their first venture into the blue. Lawson landed with scarcely a bump and taxied to the flight line before switching off and telling Rob to disconnect the communication tube before getting out. It was sweltering back on the ground. Perspiration ran down Rob's face, as he tugged off his helmet to find his hair was wet beneath it.

Lawson jumped to the grass beside him. 'That's flying. How did you like it?'

'It was far too short. I wasn't ready to come down,' Rob confessed.

'First rule of a good pilot is to be willing to return to his natural element. Men were not meant to fly, and those who are only happy in the air are fooling themselves. This is where we belong,' he insisted, jabbing his thumb earthwards. 'Any time we spend up there is a precious gift that we must never abuse. Remember that.'

'Yes, sir,' mumbled Rob, feeling he was being given a reprimand.

'Having said that, I have this gut feeling that we're going to make progress together. You've got a fair grasp of the principles of flight — quick with book learning, are you? — and you've a reasonably steady hand on the stick during turns. Surprising, when you've had no driving experience.'

'I've worked a tractor since I was fourteen.'

Lawson frowned. 'You said you didn't drive.'

'You asked about a car, sir.'

The American looked nonplussed, 'Seems I must be more specific when I'm teaching British cadets.' He nodded a dismissal. 'We'll fly again tomorrow.'

Rob returned to his quarters marching on air. Once there, he was surprised when Johnny flung himself on his bunk. His friend's face was unusually pale as he glowered at Rob and asked what he was looking so cheerful about.

'It's normally me saying that to you.' Rob threw his helmet and goggles on the bunk beneath Johnny's, then sank blissfully on to a nearby chair. After a moment or two he came out of his reverie to remember where he was and looked across at the bunks. 'What's up?'

'My lunch, that's what. I was sick all down my flying suit.' Johnny groaned. 'I still feel as if I'm going over and over.'

'Gosh, did you loop the loop?' cried Rob enviously. 'All we did was fly in a gigantic circle umpteen times, then land.'

'That's all *we* did, and my belly didn't like it one bit. As we touched ground, so did my lunch.' He groaned again. 'A fine bloody pilot I'll be. Instead of dropping bombs I'll be sent over to *vomit* on the Jerries.'

'You'll get over it, like we all did on the ship,' Rob said encouragingly. 'I felt a bit funny while we were climbing, but I soon forgot that when I took the controls.' He stretched his arms above his head in a gesture of ecstasy. 'I'd no idea flying would be like that. It's the most exciting thing I've ever done.'

'More exciting than laying a girl?' asked Johnny in retaliation, having long ago guessed that Rob was a stranger to sexual encounters.

Rob squinted at him. 'Are you sick doing that, too?'

'Very funny.' Johnny raised his head cautiously. 'I need to cool off in the pool.'

'I'll come with you,' said Rob, still thinking of the turns he had made.

'Don't you think it's time you told them you can't swim?'

'I'm not the only one. I've never seen Bunny Pershore do more than jump about in the shallow end.'

'He just likes jumping.'

'I like flying. I *really* like it!' murmured Rob, away again in his magic world of discovery. 'Who'd be an engineer when he can be a pilot?'

'Oh blimey, that's all I need,' grumbled Johnny, sitting on the edge of his bunk. 'For weeks you've been moaning that the last thing you want to do is fly. Now you aim to be a bloody ace.'

'No, I don't. I simply want to take up an aircraft — any aircraft — day after day,' Rob replied dreamily. 'I'm sure no girl could match the thrill of that.'

Chapter Four

Jim continued his training with another instructor, and the threat of washout hanging over him. It was not a happy situation for any cadet, but for a man with the need to prove himself to a father who had never been a failure at anything it was an intolerable burden. Knowing the new man, Clint Lawson, would have been briefed on why Grogan had refused to continue teaching him, Jim responded stiffly at their introduction. However, Lawson gave no signs of undue censure as he discussed his pupil's skills and weaknesses at the flight line.

'You know, it's easy enough to take this machine off the ground. Once she starts running along with her propeller whirring, up she goes. In the air, any pilot with basic knowledge can keep her going for as long as the fuel lasts. Bringing her down, now, that's altogether different. I've seen men do just about everything trying to land this lady. Swerves, skids, bounces, pancakes, whirligigs; broken wings, busted undercarriage, smashed nose, ripped-off tail. Oh boy, the contest between man and flying machine is at its greatest when *he* wants to return to his own element and *she* turns fickle.' His attitude eased Jim's tension. 'Seems we have to concentrate on showing her who's boss. Get on up in that cockpit and let's fly!'

After take-off, Lawson said through his speaking-tube, 'What I want for us to do today is circuits and landings — nothing else. Once we've licked that, we can go on to those manoeuvres you've already cracked.'

Jim's heart sank. Right back to basics! He would never solo at this rate. His expression was all too obvious to the man up front, but the voice in Jim's ear was impassive as Lawson said, 'Some of those guys I mentioned just now who skidded and bumped and swerved? Bin flying now for years. It's like I said; landing's a bitch. We all have trouble with it.'

For an hour they joined the others on the wide circuit encompassing four outlying fields used for practice landings, but despite Lawson's words Jim was tense remembering how he had almost landed on Brad Halloran's crashed aircraft. It was an exceptionally hot day and he sweated profusely in the execution of 'bumps', as these frequent landings were called by the cadets. Gliding down into first one field, then another, when the heat and humidity seemed intolerable, only to take off again to prepare for the next landing on the circuit, persuaded Jim he had made a grave mistake in his choice of career. Flying had suddenly become totally unenjoyable. Why had he ever thought it the gateway to freedom? Where was the thrill and elation of becoming a lord of the air when all he did was take off, fly on a straight leg, then go down again?

Hot, tired and dispirited, Jim returned to Carlstrom and made his worst landing of the afternoon in front of some interested RAF cadets. After climbing from the cockpit, he stood impatiently while his instructor scribbled his comments, then was astonished by the man's words as he glanced up.

'When I was a schoolkid I had a bad time because my old man was the head teacher. See, everyone supposed I'd be top of the class. So did I. But it turned out I couldn't do math like my dad, nor history. Hell, that list of presidents! I knew their names, but could I remember the dates? As for literature, I had no interest in it.'

Lawson leaned against the fuselage and fixed his pupil with a stern gaze. 'Near my home was an airfield. I'd go there when school was out, to watch those engine-driven birds rise into the sky, and I'd tell myself one day I'd take one up. Well, I've been doing that for more'n twenty years.' He pulled off his helmet and wiped his brow with the back of his hand. 'Now, my old man can still solve complicated math problems, he can recite the names and dates of our presidents, he can even quote Mark Twain word perfect. But he can't fly an airplane. I can do those school subjects mediocre — enough to get by — and I *can* fly. See, J.T. Benson, soon as I stopped trying to be what everyone expected, I got along fine.'

In no mood for sermonizing, Jim stared back without a word in lengthening silence, until Lawson nodded. 'That's it for today, but hear this first. You're a punishing athlete and almost certainly the most popular cadet on campus. You have the right qualities for leadership, so there's no reason to suppose you won't reach high rank one day. Alongside all that, try to accept that you'll probably never be more than a competent pilot. None of us can excel at everything in this goddam life.' He began walking away. 'I'll see you tomorrow ... if you can spare the time.'

'Mr Lawson,' called Jim, and when the man turned, added gruffly, 'an apology from me is probably in order, sir.'

The instructor nodded. 'Better still a change of name.'

*

The canteen was fairly full that evening. The RAF cadets were voluble over their first ventures into the air, and shed some of their reserve. Wary exchanges were made between them and those Americans enjoying ice-creams at the counter, and flying talk then bridged the gap. Soon, a definite softening of attitudes heralded the beginnings of integration between the more extrovert men on both sides. A sing-song started when an RAF corporal put his own words to a well-known music-hall favourite, and his colleagues joined in.

O-o-h, he flies through the air with the greatest of ease:
The daring young man with a girl on his knees.
He should have flown solo but who gives a damn?
The Wingco is fa-a-r away.

Not understanding what a 'wingco' was, the Americans nevertheless added their voices to the ditty. Then they introduced several of their own rowdy versions of military songs, and their British colleagues joined in with gusto. Not wishing to put a damper on the high spirits, Gus Buckhalter suggested that Jim and Bucket should take over the musical interlude before it got out of hand and upset the two women behind the counter.

For more than half an hour Bucket let rip on the drums while Jim played his saxophone along with another cadet who could make a trumpet sound sweet or martial. The young men eager to let off steam gathered around, tapping their feet and clapping their hands, and the roistering gradually quietened.

The evening suited Jim's mood admirably. Whenever he felt low he needed to chase away the blues with activity, preferably in a woman's company. That being denied him, the uninhibited singing of masculine songs with close companions released his tension. However, the moment he took up his saxophone and made sweet music he grew mellow. A comforting warmth crept over him, and his sense of failure was eased by it.

He was not so lost in his music that he did not notice one abstainer from the general enjoyment of the amateur group, and by the time their

56

captain began flicking switches to warn them that lights out was just fifteen minutes off, the Englishman had already left.

Jim and Bucket had discovered a shadowed corner at the end of their accommodation block, and they frequently slipped outside on hot nights to take advantage of the breeze, knowing they could not be seen from the road behind their living quarters. Bucket was still fired up by his session on the drums. He smoked a cigarette with quick inhalations as he enthused over some of the numbers they had performed. Jim remained silent, letting his friend talk the excitement out of his system, while enjoying the sensation of wind ruffling his hair. It reminded him of his mother's fingers doing much the same when she had said goodnight to him in the nursery. When girls did it they were encouraging ravishment, but the breeze created that soothing quality Maybelle Benson had used towards her small son. Jim suddenly longed for her as he had not done for some time.

'You're quiet,' said Bucket.

'Haven't had a chance to say anything yet.'

'How'd it go today?'

Jim sighed, linking his hands around his bent right knee. 'I wondered when you'd get around to asking.'

'Saw your face when you left the flight line. Guessed it'd be wise to wait a while.'

'You guessed right.'

'So what did he tell you, this new instructor?'

'To change my name.'

'That figures. I heard he was one of the best.'

For almost thirty seconds Jim gazed across the distance to where the tall outlines of hangars rose darkly against the starlit night. Then he said, 'If I fail this course I'll never be able to face him.'

'Lawson?'

'You know who.'

Bucket shifted his position as he bent to his cupped hands and lit another cigarette. After exhaling smoke, he said conversationally, 'You better hadn't fail or Lawson'll be out of a job.'

There was a strong enough hint in that comment to force a confession from Jim. 'I'll admit I enjoy the sensation of power — what man doesn't? — but I couldn't destroy a man's life in my climb to the top.

That's why I'm damned certain I don't want to run his company. He can't see things my way ... and if he did, he'd say it was weakness. If I fail as a pilot he'll say the same.'

'You won't fail.'

Jim glanced at his friend's face, which was faintly illuminated by the glow of his cigarette. 'Because I'm James Theodore Benson the Third?'

'Because you badly need to succeed. Lawson's right. Forget who you are and remind yourself you're in good company. There's Frank, Chuck, Webb, Mitch, Pepe and the two Karls to solo yet. Stop thinking of your old man and show the RAF guys what you can do.'

'There's one I'd certainly like to ...' He was about to say 'impress', then decided it was the wrong word.

'To what?'

Jim shrugged, his gaze still on the dark bulk of the hangars. 'That one Jordan introduced to us at the pool the first day. Big feller; brown hair, rarely cracks a smile, moves slow but has sharp eyes.'

'What about him?'

'Gus and I caught this mussed-up guy in a crumpled suit puking behind the British quarters just as they were all coming in. We thought he was one of the locals brought in to get the place ready. Gus told him pretty smartly to clean up his disgusting mess, and I think I said something about British flying cadets about to occupy the place he was fouling up. He darn near folded at the knees before we walked off. I might not have recognized him if he had behaved normally, but when I shook his hand he turned it into a trial of strength. That made me take a closer look, and I thought the glare he gave me was a warning not to mention the embarrassing business that morning.'

'You mean *he* was the guy chucking up behind the huts?'

'I made some comment that he probably had mixed feelings about being here.' Jim could see again that inexplicably steely-eyed look in response. 'He told me his feelings were not in the least mixed, and wouldn't change. I don't know who the hell he thinks he is.'

'Why don't you ask him?' suggested Bucket mildly.

Jim ignored that. 'Yesterday there were news photographers taking pictures of the British men, so one of them has me and Gus up there on the flight line to get some shots with them. "Hands across the sea; American general's son greets the brave boys from over there. J.T.

Benson extends a welcome to the RAF." You know the kind of line they like.'

'You told me all this once,' Bucket said dryly

'I didn't tell you Old Sourface was there showing his feelings were still not mixed, and when they set up a group with Gus and me in the centre, he walked away from it.' Really irked by now, Jim added, 'He did the same thing this evening. Although he didn't sing, he actually smiled once or twice. When Gus asked us to play, and everyone gathered round, he got up and left. I don't know what's eating him, but if he can't get over being caught vomiting when he's here to be some kind of Air Force hero, he'll never make it. The RAF must be desperate if he's all they can get to fly their Spitfires.'

'So what d'you care? You won't be flying with him.'

*

On the following two days Clint Lawson decreed that Jim must concentrate on landings until he rid himself of his hang-up over them. Schooling his frustration with difficulty Jim finally lost the battle when, at the conclusion of the lesson on Saturday, the instructor told him one more hour on the circuit should be enough.

Walking across the grass towards the flight office where a few British cadets were clustered ready for their lessons, Jim said heatedly, 'I'll be able to land with my eyes closed by then.'

Lawson said, 'That'll be an advantage. When you move on to Basic, you'll do night flying. That'll be a lot like landing with your eyes closed.'

The older man walked away, leaving Jim depressed. If he could not successfully bring a Stearman down in perfect visibility how would he land a more complex machine in the dark?

Back in their quarters to change ready for their weekend of freedom from discipline, Gus pulled on his trousers, asking sympathetically, 'Bumps again, J.T.?'

'It's all Lawson can think of.' Jim dragged off his all-in-one flying suit, which became stuck over his boots. It seemed the last straw. 'Hell, I'm taking myself to Palm Beach for a coupla days,' he grunted, struggling to free the garment. 'How's about it, Bucket?'

His friend shook his head. 'I've promised myself a visit to Patsy May, and if you're going to be away I might stand a chance of a little cosy romance.'

Gus buttoned his shirt. 'Nothing like that for me. Pick up a hellcat of a cousin, then join the family at an official dinner to mark the twenty-fifth anniversary of my old man's entry into the army. The only thing to mar the occasion will be that his son has chosen to join a crazy outfit called the Air Corps which no real soldier can take seriously. The whole family will make me aware of that.'

'Seduce the hellcat cousin and show them just how crazy airmen are,' grunted Jim, tugging off his boots and throwing them one after the other into his open locker with a sportsman's accuracy.

'You haven't seen her,' said Gus with a shudder.

'Are you coming?' demanded Peter impatiently. 'If you want a ride to Sarasota I'm leaving now.'

'So long, guys,' said Gus, catching up his bag and following his friend outside. 'Duty calls.'

Watching their retreating figures, Bucket mused, 'Can you imagine any father not being proud of *him*?'

'Yes.' Jim padded to the bathroom for a shower. 'Fathers are like that.'

Bucket followed and leaned against the door jamb. 'Sure you want to go chasing over to Palm Beach? I'll share Patsy May with you.'

'I want to shake the dust of this place from my feet,' Jim said above the running water. As he soaped his muscular body and massaged his scalp, he felt that desire even more urgently. Carlstrom was getting him down. He needed some freedom.

From the moment he passed through the gates and headed east, a sense of release washed over him. He drove even faster than usual, revelling in handling a superb machine with skill and precision, and without a voice in his ear undermining his mastery of it. He arrived at the beach house in time for cocktails with a redhead who knew how to make a man make her enjoy herself. Liza Polanski would leave any partner for Jim and, the moment he appeared on the beach in brief swimwear with a towel around his neck, she ran along the sand to greet him in just the way he needed.

Jim's natural confidence returned as he swam, surfed and played with the wilder set in that millionaire's paradise resort until the sun went down. Then it was dining and dancing through the early hours with Liza in a dazzling silver dress, whispering provocatively in his ear and running her fingers through his thick hair. Jim took her back to the house for the night. Carlos and Maria Martinez, the resident valet and housekeeper, were used to finding a woman in Mr Jim's room in the morning, so they took little notice of a female voice softly laughing when he came in.

Jim slept well — he usually did after enjoying a woman — so he was shaken awake by Carlos long before he was ready. Reluctant to fight off sleep and hazily aware of a tempting female body beside him, Jim could not initially think where he was. Then some insistent words penetrated his muzzy brain.

'Mr Jim, your father is here.'

His eyes shot open. 'He can't be.'

The Mexican's face was serious. 'He came in fifteen minutes ago. He wants to see you. *Now!* You don't come down, he'll come up, he says.'

Jim sat up with his head in his hands and groaned. 'Get me some coffee while I take a shower, and for Pete's sake stop him coming up. Better still, I'll lock the door.'

'How I bring coffee in if you lock the door?'

Getting from the bed, Jim groaned again. 'I'll leave the door. Just get that coffee, strong and black.'

It was more a swift dousing than a shower, and the coffee did little to clear his head, but Jim felt better for both when he pulled on undershorts and wrapped a white robe round his damp body before going barefoot down the polished wood stairs to a room with so great an area of glass there was a total view of the ocean. Theo was seated at the circular table on which stood a jug of orange juice, a tray bearing a silver coffee pot and elegant cups, dishes of eggs, ham and crispy potatoes. There were three place settings. Jim stared. Surely his father had not expected him to bring Liza down for breakfast!

'Thought you might be here,' Theo said darkly, no hint of a smile on his freshly shaven face. 'Arcadia's too damn near. Easy to play hookey.'

'I'm not in the third grade, sir,' Jim protested, conscious of the dark stubble on his own face, and of his bare feet. 'This is my weekend leave. Everyone gets out on Saturday and Sunday.' When Theo said nothing, Jim added, 'If I'd known you wanted me to join you for breakfast, I'd have dressed.'

Theo glared. 'I thought military men rose early and got on with the job.'

Still worried about that third place setting, Jim crossed to the table, seeing nothing of the breakers crashing on to the beach or of the clear, pale skies of sunrise. 'We're up at five every day except Sunday, and we're hard at it until lights out. Is this a short vacation from your campaign trail?'

'It is not. *I* don't get weekend leave. You'll know what work really is when you join the company next year.'

With his mouth open to deny that he would, Jim was prevented from speaking by Shelley's voice from the staircase. 'Don't shout at the poor boy, Theo. He's only just woken. Good morning, Jim. Forgive your father. He's apt to be a bear at breakfast. Pour some coffee, darling. You look as if you need it.'

Jim felt too unsettled to sit so he stood by the sweep of windows to drink his coffee, acutely conscious of Shelley's scrutiny as he waited for Theo to give his reason for being at this house he rarely used. When he did explain, it took him by complete surprise.

'The campaign is a washout. I've sacked Menzies and his pathetic tribe. They couldn't get a monkey elected to the ape house. Shepherdson's in touch with the new man, who's bringing his committee here this morning. I need to be out of circulation for a while. No one saw us drive in. Warner's putting it out that Shelley's suffering from a fever and I'm by her bedside. It's good to present the image of a loving husband.'

Shelley glanced up from buttering a biscuit. 'But you *would* be at my beside if I had a fever, *wouldn't* you, Theo?'

'Don't be irritating. This is not the time for your curious sense of humour, Shelley. If I don't get the show on the road you can kiss goodbye to shopping with the First Lady,' Theo snapped.

Jim was overcome by the notion of his father *not* being elected senator. What a piece of good fortune it would be. Theo could devote himself to his company and would not need his son in the boardroom. Suddenly, the future looked brighter. Jim even managed a relaxed smile at Shelley as he made to pour himself more coffee.

The pleasant hiatus was immediately broken when Theo said harshly, 'I want you away from here before Shepherdson arrives with the new committee. I need you to be seen as a dedicated flier; and one of this country's military defenders. How the hell is it going to seem if these men turn up to find you here looking as if you fell out of a trash can? Get your ass up those stairs and tell whoever is in your bed to disappear, and *fast*. Then you can throw on some clothes and follow her.'

Furious, and conscious of Shelley's titillation over his humiliating treatment, Jim slammed his coffee cup on the table and strode towards the stairs. Theo's voice pursued him. 'Warner's been on top line for the picture of your first solo. I told him to forget it. After all this time, even goddam Mickey Mouse could have got there. Why haven't you?'

Breathing heavily, Jim charged into his bedroom, slammed the door behind him, picked up the nearest thing to hand, and flung it against the wall with all of his immense strength. The coffee pot smashed, sending a burst of dark liquid across the cream surface. Liza roused sufficiently to roll over and ask sleepily, 'Is that you, darling?'

'No ... it's goddam Mickey Mouse.'

*

On that Sunday morning Rob awoke with feelings that were genuinely mixed. Last evening he had met the most wonderful girl in the world. True to his word, Duke Foster had taken Rob and his room-mates out to his ranch for dinner. Waiting to greet them were his wife, Peggy, his son, Mark, and a sixteen-year-old beauty named Laura. One look at the girl and Rob's toes had curled with an alien emotion, and when she had called him 'Rarb' in a soft, beguiling Southern accent he was completely lost.

All through the evening he had covertly watched her, and his heartbeat had quickened whenever she addressed him or cast him a glowing look. Although Patrick had made obvious advances to her, she had appeared to prefer someone whose rural accent somehow fascinated her. Whenever she asked him to repeat something he had said in reply to her mother's friendly questions about himself, Rob's colour had risen, making him yearn for self-assurance like Johnny's. Yet Laura had asked *him* to sit beside her on the porch to watch the sunset after dinner. Thrilled by her nearness, and by the glorious colours that stained the sky for a long while even after the sun had gone, Rob had finally understood what youth was all about.

Then eleven-year-old Mark had spoiled the wonderful evening by talking about the famous J.T. Benson, who had apparently visited the local school to demonstrate to the boys his expertise at football. The whole of Arcadia thought Benson was 'the greatest', according to Mark. Then he had revealed that Laura had a picture from a society magazine pinned to her bedroom wall. 'She's just plumb crazy about him,' Mark had said with adolescent male scorn. 'She even cut off the girl who was in the picture with him. As if he'd look twice at someone who works in the downtown dairy!'

Laura's feelings for Benson, and his own inability to swim, made Rob view the coming visit to the beach with the Fosters uncertainly. With Patrick set on getting Laura's attention as well, the outing promised to be less than wholly enjoyable. Love brought pain as well as joy, he realized.

Riding in Duke's truck, along with Mark, while the others went in the car, Rob forgot his jealousy of Patrick, who was sitting beside Laura for the journey, when they broke from the streets of a small settlement and took a rough track which gave him his first sight of the Gulf of Mexico.

The sea was the same incredible blue as the sky, as it crashed on to a beach running for as far as the eye could see in both directions. Backing the sands was a long line of palms providing a green fringed barrier to the sun. Rob climbed from the truck like a man in a trance, gazing around with eyes dazzled by sunlight catching the crests of breakers just before they tumbled on to the shore. It was like a picture in the magazines his sister loved to buy.

Duke came alongside. 'We don't get here too often — always seem to be busy. But when we do, it kinda hits us anew.'

Rob was so overwhelmed by the vivid colours of sky, sand and water that he stayed where he was, oblivious of the activity around the truck. There were birds, large brown ones he did not recognize, which glided mere inches from the surface of the sea, then climbed swiftly to keel over and dive like fighter aircraft, their long, long beaks forming arrowheads. Moments before entering the water to catch a fish, they closed their wings against their bodies to become perfect darts. With his head full of the theories of flight, Rob saw them as skilled exponents.

'What are those birds?' he asked Mark, his gaze still on the avian spectacle.

The boy halted with some boxes in his hands. 'Pelicans. They're all around here. Why?'

'They're ... magnificent,' he finished enthusiastically. 'They've mastered something we can't yet do. If we could build a plane that would dive into the sea, then surface and take off again, we could chase submarines from the Atlantic. Trouble is, the fuselage would never be strong enough to withstand the impact and ...' He continued with his wild theory unaware that Mark was watching him with something approaching awe.

'Aren't you coming in, Rob?'

He returned from his vision of arrow-shaped aircraft to find Laura and his friends already in bathing suits. The sight of Laura in a bright red garment revealing long brown legs, a great deal of her upper body and a tantalizing outline of her vital statistics drove all thoughts of futuristic flying machines from Rob's thoughts. Pin-up girls left little to the imagination, but this one was flesh and blood and Rob reacted quite violently when Patrick grabbed her hand and ran her down to the water, making her squeal.

'Hey, stop that!' he yelled, starting forward. 'She doesn't like it.'

'Yes, she does,' called Patrick, now holding her pinioned by both arms as he marched her forward. 'You're loving every minute, aren't you, Laura?'

Her response was a laughing denial whilst making no attempt to struggle, but Rob began dragging off his clothes in readiness to put a stop to what was going on.

'She's all right, Rob. Girls like a little fun. It's harmless enough, and Laura's an expert swimmer,' said Peggy gently.

The fight went out of him — how could he possibly help or impress her by merely jumping over the waves? — and he mooned about on the edge of the sand watching Patrick having fun with Laura, until Johnny waded ashore with some advice.

'Stop looking like a thundercloud and go after her. No girl would prefer that runt when there's a chap like you around.' He grinned. 'She might even forget J.T. Benson if you flexed those hefty muscles of yours — even if you got 'em in the farmyard instead of on a tennis court.'

'What a hope,' Rob said heavily, the mention of Benson adding to the loss of that enchantment he had felt on arrival. 'If I go in there with those two I'll make a fool of myself.'

'What the devil d'you think you're doing now?'

Duke and Peggy then joined them for a dip, so Rob made a pretence of politeness by staying in the shallows with his hostess, thereby solving his dilemma and further endearing himself to Laura's mother. Afterwards, they settled in the shade of the palms for something the Fosters called a wiener roast, during which Rob began to relax. Toasting frankfurters over an open fire to eat with potato salad, beans and watermelon was the kind of activity which prompted easy conversation, and when marshmallows replaced wienies on the end of palmetto sticks cut for the purpose, laughter and yells as fingers and tongues were singed removed any remaining inhibitions. The Fosters and the four British cadets had become firm friends.

After helping Peggy pack away the leftovers, they all stretched out on their towels, lethargic in the heat of early afternoon. Rob lay with his arms beneath his head, gazing at the moving pattern of palm fronds against the sky. Having always worked from early morning right through the day, he was not used to taking cat naps even after a large meal, but he was pleasantly lulled by the rhythmic sound of waves breaking as his thoughts switched from how much Jenny would love to be there to the spectacle of the diving pelicans, then to how he could show Laura he liked her.

In the midst of this difficult problem, Mark nudged him. 'Take a look at that, Rob,' he said quietly.

Sitting up and following the direction of the boy's pointing finger, Rob gazed spellbound as several dark shapes arched above the surface of the sea no more than a few yards from the shore.

'Dolphins,' said Mark. 'Look around. There's a lot. Fish must be shoaling out there.'

Before Rob's delighted gaze two dolphins suddenly leaped clear of the water before crashing back into it, sending spray flying. Unaware of moving, Rob found himself standing with water lapping over his feet as he scanned the rolling surface for the next sighting of these beautiful creatures. Ridiculously, he felt a lump forming in his throat as he watched the spectacle being repeated several times.

'They're great, aren't they?'

He turned to find Laura beside him. 'I've never seen any before ... and I'll never forget the first time I did.' He looked back at the sea. 'I can't wait to write to Jenny about today.'

'You're very fond of her?'

He nodded. 'She's all the family I have.'

'You're very fond of simple things, too. I can tell that by the way you enjoyed the sunset yesterday, and now the dolphins. I like living here instead of in a big city, so I suppose I'm a country girl.' She paused for a moment. 'And you're a country boy.'

Losing interest in the dolphins, Rob said, 'It's a different kind of countryside where I come from.'

'Would I like it?'

'Not with the war on at the moment.' Laura began to stroll along the shoreline, so he fell in beside her. 'But there's no place like Thoresby when there are buttercups and daisies all over the meadows, and the fruit trees are a mass of blossom. Or on a summer's day when everything is so green and the birds fly to roost as late as ten o'clock. And you should see it in the autumn when the leaves turn yellow, orange and red. Our valley is magnificent then.'

His pulse quickened as Laura's hand slid into his in a gesture of comfort. 'Are you so very unhappy here?'

His ready colour rose. 'I didn't mean to suggest ... your parents are being so nice, no one could be unhappy.'

'But you must sometimes feel homesick. I couldn't bear to be so far away from all this.'

'You would if you had to.'

The day became even more magical as the hot breeze ruffled his hair and burned into his skin, while a sweet, gentle girl walked so close beside him their bare arms touched. When they eventually turned they found the others were mere dots in the distance.

'Your parents will be anxious about you,' said Rob in dismay.

'They might be if I was with Pat, but Daddy says you're a good, steady lad.'

'I expect that's because I know about farming,' he replied awkwardly, fearing she was laughing at him.

'You're not a farmer now.' She stopped to study him. 'Is it very difficult to learn to fly?'

'I don't know, I've only had two lessons. There's a lot to remember, and these are the simplest kind of aircraft. It'll get more difficult.'

'Do you mind having to leave your farm to do that instead?'

'No,' he said fervently. 'You've no idea how it feels to get up to several thousand feet and look down on all this. I don't want to come down again.'

She laughed softly. 'Rob, the angel.'

Looking down at her sunkissed face surrounded by dark tumbled hair, a sudden surge of desire made him unusually eloquent. '*You're* the angel, Laura.'

It was her turn to blush, and she turned away, leaving Rob mentally kicking himself for upsetting her and spoiling everything. Yet he had not, for after walking in silence for a while Laura glanced up with a smile. 'I thought I'd never get to know you. Your friends are so talkative, but you hardly say anything when we're all together.'

'I hope I haven't seemed rude,' he said hastily.

She shook her head. 'Just rather sad.'

An extra-large wave crashed beside them to engulf Laura as far as her waist. Rob grabbed her instinctively as the receding water almost dragged her off her feet, and he held her steady while she laughed up at him. She looked so lovely with her eyes sparkling and her tanned skin glistening with droplets of water that Rob said impulsively, 'I'm not sad today. I've never felt as happy as I do now ... with you.'

They gazed at each other with the pull of youth and the fascination of alien cultures strong in them, until Laura asked softly, 'Do you have a girl in England, Rob?'

Still beneath the spell of this heady day, he shook his head. 'I was so busy studying I didn't have time to get to know any.' Then he could not stop himself asking, 'What about you and Benson?'

Her cheeks grew rosy as she gazed out over the sea. 'He's every girl's dreamboat, that's all.' They walked on for a short distance, then she gazed back at Rob, her colour still high. 'There's a dance next Saturday night in town. Would you like to take me to it?'

'Yes, *please*,' he said, the sun, the azure sea and the green palms doing a joyous whirl before his eyes. If he had been a dolphin he would have leaped clear of the water with the sheer exuberance of life.

Chapter Five

A severe storm hit southern Florida in the early hours of Monday morning, coming in across the Gulf of Mexico. The area around Miami took the brunt as it crossed the peninsula, leaving devastation in its wake. The RAF men saw the other face of the Sunshine State as leaden skies, torrential rain and high winds turned their airfield into a swamp and put an end to outdoor activities for three days. On the third, the rain stopped and the sun broke through, but the field down by the flight line was like a steaming sponge. The swimming-pool was full of arboreal debris, and the tennis courts were flooded.

Jim's black mood on returning from Palm Beach deepened further. Three days with no chance to gain that coveted solo! With no outlet for his immense physical energy, he was like a volcano waiting to erupt.

Rob was also in something of a ferment. Bursting with impatience to get back into the air, hating the dreary hours of tempestuous weather following the glory of his day on the beach, he faced a serious problem. He had no idea how to dance, yet he had agreed to take Laura to one. He turned to Johnny for help, but adamantly refused his friend's advice to go to the canteen where there were records to dance to.

'I'm not a fool,' Rob said. 'I'd be the laughing stock of Carlstrom if I let you waltz me around over there.'

'A lot of them dance together, you mutt.'

'They're doing that jig they're so fond of; they're not holding each other in their arms.'

'You mean the jive. It's the latest thing over here.'

'*I'm* never going to do it.'

'You couldn't,' his friend retaliated bluntly. 'You're too big and slow. You've got to be really nifty. Buck's teaching me.'

'You're getting very pally with them, aren't you?'

'Why not? They're okay.'

'*Okay*!' Rob repeated emphatically. 'You don't have to start talking like them.'

'Do you want me to help you or not?'

'Yes, but I'm not going to the canteen to make a fool of myself.'

Their first attempts were chaotic. Rob fell over Johnny's feet so often that his friend seized upon Patrick, who came in looking like a thundercloud, and insisted that he was about Laura's size and would make a better partner for Rob.

'Some other time,' growled Patrick. 'I'm not in the mood. In any case, you surely realize Laura only asked Rob to partner her because she wants to make me jealous. It's what all girls do and I've seen through her little game.'

'Is that why you're looking so fed up?' asked Cyril, writing his daily letter to Norma.

Patrick flopped on his bunk. 'They never give it a rest, do they? Buckhalter's just given me demerits for going around with my tie only loosely knotted. That means I'll have to walk the ramp on Saturday after ground school.' His friends made sympathetic noises, and he aired the rest of his grumbles. 'Benson's always pulling me up for the way I talk too much during meals, and Bernstein reckons I left dust beneath the bunks this morning. That's twice this week.' He gave a sour grin. 'I'm getting my own back at the poker table, though. I won fifteen dollars tonight.'

'Be careful, little Pat, they're sharper than you think,' warned Johnny. 'They may be leading you on, ready to take you for the lot when you're not expecting it.'

Patrick shook his head. 'I may not be brilliant at sweeping the floor, but I am at sweeping the board. My dad and Uncle Bob used to play poker with their pals every Saturday night in Gran's parlour, and I used to watch. I know what I'm doing with cards in my hand. I don't let the Yanks get away with much. They think it's beginner's luck so I let them go along with that idea.'

Cyril said, 'There's a notice in the canteen saying gambling for money is forbidden.'

'So what?' Patrick retorted. 'We're all doing it on the quiet.'

'Don't let Buckhalter or his cronies find out or you'll be in real trouble,' Cyril persisted.

'Get on with your passionate outpourings to Norma and credit me with some intelligence. Who's going to inform Buckhalter? Half the upperclass men are in on it. He wouldn't shop them, so I'm safe enough.'

'Are we having a dancing lesson or listening to Pat's wicked nightlife?' demanded Rob. 'I've only got five days to learn how to be a Fred Astaire.'

'That you'll never be, you great gallumping erk,' Johnny told him equably. 'By Saturday you might be able to waltz, but don't count on it.'

Much of Rob's free time that week was spent in their quarters pursuing the art of dance. With Johnny humming popular melodies, Rob allowed himself to be pushed and pulled around the room holding his friend's waist. He enjoyed no aspect of it and could not understand why ballroom dancing was so popular. The only reason he persevered was that the notion of holding Laura in his arms was so enthralling he was prepared to do almost anything to achieve it.

On Thursday flying was resumed, but the three-day break had affected the cadets adversely and most of them performed badly that day. In contrast, Rob was possessed by increased elation during his lesson, and Clint Lawson commented on it when they landed.

'The climb was too violent for a first attempt. You veered too far off course, but I guess you rectified it without much trouble when I signalled. Go a little easier on the stick. I told you before that an airplane is like a woman. Treat her gently to get the best out of her. Time enough for strong-arm stuff when you're in combat in a machine that outmanoeuvres any other. You'll be doing that soon enough.' They began walking across to the flight office. 'You're very sparky today. I was young myself and recognize the condition, but don't ever let thoughts of a pretty girl interfere with your concentration. You'll be of no use to her on crutches, or with a broken neck.'

The warning was not needed. Although Rob's thoughts now mainly concerned Laura, he always became single-minded during his study periods and whenever he climbed into the cockpit. He proved this the following day when he earned cautious approval from his instructor at the end of his lesson, on his grasp of the essentials for landing.

'*Ease* her. *Ease* her down. You're still too heavy-handed on the stick, but you've done well enough.' Lawson pulled off his helmet and smiled. 'Take things nice and steady and you'll form a partnership with airplanes that's more enduring than a fling with a beckoning woman.'

Rob smiled back wryly. 'Flying comes easier to me than dancing. I can't get the hang of *that*.'

'I never could, either,' Lawson confessed, unfastening his parachute at the end of his afternoon's tuition. 'You stepping out with your girl this weekend?'

Surprising himself, Rob began confiding his fears to this man he found easy to like. 'She asked if I'd take her and I said yes, forgetting I'd have to dance with her. I'm trying to learn by tomorrow.'

Lawson laughed. 'Oh my!'

'I'm not much good so far.' Rob shrugged out of his own parachute as they walked in the late afternoon sunshine.

'Take a piece of advice?' asked the older man.

'Isn't that what you've been giving me for the last hour?'

'You don't *have* to listen to this. The lesson's over.'

'Then it's good of you to offer it, sir.'

They were almost upon the cluster of cadets and instructors checking in at the office before dispersing, so Lawson halted and put his hand on Rob's arm. 'Never struggle with something that doesn't come naturally. Stick with what you do best and to hell with all else. I know a born flier when I see one. You'll do all right without dancing ... and if she's any sense she'll see that.' He nodded a goodbye.

After his flying sessions Rob liked to shower, then walk around the perimeter to unwind and reflect on all he had done during that thrilling hour. There were few opportunities for solitude during a day that began at dawn and put heavy demands on young men striving to learn an exact skill within a short time. The British cadets rarely lost sight of the fact that they were being trained for war, and would soon be facing enemy bullets while trying to remember all they had been taught. This had been brought home to Rob by Clint Lawson, and it was in his mind as he returned to the flight line for his walk before supper. The long line of Stearmans turned into Spitfires in his mind's eye. It would be wonderful to fly one, but how would he be in the face of the enemy? Did he have enough courage? He had never killed anyone. How would it feel to know he had brought another man's life to an end?

'Wotcher,' said Johnny, falling in alongside Rob and bringing him out of his dark reverie. 'You missed the chance of fame by flying last today. A photographer from a swanky magazine was here taking pictures of some of our chaps. She wanted good-looking ones so's they'd fit in with all the glamorous society people on the other pages. She might have picked you. You're not bad compared with some of our ugly blokes, but you always push off whenever a camera appears.'

'I can't see any point in it,' Rob replied, wishing his solitude had not been broken. 'We're here to learn to fly, not to make ourselves look silly doing some of the antics they suggest. Burke and Willis were put on horses each side of that cowgirl last week.'

'They didn't mind. Why should you?'

'What I think is plain daft is that we had to wear those thick civilian suits to travel from Canada, and we're dressed in American uniforms here, yet they're putting in all the papers that we're RAF. I thought that had to be hushed up because of neutrality, so I don't understand why they do it.'

Johnny shrugged. 'You don't understand anything unless it's to do with flying. You know that bit about all work and no play? You should get your nose out of flying manuals more often during evening break and join the rest in the canteen.'

'And gawp at *him* playing the saxophone? No, thanks.'

Stopping to face Rob, Johnny said, 'You've only spoken to him once, and he was friendly enough.'

Rob stepped past him and continued walking. This was the most relaxing part of his day and he wanted to enjoy it to the full. Although there was a great difference between Arcadia and Thoresby, it was possible in the peace and quiet at the end of flying to pretend he was back in the village that had been his home for eighteen years. On the far side of the airfield a hawk was hovering, watching for an unsuspecting creature that would make a meal. They did that above the fields of Darston Manor.

Johnny came up with him again. 'You didn't answer my comment about Benson. He's going to be here another five or six weeks.'

'Unless he gets washed out. He's under review already.'

'You should sympathize, not condemn.'

'Now you sound like the Padre!' He sighed. 'If you must know, it annoys me to see everyone, including some of our own chaps, hanging round him when he plays tennis or basketball. And why does he have to be in every photograph the newsmen take?'

'He's their hero.'

It was said in casual manner, but Rob rounded on him. 'They don't know what the word means.'

'Oh, come off it! He gives others the benefit of his skill. If you'd ever watched him you'd know he's happy to coach anyone who wants to improve their game. All right, so he knows he's good, and maybe enjoys an audience when he gets on the tennis court, but so would I if I could slam a ball across the net with the power he puts behind it.'

Rob walked on silently, unsure just why his initial resistance to Benson had deepened to dislike. He had never before felt such an immediate aversion to a person, especially one who was universally popular. The best he could make of his feelings was that he had been taught to respect the gentry, not idolize them. In his world, the Guthries had been the examples to follow. The backbone of England, Fred had maintained. People of principle and integrity. Sir Charles and his wife certainly recognized their place in society, but they had a quiet dignity and were treated with equally quiet respect. Villagers had never flocked around them each day to hear them hold forth; no one turned out to watch Sir Charles play golf. Young girls did not have cuttings from magazines showing him and Lady Guthrie at the county ball. Rob supposed they might have had postcards of Robert Taylor or Clark Gable once, and the boys their pictures of cricketers, but those had been replaced by postcards of Spitfires, tanks or submarines, and the cuttings now contained accounts of fiercely fought battles.

The truth was suddenly in the open as Rob remembered a woman and a small girl picking roses from a bush growing amid rubble, and he again visualized Liverpool ablaze beneath the dark, droning silhouettes of German bombers. The real heroes were ordinary people from all walks of life, who were having to do the most terrible things in order to keep their country free; not wealthy, influential, too-handsome men whose activities on the sports field and in the swimming-pool made them some kind of demigods. The hallowed J.T. Benson was learning to fly as no more than an interesting sideline. He would not be using his new skill against an enemy who had killed his loved ones and laid waste half his country.

Rob slowed and turned to Johnny. 'Thoresby was never bombed, but London has been. You've forgotten that, haven't you?'

'No, I haven't bloody forgotten,' Johnny returned, 'but I don't have to dislike a chap because he's good at tennis. It's not *his* fault the Jerries are bombing London. Look, we can't do anything for the folks at home until we've qualified as pilots and are sent back at Christmas. The Yanks have made it possible for us to train here in peace, so the least we can do is show them a bit of friendly gratitude.'

'I don't have to touch my cap each time I pass Benson.'

'Are you suggesting I do?'

Rob sighed and continued walking, his elation after flying completely ruined. 'You've just said we've got to qualify before we can help back home. I'm concentrating on doing that, instead of sitting in the canteen hearing them tell us how much bigger and better everything is in America,' he explained. 'They're here for the fun of it, that's all. It'd be different if they meant to help us fight instead of adding flying to their list of things to brag about.'

Johnny said, 'If you spent more time with them you'd know they're all eating their hearts out to go into action. They don't say much but they'd give their eye-teeth to be in our shoes.'

Rob shook his head vehemently. 'The only shoes they'd like to be in are Benson's. If he's their idea of a hero, then God help them if they ever do go to war.'

Unused to such sentiments from a normally placid man, Johnny responded heedlessly. 'I don't know why you're so worked up about it. You've been down on the farm away from air raids and miles from any form of danger. The war's hardly touched you.'

Rob felt himself grow cold as he stared at a man who was the closest to a friend he had ever had. 'My parents were visiting my grandmother in London six weeks before Christmas when her house got a direct hit. I had to identify their bodies. That's when I saw what the Jerries had done to your home town.'

Johnny took a deep breath. 'Oh God, my bloody great mouth! You said your people were dead and I thought they'd ... they'd been ill ... something that had happened a time ago. Why didn't you tell me this before?'

'Because I prefer not to talk about it.'

'But we're chums,' Johnny protested. 'You could've told *me*.'

'It wouldn't have changed the way you feel about your new American friends.'

'No, but it helps me understand why you sometimes like to be alone. You should have said something before, you mutt, instead of letting me sound off like that.'

Rob turned away and headed for his quarters. 'That's another of their expressions. You're beginning to talk just like them ... and don't say anything to anyone about my family, please, or you can forget about being chums.'

When they were halfway across the field Johnny broke the silence in quiet tones. 'This place is a paradise, I'm starting to talk like I'm from Noo York, and I'm getting keen on the rich food, but each time we fall in to raise and lower their flag I feel bloody homesick. I lie there after lights out thinking about fish and chips wrapped in newspaper, or a bit of my Aunt Vi's roly-poly with custard. I long to read an English newspaper and hear a cockney bus conductress saying, "Where to, luv?" There are even moments I wish I hadn't volunteered just so's I could sometimes walk along the Embankment. Dear old dirty brown Thames with tugs and barges chugging through the fog. It doesn't sound much, but it's home.'

Rob was astonished. Johnny had just confessed to feelings no one would guess he had. They had almost reached the accommodation blocks where the cadets were preparing to go to the dining hall for their supper, when Johnny added, 'Don't take it out on the Yanks, Rob. They didn't wipe out your family.'

'They could help us prevent others being wiped out,' he replied doggedly.

'Give 'em a little longer and they will.'

*

Jim and his room-mates studied for the obligatory period after supper that evening, and the silence was only broken by sighs of frustration, the scratching of pens on paper, and the turning of pages. He tried to concentrate, but found it even more difficult than usual. He needed that solo flight so badly that his anxiety was driving it further away. In the air he was steady and sure. It was when he began to descend that the jitters started so that he became heavy-handed at the controls. Until he had flown solo he would remain under review ... and slightly less able than Mickey Mouse!

He had heard no more from Theo. The papers duly reported the progress of the beautiful Shelley Benson's supposed fever, but mentioned nothing of the new campaign team. Jim fervently hoped his father would not be elected, but Theo always got what he planned for and this was his most glittering prize. Winning his wings was surely his own glittering prize, so why was he taking so long to conquer the basics of flight?

'Time's up, guys,' said Peter Kelsey, shutting his manual with a snap. 'I can read the theory of powered stalls all night and I still won't carry one off in copybook fashion tomorrow. Something happens to me when I get into one. I seem to freeze.'

'First time you tried it, today. Give yourself a chance,' reasoned Gus.

'I have that pleasure to come next lesson,' said Bucket with a frown. 'If I'd known there was so much to flying I'd have joined the Infantry instead. Been walking since I was a year old.'

They all laughed save Jim. Would he ever get around to powered stalls? Maybe he should have joined the Infantry.

Peter put away his books and announced that he was off to the canteen for a game of poker, to which the Cadet Captain replied that he hoped there was no money involved. 'You know the rules, Pete. No gambling.'

'Oh c'mon, Gus, we play for ice-cream stakes. Everyone knows that.'

Gus grinned. 'It's what's tucked under the dish I'm concerned about.'

Peter grinned back. 'Concern yourself about my powered stalls instead.'

He went out, and Gus said with a sigh, 'I know there's more than one little syndicate operating over there most nights, and I'm supposed to break them up. They keep it under wraps, so I turn a blind eye and risk being put under review if the CO should hear about it.'

'He won't,' said Bucket, busy at his locker. 'The guys have to let off steam somehow, and poker's better than some other ways. Let it ride, Gus.'

The general's son sighed again. 'They've pulled in some of the British cadets. They don't have the money we get. I can't have them running up debts.'

'They know what's what,' said Jim firmly. 'It's not up to you to keep them out of trouble. Why care, after the way they ignored some of our rules at the start? If they get hoodwinked by some of our hardened poker players, it'll cut them down to size.'

'They're okay,' said Bucket good-naturedly. 'I know some of them are a bit rough and speak a language we don't recognize — hell, the one from Scotland could be talking Chinese for all I understand of him — and one or two have the idea this is still one of their colonies, but on the whole they're trying to fit in.'

'Except Stallard,' Jim put in sharply. 'He has no intention of fitting in. I sit at his table for meals, as you know. Old Sourface concentrates on his food and rarely joins in the conversation. I don't know what's bugging him.'

'Maybe he's the strong, silent type,' suggested Bucket.

'He looks strong, sure,' said Gus, 'but I've marked him down as one of the Britishers who'll never last through Basic. He's something of a loner, and one of the essentials for a good pilot is to be able to lead a team. What use will he be in a bomber if he can't inspire his crew?'

'Perhaps the RAF'll give him a fighter,' argued Bucket. 'All the great pioneers of the air have been loners; men and women with a free spirit.'

'You're surely not grouping Stallard with them?' grunted Jim. 'I heard somewhere that he was a farmer. It's my guess he's from some hick town where people keep to themselves and run strangers off their territory at the end of a gun.'

'By all accounts he's no fool in the air,' Bucket murmured.

'With luck he'll stop up there one day and not come down.'

Gus looked at Jim in surprise. 'You're not letting him get to you, surely? Everyone on campus thinks you're the tops. Why worry about the one guy who doesn't? That's his loss.' He yawned loud and long. 'I'm hitting the sack. Big day tomorrow. Grogan wants me to simulate an emergency landing. If I don't get an early night it won't be a simulation.'

Feeling restless, Jim announced that he would take a jog round the perimeter before turning in, and Bucket offered to join him. In shorts and vests, they set off in the afterglow of sunset in companionable silence, although Jim's thoughts were not easy companions. Stallard *was* getting to him, and he deplored the fact. As Gus had said, why worry about the one man who held aloof? Jim had every advantage over the Englishman, yet the tilt of Stallard's head and the set of his mouth suggested otherwise. It was ridiculous, of course. The man had been caught in a humiliating situation on his arrival, but he had neither the polish nor the grace to put the incident aside and forget it. It did not occur to Jim that he, himself, could not forget it or put it aside.

Annoyed that the bovine ex-farmer should rattle him so much, Jim lifted his head to gaze across the grass towards the hangars and was shaken by what he saw. The sun had gone behind the trees to leave a vivid orange-red light. Jim was no aesthete and hardly ever noticed the spectacular sunsets in this Southern state, but tonight the afterglow cast a lurid reflection over the line of Stearmans so that they looked as if they were on fire.

Jim had a momentary insight into why Stallard might behave as he did; why there was a certain reserve beneath the surface mien of the British cadets. Learning to fly was a deadly serious business for them. As soon as they gained their wings they would be sent home to kill or be killed in the air. If they witnessed this sunset trick of turning aircraft into flaming machines, their blood must chill.

At that point, Bucket also became struck by the sight, and slowed. They both came to a standstill.

'It's kind of sobering, isn't it?' murmured Bucket, gazing ahead.

Jim sighed. 'I've had it all wrong, you know. My old man gave me a time limit in the air force, and I've thought only of that ultimatum; of showing him who's boss. I've somehow forgotten our real purpose in being here. If we get into this war I'll be a fighting man; pilot of a warplane. That's what I should be aiming for. Learning to fly isn't a means of getting my own way, it's fulfilling a pledge to my country.'

Bucket reached up to muss Jim's damp hair. 'You've known that all along, kiddo. You just lost sight of it for a while.' He put on a spell of exaggerated panting, then said with a grin, 'Can we now go to roost? I'm dead on my feet.'

Jim grinned back. 'Race you home.'

*

The dance hall was packed. Since Carlstrom Field had reopened, social events in Arcadia had flourished. One hundred and fifty young men seeking escape from the demands of their daily routine threw themselves fully into any entertainment offered, especially if there was a chance of female company. The local girls were highly delighted by this military invasion, and most thought fliers even more exciting than rodeo stars.

This caused jealousy and resentment from those who had had the field to themselves until three months ago, and nowhere was this more likely to flare up than at a public dance. Although the cadets were out of uniform, they were easily identifiable by their severe haircuts and well-pressed clothes. The British men had had an opportunity to buy suitably light outfits, and a large number were there on that hot Saturday evening with the daughters of families which had hosted them the previous weekend, and with the girlfriends of those daughters, who also wanted to meet the foreign fliers.

Jim had not been keen on the idea of attending the dance, but Bucket had eventually persuaded him to go and release his tension with simple fun. They arrived some time after the event had started, knowing things would have warmed up by then. Jim could always take his pick of the girls — they practically mobbed him whenever he appeared — but he chose his partners with care. He enjoyed dancing, but only with girls who could follow his guidance with expertise. His great love was the jive. The rhythmic beat, the body movements required, the sense of mastery as he swung his partner in the air, all greatly appealed to him.

Soon after he arrived, the band struck up a jive number and there was a general rush to the dance floor, which enabled Jim to witness a small scene being played out at the back of the hall. A slim brunette was tugging at the hand of a reluctant partner. The man resisted, shaking his head at her verbal and physical coaxing, until she broke contact and turned her back in frustration. She appeared to find the beat irresistible. Her body swayed automatically as she watched the fast and furious gyrations of the dancers.

Jim moved towards her on impulse. She had not been among the eager girls who had clustered around him on arrival; he would have remembered that vibrant pink dress. The cowboy who had brought her here must be a dog in the manger. Jim nevertheless approached the girl with utter confidence. It would be only a Goliath or a fool who would stand in the way of J.T. Benson. Only when he was almost upon the girl did he recognize the man standing red-faced behind her as Stallard. Astonishment over his presence at such an event mingled with disparagement for a man with total lack of social graces. He should have stayed in Hicksville where he belonged. Giving the Englishman no acknowledgement, Jim took the girl's hand and drew her forward.

Turning as pale as Stallard was flushed, she gazed at Jim in disbelief as he smiled and said, in the language of swinging youth, 'Let's show them how, baby.'

She was a natural dancer, twisting and twirling with graceful speed, her skirt flying up to reveal shapely legs. As Jim swung her back and forth, his hips swaying and his feet moving expertly, the insistent beat of the music brought the familiar desire of youth. She was very easy on the eye, and too breathless to giggle.

When the number ended, Jim took her hand to lead her towards the band. 'I'm not letting you go yet.'

She went willingly, her eyes glowing with admiration, her cheeks flushed with excitement as she gazed at him. 'You're a *wonderful* dancer.'

'So are you ...?' He raised his eyebrows and she gave her name. 'Well, Laura, the evening was kind of dull until now.'

She studied the floor as her flush deepened, then glanced from beneath her lashes to say, 'I didn't know anyone could swing me around as much as you did. It made me tingle all over.'

His deliberate words revived her shyness. 'I usually manage that without giving dance lessons.'

To calm the excitement, the band struck up a dreamy foxtrot. Jim pulled Laura close before she had time to think, and as they moved across the floor he felt the girl trembling in his arms. He murmured in her ear, 'Why haven't I seen you around town?'

After a moment, she said against his shirt, 'I've seen you ... several times. The best was when Mom and I came to the school one Saturday to collect my brother. You were showing him how to catch on the run.' She tilted her face up to his. 'We watched for more than ten minutes. You made it look so easy.'

'It is easy.' He drew her even closer. 'What perfume are you wearing? It's very seductive.'

'Is it? Is it really?' She started to tremble again. 'It's called Lotus Blossom.'

All Jim could smell was the warmth of her skin and the shampoo she had used on her hair, but it was a good line that invariably worked. The mixture was pleasantly erotic; her body was hot and firm beneath his hands. Dancing suddenly lost its appeal. 'Let's go somewhere quiet where I can get to know you better,' he murmured. 'We'll drive to the river. It'll be cool and peaceful there.'

Giving her no chance to resist, he danced her to one of the doors standing open to let in air and led her to where he had left his car. She hesitated momentarily to glance back at the hall where dancers were now drifting from the floor with a surge of laughter and conversation, but Jim urged her forward with his arm around her waist, and then settled her in the passenger seat with as much body contact as he could contrive. He shut the door and headed round the bonnet, saying, 'Prettiest thing I've had in here beside me for a long while.'

At that point he was halted by a figure appearing from the shadows, and there was no mistaking that measured British accent as he demanded, 'Where are you going with her?'

Jim looked the Englishman over with amused deliberation as he stood blocking access to the driver's door, his eyes more steely than they had ever been. 'What's that to do with you, pal?'

'Miss Foster is with me.'

Jim laughed at the absurdity of such a notion, knowing he had control of the situation. Leaning against the car he folded his arms nonchalantly. 'I'd say it's clear enough she's with me. She's sitting in my car.'

'Only because you dragged her out here. I saw you.' Stallard was surprisingly worked up. 'I don't know what game you have in mind, but you're not playing it with Laura.'

'How do you aim to stop me?'

The other man advanced belligerently. 'We're off camp and out of uniform. I could knock you out cold, Benson, believe me.'

'I'd like to see you try. You'd be flat on your back before you had a chance to make a fool of yourself ... yet again!' Laughing, Jim bunched his fists. 'Are you man enough to risk it?'

That cold, hostile stare took away Jim's sense of amusement as Stallard said, 'My father always claimed punch-ups create bullies, not men. I'll just take Miss Foster back to the dance, and you can keep away from her for the rest of the evening.' He walked round to the passenger door and opened it. 'Come on, Laura.'

The girl did not move as she saw the realization of her wildest dream about to be crushed. Stallard repeated his invitation to go with him, adding, 'I promised your father I'd look after you and see you safely home.'

Laura reacted to that like any girl in the grip of hero-worship. 'I'm not a *child*. I don't need a nursemaid.'

Completely thrown, Stallard remained where he was, still holding the door open. Jim thought him excessively dumb if he could not see that his behaviour was destroying Laura's self-image of being irresistibly desirable to someone she had worshipped from afar, and was reducing her to the small-town adolescent she was. She would hate him for it.

'Go away, Rob,' Laura ordered fiercely.

'I can't let him take you off. He has a bad reputation,' he insisted with blind perseverance. 'I promised your father ...'

'*Go away*!' she repeated, almost in tears. 'You're spoiling everything.' She pulled the door from his grip, slammed it, then turned her back on him.

'You heard the lady,' said Jim with great relish, as he slid behind the wheel. 'She doesn't need a nursemaid — especially one who talks big, then backs off.' Putting his convertible into reverse, then immediately into an accelerated U-turn that sent dust and grit flying up over the sturdy figure left standing in the light spilling from the hall, Jim drove off, smiling over the self-induced mortification of his rival. Then he discarded the word. Stallard was no rival; the balance was too uneven. He was more a thorn in his side, and a very small thorn, at that.

Chapter Six

Rob surfaced from sleep to find Johnny vigorously shaking his shoulder. He did not understand why his friend was also hitting his head with a hammer. He was not normally sadistic. Then Johnny jerked off the sheet and announced that Flying Cadet Stallard had either to get up and dress, or to report sick. 'If you do that you'll be in even more trouble than you are already, because a drunken hangover is classed as a self-inflicted wound.'

It was then Rob knew that the hammer was inside his head and that if he tried to move he would be sick. 'Fetch a bowl ... *anything*,' he groaned.

Johnny provided a receptacle fast. When that was over Rob felt slightly better, and the hammer blows had softened somewhat. He peered cautiously at his friend through bleary eyes as he sat on the edge of his bunk in his underpants. Johnny's mouth looked a funny shape.

'What happened to you?' Rob asked.

'You happened. Don't you remember?'

'Remember what?'

'You soon will when they give us what for.'

Wincing from a curious pain in his right eye, Rob tried to focus more clearly on Johnny's face and noticed that his lower lip was puffy above a bluish bruise on his jaw. 'What've you been up to ... and who's going to give us what for?'

'Oh blimey, you don't remember, do you? Last night you came back to the dance hall and began drinking as if prohibition was starting at midnight. Three or four beers and you were out of control. You'll have to learn to hold your liquor before you're much older.'

'Oh lord,' groaned Rob, as memory began returning. Benson had made a fool of him. No, he had made a fool of himself in front of the American. And Laura. 'Did *she* see me like that?'

'Who?'

'You know who.'

Johnny shook his head. 'He must have taken her home. I heard from your own lips that Benson had kidnapped her and you were going to punch him on the nose when you caught up with him. You informed everyone within earshot that you were going to sort him out good and proper. You created merry hell, chum. Cyril and I tried to get you outside to cool down, but you were fighting mad and shook us off. That's when it happened.'

With a sinking heart, Rob asked, 'When *what* happened?'

'Pulling free of us, you lost your balance and grabbed at the nearest means of support. It happened to be Brad Halloran, whose temper has been on a short fuse since his crash grounded him, and his beer slopped over the back of a girl standing next to him. Her boyfriend, a strapping ranch hand, grabbed Halloran by the shirt and gave his opinion of military fliers, nose to nose, then invited him to step outside. Halloran quickly suggested you should take his place, and his pals backed him up. I wasn't standing for that, so I said if Yanks made a habit of walking off with another chap's girl, their sense of fair play was pretty dismal.'

Rob heard all this in dark dismay. How *could* he have started something like that? From the day of their arrival in Canada it had been impressed upon them by their own RAF officers that they were guests in this country, and should behave in sober and respectful manner. He would be in big trouble now.

'At that point, you decided Halloran was Benson and threatened to punch *him* on the nose. With the rancher wanting to take him outside, and you threatening to duff him up, Halloran's solution was to tackle you first. You hit the ground, I hit Halloran, his pal hit me, and the rancher hit anyone within reach. Anglo-American relations suffered a nasty setback, until Bucket and Freddy Goodall decided to intervene. Someone had already called the sheriff, unfortunately.' Johnny sighed. 'Everyone's confined to camp today, and you, me, Halloran, his pal Mick, and that Scottish firebrand McIntosh are for it. We all go before the CO right after breakfast. You have to see our new liaison officer, who arrived this morning, after the disciplining.'

Fearing he was about to throw up again Rob staggered to the bathroom and stood beneath a deluge of cold water until the nausea passed. He had ruined everything. How *could* he have been such a fool? He would be washed out, reclassified and sent home. It was what he had wanted until the day he first climbed into a Stearman and rose into the blue. The CO was certain to adopt the sternest attitude towards a man who had started a public brawl. Rob could hear his father saying, 'I never thought a son of mine would drink and fight like a common navvy.' Closing his eyes as he leaned against the wall, Rob feared he would lose the greatest source of fulfilment he had been offered, and it would be because of a pretty, heartless girl and a bastard named J.T. Benson.

Two hours later Rob emerged from the CO's office offering up a heartfelt prayer of thanks. He was still Flying Cadet Stallard, although his place on the course was now under review until he had proved that he was a sober, responsible man fully conscious of his status as a trainee pilot. Along with the other culprits he was on extra drill for a week, including next Sunday, which meant they were virtually confined to camp for another weekend. In addition, because of his drunkenness in a public place, Rob had to undergo parachute punishment at sunset. Yet he would gladly have suffered worse just so long as he could continue flying.

His sense of relief was shortlived. He went from the CO's office to another set aside for the RAF liaison officer, Flight Lieutenant Chalmers. The dark-moustached man looked very hot and very annoyed as Rob saluted and waited, standing stiffly to attention.

'Stallard, is it?'

'Yes, sir.'

'That name will be engraved on my mind for the rest of my service career. I arrived at Arcadia station at six a.m. today after an appallingly long journey from Canada. I was met by Lieutenant Brophy, who regaled me during the drive with the details of a punch-up at a local dance started by an RAF cadet who was paralytic. The *sheriff* had to be called out! Have you any idea how I felt on being told that news, Stallard?'

Rob's colour began to rise and his cheeks were a fiery red before Chalmers ended his hostile silence with further condemnation. 'You are an utter disgrace to the badge you wear in your cap. You have let down the Royal Air Force in the eyes of our host nation. You have given the Army Air Force and the people of Arcadia the impression that British cadets are drunken louts who have no idea how to behave as gentlemen should. You are not only training to be a pilot; as a cadet you are also a potential officer. The Americans are very hot on that side of their training, and I expect any British cadet to live up to their high standards.'

He sighed deeply as he gave Rob another hostile glare. 'I understand the CO has been lenient enough to allow you a second chance because one of the Americans has been so treated. He has bent over backwards to be fair, which I think is very decent of him. *I* would have had you lashed to a gun carriage and flogged,' he added furiously. 'I'll be watching every move you make from now on, Stallard, and for even the smallest transgression I'll have your guts for garters. Now get out of my sight!'

Rob walked very slowly back to his quarters, feeling the way he had been made to feel during his first year at Darston Grammar with schoolfellows from wealthy families. Chalmers had reduced him to a village yokel who did not measure up to his betters. He burned with shame. His father would be turning in his grave.

Halting by the empty swimming-pool, he gazed into its depths, seeing the socialite Benson cavorting before an audience of admirers. Shame turned into anger. Johnny said the American was not on campus, so he had stayed overnight somewhere. With Laura? She was welcome to 'every girl's dreamboat'. Between them, they had humiliated him into losing his temper and he had just been further humiliated because of it. They had almost robbed him of the greatest joy of his life. He would not allow Benson to drive him to such madness a second time ... and he would never touch alcohol again.

His friends diplomatically ignored Rob and pretended to be engrossed in their various tasks, as he stripped to his underwear and flopped on his bunk to stare at the one above his until lunchtime. It was not until they went across to the Mess Hall that Johnny asked how the interview with their new liaison officer had gone.

'He wasn't too happy,' Rob said briefly.

'Ah ... I see.' They went to their usual table and sat. 'Eat hearty, lad. You might not have the strength for any supper after your sunset jog round the perimeter.'

'That doesn't bother me. What does is that Benson will find it highly amusing when he drives that swanky car back here and learns what happened.'

'It'll be a nine-day wonder,' Johnny said soothingly.

'Not to me. And I'll make sure he knows it.'

When he walked out to the flight line that evening, Rob feared there would be an audience to watch his punishment for something which had also deprived them of their one full day's relaxation. They might enjoy seeing him stagger around the perimeter, weighed down by a parachute, trying not to fold at the knees before completing the circuits. It was possible in this humidity.

The only person to watch him was a very annoyed drill sergeant, who handed him the bulky parachute pack without a word. As Rob jogged around the familiar field he kept his mind off the physical toll by focusing on the long line of Stearmans. One of them was still his for the taking tomorrow, so he gritted his teeth and forced himself to keep going with that prospect to relish, and with the vow that Flight Lieutenant Chalmers and the Commanding Officer would find him an exemplary cadet in the weeks ahead.

Sweating, panting and thankful it was over, Rob handed the parachute back to the unsmiling sergeant and headed back to his quarters. His eye was now throbbing badly. When he gently touched the area around it, it felt tender and puffy. Halloran could pack a punch, even with his other arm in plaster. Still, Johnny had made a mess of Halloran's nose. He must remember to thank him when they were alone.

Rounding the corner of the accommodation blocks, Rob came upon Benson walking from the pool in swimming trunks, having cooled off before supper. The American's gaze flicked over Rob's dishevelled appearance and lingered on the black eye before a derisive smile touched his mouth. Rob would have passed without a word, but that smile touched a raw nerve.

Blocking the other man's path, he said heatedly, 'You don't take any of this seriously, do you? Learning to fly is just something else to fill your idle life; to show off about.'

Benson's smile faded. 'You made a big enough fool of yourself last night, without adding this.'

'How well did you come out of it? Don't tell me you wanted to talk to Laura about aeronautics.'

'Grow up, Stallard.'

'That's rich, coming from you, Benson. You're so juvenile you need to have everyone gawping at you, telling you how wonderful you are. Laura included.'

'She didn't seem to think you were very wonderful after bragging that you could knock me down, then backing off when I told you to try.' Again that smile. 'You'd have been out cold before you had time to think. Halloran proved that.'

'Leave him out of this. *He* didn't go off with the girl I'd promised to see safely home.'

'She made it obvious whose company she preferred,' said Benson. 'Now get out of my way.'

'Whatever you got up to with her, I hope she now knows what you're really like,' Rob said with an unwelcome echo of his overwhelming attraction on first meeting Laura.

'What I did was to spare her being caught up in the brawl I hear you started. I guess you were also drunk when you threw up behind the hut on that first day. You'll never make the grade here, buddy. Our standards are too high. I'm amazed you're not already on your way back to Canada.'

'I'm under review, which you've surely also heard. That's because an American was also given a second chance,' Rob said grittily. 'That makes us even.'

'*Nothing* would ever make us even,' he replied with heat. 'You're just a cowpoke from Hicksville.'

'And you're an immature lump of muscle and good looks relying on your name to get you by. People like you make me sick!'

'You do the same to me, Mister!'

They stood measuring up to each other in the crimson-flushed dusk, two powerful men oblivious of being watched from rows of windows as their dislike of each other deepened.

'I don't know who the hell you think you are,' Benson continued, 'but I know what I'd do with you if you British guys were tough enough to stand up to hazing. You'd get a lesson you'd never forget from me.'

Holding on to his fading control, Rob said, 'We're all tough enough for anything, but back home we stopped doing things like that in the sixth form. We're now too busy shooting down the enemy, dragging bodies from burning buildings, and searching through rubble for children buried alive. We're fighting for our survival!'

Benson's eyes flashed with anger. '*You're* not! You're getting drunk and making a nuisance of yourself. All you RAF guys are over here, courtesy of Uncle Sam, enjoying all this great country has to offer while being taught by the best fliers in the world.'

'So how do you think the RAF stopped a German invasion last year without their help?' Rob demanded hotly.

'They must have had better men than you in the ranks,' Benson whipped back. 'You'll never join them, Stallard. You haven't the guts. *Any* air force would have to be desperate to take you.'

Rob met that head on. 'I'll bloody well join them, Benson, and I'll do it on merit, not because my father's going to be a senator. You're the one without the guts. Even the best fliers in the world haven't had much success with you, have they?'

'You redneck *bastard*!'

'Call me what you like, but the RAF is more interested in how good a pilot a man is than in the colour of his neck.' He began turning away, knowing Benson was finally rattled. But he gave one parting shot. 'If you'd ever seen an American city ablaze beneath a skyful of bombers, you'd know just how desperate we are.'

*

On Wednesday morning Jim awoke with a feeling of quiet excitement. Today he would fly solo. Clint Lawson had announced yesterday that after a circuit or two he would vacate the front seat. Landing was still Jim's weakness but the instructor was satisfied that he could now do it safely, if cow-handedly.

After the usual dash to reveille, and the frantic tidying of quarters, Jim marched to the Mess Hall for breakfast. All through this meal, which was usually fairly lively because the cadets were refreshed and discussing the day's routine, Jim was conscious of probably the only man present who ate in comparative silence. Even down the length of the table Stallard's straight gaze lost none of its coolness.

Stallard suspected him of trying his luck with the Foster girl. So he had, but her small-town morals had soon overridden her hero-worship, and he had driven her home seething with the knowledge that the elegant, sophisticated Shelley had offered herself on a plate and he had turned her down, while a kid with straw in her hair had given J.T. Benson the runaround. He preferred the Englishman to believe what he did about that evening.

While they were all taking a breather between classes at ground school, Jim was surprised to find Lieutenant Brophy approaching him. Although the officer was half smiling, Jim's heart sank. He was still under review, and this could surely only mean further trouble in store. It was, but not the kind Jim had imagined.

'Benson, we have just heard your father is on his way to Carlstrom. He'll be here in time for lunch.'

'But I'm flying solo this afternoon!' Jim protested in utter dismay.

Brophy's smile broadened. 'The most fortuitous day for him to honour us with his visit.' He turned away. 'You'll be free to spend some time with Mr and Mrs Benson when flying ends.'

Jim followed him. 'Why's he coming *here*?'

Surprised by Jim's tone, the officer stopped. 'You'd not heard your stepmother has recovered from her fever?'

Recalling Shelley's radiant appearance at Palm Beach, Jim merely shook his head.

'I see. As I understand it, Mr Benson is due to speak at a campaign rally tomorrow night. He's taken time out on his way through to look us up.' He gave a nervous grin. 'It's an unofficial stopover to get an insight to the training we give here. No need to roll out the red carpet.'

Jim felt like rolling out the dynamite fuse. Why today? What was really behind the visit? Theo never did anything without an ulterior motive, and he would expect a metaphorical red carpet if not a real one. He always did.

Throughout the remaining lectures Jim's attention wandered disastrously. He could not believe Lady Luck was treating him so badly. His confidence crashed to rock bottom. With Theo and a retinue of others watching his solo, he was certain to make a kangaroo landing. Knowing he was under a microscope would be sufficient to ruin any hope of a smooth touch-down. So much for Lawson's advice to forget who he was! Out there today, the entire complement at Carlstrom, right down to the girls in the canteen, would be made aware of it. Damn Theo! How *could* his father do this to him?

*

92

As Rob waited at the flight line that Wednesday he was thinking of Jenny. Her first letter had reached him this morning after travelling for three weeks all over North America. He had read it avidly.

Rationing is getting tighter, Rob. The troops have extra, as they should, but I don't know how the men and women who work long hours on the land and in factories manage on the meagre allowance. We're lucky to be living in the country, with plenty of pullets and eggs. Jack and old Claude shoot rabbits — there are millions *of them this summer over by Darston Copse — and Sir Charles now allows the Hobson brothers to catch and sell trout from the stretch of river running through the estate. The vegetables you planted before you left are doing well, and from the amount of blossom on the trees we should have a good crop of fruit.*

I'm really enjoying my work for Lady Guthrie. She's so pleased with my secretarial skills she's giving me more and more to do. It's so interesting. By the time you receive this you'll have started flying. How do you like it? Can't wait to get your next letter so I can tell everyone about it. I'm so proud of you, Rob, and so's everyone in the village. I know you don't like fuss, but when you come home you'll get such a welcome from us all.

I received your letter from Canada. I'm not surprised you were all sick on the boat with so much chocolate available. Doubtless you all made pigs of yourselves! And oranges, bananas and huge steaks! I'm so envious. I can't now imagine streets all lit up at night, and masses of cars with full headlights. I suppose poor old England will get back to that one day, but it doesn't seem likely for a long time.

Although Rob felt distinctly homesick while reading his sister's news, he soon realized she described a world presently lost to him. Thoresby was so far removed from Arcadia that it was now his home village that seemed a storybook place. Reality was a room he shared with three others. It was long hours of studying theories and facts, followed by the indescribable thrill of putting them into practice. Reality was brilliant sunshine, punishing heat, palm trees, dazzling sea and dolphins leaping with balletic grace. It was flaming sunsets and parachute punishment. It was a total change of identity. It was also men like J.T. Benson, and the threat of washout hanging over him. Even so, as he waited in the hot sunshine for his turn to fly, there was no place on earth he would rather have been just then.

When Clint Lawson called for his next pupil as he took a much-needed iced drink between lessons, Rob's eagerness was so acute that he trotted the short distance to his instructor.

Lawson grunted. 'Keenest trainee I've ever come across, but give me a chance to get my breath back. It's hot up there today.'

'I missed out on Monday and Tuesday, so I've time to make up, sir,' Rob explained.

'And whose fault was it you missed out?' came the stern question. 'I knew that eye was too puffed and bloodshot to be of any use to you, and the altitude would have made it worse.' He drank the rest of the water in one gulp. 'Never fight over a woman. While you're hammering it out with your rival, she walks off with some other guy with more sense. Yes, I know I said all that before, but sound advice has sometimes to be repeated to healthy young fellers before it sinks in.' He frowned. 'When it comes to flying you hear everything I say first time, but I suspect your pa forgot to tell you much about the pitfalls of life, and you ain't much interested in hearing about them from your flying instructor.'

'No, sir, it's just that —'

'You can't wait to get off the ground,' Lawson finished for him. 'I know, I know. You have a love affair with the flying machine, but I'll tell you this. When a man is happier up there than when he's on the ground, he can be mighty lonely down here. Flying is a dangerous business — never lose sight of that — and you're going back home to the most dangerous form there is. You're no fool. You know what your chances are. Your love affair could end mighty quick. When a born flier is permanently grounded he needs people to bring him down to earth, otherwise he has nothing left to live for.'

Rob was impatient to get on with his lesson. This man had refused to let him fly on two days, and they had lost three last week due to the storm, which meant that all he had had so far was five hours in the air. 'I'll face that when and if it happens, sir.'

'I think you should start giving it some thought now.'

'I'm not very relaxed with people,' Rob confessed, reddening.

'You're fine with me.'

'Because we work together and both love flying.'

'I have a wife and two daughters I also love. And a number of friends I'd pretty near die for. Loosen up some and don't make things too hard for yourself. You're already under review, and there's a testing few months ahead of you before you can win your wings.'

'Yes, sir.'

The older man reached out and clapped Rob on the shoulder. 'Okay, Stallard, let's get to work.'

They spent the usual few minutes discussing manoeuvres and the route to be followed for the lesson, and Rob participated eagerly. Pointing at the map, he said, 'If I dive, then flatten out here over the lake, it'll take me very close to that tower just north of the highway. I almost hit it on Friday.'

Lawson nodded. 'Just testing your memory. Keep on the correct course *with no deviation* today, and there'll be no problem. You made a good job of just missing the tower, but I don't want another demonstration of that questionable skill. It's too hot for further excitement.'

Rob grinned. 'Thank goodness. I didn't much enjoy it. And I found the left turn over these trees difficult, because at low altitude the horizon is obscured for a while,' he added, sobering. 'I lost too much height, if you remember, and you took the controls.'

'I didn't fancy coming home with a bird nest on the undercarriage. Now, see here, how d'you imagine we fly in clouds or at night when there's no horizon visible?'

'By watching the instruments.' Rob sighed ruefully. 'How could I have forgotten that basic rule?'

'Because the horizon is always so visible around here. You'll have to rely on instruments far more when you do night flying.' He folded the map. 'That's a long way off and you have a lot to learn here first. Come on, let's fly.'

The moment the huge radial engine burst into bellowing life, Rob's pulse quickened and the usual heady mixture of apprehensive excitement and a sense of mastery rushed through his body to fire all his senses. He had come wonderfully, gloriously alive! With the pre-flight checks done, Lawson gave his pupil permission to take off. It was permission to become lord of the air once again. Rob slowly opened the throttle, revelling in the guttural roar of the engine and the back-rush of air from the racing propeller. Easing back on the stick and watching the field ahead by leaning well over the side of the cockpit, he took the machine from a lumbering run into the air as smoothly and sweetly as any instructor could wish. It was not until he had climbed to eight hundred feet that a voice said in his ear, 'When you can do that in a military fighter at night you can pat yourself on the back. Don't do it now.'

Rob nodded at Lawson in the mirror. That was the American's way of cutting him down to size. The copybook take-off nevertheless pleased Rob so much that he smiled as he circled, slowly climbing to the required three thousand feet, then levelled off.

'Increase your speed by ten. Keep her nice and cool.'

Rob made the adjustment, then went into a right bank that would put him on the correct course for the lake where he would execute the dive, well clear of the tower today. He flew on, alternately watching the horizon and his instruments until the sparkle of water became visible ahead. He glanced up at the mirror and Lawson nodded.

'Take it in your own time. If you're not happy, make close circuits and go down when you are. Watch your compass, and remember your stall speed as you pull out of the dive. Once you lose the horizon behind the trees, fly on your instruments. They won't let you down ... and don't forget I'm up here to get you out of any jam in one piece. Okay, it's all yours.'

Biting his lower lip in concentration, Rob mentally reviewed all he had been told and prepared to dive without further eye contact with his instructor. He had been given control of the aircraft, so he would fly it without assistance until he had completed the manoeuvre, on that he was determined. Once into the dive, his excitement mounted as the windrush increased and the lake appeared to rise to meet him. He had everything under control, and the Stearman which lumbered in elephantine manner along the grass became a graceful, obedient machine swooping from the heavens. Rob found himself laughing softly with sheer exuberance, and momentarily visualized the pelicans he had seen diving so spectacularly. Did they feel this same elation as they plunged?

It was controlled elation, however. Rob was monitoring the dials on the dashboard in front of him, and keeping a constant eye on the water as it appeared ever nearer and larger with every hundred feet he dropped. The tower he had almost hit last time rose well away to his right, but the thick block of trees lay ahead where he must pull out and make the awkward turn he had muffed on Friday. He would rectify that mistake today. Remembering the risk of stalling, Rob watched the speed indicator and the altimeter like a hawk as he levelled out over the lake and almost immediately went into the turn biting his lip so hard it hurt. The trees dropped away as he successfully completed the difficult turn and put the aircraft on the heading he had been given.

Laughing softly, Rob glanced up at the mirror for Lawson's usual nod of approval. It took a moment or two before he realized something was wrong, and some moments longer to accept that the older man was not simply taking a nap. Lawson was slumped forward and very still, held in position by his harness. It was impossible to see his face, but Rob had no doubt his eyes were closed. Dear God, had the man collapsed because of that dive?

Momentarily paralysed with shock, Rob stared at the inanimate figure in the front cockpit. Then a lurch, together with a surge of engine noise, broke through his mental hiatus to bring awareness of his predicament. Thoughts racing, he saw that he was now flying dangerously low and some way off course. His speed had dropped to near stalling point, and the dreaded tower rose about a mile and a half dead ahead.

'Oh, Christ,' he muttered, 'what the hell am I going to do?'

What he did was to increase his engine power quite considerably with a sense of panic, then embark on a climb, hanging over the side with his goggles pushed up to his forehead, until he saw the tower pass beneath the Stearman. *Speed, height, attitude. Always keep them in mind*, he mentally heard the instructor say. Eight hundred feet. A thousand. Make it two to be on the safe side! Lawson was now lying back in his seat, the climb having brought his head up, and he was still unconscious. Sweating profusely, and licking his lips with a tongue that felt like sandpaper, Rob levelled out at two thousand feet. At that height there was little risk of hitting anything, so he felt marginally happier while he came to terms with his options. There was only one, of course. He must get on the ground as soon as possible so that Lawson could have medical treatment.

'Oh, Christ,' he muttered again. He knew how to land when being talked down — he had also done it several times without oral help — but the instructor had been there to take over, if necessary. Going in cold, with a sick man up front, was not an attractive prospect. *First rule of a good pilot is to be willing to return to his natural element*. Today was the first time this pilot wanted more than anything to return to earth.

Now that his stomach was churning less violently, Rob took several deep breaths and faced the inevitable. A quick glance at the fuel gauge showed it to be half full. No problem there. He had lost all sense of compass direction and Lawson had the flight chart, so navigation would have to be by the naked eye. There were few landmarks in this flat area, but Rob had flown over it five times and had a general idea where Carlstrom lay in relation to the lake. The airfield stood out as a wide green space just a few miles from the built up area of Arcadia. He could not possibly miss it, and when he neared there would be other Stearmans circling to guide him. Panic overtook him once more. Dear God, how could he land and keep his eye on a skyful of other cadets at the same time?

Telling himself sternly that he must worry about that only when he reached Carlstrom, Rob gazed around to get his bearings. Sweat was running into his eyes to cloud his vision, but when he replaced his goggles they steamed up to blind him altogether. It was then he realized tension had turned his body into a furnace, and his flying suit was so wet it clung to his skin.

Speed, height, attitude. Watch your direction and remember your stall speed. Turning into the sun, Rob flew straight and level until he saw a long, unbending road cutting between the orange plantations. He sighed with relief. The road from the coast to Arcadia. If he overflew it he would come to the town, and Carlstrom would lie a few miles on to the right. His mouth still felt unbearably dry, but his legs had regained their strength after turning to rubber. It was heartening, because he would need them on the pedals when he touched down. Dead ahead he spotted one of the outlying fields used for 'bumps' and was tempted to use it, but Lawson needed a doctor as soon as possible so it would have to be Carlstrom.

His back was aching unbearably; his jaws were tightly clamped together. The stick appeared to need more strength to move it than at any other time, and his hands were so wet within his gloves he had difficulty gripping it. As Arcadia hove into view his stomach began to churn again. He would be over the airfield within ten minutes. God, could he really land this thing on his own? There was not only his own safety but that of a sick man to consider. Clint Lawson would expect him to carry it off successfully, and he could not let down the man who had faith in him.

Nearing the airfield, Rob saw with dismay what he feared. Blue and yellow aircraft were all over the sky as lessons continued. How could he watch the circling Stearmans and his instruments at the same time? The answer came immediately. He could not, so he must trust the instructors in the other aircraft to keep clear of *him*. When they saw a machine coming in early and cutting right across the circuit they would surely realize there was an emergency, and hold off. His priority was to get down fast.

With this firmly in mind, Rob mentally ran over the routine for landing. Close throttle, trim elevators, monitor speed and height, ease back on stick to raise nose, apply rudder brakes, pull stick right back to chest, taxi to a halt. Those were the mere basics, all he must do now was to carry them out without a smash-up at the last. Aware of circling machines all around him, Rob flew steadily to the far end of the field and turned on to the general approach path knowing he must do this at the first attempt or he might not have enough nerve to go through it all again. He had descended to five hundred feet, scaring the occupants of half a dozen other biplanes in the process, and he now closed the throttle to start the glide, his left hand on the elevator trim, his right curled round the stick, his feet lightly on the rudder pedals.

Watch your speed. Easy movements. Nothing violent, now. Bring her down nice and steady. A Stearman flew across his nose too close for comfort. Rob was vaguely aware of a figure in the front cockpit shaking his fist, but his own attention was on the pointer showing his speed and on the little black ball indicating balance. It was rolling from right to left quite dementedly as Rob struggled to keep his wings level, while he dropped lower and lower. Every moment or two, he gave a swift glance over the side to ensure that the field really was there beneath him. He had drifted slightly to the left, but there was a lot of field to play with. A lot of field to crash in! He dashed a gloved hand across his eyes once more to clear the sweat running from his forehead. Christ, the ground was already much nearer than he had thought.

The altimeter showed two hundred feet, then a hundred. *Ease back and bring up the nose. Too late! I have control.* Rob pulled on the stick. Nothing happened. The field was flashing past almost beneath his feet, Panicking, he tugged hard on the stick to prevent the aircraft from going nose first into the ground, then he grew alarmed as she began to rise in a gentle climb. *Nice and easy. Nothing violent.* Biting his lip hard, Rob forced his hand forward very gently. The aircraft levelled, dropped her nose again, then touched down with a shuddering thump that jarred Rob's every bone. Arching back as he hauled the stick hard against his chest and simultaneously pressed down on the brake pedals, Rob worked his feet alternately in the fight to maintain a straight path. Heading inexorably towards the hangars, the Stearman veered to the left despite Rob's efforts. Then, through his crowding thoughts came clarity. He killed the engine and the biplane slowly and safely trundled to a halt. Rob closed his eyes and offered up a silent prayer of thanks to whichever angel watched over pilots.

Chapter Seven

As the upperclass men marched to the flight line, Jim knew everything he had learned about flying a Stearman had gone from his mind. He could not even visualize the controls in the cockpit, and two thousand feet seemed a great deal higher than before. For once, he could not respond easily to his fellows when they promised him a ducking after his solo. There had already been forty-seven baptisms of triumph. Maybe Mickey Mouse should give it a miss.

When they arrived beside the flight office there was a curious atmosphere that did not appear to be due to the presence of Theo, Shelley and the dogged Jerry Warner. They were certainly there with their retinue, but all their attention, and that of the cadets, was on the sky. Jim glanced up and saw a Stearman steadily losing height as it flew across the regular circuit in total contravention of the rules applying at Carlstrom. It passed dangerously close to several others as it crossed the field, then made an alarming spiralling turn to line up with the normal approach path. It was coming in early even for the first of the present session, which suggested trouble of some kind. The machine was yawing badly, but that was not uncommon when a cadet was at the controls. Jim had done it often enough himself.

The mechanics and engineers were lined up by the hangars, hands shading their eyes to watch, and the CO was in conversation with the Chief Instructor as both men studied the unusual behaviour of the aircraft. As it was approaching head on, it was impossible to see the identifying number, but there was nothing uncertain about the pilot's intention. He was going to land, and fast.

Sensing a drama, Jim's gaze followed the rapid descent of the Stearman and he remembered Brad Halloran's crash. There had not been one since then. Was the trouble-free period about to end? If there were two people aboard, the instructor would have the controls, yet even the most experienced pilot could be defeated by a faulty aircraft. He held his breath as the biplane looked set to go nose first into the ground, then performed the high balloon movement every cadet dreaded — J.T.

Benson particularly — before thumping on to the grass with such force that those watching gave a concerted groan. The undercarriage miraculously survived as the machine ran towards the hangars in a pronounced veer to port.

Silence fell as every man on the ground stood rooted to the spot in the appalled certainty that the Stearman would run headlong into three parked machines presently out of service. It was now possible to see that the figure in the front cockpit was slumped sideways, and the silence was suddenly broken by excited exclamations. A cadet must be at the controls! There was a general movement forwards when the sound of the engine died and the aircraft slowed to a halt out on the field, a safe distance from the hangars.

Standing silent in the midst of a voluble group, Jim saw the figure in the rear cockpit signalling energetically that help was needed for the man up front. People converged on the aircraft as the cadet began to climb out to the wing, where he leaned over the motionless figure until others reached him.

'Looks bad,' someone alongside Jim commented. 'That chap is most likely one of ours, but I can't see who. I wouldn't have been in his shoes over the past half hour for all the tea in China.' He gave a nervous laugh. 'I suppose you could say he's the first of our lot to solo. After only a few hours, that must be a record for the combined course.'

Jim grew even colder. Men were lifting the instructor from the cockpit while the cadet looked on, when Jerry Warner was suddenly there with his camera, scooping an exclusive. It brought home to Jim just how the PR man had landed the job with Theo. He was utterly ruthless. Never mind that some poor devil had almost killed himself trying to land with an unconscious instructor, or that medical help was being called for as the sick man was carried to the flight office. Jim's blood almost froze as he watched his father approach the cadet being questioned by the Chief Instructor, and proceed to hold centre stage while Warner took pictures from every angle of the smiling political candidate shaking the hand of the hero of the moment.

Information was being passed around the excited cadets as those nearest the tower learned what had happened. Jim's British neighbour told him Clint Lawson had apparently passed out during a dive over the lake. The doctor was on his way, but it seemed serious.

'Look at that moron out there taking pictures,' he continued indignantly. 'They might let the poor devil recover before putting him through that. I know what he did was a good show, but I don't suppose he's feeling too hot right now.'

Jim's stomach muscles began to tighten painfully as he watched Shelley being drawn forward to pose beside the cadet, who had now pulled off his helmet and stood like a man in a daze. Then someone hurried from the office to speak to the Chief Instructor, who took the cadet's arm and led him away from Theo and his committee.

Jim then saw the man's face clearly. It was very pale, and blood trickled down his chin from a cut on his lower lip. Those eyes, normally a cool grey-green, now resembled huge dark pebbles. He walked like an automaton, his leather helmet dangling from his loosely curved fingers, his flying suit clinging wetly to his body as he was guided towards the door of the office. Jim stared at the Englishman who had disturbed him from their first meeting. How *could* Stallard have done what they had all just seen him do?

Someone grabbed Jim's arm and began dragging him forward. 'One moment! Just one more picture!' yelled Warner to the pair about to go inside. 'It'll take no time at all.'

Comprehension overtook Jim at the last moment, and something inside him broke. Yanking his arm free of Warner's grip, he shouted, 'No! For Crissakes, no!' Turning, he pushed his way through the cluster of cadets and began walking fast towards the far side of the field. Now as hotly furious as he had been cold before, Jim craved violent action of some kind, so when a hand fell heavily on his shoulder he spun round to throw it off with aggressive force. He found himself facing someone as full of rage as himself.

'What the hell are you playing at?' roared Theo. 'Everyone saw you refuse to shake that man's hand. No son of mine deals out insults like that.'

Breathing hard Jim said, 'I'm no son of yours if you expect me to further your campaign with tricks like that. That poor bastard was in a state of shock and you were *using* him.'

'We were merely on the spot,' snapped Theo, his face working. 'No one knew he was going to pull off something sensational today. He's a hero and I happened to be on hand to congratulate him.'

'A man could be in there *dying*, for all we know,' yelled Jim, pointing unsteadily at the distant office. 'Everyone saw my father making political gain from that. You disgust me, d'you know that?'

'That's nothing to what you'll do to the other men here when word gets around. Some cadet still wet behind the ears — some *British* cadet, mind you — hits the headlines with a great flying stunt, and James Theodore Benson's son, *who still hasn't made it solo*, publicly turns his back on him. How d'you think *that* looks?'

Jim closed on his father, fists clenched. 'That wasn't a *flying stunt*; it was an unavoidable bid to get back on the ground by someone faced with a desperate emergency. It could have happened to any one of us at any time, and we'd each do the best we could. He stayed calm and made it down. He did great ... but he's not a showman carrying out death-defying feats. I know him. When he sees those pictures splashed all over, he'll just about throw up.'

'That's too bad,' Theo sneered.

'Here's something else that's too bad. I'm through helping you to get where you want. From now on you're on your own, while I concentrate on getting where I want to be. And it isn't in the boardroom of Benson Pharmaceuticals,' Jim said with vicious emphasis. 'You'll have to get yourself another son to take over the company. You're not too old, and a pregnant wife would give you all the family image you need. It would also help to keep Shelley occupied, which would be a good thing because the next guy she makes a play for won't be inhibited by filial loyalty.'

With that parting shot Jim turned and walked away, punishing the palm of his left hand with repeated heavy blows from his rolled helmet and goggles. He had reached a turning point and was scourging past weakness from his system. All the time he did it, Jim could visualize Stallard's pale face and shocked eyes the moment before he had pulled free of Jerry Warner and made off through the crowd.

*

Rob remained in the flight office after the ambulance had taken Clint Lawson to the sick quarters. He felt incredibly tired, so it was easier to stay on the hard wooden chair than to make the effort to go outside and face the crowd again — especially the large, floridly handsome man who had grabbed him while he was trying to get help for Lawson. Benson's influential father, presumably, since he had had in tow the photographer

104

so often on the heels of every girl's dreamboat. Confused, concerned about the sick instructor, Rob had been manhandled into poses with the prospective senator when he should have stayed with Lawson. The man's renowned son had walked away rather than feature in more pictures. Rob would like to think that it was because J.T. Benson felt that the tragedy of what had happened was not a subject for cheap publicity, but he thought it more likely that the man was simply unwilling to be photographed shaking the hand of a redneck bastard.

There had been a press of sun-tanned men in expensive suits around Benson's father. They had crowded Rob. Voices had shouted at him: the noise of the Stearman's engine still throbbed in his ears. He craved silence and rest now that Lawson was under medical supervision. Tilting his head back against the wall, he closed his aching eyes.

'Come along, Stallard, I'll drive you to your quarters.' A voice from seemingly far away forced Rob's lids up some moments later. Flight Lieutenant Chalmers was standing before him. 'You can't stay there all night. On your feet, man.'

Struggling upright, Rob felt his muscles protesting as he followed the liaison officer through the door, noting thankfully that the crowd had dispersed. The aircraft were neatly lined up ready for tomorrow; all except one standing out on the field. Rob stared at her. Had he really brought her down in one piece?

It was a short distance to his room, but Rob was glad of the ride in blessed silence. Only when he pulled up beside the accommodation block did the officer turn to speak.

'You don't do things by halves, do you, Stallard?'

'I hope Mr Lawson will be all right,' Rob murmured, wondering what the other man meant.

'When I get any news I'll pass it on to you. I should have an early night and forget the study period for once.'

'Yes, sir.' He began to climb from the car. 'Thanks for the ride.'

'I doubt you'd have got here on Shanks's pony ... and Stallard!'

He bent to the window. 'Yes, sir?'

'That was a good show. I think you can regard yourself as no longer under review.'

Rob's smile was so wide it went past his ears and met at the back of his head. 'Thanks a lot, sir.'

When he entered his room Johnny, Cyril and Patrick were all reading. Without taking his attention from the Western in his hands, Johnny said, 'Bathroom's all yours. Buck up! Crowther'll be coming to march us over for supper in fifteen minutes.'

Rob was elated, but he was also very tired. Could he possibly march the short distance to the Mess Hall? A shower did wonders, and so did clean clothes. By the time the Cadet Platoon Commander arrived to fall them in hunger had overridden weariness to allow Rob enough energy to go in search of food. When they arrived at the large, airy dining hall it was almost full. They must be the last contingent tonight. No sooner had they entered than a deafening knocking sound began. Rob's fellows all dashed for their seats and increased the noise by also banging their spoons on the table and stamping their feet. Left standing alone, Rob realized all faces were turned his way, and he then grasped what was happening. Flushing a hot red he made his way to his usual seat at the end of the table, hoping they would stop when he sat down. Deeply embarrassed, he nevertheless felt a surge of warmth over the simple tribute offered by every cadet present.

On the following afternoon, during a break between lectures, Rob was allowed briefly to visit Clint Lawson.

The instructor looked strained, but he summoned a smile. 'Good of you to come.'

'I've been worried about you, sir.'

He indicated a chair beside the bed. 'Stay awhile?'

'I've got to get back for the armaments lecture,' Rob told him, ignoring the chair and the real reason why he had been told he could not stay for more than a few minutes.

'Sorry to do that to you yesterday.'

'You weren't to know.'

'Nothing showed up at my last medical. It must have developed in the last coupla months.' His frank gaze held Rob's. 'I can't get to grips with the knowledge that I've been risking cadets' lives day after day. I could have killed someone out there.'

'You weren't to know,' Rob repeated awkwardly.

'Lucky it was you I was with when it happened.' He gave a faint smile. 'I take it you missed the tower after the dive.'

Rob smiled back. 'Good job you didn't see some of the things I did later on, sir.'

After a moment or two, Lawson said, 'This is the end of flying for me.' Knowing it to be the tragic truth, Rob remained silent. 'Remember what I said to you about when a born flier is permanently grounded? Well, I have a family and friends to see me through this. You know full well that when you go home the odds'll be stacked high against you. I can't do anything about that, but please take my advice to loosen up and let people into your life. You'll maybe need them before too long ... and you're sure worth knowing. Goodbye, son, and good luck.'

Rob shook his hand, feeling choked. 'Good luck to you, sir. Even born fliers need good teachers and I had one of the best. I won't let you down.'

'I know. You proved that beyond doubt. Thanks.'

Rob remained for a while outside the building, sobered by Lawson's words. Then he returned to ground school, sensing that he had lost more than a flying instructor.

*

On the morning after the drama surrounding Lawson, Jim and the other two Americans who had not yet soloed were told that unless they did so by Saturday they would be dropped from the course. Jim hastened to point out that he would have done his solo if Lawson had not collapsed just prior to his lesson. He was then informed that if after one circuit his new instructor agreed, he would be sent up alone that afternoon. The ultimatum did not unsettle Jim. He went through the morning lectures coldly determined where formerly he would have been full of nervous agitation. Today he would achieve what could have been his long ago if only he had put his mind to it. Something that almost broke his new calm mood was the sight of the day's newspapers when classes ended for lunch. The front pages all recorded the drama at Carlstrom, with Jerry Warner's on-the-spot pictures syndicated nationwide. The 'British hero', as every edition dubbed Stallard, gave the impression of being overwhelmed by being congratulated by a prospective senator. His dazed, wide-eyed expression was turned on Theo in the picture carefully selected by the new campaign team. There were others showing Lawson being lifted from the cockpit, the aircraft standing alone out on the field, and the CO speaking to Theo — more probably the other way round, Jim guessed. One picture even showed James Theodore Benson II with his beautiful, compassionate wife at the bedside of the afflicted instructor.

Jim dared not guess Stallard's reaction to it all, or how the Englishman would feel on climbing into a Stearman this morning. The thought did not bother Jim for long; he was more concerned with his own impending lesson. Although he had generously joined the 'spoon and stamp' accolade for Stallard last night, the man had bested him and Jim's fighting hackles were up. His greatest sporting talent was to wrest victory from certain defeat and he meant to beat the man at his own game. No, more than that. To trounce him thoroughly, through merit and not because his father aimed to be a senator!

Jim's new instructor, Jess Hobson, was only a few years older than himself and a fellow athlete. He greeted Jim genially. 'It's a pleasure to meet you, J.T. Benson, and more comfortable to do it here than on a tennis court or football field. I've been reading reports on your progress and it looks fair enough to me. Landing's always a bitch in these machines. Some get it straight off, others fancy-foot around for weeks. From Lawson's comments, seems you finally broke the jinx start of the week. Guess we'll fly one circuit dual, then I'll climb out and you can take the ship around alone and have some fun. How's that sound?'

'Pretty good, sir,' said Jim, exuding health and confidence as he smiled. 'First lesson together and I'm going to pitch you out after one circuit. Don't take it personally.'

Hobson climbed aboard. 'I only do that when the student pitches me out in mid-air.'

In that mood of easy rapport Jim taxied out, took off to fly a perfect circuit, then landed with such assurance he could not believe he had had so much trouble for so long.

Hobson said into the speaking-tube, 'I have no problems with that circuit. She's all yours, Benson. Go and enjoy yourself.'

It seemed strange with an empty cockpit ahead, but excitement bubbled in Jim, despite having waited so long for this moment, as he taxied to the take-off point and flew the required circuits according to the rules. In so doing he came to terms with another jinx. He was going to have a career as a military pilot and let no one try to stop him. There was no power greater than personal determination, and Theo had made him a present of it yesterday. Lawson had suggested he change his name: all he had needed was a change of attitude.

The entire upper class turned out for the ceremonial ducking at the end of that afternoon. Jim made a fun occasion of it by pretending to flounder in his sodden flying suit, calling for help, which everyone laughingly refused the finest swimmer among them. Hauling himself from the pool Jim stood for a moment silently dripping, before asking with a grin that those who had thrown him in should be the first to congratulate him. Everyone swiftly denied being responsible and they began to close up to protect the culprits as Jim advanced head down, his powerful shoulders ready to charge his way through to reach his room-mates. Amid much horseplay and hilarity, the assembly degenerated into a mêlée, which ended with Jim getting a second ducking as a sign of the affection in which he was held. It was a tremendous salve to his pride.

On the following day the Americans flew in the morning, and clustered around the pool to relax after their afternoon classes, which were getting more and more complicated. Jim and his intimates decided to dry off and whip together a team for basketball before changing for supper, and they were in the process of getting volunteers when they heard concerted shouting and cheering. Glancing up, Jim saw a surging group of cadets high on excitement heading for the pool, their voices identifying them as RAF men returning from the flight line. Memories of Halloran's ducking told Jim this was another such moment. He knew who it had to be.

The group arrived beside the pool, where the victor was seized by hands and ankles. Vigorous shouting sent the whole group shuffling to the shallow area, then surging back to the deep end. Jim saw the one named Bradshaw waving his arms wildly as Stallard struggled like mad to break free. Jim's lip curled. How typical of the man!

Came the concerted chant: 'ONE, TWO, THREE! Oh-h-h, he flies through the air with the greatest of ease!'

Stallard hit the water and sank; then surfaced with arms flailing before going down again.

'He can't swim!' came Bradshaw's desperate cry above the laughter. 'He told you that!'

'He thought he'd get out of it,' retorted one of the excited ringleaders. 'No such luck.'

'J.T. tried that game yesterday,' called Grant Jordan, laughing. 'Give him time. He'll give it up and come on out.'

As Jim made to turn away he was astonished to see Bradshaw and the little man Bryce, who shared their room, jump in and thrash their way to where Stallard had again surfaced in a semblance of panic. Before the Londoner reached him, Stallard had once more become a dark shape underwater, his legs and arms now moving less energetically. At that moment Jim realized incredulously that the Englishman really could not swim, and was in danger of drowning. His friends' skills looked inadequate, especially when hampered by flying suits.

Running along the side of the pool, Jim took a flying dive into the water and struck out for the spot where Bradshaw was now being dragged under by the man he was trying to help. Bryce was helplessly treading water nearby.

'Leave it to me,' Jim cried, as the Londoner struggled to keep his own head above water. 'Soon as he lets go, swim for the side.'

Curling over, Jim dived to where Stallard was clutching his friend's leg with the grip of pure panic. Reaching the drowning man, Jim used the side of his hand in a self-defence chop they had been taught at college. It worked even underwater. Stallard's hand opened to release Bradshaw, but he then grabbed at the other shape he saw beside him. Jim was ready for that. He had qualified at life-saving years ago, but this was the first genuine victim he had ever encountered.

The Englishman was strong and panic made men even stronger but, as he had swallowed a lot of water and was hampered by his heavy clothing, Jim was able to overcome Stallard's resistance before his own need for air became vital. Using his powerful muscles to rise to the surface supporting Stallard, Jim slowly towed him to the side where silence had fallen. It remained as many hands pulled the half-drowned man out and laid him on the paved surround. Jim heaved himself from the water and immediately began resuscitation, watched by men awed by what had happened. Stallard looked frighteningly near to death, but Jim knew the man was far from lost as he pressed rhythmically on his chest to expel water from his lungs.

Before long Stallard began coughing and retching, turning his head aside to spew liquid from his mouth. Jim glanced up at the surrounding ring of concerned faces. 'He'll be okay now.'

'He *told* them to put him in the shallow end,' insisted Bradshaw standing dripping a few feet away. '*He* told them, and *I* thought they knew he couldn't swim. Thank God you were on hand.' He took a deep, rasping breath as Jim got to his feet. 'You're pretty nifty at rescue. Thanks.'

Jim frowned. 'Because I put on an act yesterday, everyone thought he was doing the same. I'll never do that again.'

Stallard had now recovered enough to struggle to a sitting position, although he still looked ill. His fellows were all talking at once to him, trying to explain and apologize, but it was doubtful if he took much of it in. He started to get to his feet and was helped by those around him until he stood rather unsteadily, recovering his senses slowly.

At that point, Gus pushed through to ask curtly, 'You okay now?' Receiving a slow nod, he looked around at the British cadets. 'That was a crass, damn fool thing to do! Before you dunk anyone again make certain he can swim ... and if he says he can't, *believe* him.'

He was really worked up, and Jim could understand why. As Cadet Captain, Gus would be asked to explain how such a potential disaster could have happened. Jim had never seen him so angry.

Turning on Stallard, Gus demanded, 'Why the hell have you risked this happening? Each man jack of us has a responsibility to himself and to his fellow cadets. I have said repeatedly that we're ready to help you RAF men in any way we can. Any one of us would have taught you to swim.' Gus was the son of a general, and the fact had never been more apparent. 'You've made it clear from the moment you got here that you prefer your own company, but no one can survive alone ... and you sure as hell nearly didn't a few minutes ago. Get wise and start learning a basic and necessary skill. You have Mr Benson's expertise to thank for the fact that you're still alive.'

Stallard's eyes, even darker with shock than they had been after landing with Lawson, fastened on Jim for a long, dazed moment. Then he rasped, 'Thanks ... I ... thanks.'

Jim studied the white-faced, drooping figure and saw again a redneck in a shapeless grey suit throwing up behind a hut. Stallard might be a hotshot pilot, but he was not much of a man in any other respect. Giving a brief nod of acknowledgement, Jim turned away and headed for his room.

*

Rob was helped to their quarters by Johnny and Patrick. He there brought up the remains of his lunch along with a quantity of pool water. As he dragged off his sodden clothes his teeth began to chatter and his body to shake. He was still beset with fear. Drowning was a terrifying sensation, which he found difficult to shake off. In consequence, he remained in a daze as his friends wrapped him in blankets and tried to persuade him to lie down.

'No, no,' he murmured, resisting their hands. 'There's still water in my lungs. I'll choke.'

'No, you won't,' soothed Johnny. 'You'll cough it up in a minute. I'll get a bucket ready.'

Cyril entered, looking glum. 'I've been down to the office. There's still no letter from Norma. I hope she's all right.' He pulled up at the scene. 'What's going on?'

Patrick supplied the details, adding, 'Johnny and I did our best, but we're not expert swimmers. Benson made it look easy.'

'He makes everything look easy, except landing a Stearman,' grunted Cyril. 'I know why. I can't get the hang of it myself. You all right, Rob?'

'Does he look all right?' demanded Johnny returning with the bucket.

Patrick stripped off his own wet things and headed for the bathroom. 'I think Beastly Buckhalter went too far ranting at Rob while he was still trying to recover, and in front of everyone, too. All that tripe about preferring his own company! I know Rob's an old sobersides and would rather read Edgar Wallace in here when we go to the canteen, but what's it to do with Buckhalter? We're individuals, not bloody robots.'

'Buckhalter's the chap who'll get it in the neck if the officers get to hear about this,' mused Johnny, standing dripping in the centre of the room. 'You know how hard the Yanks come down on anyone who doesn't "measure up". Dust beneath bunks and near-drowning both rate as that.'

Patrick poked his head round the bathroom door. 'Maybe *he'll* be given demerits and have to walk the ramp. See how he likes it.'

Leaning back against banked pillows with his eyes closed, Rob begged wearily, 'Drop the subject, can't you? You only hold a post mortem when someone actually dies.'

'But for your arch enemy you might have,' Patrick pointed out as he returned to dress for supper. 'And from the look on Benson's face when you thanked him, he wasn't all that pleased about what he'd done.'

Voices faded into the background as Rob recalled those moments of return from the black abyss. The Cadet Captain had started bellowing at him in front of fifty or more cadets, his authoritative voice further magnified by the echo of a pulse thundering in Rob's ears. Through the tirade had come a suggestion that Benson was responsible for saving his life. Yet there had been disparagement in those familiar dark blue eyes as Rob, confused and weak with the remnants of fear, had mumbled his thanks. At least, he thought he had.

Only after he had violently ejected the remaining water in his lungs did Rob remember that he had flown solo today. Was it only two days ago that he had brought Clint Lawson safely to the ground and earned the acclaim of every cadet on the field? An event that should have been a golden milestone in his life had brought a frightening shave with death and public humiliation in the presence of men who had recently admired him. J.T. Benson had been a part of that. It cancelled out his triumph in flying solo in record time, in the same way that the newspaper pictures of Benson senior had reduced the drama of Lawson's mid-air collapse to a Hollywood-style stunt.

*

On Monday, the two Americans who had not flown solo left Carlstrom, having failed the course after just six weeks. It sobered everyone considerably, including those men who were doing well. Spirits plunged further when, during that week, one upperclass and two British cadets were placed under review for careless flying or reprehensible behaviour on the ground.

Brad Halloran was declared fit to take to the air again, but he had lost so many flying hours that the Chief Instructor ruled that he should be given the advantage of joining another course starting from scratch. His departure unsettled everyone further. Brad was a daredevil with a lively personality, who had inspired others in spite of his crash. With less than three weeks before they moved on to Basic, the Americans began wondering uneasily who would be the next to go. It was a cadet from Manchester, who still suffered so badly from airsickness that he begged to be reclassified.

During the ensuing days, the personal hostility between J.T. Benson and R.N. Stallard extended into professional rivalry. Having first soloed only a day apart, the pattern appeared set. Rob's ability quickly to absorb all he was taught in ground school, in addition to his greater natural skill as a pilot, meant that he soloed at each stage no more than a few days after Jim. It had begun as pure chance, but after it happened again each man was seized by the desire to prove himself the better in the air. Jim worked harder than he had ever done. With grim glee Rob kept apace, outstripping the others on his own course in the process.

Although still at the same table for meals the pair contrived to avoid each other at all other times, and the next two weeks heralded a more settled period for Rob. Apart from petty misdemeanours which led to a walk on the ramp during his valuable free time, he kept out of serious trouble. He made no attempt to learn to swim. The pool was always full of experts somersaulting or racing its length with effortless strokes, and Rob had no intention of humiliating himself further in their midst. He knew the RAF would teach him during the course on survival, so he would wait until then.

When first Johnny, then Patrick, flew solo, Rob watched the dunking ceremonies with dark memories of his own. The general enthusiasm for the ritual had diminished, however, so that when ten cadets soloed on the same day they were simply pushed in and left to sort themselves out. Cyril still could not land well enough to be sent aloft on his own, and his room-mates agreed that he never would while he was so besotted with his Norma. On those days he had no letter from her he was distracted during lectures, and when several arrived at once he could think of nothing but the passionate things she had written.

'That girl will be the death of him if he doesn't watch out,' Johnny prophesied.

Girls were proving the reverse for Rob, who had discovered there was another kind of love in his life besides flying, which filled him with delight. It occurred at weekends when he and his three friends were taken by the Fosters and others for boat trips, beach barbecues, a hoe-down, and all manner of simple outdoor fun enjoyed by Floridians. They had even been promised tickets for the county rodeo at the end of the month.

Laura had been superseded by her friend Sadie, despite the former's pink-cheeked apology and her confession that she had replaced Benson's

114

picture on her bedroom wall with the newspaper cutting of Rob. Sadie had shown Rob how to recognize sharks' teeth and sand dollars as they had walked hand in hand along the shore, and he had been captivated by her long blond hair and blue eyes. On the following Saturday he had fallen in love with Ria. She had sat very close to him while toasting marshmallows at an open fire, beneath a moon so large he could almost touch it. When she fed him with a warm, melting marshmallow so that her fingers brushed his lips, Rob knew he had been missing one of life's greatest pleasures while studying so hard to be an engineer. Lying in bed that night, gazing at the moon through his window, he decided that if he was going to fall in love with every American girl he met, he had better have a few lessons on that subject as well as flying. Johnny maintained that sex was just as exciting, so it was time he found out.

*

For Jim, the run-up to the end of the course was less relaxing. When he realized the Englishman had the right to consider himself his rival professionally, if not in any other respect, the compulsion to beat him burned even hotter. Jim schooled himself to comply with his instructor's orders to the letter, but Stallard nevertheless advanced at the same rate, like a bad-tempered terrier snapping at Jim's heels.

On the day before the upperclass men were to move on to Basic at Montgomery, Alabama, they were sent aloft for a two-hour solo in which they were to practise all the manoeuvres they had been taught. Jim felt lighthearted and carefree as he followed his desire to swoop and climb at will. This was flying as his spirit perceived it. He revelled in the spell of freedom, knowing it would be back to orders at the new field.

For just over an hour Jim threw the Stearman about the sky in loops, rolls and the dive known as the falling leaf. The sun was high. It flashed and dazzled as he spun, but he was sufficiently confident not to let it bother him. He was also quite used to the brief cessation of the engine during a slow roll, which momentarily cut off the fuel supply.

While coming out of one of these rolls, Jim was shocked by continuing silence. The Stearman's robust engine usually roared loudly, so that in the frightening hush Jim could hear his heartbeat thundering instead. As the aircraft began to lose height, all he had been taught formed a bottleneck in his brain to prevent any single fact from emerging. Staring at the controls and instruments, he struggled against the hiatus in his mind. When he broke it, he acted instinctively and pushed the nose down sharply. After what seemed like an eternity the engine coughed, then roared into life again as the dive corrected the problem. Levelling out, Jim finally took his attention from the controls and gazed around to get his bearings. Panic returned with a rush. There was a Stearman heading right for him!

Knowing he had momentarily forgotten the cardinal rule of constantly keeping watch in the sky for other aircraft, he nevertheless instinctively yelled blue murder at the pilot who kept on coming. After several hung seconds during which his reflexes worked faster than his brain, Jim banked sharply, to find himself blinded by the sun as he waited for the inevitable crash. With blood racing through his veins, he grew aware that a collision had miraculously been avoided by his instinctive manoeuvre. He thanked God the damn fool who had almost flown into him had not banked in the same direction. Their careers could have ended abruptly.

Climbing to his original height before the engine cut out, and circling to get the sun behind him once more, Jim glanced around at the blue and yellow biplanes making the circuit. There was no obvious indication of which cadet must now be messing his pants with fright. Spared that indignity himself, Jim instead suffered a bout of intense nausea that caused him to vomit over the edge of the cockpit. Recovering, he fought the urge to land immediately. If the other man was set on staying airborne, there was no way J.T. Benson would show he was chicken. However, for the remaining thirty minutes of his session he circled way above the others, in a cold sweat in case the engine cut again.

Back on the ground he reported the problem with the engine and was told he should have come straight in. He said nothing about the near-accident. Why get himself and some other cadet into unnecessary trouble on their last day here? The dangers of what he was doing had been brought home to him, however, and he was quiet as he and his friends stripped off their overalls to take a shower.

'What's eating you?' demanded Bucket, studying Jim's face. 'Don't tell me you're heartbroken over leaving tomorrow.'

At that moment, someone appeared at the open door and stepped inside. White-faced, and breathing fast, Stallard focused on Jim. 'You could've killed me, you bastard. You could've *killed* me!'

Gus edged forward. 'These quarters are off limits to you.'

The Englishman rounded on him. 'Don't talk to me about your petty rules. You bawled at me that I had *Mister* Benson to thank for saving my life in the pool. Today, he almost took it. But you won't humiliate *him* in front of the whole bloody camp, will you? He's treated like God Almighty here.'

'You're out of line, Stallard,' snapped Gus, uncomprehending but upholding his position as Cadet Captain.

Jim noticed that Stallard was shaking as he turned his back on Gus and approached. 'I knew you'd never take the fact that I, of all people, could beat you hands down in the air, but what you did was bloody criminal! You should be permanently grounded.'

Knowing Stallard must have been the idiot flier of this afternoon, Jim retaliated heatedly. 'Hell, you came straight at me!'

'*I* don't play stupid games in the air,' was the equally heated retort. 'You came out of the sun. I couldn't see you until you banked right across my nose.'

Realizing the probable truth of that, Jim defended himself with vigour. 'My engine cut. I was in trouble. It must have been obvious. You should have stayed well clear.'

'I couldn't bloody *see* you!' he raged. 'You *knew* that. You wanted to give me a fright? Well, you did. But if I'd panicked I could have ended up a pile on the ground. There was nothing wrong with your engine. God, I heard it loud enough as you swept past with feet to spare.' He took a deep breath to steady himself, then resumed the attack. 'I checked the number on the side of that Stearman and asked who had been flying it when I landed. The great sporting hero,' he said with biting contempt. 'You played the dirtiest trick in the book on me this afternoon.'

Jim lost what remained of his temper. 'I never play dirty. *Never*! D'you think I give a shit about your hotshot flying? I didn't know *who* was in that Stearman.'

Stallard gave him a long, steely look containing more hostility than ever before. 'If that's true then you did it for kicks just to scare the living daylights out of some poor blighter. *That's bloody criminal*!' His voice was deeply unsteady as he added, 'One day, the real world will catch up with you, Benson, and I hope it knocks you from here to kingdom come.'

There was silence after Stallard walked out, and Jim looked around at his friends defensively. 'I reported the engine trouble. They're having it checked out.'

'You should have reported the rest,' Gus said quietly. 'These things have to be recorded.'

Swallowing, Jim demanded, 'You believe that moron?'

'I believe it was an unavoidable incident.'

'*He'll* never believe that,' said Jim in disgust.

'Will you?' asked Bucket with gentle intuition.

Chapter Eight

Sergeant Pilot Stallard arrived in London at the start of December 1941. He bore little resemblance to the numbed farm worker who had stepped around blanket-covered corpses in a leaking hall, seeking three members of his family, yet his pleasure at being back in England was as great as he had known it would be. While waiting for a ship, he had been selected with seventeen others to accompany Canadians ferrying bombers across the Atlantic straight from the factory. They had all jumped at the chance to get home more quickly, and Rob had been thrilled by his first flight in an operational machine, even though they encountered no opposition from start to finish.

He was shocked by the vast areas of rubble, the many buildings shored up and heavily sandbagged, the grey armada of barrage balloons overhead, the scarcity of cars, the overwhelming number of people in uniform, and the general drabness of a capital city with Christmas not far off. In Canada there had been glitter galore.

There had also been snow, so this bitter winter weather was not as great a shock as it might have been if Rob had flown direct from Florida. All the same, he was glad of his heavy greatcoat, woollen socks and gloves as he sat in an unheated, blacked-out compartment of a train trundling through to Yeovil in the late afternoon. On the facing seat two pale-faced girls wearing cheap tweed coats giggled and whispered to each other in the hope of catching his attention. The large woman next to Rob clicked her tongue disapprovingly, and remarked to her companion that girls had no shame these days. Two schoolboys in opposite corners argued about the respective merits of the Spitfire and the Hurricane, casting self-conscious looks at the sun-tanned pilot they hoped to impress, while a frail man whose hands constantly shook muttered under his breath about servicemen taking up so much room with their kitbags, packs and everything but the kitchen sink.

These people looked dowdy and sallow, but they all spoke the way Rob spoke. The train was cold and in need of refurbishment, the cheese sandwich at Waterloo Station buffet had tasted like a slice of rubber between two layers of wet flannel, and a glance behind the shutter over the window showed Rob it had now begun to snow, but this was *home* and he rejoiced at being here. He was also proud to be wearing wings and three stripes.

At Yeovil, Rob waited forty-five minutes in a snowstorm for a branch-line train that would take him to Darston Chase. When it arrived it was packed with servicemen on pre-Christmas leave. Fighting his way aboard, he stood almost nose to nose with a sailor for the fifteen-minute journey, so he could not avoid the man's cheery chatter. He answered absently, all his thoughts on his reunion with Jenny. He had written that he should be with her by Christmas, and he had telephoned from Waterloo to warn her that he was already here. There had been no answer to his call, so he had boarded the train waiting at the platform without further delay.

In his luggage he had a leather handbag, a pink floral scarf and a bottle of perfume called Tonight at Nine. Johnny had advised him on the latter, because his mother had once been taken on by Selfridges for the Christmas rush and served on the gift counter. Rob had chosen the bag and scarf with the help of a girl called Nancy Beth, and he was certain his sister would like them. He also had with him some oranges and chocolate for her.

At Darston Chase, Rob struggled from the train to find several inches of snow on the ground. He thought briefly of North American horror at the absence of taxis, but he was undaunted. The covering of white enabled him easily to see the way as he shouldered his kit and set out along a familiar route. As he trudged, he wondered about the Operational Training Unit to which he had been posted. He now faced enormous demands on his newly learned skills, but Rob welcomed them. He could finally start to hit back at an enemy who had killed three-quarters of his family.

As he progressed, Rob forgot all else in the pleasure of seeing again familiar landmarks which held such strong memories. The nearer he drew to his home, the further Florida receded. Passing Darston Estate, he could not resist stopping to gaze out over the snow-covered meadows where he and his father had worked in harness. Nostalgia flooded through him. This was where he belonged; his roots were in this corner of England. It was wonderful to be back.

As he approached the cottage, Rob smiled over the surprise Jenny would have when she opened the door in answer to his knock. However, it was not she who did so; it was a plump stranger who stared in faint alarm at a large figure covered in snow.

'Yes? What d'you want, then?' the woman asked in a broad accent. 'You lost or somethin'?'

He stared back at her. 'I'm Rob Stallard. I live here.'

Her expression changed to one of concern. 'Oh, dearie me! Didn' you get your sister's letter, then? Oh my, now here's a terrible mix-up! So you doan know where Jenny is now?' She stepped back. 'Just you do come in out of that snow. You poor man, with all that on your shoulders.' Twisting her head, she called out, 'Jack, here's Mr Stallard thinking he's at his home. He didn' get Jenny's letter. Leastways, seems he didn' cos he's turned up here.' She began walking in to the familiar parlour, leaving Rob unable to think straight. 'From what Jenny did say to me yesterdee she's not expecting him. Jack, do you telephone up at the Manor, and let them know. Come on in here, Mr Stallard, and put all that heavy weight down. You look frozen to the marrow, poor dear. I'll brew tea. I dessay you'll make short work of one or two cups.'

Totally dumbfounded, Rob left his kit in the stone-floored passage, then entered a parlour that was not in the least familiar after all. Hardly had he registered the fact that the furniture his mother had kept beautifully polished was no longer there, when Jack Morrison walked through from the kitchen, an uneasy smile lightening his expression of concern.

'Well, here's a surprise! Jenny told us you were overseas.' He seized Rob's hand and shook it. 'You've had a bit of a shock finding us here, that's plain. We moved in six weeks ago after our wedding. Your sister wrote to tell you about it.'

'The letter's probably chasing all over North America after me,' murmured Rob, feeling giddy in the sudden warmth after the bitter cold outside. 'Where *is* Jenny?'

'Up at the Manor. Look, why not take off that wet coat, sit down here and let Mona bring you a cup of tea while I get through to tell them I'll be driving you up there in ten minutes or so? What a night to arrive home!' He walked to the table and picked up the receiver of a modern telephone.

Where was the old wall-mounted equipment, with the cone-shaped mouthpiece Fred Stallard had always shouted into in the belief that his voice had to be heard some distance away? Rob gazed at the Morrisons' furniture and their picture of St Paul's Cathedral. What had happened to the chenille table cloth, the china shepherdesses, and *The Stag at Bay*? This had been the Stallards' home all his life. He knew every corner and cupboard; every sound and smell. He had helped Dad repair the roof and whitewash the interior. Every year Mum and Jenny had bottled fruit and made jar after jar of jam to store in the huge, cool larder. In the bedroom above him he had studied until his brains felt addled and his eyes ached. He had walked from this cottage behind the hearse carrying the bodies of three beloved people. He had left his sister here with freshly painted walls and a full supply of logs. He had dreamed of home all the time he was away, yet it was not his but the Morrisons'.

'You all right, Mr Stallard?'

Rob focused on Mona Morrison's face as she held out a cup of tea. 'What's Jenny doing at the Manor?'

'Do you sit down,' she said kindly. 'Must be strange findin' me and Jack where you thought to be stayin'.'

Rob sat in an unfamiliar chair because she waited for him to do so. Then he took the tea, but left it untouched while listening to Jack trying to explain the situation.

'Maybe you'd break the news to Jenny, sir, and say I'll bring him to her as soon as he's had a cup of tea.' He gave a light laugh. 'No, I'll wager he hasn't forgotten the taste after being away so long. He's walked from the station with all his gear, and he looks rare done in. Finding the wife and me here hasn't helped. Shame he never got his sister's letter, but she'll soon explain. Yes, sir, in about ten minutes.'

He approached Rob's chair, rubbing his hands together. 'There, that's done. Drink up! Jenny'll be jumping over the moon until she sees you.'

Rob put the cup of tea on the sideboard as he got to his feet, asking yet again, 'What's she doing there?'

'Lady Guthrie has taken her on as a full-time secretary and given her two rooms at the Manor so she can work in the evening and weekends, if need be. Jenny was all for it. This place had grown too much for her with no man to do the heavy work, and when I asked Mona to make a match of it we needed a cottage handy to the estate.' Noticing Rob's bleak face, he added, 'We didn't turn her out, Rob, don't you be thinking that. It was Jenny suggested the arrangement.'

'I see.'

'Look, I'll just run the truck out of the shed and we'll get going.'

Snow was lying several inches deep in the lane. Jack made a few comments about the problems that would pile up if it continued for long, but otherwise it was a silent drive. Rob's return home was ruined. He had no home, apparently.

When they got there Jenny was waiting in the porch. She began waving excitedly, and Rob forgot all else as he jumped from the truck to enfold her in a bear hug, leaving Jack to unload his kit and dump it on the step beside them, then drive off, his cheery farewell unheard.

'Look at you!' cried Jenny, her eyes glowing with excitement as she held Rob at arm's length. 'You seem to have grown even bigger, and you're so brown! Congratulations on getting your wings. I'm so proud, I tell everyone I meet. And you're now a *sergeant*!' She hugged him again. 'Oh Rob, I can't believe you're really here. Why didn't you let me know you were coming?'

'I wrote saying we hoped to be home for Christmas, then I was given the chance to ferry a new Hudson over so I'm here before my letter reached you. And before yours reached me,' he added, recollection returning. 'Can you guess how I felt when I found the Morrisons in our home?'

Jenny drew him further into the spacious hall. 'Come inside, I'm getting frozen. We'll look in on the Guthries for a few moments, then go upstairs and have a lovely long talk. I'm dying to hear about America. Mrs Brumby's been told to send up two meals tonight, but I'll make some tea first. We don't eat until seven-thirty, and you're certain to be hungry. I've biscuits and a plum cake in my room. They'll keep you going until dinner time.'

Rob pulled up, bringing her to a halt. 'What's going on, Jen? Stallards have never treated the Squire's house as their own. That's what you seem to be doing ... and how long has supper been called dinner?'

At that point, the door of the sitting room opened and Molly Guthrie came out. 'I heard voices and guessed you had arrived, Robert. Welcome home, even on such a wintry evening. Please come in for a quick word with Charles before you go upstairs.' She moved further back into the open doorway. 'He's recovering from a bout of 'flu, but would so much like to greet you. He's been very irascible all day — longs to get out on the estate, as you may guess — so it'll cheer him to see you. You can get together for a longer chat in a day or so.' Her smile was warm and friendly. 'I'm sure you're eager to tell Jenny all the things you've been doing. We won't delay you for long.'

Rob had no choice but to go into another room of the large manor which he had rarely entered when he had worked for the Guthries. Although he was no longer their employee, it still felt wrong for a Stallard to be there.

Sir Charles certainly did not look well, but his long face lit with pleasure when he saw Rob. 'Very good of you to spare me a few minutes when you've not seen your sister for seven months.' He stretched out his hand. 'Congratulations on winning your wings. I'm very pleased for you, Robert. Very pleased indeed.'

They shook hands. 'Thank you, sir.' Rob stood beside the invalid's chair uncertain what to say next.

'How d'you like flying, eh? Taken to it like a bird, I suppose.'

'Not exactly, sir. I need a machine to help me do it.'

Sir Charles laughed. 'Quite so. How adaptable *homo sapiens* is! One minute a man's managing my herd, the next he's defying gravity in a flying machine. I suppose you're not allowed to say where you've been posted.'

'An operational training unit, sir.'

'Well, I wish you the best of luck. Wherever you've been since May, the climate seems to have suited you. You look wonderfully fit.' A bout of coughing caused him to add, 'Could do with a spell there myself. This damned influenza! Haven't been able to get out for ten days. Jack's keeping things running, but I hate being cooped up indoors. The new herd is coming along well ... but there, I mustn't keep you chatting about that when you've just arrived. We'll talk tomorrow ... or the day after.' He smiled at Jenny. 'Take your brother off, my dear. You'll have a deal to tell each other. Goodnight to you both!'

Rob followed his sister up the main staircase in a state of continuing unreality. Jenny was completely at ease in the house of her employers. She was also not the girl he remembered. Her brown hair was now swept into a shining roll halo-style around her head, and she was wearing very bright lipstick. Her fingernails were the same scarlet shade. Mum and Dad would never have approved. Within seven months Jennifer Stallard had become an assured, smart woman with a figure so well contoured by her black and white wool dress that Rob felt curiously embarrassed. He had always regarded her as his little sister. She was now a sophisticated semi-stranger.

Jenny led the way to a fair-sized room off which another led. There was a generous log fire burning in the hearth, where a kettle on a metal stand was letting forth steam. Jenny's single bed was there, with her wardrobe and dressing table, as well as two chairs from home and a bookcase Dad had made. Through the open door connecting the two rooms Rob could see a desk bearing a typewriter and a stack of papers, a wooden chest with numerous drawers, and a modern telephone.

'Take off your things and sit by the fire, Rob, I won't take long to make tea and cut you some cake,' said Jenny, walking to a cupboard on the wall behind the door she closed after him. From it she took a small teapot and the old tea caddy. The sight of that familiar black and gold tin released Rob's pent-up emotion.

'You might have had the decency to wait until I got here before handing over our home to the Morrisons.'

His harsh tone caused her to spin round, teapot in hand. After a brief study of his expression, she said, 'I didn't know you were coming, did I? In any case, the Guthries would eventually want the cottage for Jack — he's the farm manager you recommended to take your place — so I just made it easy for everyone by offering to move out before the wedding. I know it's been a shock to you, but I *did* write telling you all the details.' Her tone softened. 'It's not my fault you left before the letter caught up with you. Let's have some tea and just enjoy being together. I've so much to ask you. We can talk about the cottage later on. *Please*, Rob.'

Now he had embarked on the subject he found he could not drop it. 'For God's sake, Jen! I arrive home to find I haven't one any longer because someone else is living there, and you expect me to have tea and cake and talk about anything but that until you're ready. What's happened to the rest of the furniture Mum and Dad saved for years to buy? What about *my* things; my clothes and books?' he demanded with a renewed surge of bewildered anger. 'What have you done with it all?'

Jenny's face clouded. 'Don't shout at me!'

'I'm not. I just don't understand how you could do it. You should have asked me first.'

'You weren't here,' she cried. 'If you remember, you decided one night to turn your back on all this and join up.'

'I only went because I believed you were going to marry Phil almost immediately. You know I did.'

'And what did you think would happen to everything in the cottage if I did?' she flung at him. 'It's only because it's no longer there that you've grown so concerned. Have you once wanted or thought about Mum and Dad's things while you've been in America? No, you've been having the greatest adventure of your life.'

Jenny's words gave him pause for thought because they had hit the mark, but 'the greatest adventure of his life' had demanded all his concentration of mind and much physical effort in an environment vastly different from this. It had also involved a degree of danger. Two cadets had been in fatal crashes during advanced training; four others had been injured. Of course he had seldom thought of the familiar furniture and individual ornaments. 'Home' had been a composite abstract: somewhere to return to, a place to yearn for when the alien quality of where he was grew too strong: the scene of his past.

'I suppose I imagined you and Phil would have everything. I don't know. Perhaps it never occurred to me,' he admitted on a sigh. 'The loss of Mum and Dad so suddenly ... I wasn't thinking very straight. I just had to get away.' He sighed again. 'I'm sorry, Jen.'

'I'll pour you some tea. You look just about ready for it. As you're determined to get things straight first, I'll forget about biscuits and cake,' she said quietly.

The logs crackled and spat in the silence as Rob shrugged off his greatcoat and sat in the chair that had been his father's. This room was almost as alien as those he had occupied over the last seven months, and Jenny had brought full circle the sense of guilt he had suffered on leaving her. It was as if all he had achieved had never happened; as if he was again merely Fred Stallard's lad. When his sister offered the cup he warmed his icy hands around it, and sipped the tea while trying to order his thoughts.

Jenny sat facing him. 'Jack helped Benny Forbes move the furniture up here for me. Your clothes, books and personal things are in a room along the corridor. The Guthries offered also to have here the best parlour furniture, and things like their wedding-present dinner set, Mum's épergne, that pair of shepherdesses and anything else I considered special, or that you and I might want when we have homes of our own.'

'And?'

She faced him candidly. 'I thought they had been generous enough, so I got Frank Barstead to send one of his vans and take it into store for us. The allowance you made me from your pay to cover the rent is now settling Barstead's weekly account. I've put what's left over from it in the rent tin for you. You'd better tell the RAF to reduce the amount when you go back from leave.'

Rob shook his head. 'Tell me how much you're giving the Guthries for these rooms and I'll bump up the allowance.'

'I don't pay rent.' She coloured slightly. 'Lady Guthrie says it's foolish for her to pay me, then have some back, so she simply takes it into account when working out my wages.'

'That's not right,' he protested immediately. 'Dad wouldn't like it, you know he wouldn't.'

'Rob, Dad isn't with us any more,' she said with emphasis. 'He was a dear, kind man, but he was dreadfully old-fashioned and set in his ways. We naturally abided by his wishes when he was alive, but we have to put the past behind us.'

Rob got to his feet, unable to sit in Fred Stallard's chair during such a discussion. 'So you've put Dad in store along with his furniture, have you?'

She gazed back in shock. 'You never used to be cruel, but that was.'

'Was it? Yes, I suppose so. I just ... it's been a hell of a lot to take in on my first day back. I was expecting everything — you — to be the same.' He ran a hand through his hair. 'It was daft, because I'm not the same. Even so, I thought about Thoresby a lot — you do when you're away — and this has been a bit of a let-down. There's no place like home.'

Jenny's expression grew sad but resigned. 'I think "home" vanished along with Mum and Dad. You must have sensed that, or you'd never have been so determined to leave.'

He turned away to gaze at the glowing logs. Jenny was no longer the girl devastated by their triple loss; the sister who had expected him to shoulder all the responsibility and carry her through that terrible period last year. She had grown independent; had easily adapted to her role as Lady Guthrie's secretary and put the past behind her. He had thought he had done the same, until now.

He glanced at her. 'You've grown up while I've been away.'

She nodded. 'And you've become a handsome and very clever young pilot. The wings on your tunic look really special.'

'I love flying, Jen.'

'So you told me in every letter. And I love living here and working for Lady Guthrie. She's taken on the chairmanship of a committee liaising with an American women's organization which raises funds for British war orphans. They've even financed several batches of children shipped to safety there for the duration of the war. They find foster homes and check on them regularly. When Lady Guthrie attends meetings in London, I go with her. Along with all her other voluntary work, she keeps me very busy. I've never before felt that I was doing something really worthwhile. It's not as grand as flying an aeroplane, but it's more important than just getting married and having babies, don't you think?'

Rob countered that with 'So it's definitely all over between you and Phil?'

It was a moment or two before she said, 'His ship went down with all hands two months ago. He never came home on leave, so I didn't have to hurt him.'

Rob was deeply sorry. 'Why didn't you write and tell me?'

'I did ... in the letter that never reached you. I explained that it was one of the reasons why I wanted to leave the cottage and live up here. I let Mona have the wedding dress for ten shillings. Phil's parents said they'll never forgive me.' She appealed to him. 'It was just a dress ... and Mona couldn't get satin like that now, even if she could afford it.'

'Poor old Phil,' Rob murmured, still shaken.

'He wasn't old, he was only twenty-three,' she said sharply. '*That's* the tragedy, not some silly dress.'

Rob moved to put his arm round her shoulders. 'They'll cope with their loss in time. Then they'll see things the way you do.'

'I was very fond of Phil, but I didn't want to marry him,' Jenny said reflectively, as she also gazed at the fire, which needed fresh logs. 'Mum and Dad were all for it so I thought I was, too. When they were no longer here, and Phil was away at sea, I realized I wanted something entirely different.' She glanced up at Rob. 'Same as you did. That's what I meant about putting the past behind us. Try to understand.'

'I do.' He squatted to add wood to the flames. 'At least, I will when I've had time to think about it all. I've been travelling since seven this morning, so I don't feel as clever as you seem to think I must be.' He stood again. 'I really am fagged out, Jen. If I'm to get back to the Chase I ought to set off while the lane's passable. It's snowing really hard.'

'Why've you got to go back to the Chase?'

'I'll need a room at the Pig and Acorn for the week. That's nearer than the Wheatsheaf at Bestead.'

Jenny's smile softened her strained expression. 'You surely didn't think the Guthries would turn you out on a night like this? As soon as they got Jack's call, Mrs Brumby was told to make up a bed for you in the room along the corridor where I put your things. They knew we'd talk well into the early hours.'

'I can't stay here as a guest,' Rob protested. 'I used to work for them.'

'Now you're a pilot in the RAF. That changes things.'

'No, it doesn't. They're still my former employers.'

'One thing success hasn't changed is your dratted mulishness,' she told him impatiently. 'You can't refuse their generosity. It would be insulting.'

'But I'll need a room at the P and A for the rest of the week, so I might as well go there now.'

'Give me credit for some sense, Rob. I still know how to look after my brother, so I asked Mrs Brumby to let you have her spare room during your leave. When she goes home tonight she'll get it ready for you. You'll have the place to yourself during the day, and you can come here for the evening. It's only a short walk along the lane, so it won't matter even if the snow piles high on the doorstep.'

Her words dismayed him. 'My kit must still be out there! I've chocolate, oranges and presents for you. They'll all be frozen solid.'

They made a rush for the door.

*

The seven days of Rob's leave dragged. His hope of walking the familiar lanes was dashed by the severe weather. In Mrs Brumby's small parlour his only means of entertainment were a crackling radio and a small collection of battered romances with covers showing cool, virginal creatures on yachts or sun-washed terraces. Having discovered the joys of intimacy with a woman Johnny had tracked down on the outskirts of Arcadia, Rob found the romances ludicrous. He had never slept with a girl whom he had not paid for the privilege, of course, but he was sure most women's feelings were more earthy than the books suggested.

Sorting through his possessions, he was appalled by the darned combinations and thick flannel shirts. Had he really ever worn such clothes? He threw everything out, including Great-Uncle Herbert's pocket watch, which had never worked, and a scale model of Stephenson's 'Rocket' he had made as a boy. All he retained of his past were his engineering manuals, which he packed in his kit. Only then did he fully realize that he had no home other than a hut awaiting him in Cheshire.

He arrived at the nearest station to the OTU as it was getting dark, in a temperature of minus six, after travelling for ten hours in freezing trains. The driver who picked him up had difficulty getting through the lanes due to frozen compacted snow. Rob longed for a big, hot meal, but his first duty was to report to the Adjutant. This fair-moustached individual scowled when Rob announced himself.

'God, you must be keen! Any sensible chap would've phoned to say he couldn't get through, and taken a few extra days' leave. You can't do any flying. We've been snowed in all week.'

Wing Commander Blaine was more welcoming. 'Glad to have you, Stallard. Bit different from Florida, eh? You'll be flying a Hurricane when conditions improve, but you'll have plenty of practice before you go operational.' He smiled. 'You gained very high marks during training so you have been classified as a top-grade pilot. You'll discover that it takes more than that to succeed in combat, however. Your colleagues will bend the rules, defy accepted procedures, and do the damndest things in the air, which you'll find unsettling, but remember this. The pilot who uses his skill with intelligence and flair is the man who invariably returns to base.'

'Yes, sir,' said Rob, filled with excitement at the prospect of flying a Hurricane.

'I'm pleased to tell you that you've been granted a commission with the rank of pilot officer, effective from today. The Mess Sergeant will find you a second-hand uniform until you can get to the tailor. There's one thing I must say to you, Stallard. Your record shows you tend to prefer your own company. An officers' mess is a somewhat rowdy place, you'll find. They need to let off steam and expect everyone to join in. A squadron is a team. You have to become a full member of it to survive.' He offered his hand. 'Good luck.'

As he waited, shivering, outside the office for a jeep to take him the two miles to the country house used as the Mess, Rob remained stunned. He had been a flying cadet for six months; a sergeant for four weeks. Now he was an officer — he, Fred Stallard's son! And a fighter pilot! He could not believe his luck. Yet, as he stared out at the rows of blacked-out Nissen huts standing starkly against the snow, he recalled the sight of Mum, Dad and Gran's lifeless faces covered in brick dust, and excitement died. He was not here for the fun of it. His time had come to hit back.

*

Jim graduated at the start of December, having been retrograded at Basic due to difficulty over landing at night. His skill in every other respect was good enough to persuade his instructors that he needed only a little more time to conquer the problem. Their faith had been justified, but it meant that Bucket and Gus were a stage ahead of him throughout their training. They had all been deeply affected when Peter Kelsey crashed after failing to pull out from a dive, injuring himself so badly he would spend the rest of his life in a wheelchair. Once again the danger of what they were doing was brought home to the trainee pilots.

By the time Jim was presented with the coveted silver wings he had grown a great deal quieter. The newly elected Senator Benson used pressure of work as an excuse to be absent on a day that meant a great deal to his son. Jim knew it was Theo's way of punishing him for refusing to dance to his tune, but newspapers began hinting at an irreconcilable rift between the Senator and his son. Could it be because J.T. had been retrograded along the way? The hard-hitting head of Benson Pharmaceuticals was known to have no time for anyone who did not absolutely excel.

On that December day Jim stood on the parade ground waiting to be called forward to receive his hard-won wings, hearing Theo saying, 'After all this time even goddam Mickey Mouse could have got there.' At the end of the ceremony, when proud parents and exultant new pilots rejoiced with their families, Jim returned to his quarters, packed his bag and headed for the rail station.

The Boston house was empty, so Jim celebrated there with Bucket and Gus, who were both already with squadrons within easy travelling distance. They came for the weekend bringing the girls they were currently dating, and Jim invited a socialite red-head named Topaz he had met at a recent party. She did not care about her escort's aerial prowess just so long as she had a good time, so she was perfect for this occasion.

The six celebrated in style, and Thomas showed as much pride and delight over Jim's success as if *he* were his father. The hurt inflicted by being one of very few graduates with no one present to witness that special moment of honour gradually eased in the company of his friends and three admiring females.

They swam in the indoor pool and the men played squash while the girls lounged in towelling robes painting their nails in readiness for the evening, when they planned to hit the night spots. Boston was decorated with the aftermath of Thanksgiving and the onset of Christmas, and Jim threw himself into the pleasures of dining, dancing and charming women. When they returned to the house in the early hours, they drank hot spiced wine and toasted marshmallows at the log fire. After saying goodnight and going to their rooms, there was no one to see or care if a little nocturnal visiting took place. Thomas had retired long ago, and the host was happily tucked up in bed with Topaz.

On Sunday they all arose late and ate brunch in their robes, while they discussed what to do with the six hours before Bucket and Gus, with their girls, had to leave. Jim had persuaded Topaz to remain for the rest of his leave, at the end of which he would be notified of his posting to a squadron. She had needed little persuasion while lying in his arms last night.

As it was an invigorating winter's day it was decided that they would visit a hill giving magnificent views, and take a brisk walk. After a very fast journey in Jim's convertible they chased each other along the top of the hill in an excess of youthful high spirits, then happily crammed into the car for the return which allowed the opportunity for kissing and cuddling. When they reached the house even the driver had lipstick on his face and collar. Topaz was a very loving girl! They burst in, seeking the warmth of the fire, champagne and popcorn, but Thomas met them in the hall and one look at him halted their happy progress.

The old servant had tears streaming down his cheeks, and he had difficulty in speaking. 'Mr Jim, the Japanese have wiped out our fleet at Pearl Harbor! Thousands are dead.'

Jim grew cold as the words sank in. '*What!*'

'Yes, sir, it's war. The President is due to broadcast this evening.'

Jim looked at Bucket and Gus, both as shocked as he, and they all vented their feelings in violent language while the girls stood rooted to the spot. Topaz began to sob; a harsh, terrible sound in the shocked silence that followed the outburst. 'My brother Bobby's out there with the Navy. Oh, my God! Oh, my God!'

'Take her in there,' Jim told the other girls, nodding at the drawing room. 'Give her a drink.'

Thomas stepped nearer, still distressed. 'There's been calls for Mr Etwell and Mr Buckhalter to report back right away, sir. Came in an hour ago.'

'We'd better get going,' said Gus in a cold, toneless voice. 'This is it. No country attacks us without warning and gets away with it.'

Bucket looked very pale. 'What kind of enemy attacks first, then declares war afterwards?'

'Looks like we'll soon find out,' muttered Jim, trying to come to terms with this horror which had hurtled at them in the midst of carefree happiness. 'They'll soon discover they've taken on an enemy who'll give no quarter until they've beaten the hell out of them.'

Still stunned, the two pilots departed on the first available train, leaving Jim to make arrangements for the girls to depart for home later in the afternoon. He found the duty irksome when his mind was full of unknowns and possibilities. What about himself and the others who had graduated two days ago? Surely they would not be left to kick their heels while panic was calmed into order? It would be unbearable to watch the army mobilize while sitting on the sidelines, because he was in a military limbo.

After the girls left, Jim prowled moodily around the house, listening to the radio in whichever room he was in. Taking his uniform from the wardrobe, he hung it on the door and fingered the wings so bright and new. From out of the past came the memory of a row of Stearmans at

Carlstrom, washed by the sunset glow so that they looked on fire. He had thought then how daunting a sight it would be to the RAF cadets. It now struck deep into his own senses. Yet there was also a feeling of exultation. He was a pilot trained for combat. This would be the ultimate test for them all. It was what every one of them had longed for. When would that vital call come through?

It was two in the morning, as Jim sat eating popcorn and listening to the radio in his sitting room, when the telephone rang. He rose and lunged for it, heart hammering.

'Mr Benson?'

'Yes, *sir.*'

'This is Dwight Peterson.'

Jim waited for enlightenment.

'We met when your father and Mrs Benson visited Carlstrom Field.' A short silence. 'On the day a Britisher brought down his unconscious instructor,' he prompted.

Jim's fingers tightened round the receiver. This was not the call he was expecting. Peterson was a member of Theo's campaign committee. Damn him! Why was he calling at two a.m.?

'I've been ringing around trying to connect with you.'

'Peterson, I'm on top line to receive military orders,' Jim snapped impatiently.

'That's why I'm calling, Mr Benson. The Senator has been in conference with General Connicks this evening, and you've been assigned as a personal aide to Colonel Flood of the War Department. Your orders will come through from the Colonel's office in a day or two, once I inform his staff where you can be reached.' There was a pause. 'Mr Benson, are you still on the line?'

Jim slowly replaced the receiver and stood staring at it while passion built in his breast like a gathering storm. His father he would have defied. Military orders he could not. Theo had had his way: he had won hands down. James Theodore Benson III would be in a boardroom after all — a grounded pilot in a military boardroom. Jim now counted the cost of what he had said at Carlstrom to a man who revelled in power over others; the cost of his continued defiance. His father had just destroyed what he had struggled so hard to gain. He had snatched away his hard-won freedom. Jim's fist began hammering against the wall with increasing ferocity, and he sobbed for the first time since hearing of the death of his mother.

Chapter Nine

Jim wandered in the gentle spring sunshine, enjoying the picturesque appeal of mellow stone cottages with roofs of brown thatch standing in an uneven row beside a winding lane, which followed the meandering of a clear, shallow stream. These miniature homes were beautifully kept and the ground within their painted fences was planted with straight rows of vegetables. There were flowers which defied the demand for food, however. Creepers rambled over walls and porches in a blaze of colour. Trees were covered in pink and white blossom, wooden tubs beside front doors were crammed with the owners' favourite plants, and wild daffodils fluttered in the breeze all along the banks of the stream.

America had been at war for sixteen months, yet Jim had only arrived in England eight weeks ago at the end of February 1943, when Clancy Flood had been promoted to brigadier general and attached to the US Eighth Air Force. Jim's initial delight at finally reaching a war zone had quickly evaporated. Grey skies, sleeting rain, blacked-out streets and dreary towns where red-brick houses clung together in endless terraces now broken and blackened by air raids, all created a depressing impression of this ancient island.

When he saw London, his depression had deepened to shock. There were miles and miles of total devastation. Fifty per cent of the ruins shored up by gigantic beams were unlikely to stand for much longer; the people living and working there would surely be buried beneath the rubble when they collapsed. Important buildings were protected by sandbagged walls so that the beauty of the architecture was lost. Some of the beautiful old churches were no more than empty shells; others were used for individual prayers by the bereaved, the lost and desolate. The homeless occupied school halls, club rooms, mission huts and empty warehouses. Temporary mortuaries housed the victims of nightly raids.

Jim found it hard to accept that this had been going on for three and a half years. What if it had happened in New York or Boston or Washington? Arrival in a war zone sobered him considerably, although the British had a curiously blasé attitude to it all which he had found irritating until a woman in a shabby coat and a headscarf explained. 'When you've been at it as long as we 'ave, dearie, you'll be the same.'

Despite a strong attitude of 'What took you so long?' from certain sections of the public, and instances of misbehaviour by undisciplined boys from the more remote corners of some states, the first Americans had been welcomed with open arms by their hosts, who had faced probable invasion and years of aerial battering. The breezy lads from across the Atlantic brought a breath of fresh air and renewed hope as they gradually occupied half of England and joined battle alongside British and Commonwealth men and women. With their jaunty uniforms, relaxed manners, and gifts of food, cigarettes and items of clothing last seen in 1939 these men from the land of Hollywood films brought to the average family an insight into a country and culture markedly different despite a shared language. The elderly sometimes found it too much to take and tut-tutted. Parents of young girls were alternately delighted and worried by growing friendships with Al, Mitch or Chuck. The boys were well-off and appeared to be very important in their home towns, but America was so far away their girls would be lost to them for ever if anything came of it.

So far as many girls were concerned, 'The Yanks' were the best thing that had ever happened to them. Their drawling accents, their cockiness and their generosity bowled them over. Only the most reserved or those already deeply in love failed to be charmed by the transatlantic invaders. Engagements were broken off; marriages were threatened. The birthrate rose in disproportionate ratio to weddings. Those who had initially asked, 'What took you so long?' began to wish the Yanks had taken even longer. There was nevertheless a new optimism now the Allies were striking at the enemy together, and a little healthy competition added spice to life.

One of the greatest disappointments of Jim's new posting was that there was scant opportunity for sport. The British did not pursue it to the same extent as the Americans, he had discovered, and they all thought football was their game of soccer. When baseball was mentioned they invariably said, 'Oh, we call it rounders, and it's mostly played by girls.' Basketball was netball, and that was played by girls, too. What did the men play? Cricket, of course, 'football', and rugby in the winter. Then there were darts, skittles and shove-ha'penny in the pubs. Golf courses were mostly closed. Jim had long ago given up trying to talk about sport with the British. They embarked on memories of matches played by people whose names meant nothing to him, interspersing their monologues with phrases such as 'jolly good all-rounder', 'bloomin' nifty when dribbling up the pitch', 'unbeatable at square leg' or 'cheekiest dropped goal I ever saw'. They understood tennis, but appeared to regard it as a social get-together on those summer evenings when it did not rain more than a serious sport.

If Jim had been a member of a squadron he could have enjoyed the facilities available to men at an airbase, but a 'boardroom pilot' had none of those advantages. It was also a lonely job. J.T. Benson was no longer the clean-cut, laughing, sporting hero of a group of virile young men. He was highly thought of by his superiors, doing his job with diligence and inbred social know-how. He had been promoted to first lieutenant, with all the privileges of a personal aide, but he spent his days with men too obsessed with promotion and being noticed by the right people to share the kind of pastimes Jim enjoyed. The women were too afraid of losing their plum appointments to risk a sexual relationship with someone also on the staff.

Jim's great hope on learning he was being sent to Britain was that he would have the chance to switch to operational flying, but his forceful boss maintained that Theo Benson's boy was indispensable to him. So Jim continued to serve the sentence his father had imposed on him for daring to break loose. After gaining his wings, Jim had bought a twin-engined, streamlined aircraft and flown it with all the panache they had drilled out of him during training. While acknowledging that his instructors had been right to do so, he had nevertheless become a free spirit when flying that little machine over the country he loved and dearly longed to serve in his rightful capacity. Deprived of the opportunity to maintain his solo hours, all Jim could now do was to persuade pilots to let him take the controls for a while whenever he accompanied Clancy Flood to conferences involving a short flight.

His yearning to join a squadron remained uppermost. Bucket had been flying bombers over Germany for six months. The friends had met up in London a few weeks ago; a heavy raid had interrupted their meal at the Savoy. Bucket looked older and rather strained, but they took up the old relationship as if there had been no long absence. Even so, halfway through the meeting it became apparent to them both that carefree youth had slipped through their fingers since the day they had heard about Pearl Harbor.

As they talked about the music they had created together, the girls they had known, the hectic weekends at Palm Beach, the camaraderie at Carlstrom and various other training fields, it seemed that they spoke of two different people. Gradually, the forced recollections had sobered as they touched on Peter Kelsey's disabling crash, and Gus Buckhalter's death a week after arriving in the Pacific. He had been awarded a posthumous medal for a daring attack on a Japanese convoy. It did not seem possible that he had been wiped out so swiftly. He had had everything ahead of him; a golden life.

'Maybe his old man finally felt proud of him,' Bucket had said.

The encounter had unsettled Jim further and he was daily eating his heart out for an operational role like any aggressive, restless, twenty-four-year-old bursting with energy and the fire of patriotism. Instead, he had accompanied Flood to a meeting of high-ranking American and British air force officers at a large country house in the county of Somerset. The early stages of discussion had ended at lunchtime. Top secret talks were now under way and expected to last until tomorrow, which gave junior staff some time to relax. Jim had confiscated a Jeep and driven the few miles to a village they had earlier passed through. It was proving as enjoyable as he hoped.

Where the cottages ended he found a forge manned by a giant with little time to spare for an American in uniform who asked about the church on the opposite side of the lane.

'Just how old is it? We don't have anything like that back home.'

'From all I've heard, I doan s'pose you do. Over there it's all new ... and bigger than anything else.' He nodded his head. 'That church there was put up in thirteen forty-two. Got the original font, it has.' He prepared to turn back to his work. 'This forge is hundered year old. Bin in my family four generations. Can't match that neither, doan suppose.'

Further conversation was prevented by hammer blows on metal, so Jim crossed the lane to the church, feeling sure he had heard an accent something like that before. The moment he entered the cool interior he forgot all else but the beauty of stained glass, ancient wood and stone walls that had stood the test of time. Not normally much interested in historical buildings, he found this one affecting him. He stood for some time in the silent serenity of that tiny church, reading the commemorative plaques all along the walls, many recording the names of succeeding generations of the same families, and he found peacefulness entering his soul. For the first time since landing in this country, he found some pleasure in being here.

He left the church to step back into welcome sunshine. Maybe it was because he had seen so little of it over here that he was enjoying this bright afternoon. Summer was on its way, and this quaint village was the epitome of the popular concept of England. The war did not appear to have touched it. He had no idea of its name — all references to it had been painted over for security reasons — but whatever it was called, it resembled a place from a children's storybook. The people who lived here were probably like characters from one.

Smiling at that thought, he stepped from the lych-gate right into the path of a girl on a bicycle. Startled by his sudden appearance she swerved, wobbled, then came a cropper on the grassy bank alongside the churchyard wall, spilling the contents of the basket on the handlebars. Jim hurried to help her up, enjoying the uninhibited view of shapely legs as far as her stocking suspenders as she lay winded.

'Are you hurt?' he asked, bending over her and encountering startled green eyes as she pushed down her skirt.

'Only my dignity.'

He grinned. 'I shouldn't worry too much about that, ma'am. Let me give you a hand.'

Deprived of the sight of her legs, Jim found ample compensation when she stood before him pushing back her loose shoulder-length brown hair. A scarlet high-necked sweater moulded her breasts enticingly, and a wide black patent-leather belt on her skirt emphasized her neat waist. Jim was more than ever glad he had come to this enchanting village.

The girl treated him to a wide, friendly smile. 'You gave me an awful fright appearing so unexpectedly. We don't get people coming to see the church these days, so I hared past it without thinking.' She looked at the wings on his chest. 'You're a pilot. You haven't baled out and landed in the churchyard, have you?'

Jim shook his head, unhappy over her assumption. 'I wouldn't risk that sharply pointed weather-vane on the roof.' He moved to where a quantity of knitting wool lay scattered over the lane, and began picking it up. 'This is going to make a very jazzy kind of jacket.' He glanced up at her. 'Joseph's coat of many colours?'

She gave a light laugh. 'It's for the Polish refugees. They knit things for their children. Here, let me take that from you.'

Once the wool had been gathered, Jim picked up the bicycle so that she could stow it in the basket on the handlebars. He thought she presented a delightful picture standing with her arms filled with rainbow skeins, watching him with faintly flushed cheeks. There were no rings on her left hand.

'I envy the Polish refugees,' he said, keeping his hold on the bicycle and smiling into her eyes.

'You wouldn't if you saw them,' she responded coolly. 'Their faces are etched with the horror they've been through.' Despite that brush-off, she nevertheless seemed happy to linger. 'What are you doing here if you didn't bale out?'

'I had time to kill so I decided to explore. We came through here just after dawn, and I wanted another look at the village. What's it called ... or aren't you allowed to say? A man can't find his way around this country. All the signs are painted over.'

'You're not a German spy, are you?' she asked with a twinkle in her eyes.

'Cross my heart.'

'This is Thoresby. The church dates back to the fourteenth century.'

'And the forge is a hundred years old. The smith already told me that.' He put on a rueful expression. 'He also said everything where I come from is new, and bigger than any other.'

'Oh dear! Even down here we've heard about the way Americans talk.'

'That's because so much over here is small in comparison. Your fields are like patchwork — tiny squares divided by walls or hedges. Back home, farms are so big it can take a day or two to drive around them. Highways go on for miles, straight as an arrow, yet these lanes are —' He broke off as he saw her expression. 'Hell, I'm doing it.'

'Yes, you are ... but I know you're not bragging. My brother spent seven months in America and he told me a great deal about the vast distances, and the roads without bends in them.'

'So you're not averse to Americans?'

141

'Heavens, no. It must be a very unnerving and lonely experience to be shipped over to a foreign country where everyone's a stranger, and then be expected to fight. I know Rob took a long time to grow accustomed to the United States.'

'That your brother?'

She nodded and her eyes grew soft with affection. 'He's a pilot, too. They taught him to fly in Florida. In forty-one — when you were still neutral.'

Sensing resentment in her comment, he said, 'So you've also heard down here the phrase, "What took you so long?"'

She faced him frankly. 'I wasn't criticizing, merely making a statement.'

'Yes?'

'Yes,' she said firmly. 'But I'm afraid a lot of people do feel ... Those who lost loved ones early in the war,' she finished quietly.

'As you did?' he guessed.

'Yes.'

'I know how it is. One of my air force pals was shot down in the Pacific. He was a great guy, son of a general. Just twenty-four, with everything going for him.'

'I'm sorry. My brother's squadron is always losing crews. One night they just don't come back. Sometimes, when no one has seen what happened, it's as though they simply vanished up there among the stars. He doesn't say much on the subject but it must be a terrible strain on them. You'd know all about that, of course.'

She gazed at him with such understanding that he was driven to say, 'I'm out of it at the moment.'

'I thought that would come as a relief, but when Rob was grounded at the end of his first spell of ops he became unbearably restless and moody. Couldn't wait to get back in the air.' Her attractive smile appeared again. 'He loves flying. Mad about it. Although it was the last thing he wanted when they first sent him to Arcadia. He was crazy to be an engineer then, and moaned —'

'He was at *Arcadia*?'

'It's in Florida. Do you know it?'

'I'll say. I also did my preliminary training there in forty-one. I'll be darned! There were some British cadets at Carlstrom with us for a while.'

'That's where he was: Carlstrom Field!' she declared with excitement. 'You'll have met him. Rob Stallard.'

Jim stared at her in utter disbelief. This was unreal. This was not happening. He had walked from a village church some place in England right into the path of Stallard's sister. Things like that just did not happen. Yet he had heard of greater coincidences. As he gazed back into eyes as green but not as steely as that other pair, Jim told himself some inexplicable force had brought this about. It was not mere chance; there was surely a reason behind the impulse that had driven him back to this village.

'Is something wrong?'

Jim came from thoughts that there must be two Englishmen called Stallard who had trained at Carlstrom, and put that theory to the test. 'There were so many on the course, I don't recall his name. Does he look anything like you?'

'He's a lot taller; big and muscular. Not the kind of man to go unnoticed in a crowd.' She clearly very much wanted Jim to say that he remembered him. 'Brown hair, quite good-looking and a bit on the shy side,' she added hopefully.

Jim shook his head. 'I can't say I recollect anyone like that.'

Her disappointment was acute. 'What a shame! It's such a happy chance that we ran into each other, it would have been lovely if you knew him.'

He forced a smile. 'That would be asking too much of a happy chance, don't you think?'

'I suppose so.'

Afraid that the pause would prompt her to bring the encounter to an end, Jim obeyed an impulse to take it further. He knew she was interested in him aside from hoping he knew her brother, and he was deeply intrigued by her.

'Say, I've a Jeep around the corner. I've kept you so long from the Polish refugees, maybe we should toss your bicycle in the back and I'll run you wherever you have to go.'

'That's very kind of you, but I don't see them until Thursday. I was on my way home with the wool I'd collected from the vicar's wife.'

'Then I'll run you there. Is it far?'

'Up on the hill.'

He saw a large house standing above a sweep of lawn, surrounded by fields of infant crops. It was the only obvious one in the direction she pointed, but he felt there must be some mistake. It was much the size of the Benson house at Cape Cod.

'You can't pedal all the way up that hill,' he said in mock horror.

She laughed. 'I've done it for years. I'm used to it.'

He kept hold of the handlebars. 'Some damn fool Yank might walk in front of you again. Much better let me drive you.'

After a slight hesitation, she said, 'You told me you came here to kill time. How much?'

'Until around seven-thirty. Why?'

'Could I offer you tea? You might not know Rob, but you were both at Arcadia so that makes you one of his colleagues. It's the least I can do for someone so far from home.'

He smiled. 'There were fifty of us at Carlstrom. Just hope the other forty-nine don't turn up here one day.'

'One was killed, you said. A general's son. There might have been other casualties you don't know about. Please allow me to entertain you as a representative of them all.'

She had turned off his flippancy with a serious comment, as she had when he mentioned the Polish refugees. It was disconcerting. She was the first English girl he had attempted to get to know and he was encountering the curious reserve he remembered in some of the British cadets. One moment this girl was offering tea with wide-eyed invitation, the next she made it sound like a wartime obligation to her country's allies. Jim nevertheless agreed to her suggestion. He might never have another chance to discover something about this family, and she was extremely attractive. Another lonely afternoon wandering around this alien country had been cheered by this coincidental meeting. He would be a fool not to prolong it.

As he drove up the hill, she said, 'I've asked you to tea before I've even asked your name.'

'Suppose I said it was Rockefeller?' he replied with a grin.

'I'd have to use the best lace tablecloth. It isn't, is it?'

He cast a glance at her when he saw a clear road ahead as far as the next bend. 'I'm J.T. Benson.'

It meant nothing to her. 'How do you do, Mr Benson. Is that right? I'm not familiar with American ranks.'

'My friends call me J.T.'

'That's very American,' she exclaimed, still totally unimpressed. 'They call each other by initials in a lot of films. And by such unusual names, too. Are you Jehosaphat, by any chance?'

'Jehosaphat Tornado,' he said solemnly.

'Gracious! I think I'd better stick to Mr Benson, don't you? Oh, turn here! We've almost passed the entrance.'

He flung the Jeep round at such speed she fell against him, but it gave him no advantage. Straightening up, she said calmly, 'Sorry about that. It was my fault for telling you so late. Pull up over there by the garage. That's where I store the bicycle.'

Jim was studying the house. At home it would be called a residence of some substance. He had seen the sign at the gate proclaiming it to be Darston Manor, and there was certainly a deal of quiet dignity in its washed stone walls and mullioned windows beneath tightly packed thatch patterned by a real craftsman. Wisteria rambled over the arched entrance, great mauve blooms waving slightly in the breeze, but the romantic olde-worlde atmosphere was kept at bay by an open door in the extensive garage which revealed piled cardboard boxes marked: MAKEPEACE REFUGEE FUND — CLOTHING ONLY and by others marked BANDAGES AND DRESSINGS.

As he lifted her bicycle from the back of the Jeep, Jim remained astonished by Stallard's home. He had called the man a cowpoke from Hicksville. There had been nothing about him to suggest such a background. It had been said he was a farmer. One of considerable prosperity, apparently. The sister had a suggestion of his regional burr but she spoke much faster.

'Please come in,' she invited, waiting for him at the top of several steps while he gazed around. 'The wisteria's lovely right now, isn't it? Flowers take no notice of the war. They just keep on blooming exactly when they should, thank goodness.' Jim followed her into an impressive hall, then to a large room with a view of the village in the valley. 'I'll ask the housekeeper to bring us tea. Please excuse me for a few minutes while I tidy myself. There's a cloakroom across the hall if you wish to do the same. Do make yourself at home, Mr Benson.'

He turned to her. 'My name's Jim.'

'*Not* Jehosaphat?' she teased.

'Nor Tornado.'

'What a pity. I thought they suited you.'

She left before he could say anything more, and he crossed to the cloakroom with a strong feeling that he had underestimated the members of this family. Everything about the Stallard home suggested wealth and good taste. Back in the sitting room he assessed the worth of the paintings and ornaments, telling himself his mother would have appreciated them. The furniture was good, much of it antique, he guessed.

A plump woman of around fifty-five entered carrying a laden tray. 'Good afternoon, sir. I've not much by way of doughnuts or such, which American gentleman like, but there's scones and jam with a bit of my seedy cake. I hope that'll do.'

Jim crossed to take the tray from her, which put her in a flurry. 'I guess I've never had seedy cake, ma'am, but if that's it on the silver stand I'm certainly going to try it.'

Standing on the rug, with cheeks turned pinker than when she entered, the housekeeper said, 'Miss Stallard says you learned to fly with Mr Robert, sir. She's thrilled about it. Thinks the world of her brother, she does.'

'I guess so,' he agreed, wondering how that sparky girl could think the world of someone who never smiled. A bit shy, she had said. Downright anti-social!

'Thank you, Mrs Brumby,' said the girl as she entered. 'Oh, you've brought your seed cake! I'm sure it'll be new to Mr Benson, or do you have it in America?'

'I don't think so,' Jim said, knowing it had never been produced in a Benson home or any other like it.

The housekeeper departed, and Jim was invited to make himself comfortable. 'You haven't given me your name yet,' he reminded her. 'I can't continue calling you Miss Stallard if you expect me to eat that curious cake.'

'You don't *have* to eat it. It's nicer than it sounds, but I can always give a slice to the dog and say you loved it when she collects the tray.' She passed him tea in an elegant cup. 'I'm Jenny. As a matter of fact, my initials are also J.T.'

'That's surely an inescapable bond between us,' he said smoothly.

She gave him the cool glance he was beginning to know. 'If so, you've also one with Mrs Brumby. She's Jessica Thora.' She offered the cake stand. 'Try some.'

An unusual sensation began to stir within Jim as he took a slice of cake to put on the plate she also offered him. This girl was smart. Almost certain she had countered his overture with a smooth lie, he realized she was letting him know she was on to his game. She was attracted to him, he knew that very well, yet there was something about her poise, her disconcerting habit of leading him on then holding him off which offered a challenge. As he took a cautious bite into the cake, he told himself she had her brother's brand of arrogance, which in her was offset by warmth of personality and considerable sexual attraction.

'Do you dislike it *that* much?' she asked with amusement. 'You should see your expression!'

'No, it's ... it's fine,' he lied, his mouth full of something he thought tasted not unlike compacted birdseed.

She burst into laughter. 'It's not necessary to suffer in order to be polite. I understand. Rob had the same problem over there. His letters were full of astonishment over some of the things Americans ate. He grew used to them after a while, but never managed to accept jam and peanut butter spread together on bread. Please leave the cake.'

'How about the feelings of Jessica Thora?'

His sly thrust caught her off guard, and her colour rose slightly. 'I'll cover for you. Try one of her scones. I'm sure you'll be happy with that.'

'I'm happy enough with the tea and your company,' he said. 'This is a very charming house.'

'It's been in the family for years, along with the estate. It was built in eighteen fifty-four by the then squire. His direct heir was killed in the Crimea, so it passed to his cousin. The line has been unbroken since then.' She gave a gentle smile. 'We're fine ones to complain of Yanks bragging about how big everything is in America. All *we* do is brag about how old everything is here.'

'But you do it with such charm,' he murmured.

She changed the subject abruptly. 'Where's your home, Jim?'

He was sorely tempted to reel off the list of Benson addresses but resisted. 'Home's where the Air Force sends me.'

'Rob says the same. But where do your parents live?' she persisted.

'Washington.'

At that point there was the sound of female voices in the hall, and then a tall, silver-haired woman in riding clothes entered the room. Jim got to his feet, teacup in hand, guessing by her age that this was Mrs Stallard. She was a neatly built woman with the understated good looks he had noticed frequently in Englishwomen. American matrons made the most of themselves. Here, it was as if women thought it vulgar to emphasize their features and figures once past the age of forty. She had an undeniably lovely smile, which she turned on Jim.

'Mrs Brumby said Jenny was entertaining an American officer to tea. How very nice! How do you do. I'm Molly Guthrie.'

Not Mrs Stallard! Well, there was little family resemblance, and she had a clipped accent not in the least like the girl's warm, caressing tones.

'How do you do, ma'am.' He put down the cup and offered his hand. 'I'm J.T. Benson.'

Absolutely no recognition of that as she put her slim hand in his. 'You trained in Arcadia with Robert? How interesting, but what a pity he's not here on leave. However, I dare say you'll meet up soon enough.' She turned back to Jenny. 'Mrs Brumby is bringing another cup, dear. We met in the hall.' A little chuckle. 'She saw me stable Rambler and *happened* to come from the kitchen as I entered.' She turned back to Jim as he sat beside the girl. 'You are the first American she's seen, apart from those in films, so she was bursting to tell me you were here. I see you've embarked on a slice of her famous seed cake.'

'Oh ... er, *yes* ...'

'He doesn't care for it,' Jenny explained. 'I've promised to cover for him and vow he loved it.'

'Be careful, or she'll make one and send it to Mr Benson as a gesture to our brave allies. Better use restraint and say he thought it was quite nice.' She smiled once more at Jim. 'My husband, Charles, has a partiality for seed cake, and as we can't get dried fruit now it makes my housekeeper's life easier. It's not to everyone's taste, however, and we've not yet summoned the courage to tell her so. Please forgive my unkempt appearance, Mr Benson. We have to save our petrol coupons for essential journeys, so I ride around the village on a mare who has seen better days. Do you ride?'

'When I have the chance, ma'am,' he said, his brain working overtime to decide that Mrs Guthrie must be the Stallards' aunt.

'We still have two good hunters in the stables. You're welcome to take one out sometime. Jenny rides well. She'll show you the best country around here. Are you stationed in the vicinity?'

This charming woman was making things easy for him to advance his plans for Jenny, but he was not sure what to reply. He did not want to change their image of him as an operational pilot, yet they would surely be impressed by high-ranking names.

'I go all over the country at present, ma'am. I've been given a spell of duty on Brigadier General Flood's staff.'

'Poor thing,' said Jenny sympathetically. 'Rob said being put behind a desk on somebody's staff is purgatory. You're nothing but a grounded dogsbody.'

'Jenny!' protested Molly Guthrie with a laugh.

'Those were his exact words. You know he couldn't wait to be made operational again. How much longer is your sentence, Jim?'

He hedged, thrown by the fact that his connection with Clancy Flood had met with such a reception. A grounded dogsbody? Only Stallard could be so derisive! 'Everything's so uncertain at the moment. The prospect of landings in France grows as the summer nears. There's a big job ahead of us and every fighting man will be called to do it.'

Mrs Brumby entered with another cup, saucer and plate, gazing at Jim in renewed awe. When she left, Jenny said with a grin, 'I believe she thinks you've stepped right out of Hollywood, and you're really her current favourite, Dana Andrews.'

Molly said, 'Jenny's a terrible tease, Mr Benson. I'd say you'd be more at home with a racquet of some kind in your hand than in a film studio. Are you a sporting man?'

Jim managed a modest 'yes' by way of answer, which said much for the extent to which eight weeks in England had sobered him.

'We have a croquet set you might like to use when you come to ride,' Jenny offered.

'I usually indulge in something more robust,' he replied, stirred once more by the knowledge that she was being provocative in that intriguingly cool English fashion.

'We have a tennis court at the rear of the house,' Molly told him. 'Perhaps you'd like a game sometime. If you cared to bring a friend we could guarantee you a foursome with Jenny and Pat Chance, the vet's daughter. My husband and I amuse ourselves now and again, but we're no match for young players.'

Jim murmured an appropriate response, wondering at their expressions if he told them they had just invited a national champion to play pat-a-ball with a couple of local girls.

'Charles's game is golf, but the club was closed some time ago. I'm afraid our sporting activities have been badly hit by the priorities of the military. We're such a tiny country, open land is at a premium, Mr Benson. Golf courses have been ploughed up, tennis clubs have become barrage-balloon sites, football pitches are now vehicle depots — but you'll have seen all that for yourself. We're lucky in Thoresby, but Jenny and I make regular visits to London and have seen more and more of the countryside vanish beneath the demands of war.'

'A great deal of it is occupied by us, ma'am.'

'Yes, indeed,' she smiled, 'but you've no idea how glad we are to have you. We were reaching the end of our tether when you joined us.'

They talked for a while about the work for refugee and other organizations done by Molly and Jenny, then of the difficulties encountered by farmers over the past three years. 'Robert is so glad to be away from it, Mr Benson. His heart was never in farming, but his father did his utmost to keep him at it so that he would eventually take over from him.' She darted a smile at the girl beside her. 'He's found his true vocation, hasn't he?'

'Although he didn't think so when they selected him.' Jenny smiled at Jim. 'On embarkation leave he said everyone but himself was delighted at the prospect of his being a pilot. Once he took to the air he was in raptures about flying, and he has never come down to earth. How about you, Jim? What job were you doing before you joined the Air Force? Were you happy about being selected as a pilot, and are you crazy about flying?'

Further discussion on the subject was halted by the entry of Mrs Brumby. 'Excuse me, ma'am. Sir Charles calling from London. He won't be home tonight.'

Molly raised her eyebrows at Jenny. 'More trouble at the Ministry! Please excuse me, Mr Benson. Do come again. You're welcome to bring your friends, but ring first to ensure that we'll be here. Jenny will give you our number.'

She departed, leaving Jim with more food for thought. *Sir* Charles? Then she must be *Lady* Guthrie. And he had dubbed Stallard a redneck. How could that man have such distinguished relations?

Jenny had walked across to take from a small box on a circular table a piece of white card, which she offered him. 'These are the telephone numbers for the house, and for the office. Please don't use that line because it's given priority at the switchboard, and if they find personal calls are being put through on it we might be penalized.'

As she remained standing, Jim sensed that he was expected to leave and got to his feet. 'When I call it will be to speak to you, Jenny. I wouldn't want the girl on the switchboard listening in to check on what I plan on saying.'

She survived his charm without much difficulty. 'Then you'll have to mind your p's and q's, won't you? Have you far to drive back to your dreary desk job?'

'Another of your brother's terms?' he demanded sharply.

Her eyes widened. 'I've touched a sensitive spot. I'm sorry. I know you must hate being grounded, like he does, but at least you're safe for a while. That's how women see it.'

He tried to assess her mood and failed. 'Well, thanks for taking pity on me and inviting me into your home. I'll certainly come again when I'm free.'

He followed her to the hall, taking up his cap from the table. She turned at the bottom of the steps and offered her hand. 'Goodbye, Jim. I'm glad you came to tea, and I hope you still don't feel that I'm asking "What took you so long?"'

He took her hand and held on to it. 'I'm not certain what message you're passing me,' he said frankly. 'American girls come right out with how they feel.'

'So Rob told me. It took him a while to get used to that.' She withdrew her hand. 'You'll have to get used to English girls. We're really not difficult to understand once you get to know us, you'll find.'

She turned and went into the house, leaving Jim with that unmistakable invitation to get to know her. As he drove back through green countryside from which the sun had now gone, he reviewed the surprise of that chance meeting. How could he have been so wrong about Stallard's background? The man had behaved like a redneck. Gus and Pete had also branded him one. They could not all have so badly misjudged him. Jenny and her aunt were sophisticated and charming. The absent Sir Charles would surely be the same. So how had such a misfit entered the ranks? He must be a throwback. Jim had heard that many high-born British families now and then produced dolts. He resolutely silenced the small voice that asked how a dolt could have brought Lawson down so calmly after only a few hours' flying experience, and how he could now be flying successful missions time after time as a commissioned officer.

That same small voice could not keep at bay the expression 'grounded dogsbody' when he arrived back to find the meeting had ended sooner than expected. Awaiting him was a curt note asking why the hell he had not been on hand, and ordering him to get himself back to the office on the double. Sleeping arrangements at the country house had been cancelled; so had dinner. A British clerk clearing the conference room confided gloomily that 'the Brass' had let fly at each other and called it a day without deciding anything.

After a long, chilly evening drive Jim had to be content with liverwurst sandwiches made by his sleepy orderly. Clancy Flood had retired immediately after a substantial dinner, and had given orders not to be disturbed because he would be working through the night. To keep his mind off the rocket he was certain to get in the morning from his tireless boss, Jim lay in bed trying to concentrate on Jenny Stallard. Annoyingly, memories of Carlstrom dominated as he recalled her brother hard on his heels at every stage; especially that last day when an aerial accident had barely been averted. Pushing down a sense of culpability, Jim told himself that was in the past and was best forgotten. That bastard was on his second operational tour. The knowledge brought a return of the burning desire to win to a sportsman who now rarely graced the field.

J.T. Benson would put his head down, charge through the defence, and get himself drafted to a fighting squadron by *any* means. He would not be a grounded dogsbody when Stallard was winning all the glory!

Chapter Ten

In Wing Commander Averell's office a high-ranking officer from Group Headquarters confronted the station commander gravely. 'I know it's risky.'

Averell said, 'It's more than risky, sir. I'd call it suicidal.'

'Call it whatever you damn well please, man, but one of your pilots has to do it.'

'Shouldn't we send a back-up?'

'And maybe lose *two* aircraft? One flying at treetop level just as the sun goes down has a good chance of success, because of the element of surprise. Fast in and fast out, before the gunners catch on. Are you sure you have the man for the job?'

'No doubt at all, sir. The one I have in mind is keen, he's experienced and he's a bloody good pilot.' He sighed. 'He has as good a chance of pulling it off as any other bloody good pilot, with the added advantage that nothing ever rattles him.'

'Splendid! The Met. report is good, so he'll have everything in his favour.'

Averell stood up wearing a resigned expression. 'Will you brief him, sir, or shall I?'

'I haven't time. There's another top-level meeting with the Yanks in Somerset at fourteen hundred.' He got to his feet wearily. 'We'll never get round to landing in France until we start talking the same language. Thanks for breakfast, Dennis. Good to see you again. Give my best to Phyllis.' At the door, he asked, 'What's the name of your chap, by the way?'

'Stallard, sir. We've a surprise twenty-first birthday party laid on for him on Saturday.'

'Let's hope he makes it.' He went out.

If the visiting officer had gone across to the Mess he would have thought Averell a liar. Flying Officer Stallard had already told a cheery Australian colleague to bugger off, and the WAAF who cleaned his room had encountered a scowl when he burst in straight after breakfast with a letter in his hand and found her singing as she washed his bathroom floor. The pilot who never got rattled had received his sister's account of her meeting with an American who had trained in Arcadia with him.

He doesn't recall your name, but you're sure to recognize each other if you meet again. He's tall, dark and handsome — knows how to turn on the charm — but I liked him. His name is Jim Benson. Do you remember him at all? I was able to talk quite knowledgeably about America, of course. I don't think he enjoys being here any more than you initially liked it over there, but Molly offered to let him ride one of the geldings and I'm certain he'll take it up because he's grounded at the moment. You'll sympathize.

I sent off a registered parcel yesterday. Hope it reaches you by Saturday. It's such a shame you can't be with us on the day, but we'll have a special celebration on your next leave. How ridiculous to record your 'coming of age' when you've been doing what you have for the past year or so!

Take very great care of yourself, Rob. I'm sure they'll have a party or something in the Mess on Saturday. Try to look pleased, although I know you'll hate any fuss. We'll all be thinking about you.

Much love, Jenny.

Rob was so irate he was unable to control himself enough to make the telephone call he felt was so urgent. How the hell had Benson found Jenny? He did not believe in the 'chance' meeting, knowing that bastard's way with women. So he did not recall Flying Cadet Stallard! He would remember him all right when he next tried to charm his sister! Jenny was no fool, and she had assured Rob she was an expert at putting wolves in their place. She would surely deal appropriately with one who had lied so blatantly to ingratiate himself with her on the strength of his link with Arcadia. The bastard! The bloody *bastard*!

For almost half an hour Rob prowled around his room trying to master his rage. It seemed a lifetime ago that he had first taken to the air in Arcadia with Clint Lawson. He still passionately loved flying, but he was now more than willing to return to earth at the end of each operation. He had seen crews blown apart, others die in flames. He had watched young men come and go so fast he hardly remembered their faces. Yet he now saw Benson's with complete clarity.

Memories flooded back thick and fast as Rob stared from the window across the airfield to where mechanics swarmed over the Mosquitoes. He could visualize Benson's expression as he had sneered at 'a cowpoke from Hicksville': he recalled the sportsman's disparagement of someone who had almost drowned because he was unable to swim. Benson's behaviour with Laura Foster had been indirectly responsible for himself being put under review and confining everyone to camp for the weekend. Small incidents Rob had forgotten returned to fan his anger, but he had *never* forgotten that last day when Benson had flown out of the sun at him. Every time an enemy fighter did it, he was reminded of the first time he had suffered the fearful experience and been frightened out of his wits. Germans did it as battle strategy — he had done it himself — but that American bastard had done it for kicks.

Rob had never mentioned Benson to Jenny. He would not now go into those matters strictly between himself and the man, but he would reveal to his sister enough about her 'handsome American' to ensure he would never be admitted to Darston Manor again. By the time his call ended, Jenny would hate Benson as much as he did.

Thrusting the letter in his pocket he headed for the telephone, but as he reached the bottom of the stairs he was pounced on by a WAAF.

'Mr Stallard, I was just coming up with a message for you. The Wing Commander would like to see you right away.'

Rob swore under his breath, and the girl blushed as she gazed wide-eyed into his face. 'Is something wrong, sir? Freda said you weren't too happy about her singing this morning. Not bad news, I hope.'

'If you've ever heard your friend sing you'll know why I wasn't happy about it.' He hesitated, trying to decide whether he could telephone Jenny before seeing the CO. After all, he might have been on the far side of the perimeter track when the message came through. If it had not been for Jenny's letter, he would certainly have been outside in the sunshine tinkering with his motorcycle. He wanted to run down to the coast and have a picnic today if there was no operation planned. He liked to get away whenever he could. Johnny was now seriously courting the daughter of a local farmer so he no longer rode pillion on such sprees, but Rob found the sea irresistible and headed there when he felt the need to be quiet.

'Is there anything I can do to help?'

The breathless question drew Rob's attention back to the young blue-eyed WAAF. 'Not unless you could go to the Wingco and pretend to be me.'

The girl giggled and turned pinker. She was new and overawed by aircrew. 'The message did say "right away", sir.'

'Oh hell, I'd better go first,' he said to himself, then turned and remounted the stairs to fetch his cap. What could the Wingco want with him? He had not done anything wrong in the air that he was aware of, and he had been very careful about not revving up his motorbike outside the CO's office window. He had twice been on the carpet for that, and once for leaving a brown oily patch outside the Mess when the fuel tank sprang a leak. It was unfortunate that top brass had been visiting that day but, as Rob had complained to his intimates later, top brass ought to put up with what aircrew had to suffer, then they would really have something to complain about.

Dennis Averell looked unusually solemn on greeting him. 'Sit down, Stallard. This'll take a while.' Rob then knew he was not to be given a rocket. The culprit always stood for that. 'I've a nucleus of good, steady pilots in the squadron, but when I'm asked to produce one for a specific job I have to look for individual qualities. You've a reputation for keeping your head in tricky situations, and for expertise at low-level flying. Add your dedication to duty, which is unhampered by marital concerns and, unless you're a very crafty sod, by romantic entanglements, and you come out as the best man to take this on.'

'Take what on, sir?'

'A solo raid over Holland. I'll brief you more fully later, but I'll first explain why this has been dumped on us. The SOE cell in the area has collapsed. Someone talked. It's fouled up their plan to ambush a train tonight. The Dutch underground group active in the northern part of the country is committed to an operation of its own, so we've been asked to send over a single Mosquito to do the job.'

'What's the train carrying?' Rob asked.

'Something we ordinary mortals can't be told about.'

'So it's volatile and dangerous.'

'I didn't say that, Stallard.'

'You didn't have to. If a single Mossie is enough to do the job the cargo must be highly explosive. That means the train will be heavily armed and guarded.'

'That's the one small snag,' said Averell, with the understatement of the year. 'However, they'll be expecting a ground attack, mined bridges and so on. What they won't be expecting is a single aircraft coming at them over the rooftops in daylight.'

'We hope!'

The CO gave him a frank look. 'This train has to be destroyed. It's a no-fail operation, and I've said you can do it.'

'I can do it all right, sir. I just have my doubts the Jerries won't be expecting me.'

'You'll have to put your doubts to one side. You'll go in just before sunset, and you'll have the cover of darkness for your return. It won't be easy, but make the most of the element of surprise and you'll be fine.' He got to his feet. 'If Sergeant Reece is still grounded I'll call for a volunteer to go with you.' He gave a faint smile. 'You've already volunteered.'

Rob grinned. 'I'm always doing harebrained things like that.'

'Come to the briefing room after lunch. Meanwhile, air-test your aircraft and make ready. Don't talk to anyone about this, of course.'

As Rob saluted and made for the door, Averell said, 'I hope this hasn't spoiled any plans you had for this afternoon.'

'I was going to the coast on my motorbike. I'll get there quicker now.'

There was a parcel for him back in the Mess. Jenny's birthday present. He took from the packaging a splendid silver and enamel badge he wanted for his motorbike, and had been saving up for. He was thrilled as he turned it over and over in his hands, picturing it in place. Surely no one could have a better sister. There was a cheque from the Guthries, and a fountain pen from Mrs Brumby. He was deeply touched. As there was an hour before lunch, he decided to scribble thank-you notes there and then. Best to get them done before he went off this afternoon.

After telling Jenny it was the most marvellous present she could have given him, he added a paragraph about J.T. Benson. His fury had been dampened slightly during the flight test, but he left her in no doubt of the kind of person her tall, dark, handsome American was. He stuck stamps on the three envelopes then took them down to add to the pile waiting to be collected for mailing, before wandering out to take a look at his motorbike. He was glad the parcel had come today. If anything happened this afternoon, at least he had seen the badge and known it was his.

*

The sea was smooth and ice-blue as Rob took the Mosquito across it no more than fifty feet above the surface. 'I was going to have a picnic beside that,' he murmured.

'Messy things, picnics,' observed Charlie Reece, the navigator who had flown with Rob for four months. 'And it can get bloody cold sitting on a beach in May. Then it rains, and you get drenched. No, give me this any day. It's nice and warm in here, we won't get wet if it rains, and I had a slap-up lunch sitting comfortably at a table with a knife and fork. Bet yours was even better.'

'Lamb chops,' said Rob, flicking up the cover over the firing button and pressing his thumb on it. The guns proving satisfactory, he returned to the subject of food. 'I missed lamb chops in Florida, didn't you? They don't go in for sheep.'

'No hills, that's why. Sheep like hills.'

'I like lamb chops. Can't help what they like.'

'We had steak and kidney pie. Went down a treat. Were you going on that broken-down machine of yours?'

Rob was indignant. 'Broken-down, my eye! You won't find a smoother-running, more cosseted motorbike anywhere in the country.'

Reece laughed. 'I heard you took it to your room one night when it began to snow, and the Wingco almost court-martialled you.'

'A wild rumour, Charlie. I simply wheeled her into the Mess scullery. No one wanted to use it in the dead of night, and I intended to put her outside before the kitchen staff got under way.'

'And?'

'I overslept.' He nodded ahead. 'Coast coming up. What's our landfall?'

'Zandvoort. Should cross it in seven minutes. Nothing much there, but we alter course four degrees north-east after we pass a water tower.' He added with the weight of past experience, 'You will remember to lift up over it, won't you?'

'Can't promise. I'm not too hot with towers.' Funny how he was getting so many reminders of Carlstrom today. 'They got their timing

159

bloody tight,' he complained. 'I heard the word "sunset" mentioned. It's already pretty well vanished.'

They flashed over the Dutch coast so close to the ground that they skimmed the few rooftops and put the fear of God in the residents settling to their supper. 'There's two dogs down there will never be the same again,' mused Reece.

'All the bitches in the area will sigh with relief.'

They fell silent until the Navigator gave him the new course. Hurtling towards the water tower, Rob pulled up the nose to hop over it before banking sharply, then levelling out again, still very low.

'We should be in the vicinity in twenty minutes,' said Reece. 'Do you want to drop 'em, or shall I?'

'At this height I'll have my work cut out keeping her steady and firing the guns, without dropping the bloody bombs as well. You're sitting there with nothing to do. Make yourself useful,' Rob said with the rough camaraderie used by men facing danger together.

Reece grinned. 'Okay.'

A mile further on, Rob yanked hard on the stick as a church loomed from the gathering dusk dead ahead. Holding his breath until they cleared the spire, he muttered, 'You didn't warn me about that. Wake up!'

'It's not shown. One must have been destroyed and they rebuilt it there instead.'

'Mark it for future reference. I don't want another fright like that.'

Although he was as taut as a wire Rob was in total control of himself and his machine. He felt no fear. There was always too much to do. Flying so low demanded concentration and swift reflexes. He was good at it and got a tremendous thrill from skimming the surface with mere feet to spare, but he was now busy working out the best way to tackle this job. The element of surprise only ever lasted a short while. They might get it done before the gunners on the train woke up to their presence, but every gun post back to the coast would then be alerted and watching for them. There were also enemy fighters to consider. The cover of darkness the CO had mentioned was a myth. On a clear evening like this an aircraft would be easily visible crossing the moon-washed landscape on the way home.

'Christ, Skip, much lower and you'll be running along the tracks,' observed Charlie in worried tones. 'If you're right about this train carrying volatile stuff, we won't stand a chance if we meet it coming round a bend.'

'It's getting dark too bloody quickly,' muttered Rob, staring into the fast-gathering dusk backed by the remnants of sunset. 'You know, it's not going to be any good doing anything before we've sized up what we've got to tackle. Can't afford to make a mess of it. How much longer?'

'Unless the train's stopped somewhere, we should see it in about five minutes. See that junction at one o'clock — looks like a pile of macaroni?'

'Got it,' said Rob, noting the spot where a number of tracks criss-crossed then ran parallel for some yards before parting. 'Follow that one curving away to the right.'

Banking swiftly to do so, Rob swore heartily. 'Hell and damnation, they've put troops all along here! Whatever's on that train must be even more vital than we thought.'

A series of light vehicles mounted with machine-guns had been spaced out along the single track, presenting a formidable defence barrier within the narrow cutting bordered by dark trees. It was a veritable death trap.

Into Rob's shocked dismay came Charlie's warning. 'Target coming up in less than a minute. Shouldn't we do it straight off and get out?'

'Too dodgy,' said Rob, thinking fast as they flashed over the first of the trucks. 'Take a damn good look during this run, then I'll make a tight turn and you drop 'em as a stick along the length of the train as we fly back.'

By the time the gunners opened fire it was too late, for the Mosquito had raced past, but the rattling tattoo alerted those further along the track and the element of surprise no longer existed. Suddenly, the onset of evening was turned back to day as powerful spotlights mounted beside the guns flooded the area with white light.

'Christ, what else?' exclaimed Rob, narrowing his eyes against the glare, knowing their chances of survival were slim against this defence.

'There she is, Skip!'

Rob saw the engine at the same moment, and decided to terrify the gunners on the tender into inaction by flying right at them, his own guns blazing. 'I'll get those buggers as we go over,' he yelled above the roar of their engines.

As he hurtled over the train at suicide height, Rob felt bullets smack into the cushion of his seat, and another rip through the sleeve of his battledress to bore into his flesh. He thought he heard Charlie cry out, but he was intent on dealing death to others and kept his thumb on the firing button, cursing the brilliance more blinding than that of mingled searchlights.

They passed the long snake of trucks and hit sudden dimness which might have thrown a pilot less experienced than Rob. It was that very experience that told him they must blow the train before the inevitable happened. He was damned if he was going to die for nothing.

Going into the tightest turn of his career, he yelled, 'Are you all right?'

'Yeah, but for God's sake get a bit of height or we'll go up with it.'

'There's a one-minute delay on the fuses. Time enough for us. Make it good, Charlie. Make it bloody *certain*.' He pulled out of the turn and lined up with the track. 'Here we go, chum!'

Heading deliberately into the vivid, light-washed cutting, knowing they presented a perfect target to the rows of gunners on each side, Rob felt an unprecedented thrill of fear.

Deafened by the thunder of engines at full power, the continuous stutter of guns, the hail of bullets tearing into the fuselage, and his own pounding pulsebeat, Rob flew at the train as low as he dared. The Mosquito shook violently from the bombardment, while Rob struggled to hold her steady and fire her guns as they overtook the train in a matter of seconds. They overflew the line of trucks very swiftly. Rob felt the load leave them at the same time as he heard the yell 'Bombs away!' His reflexes led him to attempt a steep climbing turn, but the aircraft had taken too much punishment and could not obey his sure touch. Struggling to compensate for her limitations, Rob fought an additional force as a mammoth explosion sent shock waves upwards. Aware that the port engine had caught fire, Rob concentrated on keeping them safely in the air while leaving the scene. Only when he had ensured that immediate danger had been averted did he turn to his friend and navigator.

'I knew you'd make a bloody good job of it, Charlie.'

'I thought for a moment that you were going to do a hara kiri turn,' he said with an effort. 'I've never flown through anything like that before.'

'I never want to again, chum. Where'd they get you?'

162

'In the groin. It's damn painful. What are our chances?'

'Of getting back? She's never going to last out until then, so be ready to bale out if I can take her high enough. Give me the shortest course to the coast. If we can reach the sea we'll take our chances in the dinghy. If not ...'

Rob set the course, then glanced back over the region they had just left, where the dark red of fire penetrated a dense black cloud. It had happened so swiftly. Just a few minutes of his life, that was all, and he could scarcely believe it was more than likely all over. Just one train; one act of war. Would it make that much difference? It had been a no-fail op. and they had not failed. That was the important thing.

Leaving Charlie to do what he could to staunch the blood from his wound, Rob knew he could not attend to his own. The warm stickiness of blood was inside his left sleeve, and his arm throbbed. Their situation was grave. Moonlight revealed severe damage to the wings, and a howling draught around his feet indicated a problem in the belly. It was evident the tail had been shot up, and the doused fire in the port engine would have left damage to impair its performance. There was every chance it would pack up before long. All in all, it was the worst situation he had ever been in.

As they limped along at five hundred feet, Rob saw that stars were now appearing all around the sky. He liked starry nights. The darkness never seemed lonely when they were there.

'See Orion up there?' he asked, and was met with silence.

Turning, Rob found Charlie had passed out. Once again he was reminded of Carlstrom. As he coaxed the shattered aircraft mile by mile towards the coast, he recalled his apprehensive solo landing with an unconscious companion and told himself his chances of survival this time were less than they had been then. He had a long way to fly, there were men out there determined to make him pay for what he had just done, and he had to run the gauntlet of coastal batteries before he reached the sea. Although he loved to watch the sea from the shore, he dreaded coming down in the Channel, for he had never forgotten the sensation of drowning. He was sitting on an inflatable dinghy but, although he could now swim, the prospect of being afloat in a frail rubber vessel in mountainous waves filled him with a fear he never felt in the air.

So he flew on through the starry coldness knowing he must either fall victim to the ground defences or take his chances in the dark waters between the enemy coast and home.

*

Dennis Averell waited until midnight, then went to bed to lie gazing at the ceiling. The 'mission accomplished' signal had come through on time, but there had been nothing more from the lone Mosquito. He had seen a large number of young men fly off and not return, so he should be hardened to such things. Yet there had been something about Stallard; an indefinable quality that made his loss more poignant. After a year with a Hurricane squadron, where he had made a name for himself as being very steady in combat, he had been selected to fly the fast fighter-bomber proving highly successful in low-level attacks. Stallard and the Mosquito were made for each other, and he had become something of an idol to unblooded youngsters who believed his luck would rub off on them if they hung around him. It was more than luck; it was skill and experience.

Stallard was an unlikely squadron hero: a determined teetotaller who rarely gave enthusiastic accounts of his exploits after a raid, a shy, pleasant-looking chap who avoided close relationships with women, he was openly embarrassed by the admiration of boys straight from flying school. No one save his friend Bradshaw, who had transferred with him from Hurricanes, knew much about Stallard's private life. He was a private sort of man. Yet his unhurried rural accent steadied others in combat more than many a clipped, nervous, public-school voice, and his strength of purpose, which was rarely shaken, gave uncertain youngsters confidence. A man always knew where he stood with Stallard. If he did not, Stallard soon told him!

At two a.m., when the message he still hoped for had not come, Wing Commander Averell turned on his side and settled for sleep. To cancel the party on Saturday would be bad for morale, which would take a dip, anyway. It was a great pity Stallard would not be there for it: he had had no parents to give him a fitting celebration. Then a wry smile touched his lips. The young devil would probably have slipped away early. He had hated being the centre of attention.

Chapter Eleven

Rob lay in blissful serenity listening to the wonderful chorus and marvelling that there were male and female angels. He had always imagined them to be sexless, yet he definitely heard tenors, baritones and sopranos uniting in music more beautiful than any he had heard. It rose and fell in sweeping cadences, swirling all around him and filling him with undeniable emotion.

When it stopped without warning, his disappointment was so great that he opened his eyes and rolled over. Pain ran the length of his body and he let out a loud yell before flopping again on to his back, bringing further pain. This could not be heaven; he was hurting too much. So where the hell was he?

'What on earth have you been up to?'

A girl had appeared from nowhere to stand beside the bed. Rob lay in the aftermath of acute pain gazing up at her. She had a faint scattering of freckles on her face, large hazel eyes and short red-gold hair which curved forward across her cheeks. Deprived of heavenly music and confronted instead with this heavenly vision, Rob was lost for words.

'There's nothing to worry about. You're in safe hands now.' One of them was laid on his brow. 'Good, your temperature's starting to come down.'

Certain it was going up, Rob enjoyed the touch of her cool hand against his skin. It assured him that she was still there even though her face seemed to swim around in a swirl of mist.

'The doctor said his injection would keep you under for hours yet. I wasn't expecting you to surface so soon. Would you like a drink? Water or tea, *not* beer,' she said firmly.

'I don't like beer. It makes me drunk,' he murmured, wondering if she could be an angel after all.

She laughed delightedly. 'It makes everyone drunk, but that doesn't deter most men.' Fading into the mist momentarily, she returned with a glass of water and slid her arm beneath his head to raise it to allow him to drink. The movement made him giddy enough to threaten nausea, and the girl spun around with the indistinct surroundings for a moment or two when she lowered his head to the pillow again. While she and the vague outlines of furniture stopped twirling and settled an urgent thought penetrated his confusion.

'Where's Charlie? I've got to get him out.'

'Shhh, there's no need to worry about a thing. Try to sleep,' said the calm cultured voice.

Sleep sounded very attractive, but several questions were nagging at his weary brain and he could not ignore them. 'Is Charlie ... is Charlie ...?'

'Charlie's fine,' the girl assured him. 'Stop fretting or your temperature will soar again.'

Fighting the desire to close his eyes, Rob asked, 'What am I doing here with you?'

She laughed again, a delicious gurgle of sound that made him realize what he had said. 'Not much, in your present state, Flying Officer Stallard.'

Through the haze in his mind recollection began to return. They had bombed a train and been attacked on the way home. Charlie had been killed as they approached the coastal batteries like a sitting duck — a very lame sitting duck. He had tried to stay airborne for as long as possible, but the aircraft had slowly disintegrated around him over the Channel when he had been so tired and dizzy he could not tell how near to the English coast he was. He did not remember going into the drink, but he must have. So how did he come to be where he was with this gorgeous redhead who apparently knew his identity? He grew wary.

'Am I in hospital?' he asked.

'We saved you from that.' She drew a chair alongside the bed and sat. 'We found you floating off the coast first thing this morning and fished you out. You had a nasty flesh wound in your left arm which began bleeding again when we took off your clothes, but there didn't appear to be much else wrong apart from loss of blood and exhaustion resulting from exposure. So we brought you home and put you to bed. The local doctor drove over right away to dress the wound and give you a shot. Then an RAF doctor came to check on you. You were unconscious throughout, but he agreed with me that you'd be happier here than in some ghastly ward full of men worse off than you.' She smiled. 'He didn't need a lot of persuading once I got to work on him. What's causing the pain is severe muscle fatigue. Each one protests the moment you move. It'll be agony for several days, I'm afraid, but I'll keep you amused so the time won't drag while you're in bed.'

Rob's temperature had risen sharply on being told she had taken off his clothes to look him over, and it climbed several more degrees at his thoughts of how she would amuse him in bed. He strove to concentrate on priorities, but cohesive thought was difficult.

'I have to hand in a vital report.'

'Someone's coming for that. Father rang Group Headquarters and told them you wouldn't be fully conscious until tomorrow, so you've got a short reprieve.'

'They have to know right away,' he insisted.

She ignored that. 'From what Father was told, you're some kind of celebrity after what you did yesterday.'

Rob lay silent, refusing to rise to the bait. He was busily piecing together all she had told him and reaching a very worrying conclusion. She and her father — if he really existed — knew far too much about RAF affairs to be ordinary civilians. How did they know the telephone number of Group Headquarters? How had they managed to prevent him being hospitalized ... and why? The coast she had mentioned could be the Dutch one, and this could be a room in Holland. Had she been sent to charm him into giving away vital information?

'Where is this place?' he demanded suspiciously.

'Romney Marsh. We're a bit cut off, which is why we decided to put you to bed instead of subjecting you to a long wait for an ambulance which would bump you over uneven roads for ages. You looked so exhausted and tragic when we came upon you.' She gave such a warmly sympathetic smile that his toes began to curl. 'You must have had a rough time doing whatever you had done. Would you like to talk about it?'

His toes straightened abruptly. He was not going to fall for that. 'There's nothing to talk about. Who are you, and what were you doing off the coast early this morning?'

'I'm Rebecca Lambourne. I can't tell you what we were doing, I'm afraid. Father will, if he gets his way over you.'

'He won't,' Rob declared. 'No one will, so there's no point in trying.'

The girl laid her fingers against his mouth. 'Shhh, you're getting too excited. It's not good for you. While I go off to see about dinner, you'd better try to get some sleep.'

'I think it would be better for me to go to hospital. *Tonight*,' he added, testing his theory.

'It's all been decided,' she said soothingly, as she got to her feet. 'Stop fretting. It'll delay your recovery.' Pushing the damp hair from his forehead, she murmured, 'You're terribly sweet. It's going to be lovely having you here for a while.'

When the door closed behind her Rob's toes were again tightly curled. She was getting to him. Once she gave him the full works he would tell her anything, he knew he would. Torture would be easier to withstand. On that thought, he slid back into unconsciousness and knew nothing more until dawn.

*

When Wing Commander Averell himself walked into the bedroom soon after breakfast, Rob was astonished and acutely uncomfortable to be at such a disadvantage with his Commanding Officer. Was there a row afoot over this odd business, and could he be blamed for it in any way? He waited somewhat apprehensively. When the CO smiled, Rob relaxed a little. Things could not be too bad after all.

'Good morning, Stallard. How are you feeling this morning?'

'Fine, sir,' Rob lied, aching all over and weak from the effort of washing and shaving in the adjoining bathroom, after a battle of wills with the beautiful Rebecca.

Averell pulled up a chair and sat. 'I'm sorry about Sergeant Reece. He was a good man.'

'He was hit over the target, then again fatally as we neared the coast. I think I managed to get him out when we went into the drink, but I don't remember much about that last bit, sir.'

'Air-Sea Rescue picked up his body early last evening. His wife has been told.'

'They'd only been married six months, and there's a baby on the way,' Rob said heavily. 'We were a good team. It makes a hell of a difference when you are.'

The other man nodded. 'We'll find you another like him.'

'Pity about the Mossie, sir. First one I've lost. I know I've brought a couple back looking like a dog's dinner, but they did get patched up.'

'You did a good job on the train, Stallard. Men on the ground reported total success. You'd better give me the story from your angle.'

At the end of his account, delivered with his usual precise, detailed recollection, Rob asked, 'What was it carrying, sir?'

'Search me. It's only a postponement, of course. There'll be another train, another mission that dare not fail.'

Silence fell and Rob dutifully waited. What came next was totally unexpected. 'Miss Lambourne told me you initially imagined you were in captivity here. In a way you are, and will continue to be for a while.'

'I don't understand, sir. What *is* this place?'

'It's the home of Professor Russell Lambourne, in the heart of Romney Marsh. He's an eminent scientist and inventor who has been working on something in conjunction with the RAF over the past six months. His daughter is his assistant. Instead of sending her to university, he chose to let her work alongside him.' He smiled. 'Rebecca Lambourne is an extremely brainy young woman, besides being a most attractive one. Gives her rather an unfair advantage, wouldn't you say?'

'It makes her very bossy,' Rob said, dismayed by the news that she was a genius.

The Wing Commander began to chuckle. 'So that's why you apparently suspected her of being a spy last night.'

Rob felt his colour rise. 'She tried to question me on where I'd been and what I'd been doing. I'd no way of knowing who she was or even which country I was in. I didn't tell her a thing, of course. I wouldn't give that girl the size of my boots,' he finished emphatically.

'You'll have to take a better attitude than that if you're going to work with her.'

'*Work* with her? I'm no scientist.'

'You're an experienced pilot who turned up on their doorstep just when they wanted one.'

Rob responded very forcibly. 'I refuse to be experimented on, sir. I'm a flier, not a scientist's guinea pig.'

'Calm down, Stallard, nobody said anything about guinea pigs, and you've no choice in the matter. Lambourne already has permission from Group to recruit your services. You've been officially assigned to this project.' He got to his feet full of purpose. 'Lambourne and his daughter have developed a new system for attacking shipping at night. That's all I'm allowed to know at present, but you'll be given the finer details as soon as you can leave your bed. They've completed preliminary tests at sea — they were on a naval corvette when they picked you up — and it's now time to try it from the air. You appeared like a gift from heaven so they hung on to you while Lambourne checked your history with Air Commodore Griffin. Both men decided you were ideal for the job of testing this new low-level attack system.' He gave a faint smile. 'Most pilots would give their eye-teeth for a chance like this.'

'Yes, sir ... until it goes wrong and sends me down to meet Neptune,' Rob murmured, nevertheless excited about what he had been told.

'Lambourne wants to discuss everything with you here, get your opinion on what can or can't be done in a Mosquito, while one is being fitted with special equipment. I understand timing and precision are essential for success.'

'I knew it,' exclaimed Rob with a grin. 'One slip and I'll be down there with the mermaids.'

'You'd better not,' the CO returned in the same light vein. 'You've already cost the RAF one Mossie. We can't afford to lose another through your carelessness. The squadron will have to fly one short while you're on this.' He picked up his hat and gloves. 'Give yourself time to recover fully. I was told you can barely move without bringing the house down with your screams.'

Rob protested. 'She exaggerated. She's not only bossy, she's dying to mother me.'

The Wing Commander settled his cap on his head, lips twitching. 'I think you're in more danger from Professor Lambourne's daughter than from his invention. Good luck with it. I'm going to recommend you get some kind of recognition for the Dutch operation, and these tests will further boost your record.'

'Thank you, sir. I'll get started as soon as possible.'

The CO turned in the doorway. 'Happy Birthday, by the way. Sorry you'll miss the party tonight.'

Rob had forgotten he was twenty-one today. It did not seem as important as the fact that he was to test something new. Fate must have arranged for him to float past the corvette at just the right time.

He did not dwell on the fact that if the Lambournes had not been there testing their invention he would most likely be dead now. Closing his eyes against the brightness of the sun he drifted into sleep full of eager thoughts of what he would be doing in the coming weeks. These dulled the pain of Charlie's death.

His lunch was brought by an unsmiling, gaunt woman who said Miss Lambourne was 'in that outhouse of theirs working on some dratted invention with her father', which was why *she* had had to bring him his food. Rob was acutely disappointed. He also felt the housekeeper made him sound like the Lambournes' pet animal. The sight of lamb chops on the tray cheered him a little; even more so did the woman's parting words.

'She says she'll bring her dinner with yours and stop for a while this evening. There's a book here to keep you amused. Bang on the floor when you've finished, and I'll get the tray.' She went out with a sigh deep enough to impress on Rob how great a nuisance he was.

After eating his lunch he sat up for a while enjoying the view from the window, and imagining it at every time of the year. He had always liked the seasonal changes at Thoresby, but he rarely went there now. Jenny had adapted to life at Darston Manor with no difficulty, and was now almost like the daughter of the house. She called the Guthries Molly and Charles (Mum and Dad would be horrified!) and treated the place as the home it had become. Rob was glad she was happy, but he preferred to meet his sister when she was in London; neutral ground. He spent his leaves exploring the English countryside on his motorbike, staying at pubs or farmhouses. He never thought about what he would do when the war ended. There was no point.

He then remembered Jenny's account of her meeting with Benson, and his anger was renewed. She would have received his letter and would surely be left with no illusions about the bastard. That was all he could do about it for now. He was going to be out of circulation for a while.

His mind turned to the exciting prospect of testing Lambourne's invention, but as he knew nothing about it the subject was soon exhausted and he flicked through the pages of the book on the tray. It was a novel peopled by characters who spoke in profound riddles. Rob had hated English Lit. at school, and this was the kind of thing they had

171

been forced to analyse and explain. He preferred Edgar Wallace. The book slipped from his fingers as his eyes closed.

Returning to awareness Rob heard beautiful music again, and he lay in a euphoric state recognizing its true source. A man could surely be forgiven for believing himself in heaven when listening to thrilling, majestic melodies that made him tingle from head to toe. The room had darkened with the onset of dusk, and he lay back as if in another world as the sweeping sounds appeared to fill the entire house. When the piece rose in a steady climax with gathering volume, Rob felt his scalp grow cold with excitement, and a lump formed in his throat. In the ensuing silence he remained enraptured, so that when Rebecca appeared at his doorway in a fluffy cream housecoat, her hair tumbled, she became part of the storm of feeling within him.

'What ...?' He had to clear his throat. 'What was that?'

'The overture to *Tannhäuser*. Didn't you recognize it?'

He thought the music perfectly matched the sensations she aroused in him as he gazed at her. 'I've never heard it before.'

'How sad!' She came a little way into the room. 'I'm sorry you've been left alone for so long. We've been sorting out a knotty problem, but I'm all yours now.' As Rob caught his breath, she added, 'Would you like me to bring the gramophone and play you some more Wagner after we've eaten dinner?'

Wondering whether he could handle the music as well as her proximity, Rob let himself in for both. 'Yes, please.'

'I won't be more than fifteen minutes. That should give you long enough to get yourself comfortable.'

When she came, it was in company with the housekeeper, who carried a large tray bearing covered dishes. Dinner smelled good, but Rebecca smelled even better. She was wearing a black dress with a pale enamel pendant on a fine silver chain, and Rob knew instinctively that her perfume had cost more than he had paid for some on Jenny's birthday.

The gaunt woman was no sweeter with the lady of the house than she had been with Rob. 'All this carrying up and down stairs! Is it going to continue long?'

'Definitely!' declared Rebecca, setting down the gramophone. 'I'll knock on the floor when I want you. Don't forget Father's claret. Pour it into a glass to serve it, then he won't drink more than he should. It's bad for him,' she explained to Rob. 'I'll fetch some wine and a box of records, then we can get started.'

Rob wished she would not say things like that. They always put ideas into his head. When she returned it seemed that she had been referring to the dinner, for she sat beside the bed and ladled soup from a tureen into two bowls.

'I'm hungry,' she explained, embarking on hers immediately. 'When we're working we forget about food.'

'I don't think I could ever do that. Even when I'm flying I think about the eggs and bacon when we get back.'

'Most men are gluttons. Father's the exception.' As Rob was absorbing the fact that she knew a lot of hungry men, she asked, 'Did Dennis tell you what we want from you?'

Deeply struck by anyone calling a wing commander by his first name on such short acquaintance, Rob said, 'What you want and what I'll do may not tally. Until I know more about this thing with precision timing, and done a few calculations of my own, I'm not testing *anything* in my aircraft.'

She smiled. 'I told Father you'd say that.'

'When am I going to meet him?'

'As soon as you're able to come downstairs — which won't be until the middle of next week.'

'I'll be down tomorrow morning,' he said immediately.

'I told him you'd say that, too.' She was still smiling. 'You're very obstinate, aren't you?'

'And you're far too clever,' he returned. Then he lowered his spoon to add quietly, 'You are, aren't you? The Wingco said you're some kind of boffin.'

'That's nonsense! I help Father in the laboratory, that's all. Does that bother you?'

'Why should it?' he asked, knowing it did. 'Stinks wasn't my best subject at school, so I might be a bit out of my depth with this.'

She shook her head gently. 'Leave the science to Father. He needs your knowledge as a pilot. Dennis said you're some kind of genius when it comes to flying.'

'He must have been under the influence at the time.'

'Talking of which, shall we have some of this wine? Mrs Maple suspected I was bent on having an orgy when I took it from the cupboard.'

'Not for me. I don't drink,' he said, finishing his soup whilst imagining an orgy with this wonderful girl.

'Never?' she asked incredulously.

'Never!'

'Don't you get ragged by your friends?'

'They soon gave up.'

She filled a glass and held it out. 'Won't you take just one sip? Dennis told me it's your twenty-first birthday. Don't you think you should do something memorable to celebrate?'

He ignored the glass. 'Hearing that music was it. You promised me some more.'

'I've never met a man like you before,' she said, putting the glass beside her own empty plate.

'Then you're doing something memorable, too.' It was the only rejoinder he could come up with.

She remained serious. 'My mother died when I was eight. Father was desperately lonely, so I wasn't sent to boarding school.'

'You mean you went back and forth each day from here?' he asked curiously.

'We have a place in London.' She took his soup plate and uncovered dishes containing a fricassee of chicken and several vegetables, which she began serving. 'At home I grew used to being in the company of Father's friends. He was totally unconventional in that I was allowed from an early age to join them in the evening. I'm much more at ease with men than with women, and when it became apparent that I had a scientific mind it alienated me further. Girls at school found it difficult to communicate with someone they saw as a walking brainbox. Once I gained my qualifications and became Father's junior assistant, I was virtually cut off from women.'

Rob did not like the idea of her surrounded by men. 'Don't you feel lonely?'

'When we come out here I do.' She put a full plate on his table. 'That's why I'm enjoying your company.'

'But I'm another man.'

'You're different, Rob. That *is* what people call you, isn't it? I asked Dennis. You're different from lab assistants, mathematicians, *real* boffins. You're like the breath of gritty life.'

Feeling awkward, he murmured, 'Only just. If you hadn't been out in that boat, I wouldn't be.'

She smiled over the glass in her hand. 'That's why you have to be especially nice to me.'

'It's *my* birthday so it should be the other way around,' he said, and immediately wished he had not. If she was any nicer he would not stand a chance.

Fortunately, she concentrated on the meal and merely asked for details of his schooldays and family background. He kept strictly to generalities, loath as always to talk about his private life, and soon broached the subject of the book he had found so boring that afternoon. A lively argument on readable literature lasted until Mrs Maple brought coffee, cheese and biscuits, by which time Rebecca had laughingly confessed that she had never read Edgar Wallace.

For more than an hour and a half they sat with the lights low listening to Wagner, Richard Strauss, Tchaikovsky and Beethoven. Rob knew he had found an aspect of paradise as these glorious sounds swamped his senses, sometimes taking him to the verge of tears. It was not only the day of his coming of age, it was the awakening of his soul to music. He had been impervious to jazz, jive and swing; untouched by Glenn Miller, Tommy Dorsey, Vera Lynn and Anne Shelton. Thank God he had discovered this in time to start enjoying it.

Rebecca went to the gramophone at the conclusion of the 'Pastoral' Symphony and switched it off. 'I'll leave it here so that you can use it whenever you like,' she said softly, maintaining the gentle mood of the evening. 'I'm glad you find you appreciate my music so much. It's lovely having someone to listen with. It enhances the enjoyment.' She crossed to the bed. 'You look much less strained. I'm so glad.'

Before Rob knew it, she bent and kissed him on the mouth with lingering gentleness. Then she drew back and smiled. 'Don't look so shocked.'

'I've only been here two days,' he said, shaken, 'and I was out cold for most of yesterday ... Isn't it a bit soon to start doing things like that?'

She shook her head. 'I knew I wanted to do it the moment you opened your eyes and said you didn't like beer because it made you drunk.'

'That first-sight business is a myth,' he said roughly. 'I felt like that about a girl called Laura in Florida. Two weeks later I felt the same way about one of her friends, then another. I was forever doing it.'

'Poor lamb! What a terrible time you must have had,' she said with a smile.

Rob faced the night deeply unsettled. She had caught him when he was unmanned by the haunting power of the music, and by the intimacy of low lights in a bedroom. This was nothing like those youthful infatuations in Florida. He had lived a lifetime in the intervening two years so he now recognized the danger, but what hope was there for an ordinary pilot and a girl with a brilliant scientific mind? Even if there should be enough common ground, aside from overwhelming attraction and a love of the same music, there was the war. That ruled out happy ever afters.

*

Despite his iron will, it was another two days before Rob met Russell Lambourne. Natural exhaustion, and Dr Kennedy's pills, ensured that he obtained the necessary rest before embarking on involved discussions for which a test pilot needed to be mentally sharp.

Rebecca's father was not in the least like the archetypal inventor. He was a tall, thin, mild-mannered man, very aware of what was happening around him. His only eccentricity was his failure to remember names, so Rob became Bob, Ron, Roy, Ray and Reg in turn, which was disconcerting until he grew used to it. He nevertheless liked the man, even when he embarked on theories Rob's practical mind found hard to follow. Lambourne had to accept that the pilot who would test his complex equipment wanted explanations in layman's terms. Once they reached that understanding, progress was easier.

Rob found the concept fascinating and entered fully into discussing it from his angle. He had never served with Coastal Command, and his experience with targets in water was restricted to several operations on bridges over rivers, and ships in port. Lambourne had developed a means of detecting shipping at night, calculating its exact position, then firing rockets certain to find their mark. The theory was that aircraft which could fly low and fast would not be fired on because they could approach, do the dirty deed, then be away before the enemy knew what had hit them. Detection would be by means of a scanner in the nose of the aircraft, which would record the position of shipping on an instrument in the cockpit. The crew would then enter this data on the firing recorder so that the rockets would be directed straight to the target by magnetic beams.

'Our sea tests have proved the scanner can unerringly detect any vessel to within a few feet of its position,' Lambourne told Rob.

'We need you to test it from the air,' added Rebecca, less of a distraction now she wore a workmanlike white coat.

'I'm afraid it will entail flying very low,' her father said apologetically. 'We're still working on the magnetic beams. It's a very experimental theory and we've not yet been able to extend their range without losing power.'

'How low are we talking about?' asked Rob from his perch on the corner of a bench in the detached laboratory.

'We've been assured by Geoffrey Griffin that it's perfectly possible,' put in Rebecca.

'What's possible?' asked Rob, once more amazed by this girl who could use the first name of an air commodore so casually.

'A hundred and fifty feet.'

Rob was relieved. Plenty of height to play with. 'I'll have no trouble with that,' he told them both, 'but what worries me is the time factor. If we go in fast to take them by surprise, how long will we have in which to set their position on the firing recorder before we're within range? We'd be in danger of overflying the target unless the beams are really strong.'

'That's what you're here to help us with,' said Rebecca. 'We can't go any further until you've tested the beams from the air. We can then make modifications if you say they're necessary.'

Despite her presence Rob followed his usual habit of putting his mind fully to his work, and went on to discuss the complex equipment and the most convenient place to put it within the cockpit. After a further hour's discussion, he looked up at Lambourne. 'Any pilot sent out fishing would be informed of all friendly vessels in the area, which would prevent him from sinking his own ships, but can you be certain the scanner won't pick up another aircraft as the nearest target? We could have an entire squadron shooting each other up the tail.'

'Oh dear, Ron, I should think that's most unlikely,' declared Lambourne in dismay. 'The possibility had not occurred to me, but I can see you're worried about it.'

'Don't fret, Father,' said Rebecca soothingly, 'I have an idea he's just being facetious.'

'I'm not,' Rob returned. 'You've only tested the scanner from sea level on assorted floating objects. It might fasten on anything within its range, at a hundred and fifty feet in the air. Let's estimate its radius in relation to a squadron formation.'

Lambourne threw no tantrum, took no offence. He merely nodded. 'We must sort that out. There's always a way round difficulties you know.' He smiled at his daughter. 'Wasn't I correct to say he sounded the right man for the job when you told me he had a mind of his own?'

Rebecca threw Rob a challenging look. 'My exact words were that he was unbelievably stubborn, Father.'

Three days later, on the Saturday following Rob's birthday, Rebecca suggested that Rob should go with her for a walk across the Marsh while her father solved a small problem with the firing programme. It was a balmy summer day and his desire for fresh air overcame Rob's reservations about being alone with her. He was worried about the situation developing between himself and this girl who had taken him by storm. He had become one of a natural threesome, almost a member of the family. Lambourne treated him as such when they relaxed over dinner, then listened to music or chatted about country living. It seemed so right that Rob had begun to yearn for something he knew was not possible.

Within a matter of days he would return to the station to begin flying low over water to test the scanner. Once he had that technique perfected, he would take on board unarmed weapons. When the tests were completed he would rejoin his squadron. He was an operational pilot: there was a war on. It was foolish and irresponsible to give way to feelings better subdued. He had carefully avoided opportunities for Rebecca physically to worsen the situation, but she had done it with glances, provocative statements and her selection of music. He must put an end to it on this walk.

Rebecca took his hand soon after they set out along one of the safe tracks she knew well, and it felt so good he kept the contact. She spotted marsh birds and pointed them out. He saw others to show her and they stood quietly, watching them in delight as the sun warmed their bare arms and the busy sounds of marshland creatures hung in the still air. They walked on along the track enjoying the solitary wilderness of the area.

'It looks so different from the air,' murmured Rob, suddenly longing to be back up there.

'You love it, don't you? Flying, I mean.'

'It's what I do for most of the week.'

She stopped and looked up at him. 'I've watched you talking to Father. Your face comes alive when you discuss that side of his project.'

'Isn't it alive the rest of the time?'

'When you listen to music it's wonderfully dreamy. When you talk about country things it's rather sad ... and when you look at me it grows enigmatic.'

'My goodness, you seem to know a lot about my face,' he said, trying to keep things light.

'I love watching it. Rob, we've been alone here almost an hour. When are you going to take advantage of the fact?'

He knew the moment had come to say what he must. 'I told you before, it happens all the time and shouldn't be taken seriously. I'll be back with my squadron soon and you'll forget all this.'

'Will you?' she challenged softly.

Releasing her hand he began to wander on along the track, finding it easier without physical contact or direct confrontation. 'I trained with a former bank clerk named Cyril, who was almost out of his mind with passion for his fiancée. She was killed in an air raid. He then went almost out of his mind with grief. They took him off the course a month before he qualified because he was a danger to himself and every other cadet. God knows where he ended up, but he was finished at twenty because he had let his feelings get the better of common sense.'

'And you have too much of it to let that happen, have you?' she asked teasingly.

He stopped and turned to her with a sigh. 'Don't be fooled by my officer's uniform. I'm a farmer's son who won a free scholarship to a grammar school, and I happen to be good at flying. When the war ends I'll be one of thousands scrambling for a few jobs in civil aviation. If I'm unlucky, who knows what I'll be doing? We're poles apart, and we've only met because I'll be useful in testing your father's attack system. I think we should concentrate on that until I leave.'

'Fair enough,' she agreed sweetly. 'We'll forget the Wagner and Chopin records, we'll busy ourselves with mathematics on gorgeous afternoons like this ... and we'll retire early with an uplifting book each. Will that make you feel safer?'

*

Jim had a free weekend and he knew exactly how he would spend it. With the piece of white card in his hand he requested the Stallard number and waited, smiling with anticipation. The housekeeper answered the call.

'Hi there, Mrs Brumby, this is J.T. Benson. Miss Stallard invited me in to tea around two weeks ago,' he prompted when his name brought no response. 'I tried out your famous cake.'

'Yes, sir.'

Hardly encouraging, but surely the housekeeper would not be party to family affairs? 'I'd like to speak to Miss Stallard.'

'She's busy.' It was verging on the insolent.

'So am I, ma'am,' he said crisply. 'Just go get her to the phone.'

The receiver went down and he heard heavy footfalls on the polished wood of the hall. In retrospect, Jim had realized his lie about not knowing Stallard would surely be found out, and the man would give his biased opinion. However, Jenny had appeared to be the kind of young woman who formed her own opinions and was unlikely to be influenced by others. Jim had not expected contact between sister and brother to be so swift. Still, maybe she really was busy, and Mrs Brumby was merely in a bad mood today.

'Hallo.' It was very cool.

'Hi, Jenny, I guess I may have interrupted some important work for your refugees and I apologize. I have a free weekend and I'd like to take up that invitation to go riding with you.'

'The invitation no longer stands. I'm sure you must be well aware why.'

'Well, no, I'm not,' he said, riled by her tone. 'Maybe you should explain.'

'Goodbye, Mr Benson ... or isn't that title gushing enough for James Theodore the Third, son of a senator?'

Jim was left holding a dead receiver. In swiftly rising anger he asked for the number again, but eventually lost the battle of wills when the WAAC operator cut in to say that the number he wanted was not answering and she needed the line for Colonel Jasper's office. He sat for several minutes twisting a pencil in his fingers until it snapped. He was damned if Stallard was going to do this to him. The sister was an attractive girl; he really wanted to explore the relationship. He also very much wanted to go riding all around that quaint, old village. Okay, so there were other girls, and probably other villages he could discover, but he had an empty weekend ahead and he had just been given the brush-off in typical Stallard style. He was not letting her get away with it. Jenny now knew who J.T. Benson was, so he would give her a taste of American upperclass retaliation.

The village looked just as he remembered — an illustration from a collection of folk tales — but there was no suggestion of whimsy in Jim's mood as he drove the Jeep past the church and on up the hill. He would show her just who she was dealing with. Jenny's bicycle was leaning against the wall, which must mean she was still at home. A step in the right direction. He pushed the bell beside the door, which stood ajar, then went inside to wait beside the hall table. Mrs Brumby came from a far door, and her expression when she saw him gave Jim grim pleasure.

Flushing scarlet, the housekeeper said, 'I was told ... er ... there's no one at home. Nor will there be all day.' She pushed back a wisp of her greying hair in an agitated gesture. 'I don't know who left that door open, but it shouldn't be. Anyone can just walk in,' she added pointedly. 'Perhaps you'll close it behind you, sir.'

'Surely,' he said, stepping to push it shut. 'Now perhaps you'll tell Miss Stallard I'm here.'

Faced with a hundred and ninety-six pounds of solid muscle, the woman was daunted into surrender and turned on her heel. Very shortly afterwards, Jenny Stallard came down the stairs looking rather pale.

'You've got a nerve,' she began. 'However important you think you are, it doesn't entitle you to force your way into homes where you've already been told you're not welcome. I don't know how it is where you come from, but we're civilized in this country.'

'We are in mine, and we're also good-mannered enough to hear the other person's side of the story before condemning them out of hand. Lady Guthrie invited me and my friends to come here to ride or play tennis. You tell me I'm unwelcome, and the only hint I've been given of why is that I'm the son of a senator. Is that some kind of disgrace in this civilized country of yours?'

'No, but a man who is a self-glorifying liar and womanizer is,' she said contemptuously. 'You must have known I'd tell my brother about our meeting, so how you have the insufferable cheek to contact me again is beyond my understanding. Please leave!'

Roused to further anger, Jim said, 'I thought the British prided themselves on their fair play. There's not much of it in evidence here.' He went right up to her. 'So you told your brother we'd met. I guess he's responsible for this goddam reverse, but there's another side to the story and you're going to hear it unless you care to pitch me out through your door.' He narrowed his eyes. 'Even he couldn't do that, so why don't we get down to basics.'

The cold glitter in her eyes was uncomfortably reminiscent of her brother as she hesitated uncertainly. Then she spun round and led the way to a large office giving a view over the tennis court.

'Please close the door,' she snapped. 'I really don't want the entire household disturbed by this ill-mannered confrontation.' Reaching into a drawer she took out an envelope and pulled several sheets of paper from it. Turning to the last page she began to read in an unsteady voice.

'I'm very sorry indeed that you've encountered J.T. Benson. God knows how he traced you. I don't believe it was a chance meeting. He's a barefaced liar. He has more reasons to remember me than any other cadet at Carlstrom, and none of them good ones. He appears not to have told you his father is a publicity-hungry senator who, like Benson, will stop at nothing to get into the limelight. Don't let him return to the Manor, because he'll almost certainly have his personal pressman and photographer in tow. What his aim is, God knows. You claim to know how to handle wolves. Well, this one is a pack leader. He's conceited and needs constant admiration. Because he was some kind of champion athlete he was regarded as a hero over there before they got into the

war. Everyone will see him for what he is now, when he comes up against real heroes. He was a damn dangerous pilot. He could only have qualified because he's James Theodore Benson the Third! He uses his father's influence to get where he wants. With women he uses wealth and charm. He's an out-and-out bastard, Jen. Treat him as such.'

Jim demanded harshly, 'You believe all that?'

'Rob doesn't lie.'

'He sure as hell does. He has no idea what kind of man I am, because he never exchanged a civil word with me at Carlstrom.'

'Are you denying what he says? You lied about not remembering him, you ladled on the charm, you wormed your way into this house.'

Trying to control his anger, he snapped, 'I offered to drive you to your Polish refugees; you invited me to tea. No one twisted your arm, lady.' At her stony silence, he added, 'Sure I lied about not knowing your brother. I was kind of hit between the eyes when you gave your name, and when I realized you were his sister I decided it was best to keep quiet on the subject.'

'Because of all the detrimental reasons he mentions?'

'Yes, because of them,' Jim agreed hotly. 'It was two years ago and he made mountains from molehills. Do you have that expression over here?'

'We also have "Wolf in sheep's clothing". Do you?' She asked with dangerous sweetness.

Jim moved round the desk to her. 'See here, I don't give a damn about your spare horse, your tennis court or your fancy English afternoon tea, but you're going to hear the truth before I leave because I don't care to have some brother with an almighty chip on his shoulder blast me and get away with it. My father *is* a senator, and also the owner of Benson Pharmaceuticals. We're one of the wealthiest families along the East Coast. If I was so damn conceited, I'd have told you that as soon as I picked you up from the grass. I'd also have given out that I've won just about every US national tennis championship and was rated the most punishing tailback in amateur football. Sure we make heroes of our sportsmen. Doesn't everyone? Because of that — yeah, and because of my father — press photographers liked to keep track of me. The Air Force welcomed the publicity value for recruiting purposes. Did I? Not always. With my old man, it's different. He'll use anyone and any situation for his own ends. Your brother was used by him, and he lays it at my door without justification.'

He told the stiff-faced girl about the time Clint Lawson passed out in mid-air. 'My father was on the spot and stole every inch of limelight. I was so disgusted that when he tried to drag *me* across for a picture I walked away. I cut myself off from him and my stepmother that day and we've had no contact since. Stallard probably thought I'd refused to shake hands because he had just beaten the pants off me in the air. He was a natural; he beat the pants off us all.'

'Perhaps he also put your nose out of joint. Do you have *that* expression?'

'We have, and he didn't. The only thing he had on his side was that he could fly as if born to it. He was hostile from the first day. As professional military pilot cadets we'd been through harsh initial training and could handle anything. He resented that, and also the fact that we were upperclass men. He took every reprimand and punishment as a personal affront. There was an incident over a girl that he couldn't handle, because he turned it into a major drama which brought general punishment on the entire campus. I guess that one small confrontation is the foundation for his comment that I'm a wolf-pack leader, because he has no other knowledge of my behaviour with women. I admit I like girls; they usually like me. What's wrong with that? Isn't it what keeps the world sane?'

Her lip curled. 'A typically male concept.'

Jim studied her for a few moments through narrowed eyes, seeing echoes of her brother in her defiant stare and stance. Then he said explosively, 'Hell, I'm wasting my time here. Do you believe all he tells you?'

'Yes. He's always been exceptionally honest.'

'What about your parents? Don't they have some influence?'

She drew in her breath. 'They were killed in an air raid with our grandmother, just before the end of nineteen forty. Rob had to go to London to pick out their bodies from rows of corpses, then arrange to bring them here for burial. He was absolutely marvellous. I was so shocked I went to pieces. He supported me and got us through the worst Christmas of our lives, at the same time doing Dad's work as well as his own. He was little more than eighteen at the time!' The defiance in her eyes doubled. 'I think he's capable of handling as much as any American pilot cadet, don't you?' When Jim made no answer, she continued coldly. 'Rob volunteered when he was legally exempt from active service, because he wanted to hit back. I don't find it at all surprising that he was not impressed by a tennis champion, and had little time for a senator's son basking in the limelight. He was in your country to learn to fly, not to win a popularity contest.'

Her revelation was something this former cadet could *not* handle. Jim moved across to gaze from the window while he struggled to deal with the situation. His encounters with women were normally sexually lighthearted, conducted with mutual understanding of the nature of the relationship. He had never before found himself in bitter verbal conflict with one; had never confronted a girl who not only appeared to despise him and everything he stood for, but was unafraid to tell him so.

Jenny Stallard clearly loved her brother and was fiercely defensive of him. Jim had never come across a female who would face up to a man of his size and strength and give as good as she got until he backed down. He had never come across one with such unshakeable loyalty. Even Shelley would have betrayed Theo with his own son and thought nothing of it.

As he gazed unseeing at the neglected tennis court, Jim faced the fact that the women he habitually sought were as hell-bent on pleasure as he. There must be countless numbers like this Stallard girl, but his careless pursuit had taken him in other directions. He knew all about loyalty between buddies, team-mates, fellow officers, but passion other than the sexual variety from a woman was a new experience. When he turned back into the room, Stallard's sister was still regarding him with cold contempt.

'I'm sorry about your parents and grandmother,' he said quietly. 'It took me a long time to come to terms with my mother's death after a long illness, so I understand your sense of shock when healthy people were killed in such terrible circumstances. I apologize if I've reopened wounds.' When she said nothing, he added, 'It explains that remark of yours about feeling we should have taken up arms earlier. I guess I'd have felt the same in your place.'

There was no relaxation of her animosity as she stared at him, her brother's letter still in her hand, so Jim moved to the desk, feeling his way through this alien situation. 'It was a governmental decision. If it had been ours, we'd have been over here a hell of a lot sooner.' He gave a strained half-smile. 'I won't pretend it was because we yearned to save little old England, because you're certain to see through that. We were trained fighting men with no one to fight, and across the Atlantic there was a war in progress. We all badly wanted to be part of it. Hell, a number of our guys came over here and joined your outfits right at the start, so maybe you can guess how we feel when people ask what took us so long.'

If she could she gave no sign of it. Jim then realized he was dealing with someone who did not easily forgive; a girl totally immune to the fact that J.T. Benson was being uncharacteristically humble. Yet he could not walk away, for some reason.

'Okay, I'll admit we had little idea what the British cadets had left behind when they came to Carlstrom, but there they enjoyed Florida sunshine, good, healthy food and unrivalled Southern hospitality while they learned to fly. Our troops have now left behind peace, plenty and their folks to set up here as your allies, and they're encountering danger, hardship and a great deal of homesickness. They're not *learning* to fly, they're making bombing raids over Germany and seeing their buddies killed. It's not exactly milk and honey for them. I tell you, the afternoon I spent here two weeks ago was the first time since coming to this country that I really felt relaxed and at home.'

At last Jenny spoke. 'You came to this house under false pretences.'

'No,' he contradicted firmly. 'I came as an American officer who admired your village church and had several hours to fill. My only pretence was that I didn't remember your brother.'

'You must have known I'd tell him we met.'

'Afterwards, of course I did, but I didn't expect this result.' He gently took the letter from her hand and laid it on the desk. 'At Carlstrom, he was suffering the shock of losing three family members, and burning with the flame of revenge. No man in that state reacts rationally. Had he spoken about his recent tragedy, we would have understood his attitude.'

Jenny said, still defensively, 'Rob's a very private person. He hates fuss.'

'I knew that much about him. I told my father he'd resent being on the front page of every national newspaper, but he got there because Theo

Benson wanted to be there. Your brother laid the blame for that at my door.' He ventured round the desk to stand beside her. 'Jenny, there's a grain of truth in some of the things he says, but only a grain. Can you accept that?' When she refused to respond, he grew angry again. 'Listen, I didn't have to give you an explanation. I could easily have zapped you with my opinion of *him*, then walked out telling myself here was another instance of "Who needs enemies with allies like this?" I only stayed because he suggests I've an ulterior motive where you're concerned, and that's way out of line. I wanted to come back for a little more of the kind of friendly hospitality your brother and his buddies were given so freely in Florida. Or didn't he tell you about that?'

'Yes, he told me about it. He made a number of friends who still keep in touch through me. Rob's not good at writing letters.'

'He had no trouble writing that one,' Jim said, nodding at the pages on the desk.

'I'd sent him a present for his twenty-first birthday. The fact that he wrote to me instead of telephoning told me he was about to go on another operation that was particularly risky. He doesn't realize I've worked that out. When I rang the Mess to wish him a happy birthday I was told he was spending a few days at another station. That means he was so badly shot up he couldn't get back. I've worked that out, too. I'd have been told if he was in hospital, so he must be all right, but he's been away for some days without making contact, which is worrying. I don't understand what's going on.'

'Maybe it's as well you don't.' There was a silence during which Jim sensed that her hostility was weakening, so he said, 'It must be hard for women to wait at home. That's why it's important to make things as good as possible to compensate. Can't we call it quits and start all over?'

'I don't think so,' she said, but without the bite that had been in her earlier words.

'We hit it off okay before that letter arrived, didn't we?'

She folded the pages, inserted them in the envelope, and put the letter back in the drawer. 'But it did arrive, and I know how strongly he feels.'

'You let him dictate who your friends can be?'

'No.' Her eyes had lost their cold glitter and were troubled as she explained. 'Rob's on his second operational stint. He was twenty-one last Saturday, and he's one of the older pilots in the squadron. That means he's seen dozens of his friends lost in unspeakable ways. He also, quite wrongly, feels responsible for me. He seemed very tired at our last meeting. Now he's obviously had some bad luck he's deliberately keeping from me, so he'll be feeling worse.'

'And you, also quite wrongly, feel responsible for *him*?'

'I'm all he's got.' She offered her hand. 'Thank you for staying to explain. It was very brave of you, but knowing how Rob feels I can't upset him at a time when he's already under impossible pressure.'

Jim took her hand and held on to it. 'Will you at least accept that I'm not as black as he painted?'

'I'll talk to him about it when I see him.' She withdrew her hand and moved to open the office door before crossing the hall. Outside on the steps, she turned to him. 'I'm sure you'll find English people warm and friendly when you get to know them. We're not at our best right now. Maybe your famous Southern hospitality towards our boys might not have been quite so evident if there had been severe rationing, blackout and nightly air raids on Florida at the time. Goodbye, Jim, and good luck.'

He drove back with two convictions: he had made an almighty fool of himself, and there was no way he would let Stallard win this round.

Chapter Twelve

Rob headed back to his station, quietly pleased with his efforts over the past two weeks. On the first day he had made eight runs over the test area while aircraft of all shapes and sizes crossed his path. In every instance he was flying lower than any of them so the scanner did not register their presence. On the second day it did pick up two other Mosquitoes accompanying him, one at the same height and the other skimming the water. Russell Lambourne modified the apparatus so that aircraft produced a different signal on the monitor from the one given off by shipping.

To ensure that this was effective Rob made his first night-time tests, with comparative success. From then on all the runs were made during darkness, until he was able to report that the scanner had identified everything within its range. Today, he had been below cloud level over very choppy water in heavy rain and high winds, and had still managed to record the positions of the three practice target vessels the Navy moved around each time he flew over the area. The final test.

As he flew home Rob thought of the hearty tea he would have when he got in, but even that was overshadowed by regret that Rebecca would not be there while he ate it. Between test flights he had spent considerable time at Romney Marsh with her and her father, discussing small problems and giving his opinions of them. He had become an integral part of the team and now knew as much about it as the pair who had developed the theory. If it proved successful in sinking enemy shipping it would make a tremendous difference to the war. Rob often thought of Phil, lost with an entire ship's crew two years ago. If she had gone ahead with her plans, Jenny would now be a widow.

Contacting the tower and receiving permission to land, Rob then thought about Johnny's forthcoming marriage at which he was to be best man. Lucy was pretty and every bit as lively as Johnny. She was also crazy about him. They were so keen to have a family, Johnny had confided that they had started the necessary procedure. Rob sincerely hoped the bride would not have to change her wedding dress for a larger size before the ceremony next month. He thought Johnny highly irresponsible and, although Rob worried about the speech he must make as best man, he worried more about the one he might have to make to the widow as best friend.

Seeing the runway lights spring up through the haze created by relentless rain, Rob turned to make his approach as a small inner voice told him he was a hypocrite. He was himself being irresponsible each time he went to Romney Marsh, because he was finding it harder and harder to leave. That charming house had become the home he lacked; Russell Lambourne was the kind of man he would have liked as a father.

As the Mosquito touched the runway, sending up heavy spray, Rob faced the fact that the urge to perform the necessary procedure to start a family bothered him more every time he was alone with Rebecca. Her provocation was curiously naive, which made him certain she knew little about the sexual reactions of men. She was so used to being on a professional par with them that she embarked on flirtation on the same level, with trustful, assured frankness.

He taxied through the murk to dispersal burdened by the knowledge that he should be more resolute where she was concerned, but the prospect of ending their meetings was too awful to contemplate. In any case, while he was doing the tests he had to keep seeing her. Once he returned to normal squadron duties he would put an end to what was becoming a dangerous relationship. It was the only decent thing to do.

Dennis Averell was full of bonhomie when Rob arrived in his office. 'Well done, Stallard. We've actually driven the Navy to say they're impressed.'

Rob grinned. 'Wait until I start firing the rockets, sir. They might say something entirely different when something goes wrong and one hits them up the arse.'

The Wing Commander was still smiling as he said, 'Yes ... well, you'll make certain it doesn't, I trust.' He indicated a communiqué on his desk. 'Someone is coming tomorrow to fit your aircraft with the other half of the equipment. We've been asked to begin running tests with the weapons on Monday, weather permitting. As before, the first runs will be made in daylight until you're used to the system. Any problems can be ironed out before night flights, and Professor Lambourne has expressed a wish to fly with you on the initial trials.'

Rob immediately protested. 'I can't have him in the cockpit! He can talk the hind leg off a donkey.'

'I've already indicated that it's not a good idea.'

'It's a bloody impossible idea, sir.'

'Yes, Stallard, I think you've made your point. In any case, you're to go to Romney Marsh for the weekend to tie up a few small outstanding queries he has, so I suggest you absorb the information he wishes to impart and tactfully put him off the notion of flying with you.'

'I'll tell him I won't have him. He's a nice chap; he'll understand.'

'I hope so. You can go off right after breakfast tomorrow. Not before! I won't have that machine of yours revved up under my window at the crack of dawn. Why can't you get a car like civilized men?'

'I like motorbikes better, sir. Cars are too staid. I'm rather looking forward to the next tests, aren't you?'

'If it gives us a weapon the Jerries haven't got, yes.' Rob saluted and turned to go. 'How are you getting on with Miss Lambourne, by the way?'

To Rob's annoyance his colour rose, but he managed to say quite nonchalantly, 'She's very brainy, as you said, but all three of us work well as a team.'

Averell's grin showed he was not fooled, but he merely said, 'I'm glad to hear it.'

After sprucing himself up, Rob walked down to the ante-room for tea. Flying always made him hungrier than usual, so if the sandwiches had all been wolfed he would get the little blonde girl to make an extra plateful for him. He had a feeling she would do more than that if he ever asked her, but she was deprived of the joy of making special sandwiches, because Johnny had a napkin-covered supply for him hidden behind a plant.

'Wotcher,' he greeted him in Cockney style. 'Had a good time? That's what happens to chaps who want to be heroes. They have to go out on bloody awful days when we lesser mortals are tucked up snug and warm with a girlie magazine.' His grin broadened mischievously. 'And you missed some of the lambiest chops we've ever had at lunch. Couldn't save you any of those, but I put a pile of cheese and pickle sandwiches by before these gluttons ate the lot.'

'I had cheese and pickle in lieu of lunch,' Rob complained, thinking of the lamb he had missed.

'If you don't want them, I'll —'

Rob took the plate swiftly. 'They'll keep me going until dinner.'

'Was it successful?' asked Johnny, as Rob sat beside him.

'Was what successful?'

'Oh, come off it, it can't be that flaming secret.'

'It is.' He started his second sandwich, saying with his mouth full, 'The Navy were very impressed with me.'

'Then go and join them, chum, because we aren't.'

Lowering his voice, Rob said, 'They're adding something else special to my Mossie tomorrow, and I'm flying it on Monday.'

Johnny asked eagerly, 'What's special about it?'

Knowing rumours would be flying all round the station tomorrow, Rob said, 'It's a gadget that will turn us all into William Tells.'

His friend's eyes widened. 'We're going to shoot apples off Jerries' heads?'

'More or less.'

'Must be some kind of advanced armaments.'

'Must be,' agreed Rob with an air of finality, getting to his feet. 'I'm going to grab some of that fruit cake before they scoff it all. It's several hours before dinner.'

He felt mean about keeping Johnny in the dark. He would love to discuss every aspect with him, outline the problems, get his views as a fellow pilot. His excitement and interest in the experiment would be doubled if he could share them with the one man who had become his close friend. What he had no intention of sharing was the fact that at the place he vanished to every so often there was a girl who had his toes permanently curled. One hint of her existence, and his fellow officers would give him no peace.

He returned with four large slices of cake and had the grace to offer some to his friend. As they munched, Johnny suddenly said, 'I hope this smart-Alec business of yours isn't going to interfere with being my best man. Seems to me you're getting in too deep to take a day off when you want one.'

'The Wingco knows the wedding date. Anyway, we wouldn't run a test on a Saturday.'

'*We* might not, but if the Navy are so bloody impressed with you, *they* might.' Johnny frowned. 'It must be some kind of torpedo, if they're involved. You lucky bastard! I'd give my eye-teeth to be doing it in your place.'

Rob knew he meant it. 'You're getting married. Concentrate on that.'

'I've got to now.' He lowered his voice. 'Keep it under your hat. I'm going to be a father round about Christmas.'

All Rob could say was, 'Seems to me you lesser mortals have been tucked up snug and warm with more than girlie magazines while I've been out.'

'You're supposed to tell me how bloody clever I am, slap me on the back and offer to buy me a double Scotch.'

'I would if you looked cocky about it,' Rob said pointedly.

Johnny sighed. 'I didn't realize my superb potential for fatherhood. It must have happened the first time. We never expected it to be so quick.'

'I thought that was what you wanted, why you ... Anyway you'll be married well before it's born.'

'I want to bring the wedding forward, but Lucy won't hear of it. She says her parents have everything arranged for July and couldn't possibly change the date. And, anyway, what reason could she give?' He looked frankly at Rob. 'Between now and then we could do a dozen or more ops. and I might get unlucky.'

Rob was equally frank. 'You've always known that. Why start worrying now?'

'Because leaving behind a pregnant widow, or a wife and child, isn't the same as abandoning an unmarried girl who's carrying your baby.'

'Course it is!' he declared emphatically. 'Whichever way you look at it, you've duffed up some poor girl and left her stranded to cope with the outcome.'

'I might have known I'd get that reaction,' sighed Johnny. 'You're such a damn cool fish! I can't wait for the time it really hits *you*.'

Seeing that his friend was seriously concerned and worried, Rob said, 'Why not get a special licence and marry her right away without telling her parents? You can still go through all that veils and bridesmaids stuff in July. That way, everyone'll be happy and you won't get the jitters each time you take off.'

Johnny gazed at him in awe. 'You're a genius.'

Rob grinned broadly. 'I know. That's why I'm out on bloody awful days like this being a hero while you're back here fathering the next generation, and wishing you hadn't ... but I'll stand you a double Scotch tonight, if you still want one.'

A WAAF orderly approached somewhat diffidently and hovered until she caught Rob's eye. 'There's a telephone call for you, Mr Stallard. It's long-distance.'

Rob got up and went to the little booth in the hall, a slice of cake in his hand. 'Stallard here.'

'I guessed you wouldn't be flying on a day like this,' said Jenny's voice in his ear. 'I haven't heard from you for a while, so I thought I'd check on how you are.'

'Sorry, Jen, I've been out of circulation recently. I'm fine. How's everything at the Manor?'

'Much as usual. Charles is up to his eyes in forms and requisitions. Molly and I are organizing a charity dinner for the refugees. We've managed to invite some of the Polish officers from the camp near Yeovil. What's your news?'

'Johnny's just told me he'll be a father at Christmas. Stupid bastard! He needs his brain seen to.'

'Don't be such a spoilsport. Give him my congratulations. When are you going to find the right girl and start having fun?'

'Not until the war's over.'

'You might be an old man by then.' A long pause. 'I had a visit from Jim Benson last weekend.'

In the act of taking a bite of cake, Rob lowered it. 'I hope you sent the bastard packing.'

'Not exactly. He insisted on explaining about what happened at Carlstrom.'

Rob stiffened. 'Explain what?'

'How his father stole the limelight when you brought your unconscious instructor down. You didn't write anything about that to me.'

'There wouldn't have been any limelight if his father had kept out of the way. As it was, there were pictures on every front page showing him shaking my hand. He had no right to do that when a man had collapsed and could have been dying.'

'Jim agreed.'

Rob began to grow angry. 'Since when has he been "Jim" to you?'

'Since he asked me to call him that. Rob, you told me very frankly how you regard him, and he admitted there was a grain of truth in some of the things you wrote — I read him your letter.'

'I'm surprised you allowed him to give you the length of his smooth tongue after all I told you. I warned you not to let him visit again.'

'I couldn't stop him. He turned up without warning.'

'What a bloody nerve!'

'Calm down and listen,' Jenny begged. 'There was nothing smooth about the way he dealt with your points. I've met enough men to know when they're lying, and he wasn't.'

'Are you suggesting I am?'

'Of course not, silly, but he wasn't shooting a line when he told me he split with his father over his behaviour with you that day. Nor was he when he said being over here made him realize perhaps they hadn't fully understood what the British cadets had left behind, while they were coping with the demands of flying training. It's understandable, Rob. How *could* they have known when they had no experience of it? I have no real knowledge of what our refugees have left behind. If I can be forgiven for that, then so can he, surely?'

Rob did not trust himself to speak.

'Are you still there?'

'I thought you knew how to handle men like him. Can't you see he's getting round you to hit at me?'

'That's ridiculous!'

'Is it? You've just put a jolly good case for not understanding what you've no experience of. That applies to what happened at Carlstrom.' He heard her sigh. 'Jen, let's drop the subject. I just hope you sent him off with a flea in his ear.'

'I told him I couldn't be friends because you were so opposed to the idea,' she said hesitantly.

'Good. So that's the end of that.'

'Not really.' Another pause. 'A huge bouquet of flowers arrived from him today — with further apologies, and the hope that I might discuss things with you, then get in touch with him.'

'My God!' he said explosively, causing two passing pilot officers to turn and look at him. 'Doesn't *that* convince you of the game he's playing?'

'I don't think it's a game,' she responded unhappily. 'Truly, Rob.'

'Then you're a gullible fool. Why would he send all those flowers? Why would he persist in pestering a girl like you? He's the son of a senator, filthy rich and able to get any woman he wants.'

There was a spark of anger in her voice now. 'I'm not exactly a lowly serving wench. Neither am I plain and dim-witted. Is it impossible for you to believe I might actually be attractive and intelligent enough to capture his interest?'

It was his turn to sigh. 'Oh lord, I didn't mean ... As I said just now, let's drop the subject.'

'No, Rob, let's have it out,' she said vigorously. 'I liked him the first time we met. Curiously enough, I like him even more after our confrontation. He was definitely laying on the charm initially, but he dropped all that when he saw I was deeply hostile. I believe he's now sincere, and very lonely. You can surely understand that. Whatever happened at Carlstrom two years ago is surely no longer important compared with what you're doing now? In any case, you weren't your true self at the time. Jim was genuinely distressed when I told him about Mum and Dad and Gran, and how you'd had to deal with it on your own. He'd had no notion of what you'd been through, of course, and accepts that you were in a state of shock at Arcadia. As he said, no man can be expected to behave rationally under those circumstances.'

Rob could not believe his ears. 'You told him ...? How *could* you, Jen? How *dared* you tell that bastard all about my private life? You had no right ...' He was so incensed he lost control of what he wanted to say.

'I had every right. They were also *my* parents and Gran. I told him about *my* private life ... and you happen to be part of it. I wasn't betraying your stubborn attitude of keeping everything to yourself. He was running you down. I told him you were strong enough to handle anything, and gave him an example.'

'So he now sneeringly suggests I was irrational at Carlstrom because I *couldn't* handle it. Thanks a lot.'

'It wasn't like that,' she said defensively. 'Rob, if you tell me what went on between you both over there, I'll know what to do.'

'You mean, you'll know whose side to take.'

There was a short silence. 'That was unfair.'

'So was telling private family matters to someone I warned you against. I thought I made it bloody plain I hate his guts.'

Another silence. 'That's so unlike you. He can't be that bad.'

Rob was totally dismayed by evidence that Benson had so charmed Jenny despite his own letter leaving her in no doubt of his character. He had no idea what next to do about it.

Jenny continued. 'I shouldn't have contacted you like this, in the Mess, but I won't see him again if it truly upsets you. You've enough on your plate. I thought I might be able to sort out the differences between you because ... well, because Jim didn't seem to be as bad as you described in your letter. When he arrived I was extremely rude. You should have heard the things I said to him. Most men would have either snarled back, or left with their tail between their legs. Jim did neither. He naturally defended himself, but he also tried to explain and somehow apologize. Only someone with courage and reasonable humility could do that, in my opinion. Which doesn't fit with your description of a self-seeking, womanizing liar, does it?'

Rob had had enough. It had been an exacting flight this afternoon, and he needed to relax. The pleasure over what he had achieved had been driven away; his sense of warm contentment gone. 'It sounds as if you've already decided whose side you're on, so there's nothing more to be said.'

'It's not a question of choosing sides,' she explained. 'Why're you taking all this the wrong way?'

A final surge of anger led him to say, 'Probably because I haven't J.T. Benson's courage and reasonable humility.'

'Rob, *don't.*'

'Look, do whatever you like,' he said wearily. 'It's your life. After all, I'm doing whatever *I* like without agonized telephone calls asking your permission. Cheerio. Regards to all at the Manor.'

'Take *great* care,' she begged quietly. 'I'm sorry, Rob, I didn't mean to hurt you.'

'You haven't. Johnny's just told me I'm a damn cool fish and you've said much the same. That means I'm unhurtable.' He hung up, deeply upset and sensing that Benson was coming between him and the only member of his family left.

The weather continued wet. Rob had slept badly and he rode to Romney Marsh with his head hunched into his shoulders against the rain. Just like bloody June, he thought morosely; one week summer and the next back to winter.

The Marsh was not in the least welcoming. He had to keep wiping his goggles so that he could see the track clearly. It was easy to understand why people had strayed from it and been lost for ever. The grey gloom over the whole area was extremely forbidding: Flying Officer Stallard was chilled and wet. He wished he had stayed in bed with a girlie magazine, like all his lucky colleagues who were not trying to be heroes. He also wished he had a car. Staid or not, they kept the driver dry.

Mrs Maple scowled as he entered by the back door. 'You're not going through the house like *that*! You're spattered all over with mud.' He began pulling off his outer clothes. 'You can't hang that dripping leather coat in my kitchen. I cleaned the floor before I went off last night. And those boots'll have to be left outside. Don't move another step until you've taken them off!'

The inner door was flung open and Rebecca stood on the threshold like a bright flame on a dark day, her hair glowing with amber lights and her eyes vivid with anticipation. In that instant Rob felt he had come home.

'You poor lamb, you're *drenched*!' she exclaimed. 'Come through to the fire and thaw out.' Seizing his cold hand she pulled him forward, oblivious of Mrs Maple's flustered comments. 'I know it's ridiculous lighting a fire in the middle of June, but it's even more ridiculous to freeze. I don't know why you went to the back door, you know what she's like.' They arrived before the log fire and she smiled up at him. 'You should tell her to go to perdition. I'm sure you'd tell *me* to if I bullied you like that.'

'Of course I would. You're too bossy by half. But *she* frightens me to death.'

She began untying the sodden scarf tucked into his tunic. Rob let her do it, enjoying her closeness and the faintly erotic suggestion of being undressed by her. He had forgotten the rain, the dreary day, his heavy spirits. The pleasure of being with her again, in this room with a carpet of rich, deep colours, velvet armchairs and pale walls hung with vibrant paintings, was so great it brought a lump to his throat.

'I've been longing to get back here,' he murmured before he could stop himself.

She glanced up from what she was doing. 'How much?'

'This much.' He pulled her roughly against him, forgetting his resolution to keep his feelings under control.

She eventually freed herself and turned him round. 'Go up and change. You'll feel more comfortable, and I prefer you in civvies. I do wish you'd have a sherry before lunch. It's so civilized.'

He stopped at the foot of the stairs. 'Does that mean I'm not?'

She gave a wicked smile. 'What are you like when you're drunk?'

'Horrible ... so you can get that idea out of your head.'

Her gurgling laugh floated after him as he went to the room he now thought of as his own. He kept pyjamas and a dressing gown there, as well as grey flannels, a couple of shirts and a fawn pullover. The depression that had settled over him since Jenny's telephone call had lifted.

When he descended, her father was drinking sherry with Rebecca. His long face broke into a smile as he held out his hand. 'It's good to see you, Bob. How nice of you to spare the time.'

As Rob shook his hand, he wondered whether Lambourne knew what was going on between him and Rebecca. 'Hallo, sir, how are you? My Mossie's being fitted with the rest of the equipment today. It's certain to have everyone at the station speculating, and I'll be bombarded with questions I'm not allowed to answer.' He grinned. 'I'll be the envy of every pilot in the squadron when I take her up on Monday.'

Lambourne tossed back his sherry. 'And I'll be there to see that it works properly.'

'No, sir, I can't have you in the cockpit during the flight,' Rob said firmly.

'Nonsense! I have to be there. It's my responsibility.'

'It's my aircraft. I'm sorry, sir, but that's final.'

The older man glared at him. 'And who are you to make pronouncements of that sort?'

Unperturbed, Rob said, 'I'm the chap you fished out of the drink and shanghaied into working with you. You're stuck with me now. I respect the fact that you're the expert when it comes to science, but I happen to be an expert on flying.'

'You're an extremely cocksure young man,' accused the Professor irately.

'I have to be to work on something like this. I'm a sort of guinea pig. Before long I'll have to test armed rockets. If I wasn't sure of myself as a pilot, I'd worry all the time that I'd make a mistake and blow myself to kingdom come. I have complete faith in your skill and knowledge so I think you should have enough faith in me not to interfere.'

'Interfere! *Interfere*? It's *my* invention.'

'*Yes*, sir, and it's my job to see that it works. I can best do that if left alone.'

The door burst open. Mrs Maple said, 'I've called out twice. You'd have heard if you hadn't been shouting at each other. Don't blame me if it's cold.'

'If you announced lunch in the proper manner there'd be no problem,' Rebecca told her crisply.

'I'm not a fancy French maid,' came the gruff response. 'I'm expected to do everything around here.' She headed back to the kitchen saying over her shoulder, 'No sooner have I washed the floor over than *he* comes in wet and muddy, tramping all over it. No one else would come all this way out, day after day, you know.'

Rebecca got to her feet with a wide smile. 'That's what's known as coming in right on cue. Will you two schoolboys stop squabbling and have lunch, or shall I leave you to your fisticuffs?'

'Never have a daughter, Ron. They're far too saucy,' said Lambourne as he rose rather stiffly. 'Come and have lunch.'

Rob followed them to the small dining room, where a group of covered dishes had been left on the table with a pile of warm plates. He held Rebecca's chair for her, then took his usual one facing her and shook out his napkin. There was a joint of ham stuck with cloves, and summer vegetables. Mrs Maple was an excellent cook and a tireless worker, despite her ill temper, and she was right in saying few other women would venture out on the Marsh every day. For a brief moment Rob pictured his mother scrubbing and polishing their little cottage before putting out plates of stew, which he and his father had sat to eat in shirtsleeves and braces. Another age; another life! Could he really be Fred Stallard's lad?

'Come back, all is forgiven,' said a soft voice, and he glanced up to find Rebecca studying him curiously.

'Sorry, I was miles away.' He turned to the head of the table. 'The purpose of my visit today is to get everything straightened out with you before Monday, sir. It may not work first time. These things rarely do. I want to have a number of attempts and I'll need to concentrate, so it's more important for you to be on the boat seeing what's happening to the moored target when I fire the rockets.'

Lambourne's rare smile lit his face. 'All right, have it your own way. You're a stubborn devil ... but I'm not letting you leave here until I'm certain you're fully acquainted with the facts.'

Rob grinned. 'That's a very tempting statement. If I play dumb I get to stay an extra day.'

'Ah, it's like that, is it?'

The comment was so unexpected from a man who normally thought along intellectual lines, a man who had suddenly turned into a knowing father, that Rob flushed slightly and concentrated on his lunch. He had made the comment in a joking way to show how much he enjoyed being at the house with two people he had grown fond of, but Lambourne had jumped to the obvious conclusion which meant he did know what was going on. As he ate baked ham and minted potatoes, Rob's spirits suddenly plunged again. Nothing was really going on. It was out of the question.

For the remainder of the meal Rob answered stiltedly and hardly smiled. His awkwardness transferred itself to the others and Rob was dismayed when Rebecca went across to the laboratory with them. She was a distraction he could do without today, and when her father got under way he covered ground they had trodden before.

'Sir, we've been over this umpteen times,' Rob protested.

'But it's most important to make precise calculations. If they're wrong you could hit *anything* with your rockets.'

'Including the squadron leader's backside.' Seeing Lambourne's scowl, Rob sighed. 'Sorry, I know it's important, sir — I'll be the mug aiming them — but I've got that part down to a fine art. On Monday I'll be flying with a navigator. We then have to combine the seek *and* attack systems. Until we try it we can't go any further with the theoretical side of it all.'

'Unless you listen, Roy, we'll achieve nothing,' said Lambourne irritably.

The afternoon dragged past. For once, Rob's thoughts wandered and he had to stifle a yawn more than once. The past week had been a heavy one for him. He had been out every day on tests, doing exacting work monitored by a clutch of high-ranking men expecting miracles from him. Because of its secrecy, he had been unable to unwind by talking about it with his own small group of friends. He missed that. He had not even had a navigator for company during the flights, and he missed Charlie all the more because of it. Now he had fallen out with Jenny.

The Professor went to his library after dinner to read up on a theory he felt driven to check. As Rob stood on the rug warming himself before the fire, Rebecca gave him coffee and a lecture.

'What's the matter with you today? You could have made it less obvious you were bored. As if your glum expression were not enough, you made a bad job of stifling your yawns. And each time I poked you, you only managed a toneless yes or no.'

'I'd heard it all before,' he retaliated. 'I *was* bored. Very. He was simply out to convince himself he'd covered every possibility and done his job properly. I'm already sure about my part in it.'

'Smart Alec,' she said crisply. 'Can't you understand that he's deeply concerned that something might go wrong?'

'So am I, madam,' he retorted equally crisply. 'I have to test the system with live rockets slung beneath my wings.'

She made a startling change of approach, saying softly, 'I wish you hadn't got to do it.'

'Well, you shouldn't have fished me out of the Channel that morning and kept me prisoner.'

'It was Father who asked that you should work on this with us. I had an additional motive for keeping you here.'

Uncertain how to counter that, Rob hesitated, which gave Rebecca an opportunity to get to the heart of the matter. 'Father's coy remark at lunch upset you, didn't it?'

He put his coffee cup on the mantelpiece before saying carefully, 'It made me realize I must end this before it goes any further.'

'How much further can it go?' she demanded. 'I'm completely in love with you and, despite all that nonsense you gave me about falling for the entire female population of Florida, I know you feel the same about me. There are two ways of dealing with it, and ending it isn't one of them.'

'It's the only way so far as I'm concerned,' he said heavily. 'I told you at the start how foolish it is to let feelings get the better of common sense.'

She sank on to one of the big armchairs and gazed up at him. 'So why have you been kissing and cuddling me at every opportunity?'

'You seem to know the answer to everything, so work it out yourself,' he flung at her. 'I'm no different from other men, and you've done your damnedest to egg me on. You're doing it now, sitting there all eyes and temptation.'

Soft, intimate laughter burst from her. 'You really are adorable when you get on your high horse.'

Because she was undermining his resolution so blatantly, he grew angrier. 'This isn't a game, it's deadly serious. Shut away down here you've no idea what it's all about, what it can do to people. I've told you about Johnny and the wedding next month. He's crazy about this girl, who must have egged him on, too, because she's now going to have a baby and he's worried about being killed before he marries her. He's been operational eighteen months and never let it prey on his mind before. We don't. It's just a job. If we think at all about the danger we're in, it's always some other chap who's going to get the chop.' He paused to calm himself. 'Johnny's a good, steady pilot, but for the next month he's going to have the jitters each time he takes off. That's when men grow tense and make mistakes. He thinks it'll be all right once she's his wife, but he'll be jittery until the baby's born. Then he'll be worse, because he'll feel responsible for *two* people. I've seen it happen to other men. They have half their mind elsewhere when they're flying, and when something happens, their wives have to cope with everything alone. It's not fair on either of them.'

Rebecca was no longer amused. 'You really are het up about it, aren't you? Darling, it's impossible to call a halt to love and marriage. The war might last for years yet.'

'If it does, there'll be thousands more widows and orphans.'

'You think it would be better to have a legion of brokenhearted spinsters and no hope of a future generation?'

Rob gazed at her, trying to marshal his thoughts. He wanted to sit beside her listening to music that touched his soul; to be close to her in complete accord. He longed to silence the voice of reason and surrender to the urge of youth.

'It's not only the question of the war. I told you before, I'm just an ordinary working pilot usually stony broke at the end of each month. We're not in the same league and it wouldn't have got this far if you weren't tied up with this rocket system and I had to stay here so often.' He sighed. 'You and your father have treated me like one of the family, and I'm starting to think of this place as home. That's the real trouble.'

She went to him. 'The real trouble is that you're an old-fashioned, high-principled idiot who can't see beyond the end of his nose. I love you for the person you are, not for the hope of wealth and an ancestral mansion.' She kissed him lightly. 'Anyway, I have enough money to support us *and* all our children.'

He stepped back, flushing angrily. 'That *really* puts the kibosh on it! What kind of chap d'you think I am?'

'One I love very much,' came her calm reply. 'You rattle on about what the war does to people, so I'll remind you of it. Every night, all over the world, civilians are losing their homes, their possessions and their money — everything. They survive just so long as someone still cares about them. Love's what really matters, darling. It's all that matters to *me*.'

'What if I don't come back one day?'

'I'd want to have been married to you, if only for a short time. I'd want your child to love and hold close as part of you. Ask any of those widows you're so concerned about and I'm sure they'd say the same. Life's so uncertain right now, we should have whatever happiness we can get. I want to be your wife.'

He ran a hand through his hair in exasperation. 'Haven't you heard a thing I've been saying?'

'Yes, but I'm trying to show you you're wrong.'

'I'm not.'

She gently touched his cheek. 'All right, let's drop the subject for now. I can't have you getting jittery while doing these tests, because you're worrying about what you ought to do about us. Decisions like that can wait.' She moved across to the gramophone, switching off the overhead light. 'Settle down and I'll play the Chopin piano concerto you like so much.'

'I shan't change my mind,' he murmured, loving the way the light from the remaining low lamp cast a glow over her face and sheened her hair so that it was the colour of polished horse-chestnuts.

The music worked its usual magic, as he sat with his arm around her and rested his cheek against her head on his shoulder. Tension began to drain from him. The set-to with Jenny no longer seemed so hurtful, and he had said what he had to to this girl he loved. It was the best he could do, for the moment. When the tests were over he would tackle the problem again. It would be easier to make the break when they were no longer thrown together.

*

There was a message in Rob's pigeon hole when he arrived back on Sunday evening. It was from the CO informing him that his new navigator was Flying Officer Donald Winkie and, unless it was after midnight when he got in, Rob was to seek out the man and fill him in on what they would be doing.

Tempted to ignore it although it was only ten past ten, Rob had a quick wash, then went in search of the person who would partner him in this hush-hush project. He had no doubt Winkie would be highly efficient — he would have been selected with great care — but it was such a close relationship Rob prayed they would find the necessary rapport.

The Mess was busy because, after a promising start, rain had set in again and all ops had been cancelled at the last moment. Johnny hailed Rob and beckoned him across to where he stood with his own navigator and three strangers with mugs of beer in their hands.

'Who've you impressed this time?' his friend asked slyly.

'The Wingco apparently. He's found me a new navigator.' Rob surveyed the three young officers, dismissed the pair with pilot's wings, and focused on a thin, fair-moustached man as tall as himself who was regarding him with interest. 'You must be Donald Winkie.'

'Known as Wee Willie,' he responded with a grin, and a transatlantic accent.

'You're American!' exclaimed Rob in dismay, as his hand was heartily shaken.

'No, man, I'm from Montreal, Canada.' He winked broadly. 'I don't let on to the girls. They rate us second best to Yanks.'

One of the new pilots said breezily, 'Once the girls lose their romantic illusions about you colonial *boys*, they turn to real men like us.'

They all laughed, except Rob, as introductions were made. Then Winkie offered to baptize their new partnership by buying his pilot a pint of beer.

'Make it a tomato juice and you're on,' Rob told him, deciding that he would have to tell the Wing Commander it would not work. His resolution was strengthened when the Canadian ordered 'tomayto' juice. If he also said 'okay' all the time it would drive Rob mad.

'Some popsie got you on the wagon?' asked Winkie sympathetically, as he handed Rob the drink. 'They don't understand the stress we're under.'

'They must be the ones under stress when they come across someone as bouncy as you,' Rob observed dryly. 'And there's no *popsie* involved. I never drink alcohol.' He raised the glass. 'Here's mud in your eye.'

During the following few minutes the other four men eased away in their wisdom, leaving an awkward situation of which they had no wish to be a part. There was little finesse about their withdrawal, and silence reigned between Rob and the other man as they regarded each other warily.

'The Wingco gave me an idea what this thing's all about,' said the Canadian eventually, 'but he's leaving you to fill in the details. I guess it's some means of guiding rockets to a target.'

'It *is* a means of guiding rockets to a target,' Rob informed him shortly, accepting with low spirits that Winkie now knew so much about the affair he would have to be in on it. 'We can't talk here. You'd better come up to my room while I tell you what I've done so far.'

Winkie occupied the chair, so Rob perched on his bed whilst outlining what he had done during the past days. 'Tomorrow, we start testing the entire system. I've perfected the "seek" aspect. The scanner in the nose unfailingly picks up anything in the vicinity, day or night. Once we have the position of the target we set it on the firing recorder. The rockets are meant to be guided by magnetic beams homing on the ship, so that when they're fired they should hit the target smacko!'

'Who'll be controlling that part of it?'

'You, of course. When we're within firing range — a thousand yards is most likely, but that has to be decided during our tests — I get a green light and push the firing button. The rest is a piece of cake.'

'Yeah, for you. All you get to do is push a button.'

'I also have to fly the bloody aircraft.'

'From what I've heard you can do that with your eyes closed.'

'We'll test that theory tomorrow, too, if you like. But as I'm going to have to make a turn faster than a bat out of hell to avoid being blown sky high when the rockets strike, I'll keep my eyes open, thanks. I'll tell you now, I'm not agreeing to carry live weapons until I'm certain the whole system works safely.'

'I'll second that.' Winkie then raised several points, which prompted a lively professional discussion that told Rob he had a navigator of no mean skill.

At the end of their discussion the Canadian made a wry face. 'I suppose it's got something going for it, but I can't see it winning the war for us. It's too tricky.'

'That's why we've been chosen to test it instead of more senior chaps. There's no chance of glory attached to it, and if something goes wrong we're more expendable.' Rob stood. 'Let's call it a day.'

At the door, the Navigator said, 'I think I stepped on a corn downstairs. Has some Yank run off with your girl?' When Rob gave no answer, he added, 'Is it me you dislike, or the way I speak?'

'I'll let you know by the end of the week — if we haven't been blown to bits by then.'

Winkie gave a careless salute with two fingers to his brow, but was halted when Rob called out, 'I refuse to call you Wee Willie, by the way. It'll have to be Don.'

'Okay. I'll let you know what I'll call you at the end of the week,' he said with a grin. 'If we haven't been blown to bits by then.'

That typical bantering exchange heralded the start of a partnership between two men who were not only highly skilled but extremely individual.

They test-flew the Mosquito immediately after breakfast, then spent an hour or so studying the additional instruments that had been fitted. Donald asked what they must do if the scanner picked up an entire fleet.

'Call for help,' said Rob with a grin, then looked at his watch. 'We're scheduled to do the first run at fourteen-thirty. If we take off at fourteen hundred that'll give us enough time to make a couple of circuits before we get down to business.'

As they left the aircraft and sauntered to where they had left their bicycles, Donald said, 'This reputation for low flying I'm told you have; just how low do you get?'

'You'll find out this afternoon. I forgot to tell you that when we get round to testing live rockets, we'll be flying underwater.'

In that jaunty mood Rob went to his room to wash before lunch. He was looking forward to this new phase. He very much wanted it to work. Lambourne's hopes rested on his invention so it would be a tremendous setback for him if the system was dumped. Rob knew he would feel responsible, as he had worked on it with the man, so he intended to use all his skill during the coming tests.

It was a perfect summer afternoon as they took off; the kind of day on which Rob would have liked to run down to the coast on his motorbike, preferably with Rebecca on the pillion. They arrived over the test area with ten minutes to spare, so Rob circled several times for Donald's benefit.

'We can see the target perfectly well, but concentrate on the instruments,' Rob said. 'Get on your belly and switch on the scanner. I'll make a wide sweep over the coast, then run back across the water so that it'll pick up the target vessel and give its position on this.' He tapped a luminous panel. 'I'll approach at a speed of two fifty, at a hundred and fifty feet. Soon as we get the position of the target, you activate the magnetic beams.' He banked to head over the coastal town bathed in sunshine. 'We'll do a couple of runs without firing, so we get the hang of the routine.'

'Okay.'

Rob came out of the turn, dropped to a hundred and fifty feet, checked his speed and kept an eye on the new panel low to his right as he had been doing for the past week. As before, it soon registered the position of the target and Donald read it out clearly and precisely. Turning on to the course which would take them to the target, Rob concentrated on speed and height as the yellow light appeared, to tell him he was homing in on it.

'Stand by,' Rob warned.

'Switches on,' Donald chanted.

A green light flashed. Rob mentally pushed the firing button, counted to four, turned steeply to the left and shot away towards the distant coastline.

Donald looked concerned. 'We were bloody close to that wreck down there. If we'd been doing it for real we'd be mincemeat by now.'

Rob smiled to himself. That had given the laconic Canadian a jolt. 'It's thoughts like that that constitute the thrill of it. Let's give ourselves another.'

'You're crazy.'

'Not me. I'm only carrying out orders.' Sweeping over the narrow beach, Rob asked, 'Have you got the hang of it?'

'I guess.'

'We'll do another dummy run, then have a go at hitting it.'

'Okay.'

Rob made a wide circle before turning towards the water. He approached from a slightly different direction this time and they went through the process as before. Donald was still unhappy about their height.

'You wanna be down here where I am,' he grumbled. 'When that thing explodes it'll be right beneath my belly.'

'Stop complaining,' Rob returned, coming out of his violent turn to the right. 'I'll be the one getting your guts in my lap.'

'Know what I like about you? You're so cheerful and friendly.'

'I haven't yet found anything about you I like,' he said, levelling off at three hundred feet and heading north. 'I'll approach from the opposite direction, and this time we'll fire the first clutch. After that I'll come in from the east for the second attempt. If we hit the target they'll wave a green flag. If not, it'll be red.'

'What'll they wave if we've officially blown up?'

'Your guts, chum.'

'You're a mighty cool bastard.'

'I've got to be with you beside me worrying about something that might never happen,' said Rob. 'I hope you haven't forgotten this is a *night* attack system. We'll be doing it in the dark after today.'

'At least I won't *see* the spot where Donald Fraser Winkie is going to be scattered to the four winds.'

'So long as you see what you're supposed to be doing down there, that's all I care about. I'll start the first run now.'

All appeared to go well, yet a red flag was being waved when they looked down at the observers. 'So much for a breakthrough that ensures the rockets can't miss,' said Donald in disgust.

Rob was deep in thought. He and Lambourne had estimated the range based on his own experience. How could he have been so wrong? For the second attempt Rob cut his speed fractionally, but again a red flag was waved and they flew home feeling frustrated.

Two more tests were arranged for the following morning. Until they could get it right in daylight it was pointless to begin night trials. They spent most of that evening going through the complex calculations and discussing what the flaw could be. Then it dawned on Rob.

'It's those bloody magnetic beams, of course. Once the rockets are under way, we must switch them off. What's happening is that they're still under the influence of the magnetism as we veer off in a climb, so they're damn well following us part-way up.'

'I guess you're right. Okay, we'll try it tomorrow. I'll cut off the beams when I judge the right moment. It might take a coupla goes before we get it.'

'Sure to. Nothing ever happens first time off.'

'I don't know about that. There was a girl I —'

'Spare me the dirty details of your love life. I'm too tired.'

At Rob's door, Donald said, 'I'm not keen on this low flying. I value my guts, and there's girls and adventures out there still to be discovered.'

'When I get below the yard arm you're entitled to worry, not before,' Rob returned, piling the sheets of paper on which they had scribbled notes and diagrams.

It was not until the afternoon that they managed to earn a green flag, despite turning off the beams. To do so they had been obliged to drop their speed and height, then reduce the range to under a thousand yards. By this time, Rob was worrying as much as Donald. It was cutting the safety factor very fine, and it demanded no mean skill from a pilot very sure of himself at low levels. It also increased the risk of being caught up in the subsequent explosion. He kept his fears to himself, however, because he so much wanted to crack the system for the Lambournes' sakes. He hoped further practice would improve the situation.

After four nights of tests it was worse. They only once hit the target, and even Rob was forced to admit it had grown too hazardous. Flying home on a windy, moonless night he was silent, until Donald said, 'You were really gunning for this screwy idea, weren't you?'

'I think it has great possibilities.' He changed the subject swiftly. 'Just look at those stars! Do you ever get the urge to climb up there with them?'

'I'll get there soon enough unless you lift over this church spire dead ahead,' Donald said tautly. When that was safely negotiated, he added, 'We did our darndest, Robbo. Don't take it to heart.'

They reported to Dennis Averell, who was waiting to get to bed.

'It was rough out there tonight, sir,' Rob told him despondently. 'At that height over a heavy swell it was suicidal.'

'Coming from you, Stallard, I believe it.'

'It's not only that, sir,' added Donald. 'The risk to any aircraft over the target is too high. If the rockets should hit the ship's magazine, the explosion would engulf the Mossie.'

'He's right,' Rob admitted. 'Those beams are the problem. If we leave them on, the bloody rockets go haywire. If we switch them off too soon, same thing happens. We're too close to the target to make fine calculations, and Don's got enough to do at quickfire speed as it is. Professor Lambourne said he's made a scientific breakthrough with the beams — a new concept — so if they could be strengthened we'd have more leeway all round.'

The CO got to his feet. 'Scientific breakthroughs are notorious for taking time, Stallard. On the showings of your tests the Air Ministry have decided to give the thumbs down. I had the message from Air Commodore Griffin an hour ago. He asked me to say that he knows you both will have given your very best efforts.'

Rob was deeply upset. 'I'm sure the Lambournes could come up with a solution.'

211

'Probably, but we have to get on with the war.' He gave a sympathetic smile. 'I know how you feel. Winkie, you'll fly with Grieves while his navigator recuperates from his eye infection. You, Stallard, are to take a week's leave, which is overdue because of the demands of this project.'

Rob felt no pleasure at the thought of seven days off the station. His quarrel with Jenny added to his reluctance to spend them at Thoresby, which held too many sad memories. He went to his room disappointed, depressed and feeling to blame for the failure of Lambourne's brainchild. He longed to set off for Romney Marsh to commiserate with the man, who would surely be feeling worse depression. Rob could then explain, and they could thrash out the solution to his problems with the system. Lambourne was a lonely man, set apart by his own brilliance, and Rob had found a close rapport with him. He badly needed to talk the whole thing over with the one person who would understand how he felt.

Rob also longed for Rebecca. The weather was set fair. It would be wonderful on the Marsh. They could wander hand in hand, spotting birds and butterflies galore. Then there would be dinner served by the fondly grumpy Mrs Maple, after which he and his beautiful girl would cuddle up and be thrilled by the loveliest music in the world. When he went to bed he would know she was in the room just across the corridor, and he would drift into sleep imagining how it would be if she appeared in his doorway with an inviting smile. Physically drained, he sat heavily on the bed. That was why he must not go to Romney Marsh. He had reached the stage where he could no longer trust himself with her.

Putting his head in his hands, Rob told himself Rebecca clearly had little idea what she did to him each time her eyes beckoned and she pressed her body against his. He had tried to explain his views and his financial situation, but she had worked her magic to silence him. It would be highly irresponsible to marry her, but he had reached the stage where it was that or a complete break. Fate had taken a hand to make the latter possible. He was no longer under orders to go to Romney Marsh. If Lambourne ever persuaded Group to resume tests on their system, and R.N. Stallard was again chosen as guinea pig, it would all happen far from that house he longed to regard as home. He need not see Rebecca again.

The following morning after writing two of the most difficult letters he had ever struggled to compose, Rob drove to the coast on his motorbike and spent a wretched week watching young lovers enjoying themselves.

Chapter Thirteen

Jim wangled the use of an official car for the evening by telling Clancy Flood he was taking to dinner Lady Guthrie and her niece, who were influential landowners serving on a number of committees, among which was the organization that arranged cultural visits to places of historic interest for American servicemen.

'You think I should play host?'

'No, no,' Jim said hastily. 'I'll do the groundwork, because I was once introduced to Lady Guthrie. Later, you might care to invite the whole family to one of our cocktail parties.'

The senior man looked relieved. 'Great idea. See their names are given to Roberta. I've so much paperwork I can't spare the time to dine the British aristocracy yet again. Some of them are so goddam stiff and starchy!' He gave his booming laugh. 'Now I know why my great-great-great granddaddy drove 'em back here. I just can't take to them. Sooner we get this thing over, sooner we can go home.'

'Yes, General.' Jim seized his opportunity to pursue that line. 'Have you had time to review my latest application to join an operational squadron?'

'Didn't have to review it. You're too valuable here. Told you that last time you applied. Besides,' he added, drawing towards him a pile of files marked 'Confidential', 'it wouldn't be right to put in the firing line the son of one of our most prominent senators.' He glanced up at Jim. 'I'll see you have a medal or two to take home.'

Jim set out for the evening in an aggressive mood. He was caught in a trap of Theo's making. Admittedly, his present job involved a great deal more than tactical socializing — he was cognizant of secret and confidential projects and sat in on all but the highest-level meetings — and it was a good posting, which would be welcomed by men who had been too long in that firing line to which Senator Benson's son should never be exposed. Men like Bucket, who was still taking his bomber over Germany and feeling the strain more and more. Unbidden came the words 'grounded dogsbody' and Jim felt a surge of anger.

He now regretted setting up this meeting with Stallard's sister. She had not sounded overjoyed by his invitation, and a dose of her cool treatment was the last thing he wanted after Flood's dismissal of his application. He wanted a girl to have fun with, then take to bed; a cute cookie who understood the rules. Yet, as he sat gazing from the car window at the battered streets of London on the hot, late-July evening, and saw the medley of uniforms on young men and women caught up in the war, he knew it was not at all what he needed. He longed to be let off the hook and allowed to fly. That would make life in England bearable — just.

Jenny was waiting for him in the vestibule of a small sandbagged London hotel, and one look at her told Jim she was in an entirely different category from cute cookies he had known. Wearing a dark green chiffon dress with a flared skirt, and a short cream and grey mottled silk jacket, she looked extremely striking. Her hair was drawn back into a chignon to reveal a pair of demure diamante earrings, but Jim's attention was held more by her eyes than by the jewels. They were larger than he remembered, and regarding him warily. Instinct told him to take things easy this evening. It was going to be no walkover.

'I might have known you wouldn't keep a man waiting,' he said, unsmiling. 'Thank you for agreeing to spend some time with me.' When she said nothing he put his hand beneath her elbow. 'I've laid my life on the line to requisition a car for the evening. Shall we go?' Once they were in the back seat and moving off, Jim produced a corsage in a box tied with ribbon. 'Even in war-torn London such things can still be found. I hope you'll agree to wear it.'

She gazed at the orchid as it lay in her lap. 'After you've gone to so much trouble it would be rude of me to refuse.'

'A gesture to your gallant allies?' he taunted gently.

She looked up at him. 'Perhaps.'

'I've asked a pal of mine and his girlfriend to join us for dinner. I thought you'd feel safer with three damn Yankees than with one.'

Very conscious of the uniformed female driver, who could overhear their conversation, Jenny said in a low voice, 'I came merely to straighten out a few things left unsaid. I'm not in the least afraid of you.'

'I am of you.'

'The great sporting hero; son of a senator?'

215

Jim shook his head. 'An Air Force lieutenant trying to redeem his damaged reputation.'

'You won't do it with orchids.'

'I know that. I thought it might break the ice when we met up. It sure hasn't.'

After a moment she said, 'Sorry. While I was waiting, I had time to decide this was a mistake.'

'But you didn't go back to your room and leave a note telling me to go jump in the Thames.'

'I wouldn't do that. I was going to tell you to your face.'

'And?'

'I found I couldn't.'

'I see. Now we've got that out of the way can we sit back and enjoy the rest of the evening?' Taking the orchid from the box he began pinning it on the lapel of her jacket 'Can we also forget about senators and sport, and concentrate on a junior officer on his first date with an English girl?'

Jenny succumbed. 'You have a very persuasive manner, Lieutenant Benson.'

'How else would I have had my boss believe I was undertaking on his behalf an important duty engagement which demanded the use of an official car?' He put his finger to his lips and rolled his eyes in the direction of the driver. 'Shhh, she's one of his spies.'

It brought a faint smile from the girl beside him. 'I don't think you'd have much difficulty silencing her.'

Knowing he had broken through her reserve, Jim turned in the seat and put his arm along it behind her, starting to unwind. 'Let me tell you a little about my pal, Buck Etwell, known generally as Bucket.'

'You're not serious!' she exclaimed.

'As sure as I am Jehosaphat Tornado.'

Her smile remained. 'You never fooled me over that for one minute.'

'I'm not fooling now. He and I have been buddies since we met up at Harvard. He's a hotshot on drums, so I learned to play sax. We made a neat rhythm duo. I miss that now. It was a way of relaxing during our training, and the other guys enjoyed listening.' Suddenly he recalled that night at Carlstrom when the British cadets were elated over their first venture into the air, and Stallard had walked out the moment he and Bucket began to play. 'Some didn't appreciate it, of course, and saw it as

216

—' He broke off, unwilling to pursue a line that would destroy the fragile accord between them, but she was more perceptive than he guessed.

'If you're referring to Rob, I must put the record straight and tell you he's not in the least musical. Our parents were the same. I've always liked dance bands, but he can't stand them.'

It had been foolish of him to imagine they could avoid the subject, but now it had arisen he thought it best to exhaust it before they met Bucket and Cleo. 'Have you spoken with him?'

'He's been very tied up recently,' she said in a troubled manner. 'I'm sure something special is going on, but he can't tell me about it, of course. He's had no time off during a stand-down, which is odd enough in itself, and I've had no letters from him for some while. Since his birthday, in fact. I telephoned the Mess because I was worried. He sounded tense and ... and rather wound up. It was silly of me to mention you. I should have waited until we met at a time when he wasn't preoccupied with his work.'

Jim moved his arm back to his side and straightened, disliking talk of Stallard's involvement in the kind of flying he had again just been denied. 'I guess you'd be wasting your time whenever you mentioned my name. You shouldn't let him make your decisions for you.'

'It's more or less what he said.'

'That's why you're here tonight?'

She shook her head. 'I want to get to the bottom of why he's so touchy on the subject of J.T. Benson. I know him better than anyone does and —
'

'No, you don't,' Jim put in swiftly. 'You know what he was like two or three years ago when he lived with you and your parents. You're still thinking of him as that person. He's not. Accept that, and get on with your own life.'

Her eyes were almost hostile as she studied him. 'Have you brothers or sisters?' When he shook his head, she added, 'Then don't give advice on the subject.'

He gave her back stare for stare. 'You're a lot like him, you know that?'

'That's nothing to be ashamed of.'

'Did I say it was?'

She was disconcerted and fell silent. Then she reluctantly admitted that she had quarrelled quite seriously with her brother. 'Rob told me to do whatever I choose, yet I can't help feeling a traitor by being here with you.'

'Shall I tell the driver to forget the Savoy and drive us to the Tower of London? Isn't that where they chop off heads in this country?' he asked innocently.

A reluctant smile broke through. 'After paying so much to have my hair styled for the evening, I think it had better be the Savoy.'

The car turned into the approach to the hotel at that moment, and they both laughed when the driver announced, 'We're here, sir, and there's not a scaffold in sight.'

They got out in a much more relaxed mood, and Jim bent to the window. 'Thanks, Maree. Come back around midnight.'

As he took Jenny's arm to lead her in, she said, 'I don't intend to stay here as late as that.'

'Okay, we'll take a taxi to your hotel,' he said equably, knowing they would do no such thing unless he had lost his expertise at dining and dancing with an attractive woman.

Jim had reserved a table far enough from the dance floor to be undisturbed by constantly passing couples, and Bucket was already seated at it with a brunette in cream lace. He stood as they came up and greeted Jim with a hearty hug, but he was visibly more interested in the sister of the man he had sometimes defended in the face of others' condemnation.

Jim opened the formalities. 'Jenny, this old reprobate is my pal Bucket. Don't mention the word "jazz" or he'll talk all night.'

Bucket shook her hand, grinning. 'Same goes for him with any sports, Jenny. It's a real pleasure to meet you. How's your brother?'

Jim had warned his friend of the situation existing as a result of Stallard's letter, but Bucket, in his inimitable fashion, had clearly decided to bring matters into the open right away. Jenny responded with the calm assurance Jim was beginning to know.

'He's with a Mosquito squadron. This is his second operational tour, but he's still as mad as ever about flying.'

'He was a natural. Often said to J.T. loners make good pilots.'

218

'Are you truly called Bucket?' she asked. 'I never know when to believe Jim.'

'Sure am. Began at school; never stopped.' He turned to his girlfriend. 'Honey, meet Jenny Stallard, whose brother was with us at Carlstrom, and J.T. Benson.' He grinned at Jenny. 'Cleo never believes me, either. When I told her she was going to meet someone she's adored since high school she laughed it off. Now she'll have to eat humble pie.'

'Take no notice of him, Cleo,' Jim said, shaking her hand and wishing the American Red Cross girl was not gazing at him with stars in her eyes. He could throttle Bucket for speaking words which would support Stallard's declaration that J.T. Benson was always seeking attention.

They settled at the table and Jim resisted, with difficulty, the temptation to order champagne. He was the humble lieutenant tonight. Bucket never pretended to be anything other than the engaging character he was, and any initial awkwardness was dispersed by his efforts to make Jenny feel comfortable with three Americans. Jim realized his partner for the evening was more responsive to his friend than she had ever been to him. Bucket soon had her laughing, and it suddenly hit Jim that a sensation remarkably like resentment was overtaking him. Stallard's sister was a different person with another man.

They ordered dinner, then Bucket took Cleo off to the dance floor before it was served. Jim asked Jenny to dance, but she shook her head. 'Not just now.' They sat in silence for a moment or two, then she said, 'He's a very nice man. I like him.'

'I noticed you did.'

'His girlfriend can't stop gazing at *you* as if it's Christmas and Easter rolled into one,' she riposted.

'She's a bit dumb,' he said shortly. 'Bucket usually goes for the more intellectual type.'

'What type do you usually go for?'

'Didn't your brother tell you? As wolf-pack leader I go for *anything in a skirt*.'

Colour flooded her cheeks as she absorbed that barb, then she said quietly, 'This isn't going to work, is it?'

'Not unless you can forget him and make up your own mind about me. You won't do that by spending the evening talking to Bucket, leaving me to be ogled to death by a girl who's never matured beyond high school.'

He got to his feet. 'Now, are we leaving, or going on that dance floor to start getting acquainted?'

She stood, her colour still high, and picked up her evening bag. Then she gazed at him for a long moment and changed her mind. Setting the gold purse back on the table, she walked past him towards the open area.

Taking Jenny in a firm hold, Jim led her through a break in the circling couples with expertise. They danced in silence until the melody ended and another began in response to applause. Before she could head back to the table, Jim swung her into his arms and embarked on the quickstep, holding her very close. He enjoyed her nearness. She was wearing the right amount of perfume to produce a tantalizing hint of freshly picked flowers, and she was tall enough for her hair to brush his cheeks with a soft caress. He was sorry when the band ended that medley.

They left the floor still not having said a word, and no sooner had all four settled at the table than a waiter brought their first course and another served the wine Jim had selected. After a lighthearted toast to 'The War', when they clinked glasses and drank, Cleo asked Jenny how she had met the famous J.T. Benson. Jim cursed the girl and said swiftly, 'We just happened to bump into each other.'

Jenny smiled and said, with perfect poise, 'He's trying to avoid admitting that he knocked me off my feet — quite literally. He walked from our village church just as I was cycling past, and I came a cropper on the grass. He picked me up, one thing led to another, and I asked him home to tea. Had I known he was the famous J.T. Benson I wouldn't have dared,' she explained to Cleo. 'I thought he was just a lonely American soldier far from home. It wasn't until later that I learned who he really was. Was it?' she demanded of Jim, with a challenge in her eyes.

'That's right,' he agreed, making a note to equal the score as soon as he had the opportunity. This girl was no demure, docile partner. A date with her kept a man on his toes ... and kept him intrigued.

Bucket laughed. 'A guy has to be desperate if he knocks girls off their bicycles in order to gain attention. You must be losing your grip, J.T. But you're right, Jenny. He is just a lonely American soldier. We all are, so let's have fun tonight.'

Bucket asked Jenny to dance, so Jim was obliged to partner Cleo. He found her too short, too giggly and much too clinging. Over her head he watched the other pair laughing and chatting in complete harmony, and resentment of Stallard returned. Useless to tell his sister to do as she pleased when he had already poisoned her mind. She had the same inflexibility and determination as he, so what would it take to override her prejudice?

After the meal the two women went to the powder room, and Jim launched into Bucket the moment they were out of earshot.

'What the hell are you doing? I gave you a run-down of the situation, yet you're behaving like we were Stallard's best buddies.'

Bucket lit another cigarette and leaned back, unperturbed by the attack. '*I* didn't catch him puking behind the huts, *I* didn't steal his girl; it wasn't my old man who grabbed the chance of publicity from Stallard's cool exploit with Lawson. He's got no quarrel with me, kiddo.'

And it wasn't you who almost flew into him on that last day, Jim thought heavily.

'Who'd've guessed he had a sister like Jenny?' Bucket mused. 'She's a real lady.'

'Think I can't see that?' growled Jim.

Bucket smoked with nervous movements for a moment or two, then asked, 'So what's with this date tonight? She's not your type.'

'Cleo's not yours.'

Bucket shrugged. 'She's cute and she knows the score. You can't start anything serious in times like this. Life's too uncertain.'

'For you, maybe,' said Jim without thinking.

'They could still get you with a bomb as you walk down the street.'

Jim looked up sharply. 'Sorry, I was away on another track.' He sighed. 'General Flood sat on my third application to join a squadron. Told me tonight. No reason why *I* couldn't start something serious.'

'Have you?'

'With Jenny? Hell, no!'

Lighting another cigarette from the glowing stub, Bucket said, 'So you're using her to get at Stallard?'

'*No!*'

'So what are you doing with her?'

Jim was floored for a moment or two. 'Trying to prove to her he's wrong about me.'

'You *are* getting at her brother. Don't do it, J.T. She's a nice woman.'

'She's also very much on the ball. So far, I've only got as far as she decides to let me.'

'Either you're losing your touch, or you've met a sensible female for once in your career. Be careful. Two can play at games, and she might be running one with rules you've never come across before — like her brother.'

The women returned at that point and, as the band struck up another quickstep, Jim seized Jenny's hand. 'Let's dance!'

She was happy to talk now. 'You're a polished dancer. Add that to tennis ace, top football player, amateur saxophonist, wangler of official cars and you're quite formidable. Is there no end to your talents?'

He smiled down into eyes that appeared to hold nothing but amusement. 'How good am I at persuading a girl to trust me?'

'I'll let you know when I start doing it,' she countered coolly.

They circled the floor along with other couples happy to be in each other's arms. Jim drew her closer. She did not resist, which suggested to him that she had at least stopped fighting. Even at her most hostile he had known she was attracted to him physically. That was usually his most powerful weapon, but he was prevented by Stallard's letter from deliberately using it with this girl.

Jenny spoke beside his ear. 'Bucket said you've twice applied to be operational and been refused.'

'Make that three times.'

She drew away to look up at him. 'Why, Jim?'

'Why've I applied?'

'Why've you been turned down?'

He could not resist it. 'Not because your brother was right about me being a no-good pilot.'

'I didn't think that,' she said quietly. 'Why?'

'Because I'm who I am ... and because my father has to control me as he controls everyone else within his parameters. I defied him, and he won't allow anybody to do that, so he denies me what I most want.' He drew her closer again, murmuring against her temple, 'A flying instructor once gave me the soundest advice he knew: to change my name.'

'Why didn't you?'

'Because that's no way out.'

222

Jenny then said something very surprising. 'You men have a terrible time of it with fathers. It's so unfair.'

Before Jim had a chance to pursue that comment the dance ended, and they returned to the table. The evening progressed well after that. The low lights, the sweet music, the wine and the general atmosphere of enjoying life to the utmost affected them all. As Jim watched Jenny slowly melt beneath the combined lure of these things, he faced the questions Bucket had asked. Was he simply getting back at Stallard by chasing his sister, or was he starting something serious? Midnight came and he had reached no firm answer.

They took Cleo to the flat she shared with two other Red Cross girls, and Bucket went in for a nightcap after suggesting they all repeat their evening sometime. Resisting the impulse to put his arm round Jenny as the car set off for her hotel through streets now completely blacked out, Jim did not even take her hand. He intended to see her again, so would not risk jeopardizing that vow. He instead picked up on her earlier comment.

'What prompted your remark about men and their fathers?'

She turned as if from a daydream. 'Oh ... sons are often expected to take over from their fathers when they're old enough, even when they make it clear they've set their heart on something else. My father wasn't in a position of power, like yours, but he gave Rob a very hard time.'

Back to her brother, but he had to ask, 'In what way?'

'I can't go into it. He was angry at me for telling you about our parents and grandmother. Absolutely furious. He's a very private person.'

'How can he expect people to understand him if he clams up all the time?' At her silence, he said, 'You're a little like that. Tonight you've talked about your Polish refugees, a tea party for the evacuees, cultural outings for foreign troops in England, and various movies you've seen, but nothing about J.T. Stallard. You did say your initials were the same as mine?'

'Yes, they are.'

'But not the housekeeper's?'

She smiled. 'You knew that, I'm sure.'

At that point the night was rent by the nearby wail of a siren warning of approaching enemy aircraft. Jim was annoyed. 'That happens each time I'm in town.'

'It also happens when you're not. They're not after the famous J.T. Benson.' She put her hand on his arm. 'Sorry. It was meant as a joke, but I can see you didn't take it that way. We British have a very individual sense of humour.'

The warning had come a little late. The drone of aircraft could already be heard overhead, and very soon searchlights raked the sky to fasten on the large black shapes of enemy bombers just as the first distant thud of explosions reached them.

'They're after the docks again,' Jenny murmured, gazing upward through the window at the aircraft caught in the converged beams. 'There'll be nothing left of them soon.'

Jim moved closer. 'Are you afraid?'

'That one will get me?' she asked, gazing back at him. 'There's a general belief that we'll be all right unless one has our name on it. If it has, then running or hiding won't make any difference.'

Another instance of the Stallard imperturbability, he thought, moving away again. Yet she did not appear so calm when the thuds grew nearer and nearer. 'They're bombing indiscriminately! I was starting to feel sorry for the poor devils caught in the searchlights — they're only men doing a job, and I always think of Rob caught like that and being shot at over Germany — but they're dropping them anywhere.'

The streets around them were filling with racing police cars and ambulances, and the sky to the west was now glowing orange. A deadly imitation of sunset. They were flagged down by a tin-hatted man wearing a Red Cross armband. He bent to shine a torch at them.

'I thought you were on official business, sir,' he said coldly. 'As you're not, I must ask you to leave the car and take cover. We need to 'ave the streets cleared for emergency traffic. The shelter's just down there on the right.' He addressed the driver. 'Leave the car just where it is, miss.'

'Okay, Maree, do as he says,' Jim told her.

Out on the pavement, he took the arms of both girls and walked them towards a dimly lit sign marking an air-raid shelter halfway down the street. The night air was humid and filled with the smell of burning from incendiaries giving off the fiery light which now illuminated the city, making nonsense of the blackout. The next thud shook the ground beneath their feet. Jim quickened his pace, urging the two women to reach the concrete haven, certain the bombs were falling in a straight line and they were on that line.

Next minute, he heard a curious whoosh and the shelter disappeared before his eyes as the houses standing along that street collapsed on it. He acted instinctively by throwing the women to the ground and covering them with his body, as a wall of heat hit them and pieces of debris rained all around. It all appeared to occur within a split second. Jim had no time to think, to absorb the full details of what was happening, so when he eventually raised his head he stared in shock at the place where they had been heading. There was a raging fire devouring furniture and materials strewn over the remains of what had been people's homes until a moment ago. The shelter was somewhere beneath the conflagration.

Despite the heat, he turned cold as he realized that only the grace of God had saved them from that. He grew aware of sobbing and shifted his weight from the women beneath him. Maree was shaking and tearful as she gazed at the car, which had been blown over and was now also burning.

'Oh God, I'm responsible for that automobile,' she moaned, focusing her shocked senses on the vehicle rather than the greater horror behind her. Jim put a restraining arm round the girl and held her back against his chest in comfort while he twisted to face Jenny, who was struggling into a sitting position, also covered in dust and fragments of debris. She appeared to be dangerously calm, although tears streaked her blackened cheeks as she stared at him.

'I thought they'd taken enough Stallards already, but that was ...' She put a shaking hand up to rest on his face as if checking that it was warm and real. 'Thank you. *Thank you*!'

*

It was five a.m. before Jim reached his quarters, still badly shaken and ready for several hours' sleep before reporting for duty in his office, so he ignored the message on his dresser telling him to report to General Flood as soon as he got in. The corridors had been deserted as he walked through. Who was to know what time he got back? He took off his shoes and jacket, pulled free his tie, then stretched out on the bed and fell asleep.

When he was awoken by his orderly it seemed to Jim that he had only that minute closed his eyes, but two hours had passed.

'General Flood wants to see you urgently, Mr Benson. I left a message for you but I guess you didn't see it.'

Jim yawned and stretched. 'Only just got in, Shriver. There was a raid in town.' He sat up and yawned again. 'I'll get cleaned up and then go see him. Fetch me some coffee.'

'No time for that, sir,' said the timid soldier. 'The General's been up half the night waiting for you. He ain't too happy, according to Captain Muskett. The Captain, he says I shoulda come in every five minutes to check on when you were back. He says a message gets overlooked.'

'It did,' lied Jim, 'but I'll make it right with Captain Muskett. You're not to blame.' He stood and headed for the bathroom. 'Take out my other uniform. You'll have to get this one cleaned.' As he gave himself the swiftest shave of his life, Jim wondered what the crisis could be. He had no illusions that Hitler had surrendered, or that some other momentous development had changed the state of the war. The whole place would have been buzzing when he came in two hours ago.

Shriver still looked scared as Jim dressed quickly. 'Sorry about the message, sir ... and the coffee.'

'Can't be helped,' he said briefly, 'but another time bring coffee when you come to check on me. I could've drunk two cups by now.'

The orderly looked even more miserable. 'Captain Muskett, he said —'

'Never mind.' Jim was growing irritated. He was still half asleep and this sort of incident was the worst aspect of his job. He was a trained pilot acting as a 'grounded dogsbody'. Damn Stallard!

John Muskett looked bleary-eyed and jumpy when Jim entered his office and asked, 'What's this all about?'

'Best go to him,' came the curt reply. 'He's been waiting for you since two a.m. and he's mad as a skunk.'

'He might have waited for ever if a stick of incendiaries had dropped a tad closer,' Jim informed him. 'I'm lucky to be here at all.'

'Tell *him* that!'

Contrary to his expectation, Jim was not bawled out the minute he entered the large salon serving as an office and private sitting room for a man with immense responsibilities. The General's face was drawn when he glanced up at Jim, and all he said was a quiet, 'So you finally got my message.'

'Sorry, sir, I was caught up in that raid last night.' He stood just inside the door, sensing that his boss was deeply affected by the reason for this summons. 'The car was destroyed — I'll write a full report — and I had to get the ladies to a place of safety, then back to their hotel. With taxis off the street for a time, it was difficult.'

Flood indicated one of the easy chairs facing him. 'Come and have some coffee.'

More puzzled than ever, Jim crossed to the table, which bore a tray with a large jug and several cups. He sat, gratefully poured himself some coffee, and began drinking it as he waited for the other man to get down to business.

Red-rimmed, hazel eyes surveyed him for a few moments, then the General said, 'I've some God-awful news for you, Jim. I wanted to tell you before you heard some other way.'

Jim's hand stilled as he was lowering the cup to its saucer, and a sixth sense told him this news concerned him alone. 'Is it my father? He's dead?'

Flood shook his head. 'Late last evening, Washington time, Senator Benson was visited by the FBI. At exactly the same time, the head office of Benson Pharmaceuticals was occupied by men from the Bureau who have put a freeze on all trading with the company and its numerous subsidiaries. Theo and Shelley are under round-the-clock surveillance. He has been charged with misappropriation of government funds, falsifying documents to secure contracts, and corrupt business practice.'

Jim stared at the florid face across the table without seeing it. So his father had finally reached for something and failed. He had tried to be just *too* clever, *too* manipulative. As Jim's brain slowly came out of shock it told him a number of things. FBI investigations followed a long, tortuous course, and only when the evidence was overwhelming and indisputable did they move in on the subjects of them. Even without further details he could see the truth. The company had grown too big, bitten off more than it could chew. Running for the Senate had been Theo's bid to save the sick giant. Once in power he would be in a position to influence the granting of contracts, and to buy the allegiance of ambitious juniors or men with guilty secrets in their personal lives.

Small wonder James Theodore Benson II had been desperate to use everything, including his son's military career, to be voted in.

With a sick feeling in the pit of his stomach, Jim faced the fact that, but for the war, he would have been pushed into an ailing corporation at the sacrifice of his own future. He would now have been enmeshed in these sordid revelations. There was no doubt in his mind that Theo would have kept him in the dark throughout. He could only be deeply thankful his mother had been spared the pain and humiliation. Shelley would survive intact. Women of her type always did.

'I knew Theo quite well some years back,' the other man said heavily. 'It's hit *me*, and I'm sorry to smack you with it this way, but it's going to be in the headlines over here pretty soon and I'd hate you to read it over morning coffee, along with everyone else.'

'I appreciate your gesture, sir.'

'I've arranged a flight home for you at the end of the week. Earliest I could manage. There's not much traffic going west. They're all coming over here.' Flood gave a gusty sigh. 'Every goddam healthy American'll be out of the country if this war goes on much longer.'

Alarmed at the prospect at being the only healthy American left in the country if he now returned, Jim said quickly, 'I'd rather not go back. There's no way my return could help my father, and the Press would dish up a whole lot of lies about me to worsen the situation. It's better if I stay where I am during this critical period.'

The General sighed even more noisily, and fixed Jim with a straight look. 'You've got to understand this puts a different slant on things. I was glad to keep you on my staff as a favour to your father, and because you're the right kind of young officer to impress the stiff-necked people I have to deal with ... but I can't now have Senator Benson's son working in a situation where high-level, top-priority topics are discussed and where he has access to sensitive documents.' His famous gimlet-eyed stare added to the bluntness of his words. 'You get my meaning?'

'Yes, sir,' Jim agreed woodenly, evidence of how Theo's fall from grace would affect his own standing starting to become devastatingly clear. Then, through the gathering clouds, he saw a faint light and moved in on it. 'Perhaps you'd be good enough to reconsider my application to join an operational squadron. I imagine there'll no longer be any reluctance to put Lieutenant Benson in the firing line.'

*

Rob flew back across the Channel in the afternoon after a hit-and-run raid. The squadron had been involved in a series of them throughout August because the weather had been perfect for low-level attacks on shipping. They had been very successful until today, when they had lost two Mosquitoes. A nineteen-year-old untried pilot officer had been shot down, and a more experienced man named Beamish had inexplicably failed to pull up after dropping his load, and flown into the low hill backing the harbour. His wife was due to have a baby at any hour, so half his mind could have been elsewhere. No one would ever know, and there would be four empty seats in the Mess tonight.

It had been hectic over the target, and they had only outrun the fighters by flying very fast and low on the way home. Now the danger was over, Rob sat at the controls weary and silent. Donald was also uncommunicative as he contemplated a run of bullet holes in the entrance door just ahead of his feet. A lucky miss!

Rob wondered why he had ever been so mad keen on flying. The thrill had gone out of it lately. It seemed to have gone out of everything. He had bought a gramophone and records of his favourite symphonies and concertos, but whereas he had before been threatened with dire reprisals by his less appreciative fellow officers for playing Beethoven, Wagner or Tchaikovsky at full volume, there was now silence in his room when he occupied it. Hearing the recordings made the break with Rebecca even more painful. He was even fed up with his motorbike. The badge on it reminded him of his rift with Jenny, caused by Benson.

As he followed his squadron leader in a formation which had closed up to fill the two gaps, Rob brooded on the letter he had received from her this morning in reply to his, repeating all he had told her about J.T. Benson. Newspapers had spared no details of the Senator's downfall, and were now delving into the private life of his celebrated son who, according to the more reckless editors, had been removed from his trusted position on Brigadier General Flood's staff and shunted into a secret backwater overnight. There were hints that the only 'active service' he had been engaged in was in the bedrooms of a succession of women, if he was running true to form. Rob had not hesitated to write and point out that his sister must surely now realize why he had tried to warn her of the man.

Rob had been sent a reserved reply describing the date she had had with Benson, at the end of which he had protected her during a raid by throwing himself over her to take the full force of the blast himself. She had apparently been introduced to Bucket during the evening.

Such a friendly, amusing person, who spoke your praises. He did not appear to be aware of any instances at Carlstrom which would account for your vendetta with Jim. I wish I knew what was behind it, Rob, so that I could mediate. As Jim said, how can you expect people to understand you if you keep everything to yourself?

That part of her letter had made Rob furious. How dared she discuss him so frankly with someone she must surely now acknowledge to be all he had said? The British press stated it in headlines even if she continued to disbelieve him.

There was no doubt Benson had achieved his aim in turning sister against brother, because Jenny had written that she always took with a pinch of salt what the scandal rags published.

Clearly the father has done what many men in power do, but there's no need to tar his son with the same brush. Rob, I don't want to upset you over this but I suggest you consider what we were like in nineteen forty-one and allow that Jim has changed as much as we have in two years. It might also help to put yourself in his shoes and imagine what it must do to him to have his name bandied about by every news hack around.

That never bothered the famous J.T. Benson in the past, Rob thought sourly as he recalled Jenny's concluding words before she bade him to take great care, and to visit Thoresby as soon as he had a few days' leave. Sighing, he told himself home was no longer in Somerset and, if she was going to gush over that man the whole time, he had no real wish to see his sister and continue the row.

Receiving instructions from their leader to land after himself and his two wing-men, Rob acknowledged and fell back to line up behind Flight Lieutenant Clunes and ahead of Johnny. As he did so, Donald broke their long silence.

'Fancy a trip to the Wheatsheaf after dinner? In my MG, not on that oil-spattered contraption of yours.'

'Not tonight.'

Getting together his maps, log book and instruments ready to leave the seat he had occupied for the past five and half hours, the Navigator said,

'The gang'll be going. It's the only thing to do with the rest of a day like this.'

Rob ignored him. There was only one thing he wanted to do with the rest of the day, and he had deliberately cut himself off from the girl he loved.

'You've not still moping over those tests, are you?' asked Donald. 'There'll be other inventions.' He added, as Rob touched down with a heavy bump, 'Maybe even one that'll allow to you to land a damn sight better than that.'

'If you'd shut up I could concentrate.'

After parking in his usual position and going through the familiar routine, Rob squeezed through the front access door where his ground crew had hooked up the short ladder. Pulling off his helmet, he told Corporal Fleet that one of the guns had packed up.

'There's also a hole in the port aileron, as well as those four in the door, and it's much bigger than them, so you'll have to bung it up good and proper. I'll take a look tomorrow morning.'

'Right you are, sir.'

'Wotcher!' Johnny greeted Rob, falling in beside him as the crews headed for debriefing.

'What happened to you?' Rob asked, studying his friend's oil-smeared face and tunic.

'You know that chap you hit? He hit me first.'

'Most unsporting of him,' said a South African from the middle of the group. 'He should never have started something he couldn't finish.'

The banter faded into the background as Rob covertly studied Johnny's face. He had survived the jitters and married his Lucy last month. He had been hit on numerous occasions, but had he been careless today? Had he lost concentration? Had his thoughts strayed to his lively wife during that vital time? Rob had noticed that his friend rang Lucy every evening when the station was closed for impending operations. Ostensibly, it was to whisper sweet nothings, but Rob knew the true reason was to let her know she had not become a widow that day. Freddie Beamish's wife had, just three hours ago. She did not know it yet. She was probably packing baby clothes with suppressed excitement. The child she was about to produce did not know there would be no father when it arrived in this war-torn world. Why had Beamish not taken all that into account when marrying the girl?

As he waited in the stifling hut to give his report on the raid, Rob stared morosely at the wall, where someone had defiantly pinned a poster of a nude girl with unbelievable breasts. Scribbled beneath were the words 'Isn't she worth fighting for?' That was what he needed tonight, Rob decided. He had been too long without it. A girl like that did not put a chap in a quandary about what he wanted and what his duty was. A girl like that was just right for getting it out of his system, but leaving no sense of guilt. Standing there in a room fouled by the combined smells of aviation fuel, engine oil, cigarette smoke and sweating bodies, the full force of what he had resolutely given up hit Rob. Then he remembered Beamish's wife and the news she would shortly receive. He could not put Rebecca through that, however much he might want her.

'Rob, you're wanted by the CO.'

He came from his reverie to focus on the face of Squadron Leader James Ford. 'When?'

'Now, apparently. Soon as the squadron lands, the message reads. It's just been handed to me.' He waved the slip of paper at Rob and grinned. 'What have you been up to?'

'Christ knows. It can't be the motorbike. I haven't even kicked it over for three days.'

'He wouldn't nab you the minute we touched down for that. Better get over there and find out the depth of your crime. Wee Willie can do the necessary here,' he said, quoting the name for Rob's navigator everyone but he used. 'Don't look so grim. You might have been awarded another gong to go with the DFC for your raid over Holland. That was good shooting today, by the way. Pity you hadn't got the bugger before he fixed Freddie. But at least he won't be bragging about it at dinner tonight.'

'Neither will Freddie,' Rob said heavily. 'Who's going to tell his wife?'

'I'll run over to the house this evening and break the news, unless she's in the throes of giving birth in the cottage hospital. Bloody war!'

Ford turned away, leaving Rob mentally echoing those last words as he left the stale confines of the hut. As he plodded along in his heavy boots and crumpled battledress, Rob's mouth twisted. So much for Donald's only way to end a day like this! What the hell could the Wingco want that was so urgent?

As soon as he entered the outer office Rob's heartbeat quickened dramatically. The inner door stood open, so he saw Rebecca clearly as she sat with a cup of tea in her hands. He had not arrived quietly so his presence was immediately obvious to all three in the office.

'Come in, Stallard,' called his CO genially. 'Heard the squadron arrive. You're just in time for a cup of tea.'

Flushed and completely thrown off balance, Rob moved forward with eyes only for the girl gazing at him in a manner that made his toes curl tighter than ever before.

Russell Lambourne got to his feet with a wide smile, hand outstretched. 'Hallo, Ron, it's good to see you again.'

'Hallo, sir,' Rob managed, miserably conscious of his own scruffy appearance next to the neatly dressed man, whose daughter looked unbearably beckoning in a low-cut lemon silk summer dress with pearl buttons adorning each shoulder. He addressed the girl he loved in as formal a manner as he could muster. 'Good afternoon, Miss Lambourne,'

She spoiled it by saying softly, 'You look tired out, poor lamb!'

'Sit down, Stallard,' Averell invited with a touch of amusement as he pushed a cup of tea across his desk. 'Get that down you, man; you probably need it. Professor and Miss Lambourne have a meeting in London at twenty hundred, and I thought you should hear what they have to say before they leave in a few minutes.'

'Yes, sir.' The Wing Commander's words went over Rob's head as he sat acknowledging the painful joy of being near Rebecca again. Exhausted, as usual, by the cessation of intense concentration, physical and mental strain, he could only focus on one thing at a time, and the red-haired beauty smelling of Chanel was it.

'I've solved the problems we ran up against,' said Lambourne, leaning forward in his eagerness. 'You're the one who outlined the faults with the system, so if you look at our modifications and pronounce them acceptable I can put them before the men who matter tonight.'

'Rob's the man who matters,' said Rebecca. 'He's testing it for you.'

'But he hasn't the power to give the go-ahead, my dear,' her father pointed out.

'If he says it'll work that will *be* the go-ahead,' she argued. 'The men behind desks in London have no idea what he has to do in order to get them a new kind of weapon. *They're* not taking any risks, are they?'

Rob sat on in a dazed state while his love held a lively argument in praise of him. She had not answered his carefully worded letter. Although it had been intended as a farewell, he had nevertheless waited daily for a reply indicating that she at least understood the reasoning behind it. There had been none, and he had finally given up hope, to ride out the pain of losing her. Now here she was, behaving as if his letter had never reached her and there had not been six awful weeks since he had written it.

It was an effort to concentrate on the drawings Lambourne unrolled across Dennis Averell's map-table, but Rob somehow managed to absorb the gist of the modifications and give his opinion that they appeared to address those points he had made at the conclusion of the tests. Twin beams ought to solve the main problem.

'They'd have to be tried out before we could be certain,' he added. 'I'd like to be in on it if there are any further trials, sir.'

Lambourne was re-rolling his drawings. 'If we tell them tonight that the test pilot is happy with the mods. I'm sure they'll give the go-ahead. Thank you, Roy.'

Rebecca stood and slipped her hand into Rob's. 'Have you finished with him now, Dennis?'

Rob saw his CO completely discountenanced for the first time in their association. 'Oh, er ... I suppose ... er, yes. Yes,' he repeated faintly, no less uncomfortable than Rob.

'We'll be outside, Father,' she said serenely, then led Rob firmly through the absent Adjutant's office to the warmth of a westering sun and the balm of a breeze wafting the scent of haymaking from nearby farms. If it had not been for the rows of huts, the parked aircraft, the camouflaged trucks, the men and women in blue uniforms criss-crossing between them all, it would have been possible to enjoy the bewitchment of late-summer rural England. Wartime reminders were there, however, and the strong smell of aviation fuel ruined the illusion of country peace borne on the breeze.

Rob pulled his hand free and turned on Rebecca. 'I can't just walk out on him like that. He's my Commanding Officer!'

She smiled up at him. 'Don't worry about Dennis. He's a real sweetie, who understands about us.'

'That's more than I do. Why didn't you answer my letter?' he demanded, very worked up.

'Because I wanted you to suffer a little.'

'A little? It's been *six weeks*!'

'According to your letter, you wanted to suffer for ever more,' she pointed out.

He could think of no answer to that as he gazed down into her face, wondering how he had ever managed to write a final farewell to someone he wanted so badly. 'I've missed you like hell,' he confessed.

'That's why I let it go on for so long. *I* knew what it would be like if we didn't see each other, but you didn't.'

'I had a bloody good idea.'

'Then you're more stubborn than I guessed, you adorable idiot.' She kissed him lingeringly on the mouth. 'Why didn't you write again when it got too bad?'

'You can only say goodbye once.'

After studying him for several moments with troubled eyes, she said, 'I've never seen you like this before; straight from the killing fields. You look so ... it frightens me.'

'If we weren't in such a damn public place I'd frighten you even more,' he said forcefully. 'You look good enough to eat, and I'm really hungry.'

'You always are. But you'll find your dinner more satisfying than me.'

'No, I won't. You look pretty tasty from here.'

This brighter mood brought a return of her assertiveness and she immediately put sunshine back into his life. 'I have two tickets for a charity gala on Saturday. It'll be your introduction to an orchestral concert, and you'll love the programme. Some of your favourites. Father and I are staying at our apartment in town for several days. If you're not flying on Saturday, Dennis says you can came up and stay overnight to discuss the results of tonight's meeting, if we get the go-ahead. I'll make sure you forget all that nonsense you wrote in your letter.'

The appearance of his CO and her father spared Rob a response to that provocative statement, and he felt distinctly lightheaded as Lambourne shook his hand and clapped him on the shoulder with a promise that he would get the go-ahead at the meeting. Rebecca completed that sensation by kissing him swiftly before climbing into the official car that would take her and her father to the station.

'See you on Saturday, darling,' she called from the window as the car moved off. 'Goodbye, Dennis.'

Averell turned to a red-faced Rob. 'How did it go today?'

Rob relaxed while speaking professionally with his Commanding Officer. He could always handle anything to do with flying, but kisses in front of his CO knocked him off course. 'They were ready for us over the harbour, sir. They've probably caught on to the fact that we've been going for the same kind of target lately.'

'Umm! A sign that we should change our tactics, perhaps.'

'Beamish bought it soon after his run in. Squadron Leader Ford saw a fighter after him shortly before he crashed into the hillside. Young Falconer went before he knew what had hit him. Blown to smithereens.'

'The rest back safely?'

'A bit shot up, sir, but still walking and talking.'

'Good. Cut along to the Mess and unwind. I'll do my best to get you assigned to further tests if Professor Lambourne wins them over tonight.'

'He will. He's very persuasive.'

'So is his daughter, apparently.'

To hide his embarrassment Rob saluted and beat a hasty retreat. Nearing the Mess, he became aware of a group of his colleagues, fresh from debriefing, watching his approach with broad grins. His heart sank to his boots. They had seen Rebecca and those public kisses!

He made a dash for his room, hotly pursued by laughing young men who had found an unexpectedly enjoyable way to brighten a day like they had just had.

Chapter Fourteen

On Friday they attacked the Ruhr in company with another Mosquito squadron. The Americans had been mounting massive daylight raids on German industrial targets with their heavily armed bombers aptly named Flying Fortresses, but they had taken such appalling losses that the surviving crews were being rested while morale was raised. The RAF decided to try their own hit-and-run format during their ally's lull in activity, and hit really hard.

The other squadron was to lead, and they rendezvoused just after dawn on another clear day. Rob was calm and ready for anything as he took off into a rose-pink sky, where stars were still faintly visible. He thought it a most beautiful heaven to climb into and was held silent by the superb thrill of doing so. How could he have forgotten the overwhelming joy of flying? His heart soared with his aircraft as he saw gleaned fields, the dark green patches of woodland, and the white cliffs of England lying below in the pale wash of dawn. That girl with unbelievable breasts on the poster might be worth fighting for, but this was what he fought for. Yeoman blood was in his veins, and he loved his country passionately.

'There they are,' called Donald into the silence. 'Right on the button.'

Rob could see the distant dots of the squadron they were to meet, circling to home in on them. 'They'd better not grab all the action and leave us looking like lemons,' he murmured.

'I could always make a mistake and send us on a course that would give us a mite of exclusive action,' Donald suggested.

'No one would believe you'd made a mistake. You're too bloody clever.'

'Thanks. When are we starting tests on the modified system, by the way?'

'We haven't heard yet whether Lambourne got permission.'

'Your girl must be even brainier than me. Doesn't she scare the daylights out of you?'

'Shut up and concentrate on your sums, or *you'll* scare the daylights out of me,' said Rob, neatly avoiding a conversation about something he felt was private and personal.

They crossed the sea at five hundred feet like a flock of fast, graceful birds, and continued over hostile territory in precise formation. Rob was perfectly relaxed and happy as he kept his eye on his wing-men and the one directly ahead. Tomorrow he would see Rebecca. He would spend an entire weekend with her. A warning voice told him he was playing with fire, but he really needed this to look forward to. Life had become stale lately, and it was not as if he would be living at Romney Marsh as he had before. It was only an overnight visit to combine pleasure with business. The occasional meeting with Rebecca would surely do no harm so long as he kept things under control. Everyone now knew about her, so it would not hurt to have regular dates with her. It would put the relationship on a more normal basis. He would worry about where it was heading when he felt more in the mood for it. Right now, he did not.

On nearing the target things began happening with a vengeance. The ground defences opened up, and the formation broke to present less of a target. Big guns were seldom successful against very fast aircraft, but they created a great deal of noise and distraction the crews could do without. Enemy fighters were the real danger. These appeared soon after the leading Mosquitoes began their attack, and they provided even greater distraction to those crews waiting to drop their bombs. Rob gave a burst of fire whenever a fighter entered his gunsight, but he was primed to go in on cue.

'Keep her steady,' Donald begged as they made their approach.

'Tell them, not me,' muttered Rob, struggling to do just that as the aircraft was rocked by bursting shells and the suicidal swoops of fighters passing close with guns spitting. The morning was turning into every flier's nightmare, so when Donald announced the shedding of their bombs Rob was relieved. He had already seen one Mosquito on fire, and willed its crew to drop theirs fast. A fire could often be doused. He had done it himself, and limped home. With explosive weapons still aboard the chances were less.

'You can jump about as much as you like now,' said Donald's voice in his ear.

'Not me, chum, I'm dropping to treetop level and dashing for home.'

Even as Rob spoke his senses froze. A Ju88 dropped from the sky and pounced on a Mosquito just turning in a steep evasive climb thus presenting a perfect target. The fighter hurtled towards the aircraft, which was performing a tricky manoeuvre during its most vulnerable moments directly after the run on the target, pouring bullets into the fuselage with deadly accuracy. The victim appeared to hang motionless for several seconds, the climb suspended, before slipping sideways out of control.

Rob watched, helpless and appalled, as Johnny's Mosquito began to belch dark smoke before an explosion heralded vivid flames. Burning chunks dropped away from the doomed machine as it slowly broke up and spiralled down into the inferno being created on the ground. The cockpit became a ball of fire that threw off flaming fragments in every direction, before it was swallowed up within the pall of smoke over the target area: a brilliant glow suddenly extinguished as if it had never been there in the savage sky.

'Rob. *Rob!*' A hand gripped his arm, and a familiar voice said, 'Let's go home, shall we?'

He came out of shock aware of a screaming noise, then realized he was in a fast dive heading for a heavily built-up area. Pulling up the nose, he levelled out very close to the ground and turned on the course the voice gave him, leaving the glare of fire behind as he raced for home.

Merciful numbness enabled Rob to sleep the sleep of exhaustion that night. In the morning he telephoned Rebecca to tell her he would be unable to arrive in time for dinner.

'Is everything all right, darling?'

'Something's cropped up, that's all.'

'Get here as early as you can. We don't want to miss the start of the concert. I'll give you some supper afterwards. Can't promise lamb chops. Scrambled dried egg is more likely,' she added with a chuckle. 'See you tonight.'

Rob stayed on the station until lunchtime, hoping for a message that would put an end to the horror deep within him. Johnny had a lovely young wife, and he was going to be a father just before Christmas. Men had walked away from the most terrible smash-ups before now. Everyone had imagined Stallard was a goner a few months ago. He had instead been snugged up on Romney Marsh with a stunning redhead. Johnny had better not be on that game. He was a married man.

Rob eventually set out to visit Lucy, attacking the roads as if to punish them for suggesting his friend would never follow them to his house again. Only half his mind was on his journey. The other half was reviewing a kaleidoscope of memories. Johnny had determinedly become his friend at Carlstrom. They had waltzed and foxtrotted in each other's arms in that sun-drenched room where they had also grappled with the complexities of aeronautics and navigation. Johnny had tried to save him from drowning, until the famous J.T. Benson had taken over. Johnny it was who had found an obliging woman to initiate his friend into the delights of sexual intimacy. They had both studied, flown and played all across the state of Florida, and they had stood side by side for the presentation of their wings.

Rob gulped in air to relieve the pressure in his chest as the memories switched to home, and wartime flying. Many had been lost in the skies over Europe but Johnny had remained. He was always there on clambering down that short ladder from the cockpit, grinning and saying, 'Wotcher!' Rob had stood with him at the altar, and then said some very rude things about him at the reception. He had already been designated godfather to John Percival Bradshaw the Second. How they had laughed over that! It was to Johnny that he had reluctantly confessed his feelings for Rebecca after those public kisses.

Lucy was incredibly composed as she kissed his cheek and said she was glad to see him. Her big blue eyes searched his face, which seemed to have frozen into immobility. 'Johnny and I had so little time together. You surely knew him better than I did, Rob.'

'No,' he said hastily. 'Well, in a different way. He *loved* you.'

'And he always will, now. I shan't have to worry about time changing what we had.' She sat on the chintz-covered settee and patted the space beside her. As he perched on the cushioned seat, she asked, 'You saw what happened?' When he nodded, she said, 'Tell me honestly whether or not he would have suffered.'

Rob visualized that flying funeral pyre and lied. 'It was far too quick.'

'Thank God!'

Closing his mind to the thought of Johnny, and Bob Reynolds fighting to get out and screaming with agony, Rob asked, 'What ... will you be all right ... with the baby, I mean?'

She gripped his hand. 'I haven't told Mummy and Daddy yet. I wanted to be alone last night, and I think I'll leave it another day. I need to have a while longer in this dear little house I shared with him. Can you understand that?'

'Yes,' he said with perfect truth. 'I think you should stay here for as long as you want to. Is there anything I can do?'

'Come and see me sometimes. Talk to me about him; about the things he didn't have time to tell me.'

'Of course I'll come. I promised him I would.'

Her eyes began to swim with tears. 'So you discussed it?'

He groped in his inside pocket. 'There's a letter. We all write one when we go operational.' He put the crumpled envelope in her hands together with a signet ring. 'He always took it off when flying.' Lucy's tears began to overflow and Rob wondered what he should do about it. 'Are you all right?'

Gazing down at the envelope, she said, 'This must be very painful for you, and I'd like to read this by myself. Do you mind going now, dear Rob?'

At the door, he said awkwardly, 'Ring if you need me.'

He was so late arriving at the Lambournes' flat that he had time for no more than a wash, a change of shirt and a cup of tea that he drank too fast, burning his tongue. Rebecca looked wonderful in a long black dress cut very low. Rob longed to suggest they forget the concert and stay where they were, but she swept him along in her usual fashion.

'I've ordered a taxi. It's no use trying to pick one up in the streets. The Yanks are given priority.'

'They give bigger tips.'

Rebecca sat close to him in the taxi, and he took her hand, enjoying her perfume. He was about to kiss her to compensate for the inadequate one she had given him on arrival, when she asked what had made him so late. For thirty minutes he had almost forgotten. Now she had reminded him, and the limbo had ended.

'Something came up.'

'Father hung on as long as he could, but he had to leave in time to deliver his lecture. I didn't expect you to arrive on that noisy machine of yours. Why didn't you travel up by train in a civilized manner?'

'For the same reason I don't drink sherry, I expect.'

She began to chuckle. 'I love you in your mulish mood. Winning you over is so much fun.' He gazed out of the window, knowing he was not up to a gala occasion, and she asked, 'What's wrong, darling?'

She had to repeat the question, with growing concern, before he turned to her and forced a smile. 'You look so gorgeous, you should be with a chap who knows what's what. The thought of a gala, with you looking like that, is making my knees knock.'

'Is this the man wearing a DFC ribbon; the man who carried out low-level tests with an untried weapon system?' she teased gently.

'I know what I'm doing then. I'm not sure about tonight.'

'I am,' she declared. 'You're going to have the most wonderful time of your life.'

The glittering vestibule behind the blackout curtains was crowded; the vocal volume was deafening. The women were richly dressed and hung with jewels. The men wore tails or uniform with medals. A flying officer with a single ribbon on his chest was very small fry, Rob realized.

Rebecca appeared to know everyone and was accosted by far too many men with the prefix 'Doctor' for Rob's liking. Presumably, they were the boffins she had mentioned, for they were not in the least interested in a mere working pilot.

Gazing around in growing boredom, Rob saw, with a sense of shock and dismay, his sister and Molly Guthrie. They were standing with a group of American officers. Jenny looked animated and extremely attractive in a long dress of blue shimmering material. She was laughing up at a blond giant with wings on his chest, which made Rob see how very easily she had gained social assurance. She looked right in a company such as this. She also appeared to have a marked partiality for Americans, he thought heavily, although Benson would no longer be welcome among these people.

Jenny had not seen him, and Rob was wondering about the best way to handle this situation when the group shifted slightly and he saw a face he knew. Buck Etwell was now a captain. He looked older, but Rob clearly remembered that good-natured face and the shock of ginger hair. He remembered the pilot standing beside him, also from Carlstrom days. Jordan from Nashville, who had introduced his hero and Bucket on that first day. What did he think of Benson now?

Rob spotted Pat Chance, the vet's daughter, with the group. Good God, had the whole of Thoresby turned American? It was then that he decided not to approach his sister. It would be too awkward for them both, especially with Bucket and Jordan there. Watching her with a hollow feeling in his stomach, Rob acknowledged that the girl who had been so close to him throughout their youth no longer existed. She was now Jenny Guthrie in all but name.

Rebecca touched his hand. 'Rob, they're taking their seats. Thank heavens! Wasn't that pure purgatory? Were you terribly bored?' When he nodded, she squeezed his hand. 'Poor lamb! We had to go through it so that we can hear the concert.'

Rob began to thaw out a little once the conductor entered and the lights dimmed to bring a welcome hush. When the music began, the tenseness of his body gradually eased. Stirred by the sound of a huge orchestra playing the kind of music Rebecca had introduced him to, Rob still could not entirely forget that his sister was sitting somewhere near.

Being a gala programme, it contained patriotic tributes, and the power of the music soon enchanted Rob to the exclusion of all but the vibrant girl sitting beside him. They stayed in their seats during the interval, holding hands and discussing the items they had heard, as well as those still to come. The hot, airless atmosphere, the richness of gilt and crimson, the stark contrast of white shirtfronts and black coats in the orchestra, the dazzle when brass instruments caught the light, and the great tide of glorious sound that washed over him, all combined to break down the wall Rob had built around himself since he had watched Johnny's Mosquito go down, so that he began subconsciously to surrender to each composer's ability to reach into a man's soul.

The final item, a symphony as yet unheard by Rob, was Tchaikovsky's sixth, known as the 'Pathétique'. It was listed in the programme as a descriptive and heartfelt tribute to the gallant defenders of Stalingrad during the past desperate winter. Already vulnerable, Rob fell victim to the Russian's genius, becoming caught up in the unbearably tragic themes to such an extent that he gradually turned as cold as if the blood had frozen in his veins. The stirring, martial third movement brought a pain in his chest, and during the sombre, desolate finale he saw not Stalingrad but a burning aircraft plunging into an inferno. An unstoppable wave of grief washed over him as he stared at the platform where men and women were playing the epitaph of the only real friend he had ever known, and he had to fight back his emotion because he could not possibly give way to it there.

During thunderous applause, and several speeches of thanks, Rob continued to fight it. Struggling through the tide of people to where pre-ordered taxis awaited amid all the official cars, he remained icy and perilously near to losing control. The scramble to the taxi, and the driver's cheery grumbles about there being a war on yet jewels and furbelows seemed plentiful enough, saved Rob from the obligation to speak. When Rebecca nudged him and whispered laughingly against his ear that the man probably had no idea what a furbelow was, Rob pulled back his mouth in the semblance of a smile while he prayed he would reach the sanctuary of his room before he made a fool of himself.

He gave the driver a huge tip because he was in too much of a hurry to wait for change. In the lift, Rebecca smiled up at him. 'You're very quiet.' He tried to smile back, but failed to force his lips apart this time. 'Is something wrong?' she asked. Then, more perceptively, 'Are you all right?'

'Yes.'

'You don't look all right.'

The lift stopped at their floor. Rebecca preceded him with the key in her hand. 'I know what it is. You need something to eat.' She opened the door and entered. 'Go and take off your jacket and tie, while I brew some coffee and get your supper. Ham and eggs do?'

Rob was already in the guest room, unbuttoning his tunic with frenzied haste. He was tugging at his tie when he sensed she was behind him, and swung round.

'Rob, what's wrong?' She caught and stilled his hands. 'You're shaking. Is it something to do with the concert?'

As he gazed wordlessly at her she became the only thing to hold on to. There was no one else left for him, and he had never felt so terrifyingly alone. He reached out and drew her close, trying to gain some warmth from her body as his own went through a paroxysm of shaking.

'Don't go! For God's sake don't leave me,' he said desperately.

Rebecca held him tightly, stroking his hair and murmuring soothing words until his trembling began to subside. Then she led him to the bed and coaxed him to lie on it while she removed his shoes and tie.

'Don't be afraid,' she whispered. 'I'll be here all the time you need me.'

*

There was a ray of sunshine angling through the window when Rob awoke. It highlighted one of the polished oaken knobs on the foot of the bed, and made a circle of accentuated colour on the carpet beside the crumpled heap of air-force blue that was his uniform. He could not immediately think where he was.

'I thought you were going to sleep until lunchtime,' said a gentle, teasing voice, and he turned to see Rebecca standing by the closed door with a tray in her hands. 'I brought you a cup of tea in case you were awake, but I was resigned to drinking mine in company with Sleeping Beauty.'

She looked radiant despite her no-nonsense starched white blouse and full navy skirt. Placing the tray on the dresser, she came to kneel on the bed and kiss him lingeringly. 'Good morning, darling. You look adorable when you're sleeping, but you're much more exciting awake.' She smiled down into his eyes. 'You don't do things by halves, do you? It's either goodbye for ever, or total possession.'

Rob struggled into a sitting position as full recollection returned. Dear God, he had burned their boats now! 'You were ... I'll never forget what you did for me last night,' he said roughly. 'But I should never have ... I lost control. Forgive me.'

Her lovely eyes studied him closely. 'There's nothing to forgive. You needed me.' With great gentleness she pushed back the hair falling over his forehead. 'The ghosts are still there, aren't they?'

Rob gazed back at her, trying to face the inevitability of something he had tried to avoid six weeks ago. She was right. He had needed her. He still did, more than ever now. Yet nothing had changed. He had little to offer her save a strong prospect of becoming a widow soon after being a bride, but he could have made her pregnant last night and all hope of another 'goodbye for ever' had gone.

'I know so much about you, yet so little,' she said softly. 'What happened to you last night?'

He had not been able to tell her then; he certainly could not now, when there was only one course open to them. How could he say his dearest friend had been burned alive in a plunging aircraft, leaving his wife of a few months a pregnant widow? How could he tell her such things after loving her so feverishly last night?

'It must have been more than the music to make you so emotional,' she prompted.

Seeing Lucy gripping her dead husband's letter as if holding on to Johnny himself, he merely said, 'It's been a difficult week.'

'Poor lamb! From now on I'll be there to hold you whenever things get bad.'

He drew her close, shutting his mind to everything but the warmth and sweetness of her, so that when she murmured against his bare chest, 'I'm so full of love for you I may burst with it, so you'd better marry me quickly, before I do,' he promised her he would.

*

Jim spent eight difficult weeks at a training wing learning to fly a four-engined bomber. The B-17, known as the Flying Fortress because of its immense fire power, was featuring in massive daylight raids over Germany and the Eighth Air Force was desperate for more aircraft, more crews. Their lack of long-range escort fighters left the Americans dangerously vulnerable over their targets, and the Luftwaffe attacked in force. Such continuous aerial massacre was crippling, so even a man who had been a desk pilot for eighteen months was pushed into the cockpit and told he had to 'master this goddam bitch within two months, or else'.

The B-17 was a long, heavy machine and, seated left of centre, Jim took a while to master the balance of it. This was particularly difficult when landing, and he literally had to fight for control of an aircraft which yawed and undulated disastrously. However, after five weeks, one in three of Jim's landings no longer had everyone running for cover.

The scandal surrounding Theo Benson and the pharmaceutical conglomerate had mushroomed to bring down several prominent figures on the periphery of political circles. Some smaller companies stood in danger of FBI investigation, their directors having gone on a sudden vacation and left no forwarding address. Inevitably, the newshounds had discovered that the Senator's playboy son had been attached to a general's staff in London, with access to sensitive information and secret battle plans. That he had been swiftly removed, and shunted into some backwater as yet undiscovered, only pointed to high-level manoeuvring to keep him away from any fighting.

246

The scandal rags dug into the social life of the renowned J.T. once idolized by American youth. Alongside dramatic accounts of battles at sea, German atrocities and the desperate situation in the Far East, were photographs of Jim, looking absurdly young, with society girls he did not even recall. Small incidents, the normal transgressions of teen years, were exaggerated to suggest he was the worst kind of society libertine. If the gutter press was to be believed, Senator Benson's son had been a sporting Romeo, using his good looks, his athletic body and his easy wealth to indulge his appetite for women, and his father's powerful connections to hush up the consequences. These news items were being read by the men around him.

Since the news had broken, Jim had had no contact with his father or Shelley. It seemed best for them all. Even if Jim was in a position to help, Theo would reject it. A father who could not accept failure in his son would die rather than face the boy with his own. After delayed shock, Jim was beginning to count the material cost to himself of his father's deeds. The hope of forgetting who he was and leading a separate life was now dead. He would for ever be the disgraced senator's son. Theo was right. Jim had been James Theodore Benson III from birth, whether he liked it or not, but there was now a stigma attached to that title.

The income Jim received from his mother's family was not substantial, and a great deal less than he was used to. The style of living he had known for most of his life had come to an end. The Benson properties would doubtless fall under the hammer, so there would be no family home when he returned. It was a sobering period for a young man grappling with the complications of piloting a heavy bomber, knowing he would shortly go into action against the enemy for the first time.

In October, Jim was posted to an operational base on the Devon—Somerset border, with the rank of captain. A new squadron had been formed to occupy yet another patch of England turned over to military use, and rumours flew that an invasion of France before winter set in was on the cards. Why else would there be such interest in siting several new squadrons along the south coast? The RAF had moved on to some smaller airfields in the area, also, so there must be something afoot.

Jim reported to the CO of the base on a windy day that sent fallen leaves back into corners of doorways as fast as orderlies swept them out.

The countryside was yellow and brown where harvest stubble lay bright in the sunshine against fields recently ploughed. A barrier of trees beyond the runways made a gold, russet and red streak of autumnal beauty to gladden the eyes of a rookie pilot straight from two months on the cold Northumberland coast. Jim took heart from the softer, more gentle surroundings. A new base, a new squadron, a new start.

Colonel Hoyght was a brisk, solidly built man wearing rimless glasses, who welcomed Jim with no hint of disapproval. The crisis in overall bombing capacity was so deep the commanders no longer cared about a man's character, so long as he could do his job in the air.

'Good to have you with us, Captain Benson,' Hoyght said from behind his desk, reading Jim's record. 'Straight from training wing after a long period of staff duty. That's tough on you, although you appear to have maintained your flying hours in your own time.' He glanced up and got to the point. 'Most of the men in this new outfit have seen action. You're one of four who haven't, so you'll all fly as second pilots for a while to break you in. We'll be taking delivery of more airplanes in a week or two. Then you'll have command of one with your own crew. Nine men relying on you to fly them safely there and back. It's one hell of a responsibility, but I'm confident you can handle that.' He stood. 'A word of advice, Captain. Regard those men as your family and all will be well. Treat them as subordinates and nothing more, you're in trouble.'

'Yes, Colonel, I'll remember that. Thank you.'

'You'll be assigned to a crew later today. Go settle in and grab some coffee while you get to know the men you'll be living and working with.'

His room was at the end of a long hut housing junior officers, very similar to the one at the training wing and a far cry from the spacious quarters he had occupied in his staff job, but the atmosphere of the place excited him. This was what he had wanted from the moment Thomas had announced the fate of Pearl Harbor. Dumping his bags on the bed, Jim looked from the window across the great expanse of the base. Six or seven B-17s were already on the hard standing, and more were coming in as crews from squadrons all around the country homed in on their new operational centre. Jim was stirred by the sight and sound of these camouflaged giants descending from a pale sky to touch down, then run along beside pretty English countryside. One of these would soon be his.

He was happy to act as second pilot on a few operations, until he had experienced action.

Walking across to the officers' canteen, Jim noted an area ideal for football practice. It had been too long since he worked out or joined an impromptu game. No tennis courts or swimming-pool, of course, but there was a superb new gymnasium ideal for basketball. He lingered at the doorway to gaze around with a sense of freedom and relief. He might have been rated by the training wing as no more than a competent pilot, but he was badly needed and would show them they had underestimated him. He was not yet on the losing team.

The place was filling up with new arrivals all getting acquainted and sizing each other up. Coffee and doughnuts were being dispensed by orderlies, so Jim armed himself with both and approached a group of three men relating details of the bases they had just left.

'Hi,' said one. 'Who were you with?'

'I've just finished at training wing. I was unfamiliar with the B-17. How about you?'

They had all been operational for at least six months and were eager to talk about it. Jim listened in silence before moving away to accost another captain, who appeared to have turned prematurely grey. 'It's a bit like the first day at college, isn't it?' Jim said with a grin.

'What's college?' demanded the man with a nervous twitch of the lips which passed for a smile. 'I've been doing this all my life.'

Jim tried again. Offering his hand, he said, 'I'm Jim Benson.'

His companion merely twitched his lips again. 'I'm the sap who's been through three different crews. They call me "Captain Death".' Lost for words to follow that, Jim took another sip of his coffee as recognition dawned on the other's face. 'Benson? Say, aren't you ...?'

'That's right.'

'With me an' you in this squadron, what hope does it have?' He walked away, leaving Jim watching a man as close to breaking up as anyone could be.

While he was standing on the outskirts of a group full of cheer and only interested in first names, Jim's attention was drawn to an even larger group round a captain in a well-worn leather jacket, who wore his cap on the back of his head in a rakish manner and who was describing an aerial experience with expressive gestures and great gusto. A shout of laughter heralded the end of his anecdote, and most men in the room turned in his direction with faint smiles.

'Who's that?' Jim asked his neighbour.

'Brad Halloran. He's the tops. Twenty successful missions and never lost a ship. Came in on one engine back in June. No one thought he'd do it. Number of belly landings he's made! Flown back on a wing and a prayer so often they wrote a song about it.' He laughed. 'That's what *he* says. He's a great character. Broken just about every bone in his body, and been shot in some very intimate places but still manages to keep his women happy. He's not only the hero every squadron needs, he's one hell of a guy.'

Conversation faded to background noise as Jim recalled the day he had almost landed on Halloran's crashed Stearman. The man had been retrograded, yet he had clearly bounced back with a vengeance and put all that behind him.

After dinner, the several hundred men comprising the new squadron assembled in the briefing room to be addressed by Colonel Hoyght and his second-in-command, Major Eames. At the end of the pep talk, the CO came out with the news that they would be taking part in a mission tomorrow. Jim revelled in the thought of action at last, while inwardly protesting that they had only just arrived and were not ready. When Major Eames read out the listed crews, Jim heard that he was to fly with Captain Halloran.

The gathering broke up noisily as the men aired their usual grumbles, and they filtered out to the blustery night to seek the warmth of their quarters. Halloran was not a tall man, but although Jim could not spot his head above others, he heard the unmistakable Kentucky accent in the general hubbub as well as the laughter accompanying it. That crew was more than the family Colonel Hoyght suggested, it was a minister of God and his followers, Jim thought. At least he would be safe with them. Halloran could return on one engine or one wing, apparently.

Jim tracked the hero down in his room half an hour later. Wearing just a shirt and his undershorts, with his cap still rakishly on the back of his head, Halloran was drinking from a bottle of bourbon in company with two other pilots with bottles in their hands. Catching sight of Jim in the doorway, he said loudly, 'J.T. Benson, enter the hallowed portal.'

'Hallo, Brad.' Jim advanced with his hand out. 'It's good to see you again.'

'Wish I could say the same, pal, but I guess someone has to have you.' He ignored Jim's hand. 'You heard what the Colonel said: take-off at oh-eight-thirty. Won't worry me if you don't make it, but it sure will worry Johnson Eames. Says I gotta take you under my wing.' He grimaced at his drunken friends. 'Maybe I should drop him 'long with my load when we get over the target.'

Jim struggled to stay calm. 'Should you be drinking that stuff when you're flying tomorrow?'

Halloran got to his feet and approached Jim with the bottle clutched in his hand. 'When *you've* done twenty missions, you'll know the best way to fly is with a bottle of bourbon under the seat.' He looked at the bright wings on Jim's tunic. 'I never thought you'd make the grade, even with Daddy's influence. As I recall, you were the last to solo at Carlstrom.'

'And you were the first to crash,' returned Jim.

Halloran's eyes narrowed. 'I was retrograded because of injury. I heard you were because you couldn't land at night. I tell you this, pal, you might occupy the seat next to me for a few times, but that's all you'll do.'

'Suits me,' said Jim. 'I'll get to look around so's I'll know the targets when I get a ship of my own.' He nodded at the other two. 'See you in the morning ... and you, Halloran. I only hope you can still see me then.'

When Jim reached the door, the ace pilot asked sneeringly, 'How does it feel to be a discarded hero?'

'You'll find out before long,' said Jim. 'I hope I'm around when you do.'

*

Halloran was a different man at the controls of a B-17. His eyes might be a trifle bloodshot, but they missed nothing. His hands were perfectly steady, his voice full of authority, his brain keen. The morning was crisp and clear; the sky the colour of duck-egg shells. Sitting on the unfamiliar right-hand side, Jim remained silent, watching and listening, while a new sensation halfway between fear and excitement bubbled inside him. It was the first time he had flown with a full crew, and he marvelled at the constant chatter from them over the intercom. Yet one word from Halloran and they were silenced. Jim had not even imagined the noise during operational flying. The messages and information being passed by the crew, the sudden shattering blast of thirteen guns being tested over the Channel, the roar of their own four engines and the muffled thunder of an entire squadron surrounding them. When they rendezvoused with two more, the deep roar in the skies was deafening.

They climbed and fastened their oxygen masks. Speech became muffled; voices sounded different. When they crossed the French coast it had a profound effect on Jim. He had made it, at last! He was on a level with Bucket, and could now help avenge Gus Buckhalter's early death. He felt a sudden resurgence of the zest that had been missing from his life for so long.

Their escorting fighters reached the limit of their range, and waggled their wings in farewell before peeling off to head for home. 'There they go, boys,' said Halloran. 'We're now on our own, so keep your eyes skinned ... and put away that poker game, you two reprobates back there. Bugsy, close up that dirty book you're reading before it bursts into flames and burns your hands. You'll need 'em when the enemy fighters get here.'

General laughter greeted these comments, and a few more were added to show Jim how wrong he had been about this crew. Up here they *were* a family. It was when they were safely back on the ground that their pilot was elevated to divine heights. No sooner had their own fighters departed than a swarm of others rapidly descended, and Jim then learned about combat.

It was a feeling of helplessness while dark shapes hurtled from every direction spitting hot metal. It was a thunderous, echoing staccato as all the guns aboard fired relentlessly. It was men shouting and swearing. It was thuds and bangs on the fuselage. It was the horror of exploding bombers, fighters plunging earthwards in flames; it was the sight of parachutes drifting down, only to foul up on a doomed B-17 just below them before the bombs exploded and blew men and machine all over the sky. It was the awesomeness of aircraft all around them still droning on towards the target, as relentless as the tide. It was Captain Bradford Halloran sitting calmly at the controls, exchanging messages with the leader of their squadron and his own crew throughout it all.

Worse was to come. Their navigator informed them that they would reach the target within ten minutes, and hot on his words came heavy flak from the ground defences. The glorious autumn mid-morning became a nightmare of smoke, a terrible smell of burning and over-excited voices as they were hit and set on fire. Jim glanced swiftly at Halloran, but the pilot snapped, 'They know what they're doing,' before telling the bombardier to prepare for action. The aircraft was jumping up and down so violently that Jim wondered how the man would ever line up his sights with any accuracy. Shells were bursting all around them; to their right one of their squadron aircraft blew up, the blast rocking them so badly that Halloran had to fight to avoid catching their wing on that of their neighbour.

Jim's brain and senses could not absorb the individual components which made up the next quarter of an hour; it became a medley of impressions. The vividness of fire and the darkness of smoke, the smells of sulphur, engine oil, and sweat; the thud of his heartbeat and the laboured rhythm of his breathing; the tense voices in his ears which echoed his own sensation of terrified elation; lurches and jolts; the unbelievable reality of men dying outside in the sky around them, and a curious conviction that he would not.

'Let's turn tail for home,' said Halloran's voice, bringing Jim from his dazed hiatus, 'and don't any of you screwballs relax until we get past the French coast. Okay, who's been hit?'

'Dodger and Mitch, Captain. They'll live,' came the laconic report from the depths of the fuselage.

'How's about the fire?'

'Still raging. Should reach you 'bout now.'

'As I thought. Worst crew in the business!'

Ten miles from the French coast Jim almost shot out of his seat with fright when a dark shape appeared to fly at him like a deadly missile. Something whistled past his chest and brought a cry from Halloran. Then there were shouts from the crew.

'Fighters! Ten o'clock. There's one on our tail, Jake! Look out, there's another group coming out of the sun.'

The chorus died soon after it began, and a cheer broke out as a hoarse voice exclaimed, 'There's our boys coming to meet us. They're chasing the sons of bitches off.'

Jim recovered from his shock and turned to see that Halloran had blanched with pain. One of his hands was bloody, and there was a dark stain spreading just above his waist. As Jim made to speak he was silenced by a glare from ice-blue eyes. He held the challenge with his own for several moments, then sat back and stared ahead at the distant smudge of England's gentle coastline while accepting the fact that bullets had missed him by a fraction of an inch. If he had been leaning forward they would have sunk into his flesh. It was then that he fully realized his life could end in a matter of seconds at any time from now on.

While they crossed the water Jim sat tense and worried, waiting for Halloran to tell him to take the controls. The pilot's breathing was growing laboured, even though they had descended enough to leave off oxygen masks, and it was obvious he was in pain. Jim knew they had been shot up, but not to what extent, and there must be some fire damage. He was not familiar with the names of the crew; they knew him only as a body sitting on their captain's right. He could no longer see from the oil-spattered window beside him, and landing was his worst skill. He prayed he would get them all down in one piece.

The prayers were unnecessary. To his consternation, Halloran began the familiar exchange with the tower prior to making his approach, and Jim concluded that the wounded man was going to attempt the landing. It was crazy, it was dangerous, and it was the final snub. Jim sat watching the airfield materialize in the hazy distance and wondered if this would be his first and last operational flight. With this madman at the controls it could be, but he knew better than to wrest them from him. His heart was in his mouth as they began to lose height. All manner of things could go wrong during this most delicate manoeuvre, and Halloran had crashed even the ultra-simple Stearman.

The landing proceeded. The pilot was white-faced and gasping with agony, yet he exchanged taut instructions with his crew as if all was well. The wheels went down and locked in place. The ground grew disturbingly close as Jim braced himself. Then they were down and running smoothly, chasing the bomber that had landed a minute ahead of them.

Only when they had come to a halt, and monotonously chanted the check-list necessary before leaving the aircraft, did Halloran bend painfully to pull a bottle of bourbon from beneath his seat and take a long drink. He then offered it to Jim.

'You look as if you need this.'

Jim did. He gulped from it gratefully, then handed it back.

Halloran muttered, 'If I'd been you, I'd have peed my pants during that descent.'

'How d'you know I haven't?'

A pause, then, 'You've changed since Carlstrom.'

'You haven't.'

'Humility suits you.'

'You'll never know the meaning of the word.'

'And I'm not aiming to learn. When I go it's going to be in a blaze of glory ... and with this under the seat.' He tipped up the bottle again, then wiped his mouth with the back of his hand. 'You were pretty cool up there, Benson. Next mission you can do some work, but you *land* my ship over my dead body.'

'Suits me,' said Jim.

'Now, for Crissakes get me to a doctor.'

All through debriefing Jim fought his nausea, praying he would not have to make a dash for it through the cluster of shaken, exhausted crews. Halloran had been taken off in an ambulance, so he did his best to report what he could of the past seven hours to augment the graphic words of the crew of *Bluegrass Baby*.

The minute his duty was over, Jim made for his quarters and suffered a prolonged bout of sickness. Then he lay fully clad on his bed while a kaleidoscope of ghastly images tumbled through his mind. Breaking into a sweat, he thought of when he would be given a bomber and a crew of his own to go out and do what they had just done. He had been a mere spectator today. Could he do all Halloran had under such circumstances? Then he thought of Bucket. His friend was the antithesis of the madcap former racing driver, yet he had been flying over Germany for almost as long as Halloran. The thought comforted Jim.

Bucket had been a loyal friend throughout the past difficult months. He had sustained a leg injury which had put him in hospital for one of them, and he had written and telephoned from there at greater length than he could manage from his base. Without Bucket's friendship Jim would have felt the pressure of his father's disgrace even more keenly. As he lay on his bed thinking of their carefree days before the war, he felt suddenly old. A surge of desire to recapture the gladness of living overwhelmed him. Halloran was right. If a man was certain to go out before his rightful time, it should be in a blaze of glory.

There was a tap on his door, and a voice called, 'Telephone, Captain Benson.'

How curious that Bucket should call right at this moment, as if that great longing for the old days had somehow touched him, too. Still in his flying gear Jim made his way to the telephone and took up the receiver. 'Are you still quickening the pulse rates of those tasty nurses, you old reprobate?'

'Hallo, Jim,' said a female voice he recognized with a shock.

Trying to collect his thoughts, he asked, 'How did you know where to reach me?'

'I bumped into Bucket at a concert. He told me you were at a training wing, and which one. When I telephoned I was told there was no facility for private calls. I wrote, but the letter was returned with a rubber-stamp mark saying the addressee had moved on. I then rang General Flood's headquarters — Molly got the number from one of her contacts — but that was even worse.' There was a pause for breath. 'When an English girl starts making enquiries about the whereabouts of an American officer they clam up. It's obvious what they imagine.'

'Is it?' He was still at a loss for words.

'I was so afraid you'd been posted home, I visited Bucket's Red Cross girlfriend. You remember we dropped her off at her place from the Savoy? She's no longer his girlfriend — never was, apparently — but she did know he was in hospital because they're notified so they can arrange visits, and so on. So I rang him last night and he said you were practically next door at the new base. We've heard the aircraft flying overhead for the past three days.' After several moments, she asked, 'Are you still there, Jim?'

'Yes.'

'I thought I'd driven you away with my non-stop gabble. I ... I suppose I'm nervous.'

'You once told me you weren't in the least afraid of me.'

'I'm not. It's just that I'm not in the habit of chasing after American officers.'

'Is that what you're doing?' he asked, amazed by what he was hearing.

'You promised to contact me. I want to know why you haven't.'

He sighed. 'Isn't it obvious?'

'I'm afraid not. I thought we'd sorted everything out that night at the Savoy.'

'Don't you see the papers?'

'Of course, but I don't believe everything I read in them.'

'Not even when they corroborate what your brother told you?'

'As I said, I thought we'd sorted that out.' Another short silence, then she added with a hint of desperation, 'Oh, this is awful! I should never have ... I'm sorry, Jim, you've made it obvious you don't want to —'

'Jenny,' he interrupted firmly, 'everything's a mess here at the moment. We've hardly settled in, but as soon as we get a stand-down can we meet? I'm not sure how far this place is from Thoresby, but I guess I can find out in the next day or so.' When there was no response, it was his turn to ask if she was still there.

'Of course. I wouldn't just ring off after the trouble I've taken to find you.'

'I'm glad you did.'

'I thought ... I thought you might need a friend to talk to.'

'So they were wrong?'

'Who?'

'The people who imagined something else when an English girl made enquiries about the whereabouts of an American officer.'

'Now you sound like the Jim I know,' she said crisply.

'You don't know me, Jenny. Maybe we should get together and fix that.'

'You sound very serious.' She paused. 'Are you now operational?'

'Yes.'

'Were you in one of the bombers that came over at around three this afternoon?'

'That's right.'

'Please take care. I say that to Rob. I know it's foolish, but I have to say it.'

'Say it as often as you like, if it helps. Thanks for calling me, Jenny. I'll get back to you sometime.'

'Please do. Goodbye, Jim.'

He returned to his room and settled on his bed again. Jenny Stallard had just slammed the ball back into his court when he was least prepared for it. He had believed that game over, but she had just made it deuce. She had also put some warmth back into his life. He fell asleep thinking about that.

Chapter Fifteen

During the following nine days, Jim's squadron flew twice over Bremen and once to Cologne. He had expected to take *Bluegrass Baby* in Halloran's place, but the crew were stood down and Jim flew as second pilot twice with a man called Starke, who sang to himself the whole time, and then with Dwight Carlton, the New Yorker called "Captain Death".

Although each mission was difficult, dangerous and a severe test of the nerves, that third one, sitting beside a pilot whose hands shook the moment the firing started and whose commands were nervous and conflicting, promised to be more than usually hazardous. Yet it gave Jim the chance to get the feel of command, because Carlton was more than happy to hand over to him as soon as they neared Cologne. It was the wisest decision for them both, and the crew responded better to Jim's quiet, cultured voice than to the orders barked at them by their captain. It was an object lesson to Jim, because he found that concentration allowed him to become almost detached from what was happening to others in the great aerial armada around him.

They were hit twice before they dropped their bombs, but Jim had learned from Halloran to question his crew on the damage then leave them to deal with it while he kept them in the air. It was unnerving to stay where he was while eight men somewhere in the seventy feet of fuselage behind him were dousing fires, plugging holes or dealing with the wounded.

Confidence, and the belief that the man beside him was one breath away from a complete breakdown, led Jim to suggest he make the landing. Well into the procedure, he became aware that the bomber was not responding as he expected, and he remembered the extra weight compared with the training machines. The damage they had sustained to one wing and the front turret made the aircraft pull to the left, which he had to fight to correct. His confidence waned as the ground appeared to rise to meet him. The bomber thumped down, tipped sideways, then raced forward with a wingtip scraping the runway until it slewed on to grass and turned a great circle before coming to a halt in the mud it had churned up.

At the debriefing, Jim attempted to explain why he had deposited a relatively undamaged aircraft in the centre of a grassy area used for sports and exercise, but he was interrupted by Dwight Carlton.

'It was just God-awful flying. This man couldn't land a toy airplane without smashing it up!'

'Then why allow him to land yours?' demanded Major Eames, listening in to the crews' reports.

At breakfast next morning Jim learned that Captain Death had been sent away for a rest. He also discovered that bad weather over Europe during the next couple of days would prohibit missions. Without hesitation, he dialled the number of Darston Manor, praying Jenny would be there. After yesterday's landing, and the shattering impact of the past ten days, he badly needed the gentle delight of her company.

An hour later Jenny was waiting for him outside the gates, in a mud-splattered car that had seen better days. Jim thought she looked very striking in a yellow roll-neck sweater and a brown skirt, with a multi-coloured scarf twisted into a band to hold back her hair. He went forward to greet her with a strength of feeling that took him by surprise. She threw open the door, and he got in beside this warm, sweet-smelling creature so totally divorced from the death and destruction he had witnessed lately. He took in the bloom on her cheeks, the sparkle in her eyes and the sheen of her shoulder-length hair.

She studied him as intently. 'Hello, Jim.'

'It's good to see you, Jenny.'

'I'm glad you rang. I wasn't certain you would.'

Still held by the pleasure of her youthful zest, the allure of her perfume and the caress of her softly accented English voice, all so wonderfully normal after what lay on the other side of the gates, Jim said, 'I wanted to remind myself how beautiful you are ... even when you're mad at me. Thanks for coming at such short notice.'

'I know it's not easy for aircrew to get away, especially if the weather is fine, so I dropped what I was doing and came.' She put the car in motion. 'This mist will soon clear, and it'll be a glorious autumn day. I know the perfect place for a long walk, where we can get some kind of lunch in a pub with a view for miles around.' She smiled. 'That won't be anything new for you, but I'd like to see it. Have you brought your walking shoes?'

'Always do, ma'am. Won't you let me drive?'

'Charles only surrendered the car on condition that I went no further than forty miles from door to door, and that I take the wheel. Pilots are notorious for driving like madmen.'

'You know a lot of pilots?'

'We've had a Polish squadron stationed near for some months. They never use hand signals, and shoot over crossroads without even slowing.' Her smile broadened. 'Americans are worse. They do the same on the wrong side of the road.'

'You won't draw me into an argument on that subject, ma' am.'

'I hope we won't argue about anything. I want to enjoy today.'

'So do I, so shall we tackle the thorny subject now? Then we can forget it.'

She darted a glance at him. 'You mean Rob? There's nothing to tackle.'

'He hasn't pointed out to you that everyone is now saying I'm all he claimed?'

She drew up, peered into the mist where two lanes crossed, then set the car forward. 'He wrote an "I told you so" letter, and I replied saying I judged people on personal acquaintance and not on what scandal rags chose to print. I said again that he should tell me about Arcadia so that I might understand his attitude to you. I haven't heard from him since then.' She frowned. 'I no longer understand him. His friends are being killed; he's killing Germans. In the midst of something so terrible, how can he be obstinate over events that happened two years ago?'

'I'll answer that, but not while you're driving through lanes no wider than this vehicle, in thick mist.'

Jenny soon pulled into the rutted entrance to a field and turned to him. 'I didn't come out with you to talk about Rob.'

'But I think we must,' he said quietly. 'You spoke about killing. For the past two weeks I've been in the thick of it. Jenny, I've watched the men around me; I've discovered it for myself. What we do as our duty is something apart. We don't weigh everything against constant death and consider it unimportant. The killing is something quite separate. It has to be. What happened two years ago — *five* years ago — still matters. A guy's dog gets ill; he's sick with worry. A girl writes that she's lost the fraternity pin her boy gave her; it's a major tragedy. Someone has a letter from his mom saying she can't take Pa's sloppy ways no more; he feels guilty not being there to sort them out.'

'What are you trying to tell me?'

'We have to be human to stay sane.' He fingered her hair as it lay against her shoulder. 'The time to start worrying is when we become unconcerned about everyday things. Leave him alone, Jenny.'

'But you can't, can you?' she reasoned. 'We'd only come half a mile before you brought up the subject.'

'So I was wrong. Let's now drop it.'

'Will you tell me about Arcadia?'

'No, but I'll tell you this. You seem to think this is a one-way deal. At Carlstrom I thought he was an arrogant, ill-mannered pain in the ass. I've heard nothing to make me change that opinion. Stop trying to mediate. We just can't take each other, and I guess nothing would change that. Now, either you drive on to this hill with a view for miles and concentrate on enjoying today, or you turn back and head for the base.'

For a brief moment there was a glimpse of the cool haughtiness she had displayed before, as she turned on the ignition and eased the car into the lane. They both remained silent as the hedges on each side of the road gave way to open fields and scattered cottages, before the way widened into a village square with a memorial to the dead of the Great War in the centre. Jenny turned right round the stone cross, then, with a sudden, sharp swerve, ignored the lane and continued to circle until she resumed the road leading away from the airbase.

Thirty seconds later, Jim asked, 'What made you change your mind?'

Without taking her attention from the road, she said, 'The things you said about Rob stopped me feeling sorry for you, and I saw that I had no need to compensate for his attitude. Halfway around the memorial I recognized my feelings for what they really are.'

'And what are they?'

She shifted into a lower gear with a jerk. 'If you won't reveal secrets, neither shall I. But don't expect tea and sympathy any longer. It's no holds barred, from now on.'

He smiled as his glance played over her determined profile, and his spirits grew lighter still. 'Sounds like an interesting day ahead.'

The mist had burned away by mid-morning, so they walked the crest of the hill in gentle warmth with almost an entire county spread below in the pale clarity of October. Although used to seeing the earth far beneath him, Jim was still charmed by the somnolent scene of patchwork fields in green, brown and yellow, divided by hedges or barriers of trees in autumn colours. With a pang, it dawned on him that he was twenty-four and had taken for granted the natural beauty of wherever he had been until now, when there was a strong chance that he might not see it for much longer. The recent urge to capture the gladness of life was strong in him as he halted to gaze at the scene.

'It's so beautiful I can't stop looking at it,' he murmured.

'Even though it's so small?' she teased.

He turned and took her hand. 'What we have at home may be big, but that doesn't stop it from being beautiful, too. I guess I was always so busy, I didn't appreciate it before. Maybe I'll get around to it when I return.'

'Will you have a home to go to?' Jenny asked quietly, as they walked on hand in hand.

'We owned six properties. They'll surely all go under the hammer before my father's affairs are settled.'

'I'm so sorry.'

He eased her round to face him. 'Hey, no tea and sympathy, you vowed.' His kiss was unhurried, expressing a yearning which owed nothing to sexual desire, and Jim was content to walk on with his arm lightly along Jenny's shoulders.

The pub was quaint and overlooked the valley, but the meal was disappointing. The landlord apologized to 'the American gentleman' and explained that he had had a wedding reception at the weekend which had used up most of his supplies.

Jim tasted one of some little green vegetables with misgivings, then asked, 'What the heck are these?'

'Brussels sprouts,' Jenny told him, adding sternly, 'They're very good for you.'

'Not me, ma'am.' He pushed them aside with his fork. 'They're as unappetizing as your housekeeper's bird-seed cake. The next time we come out for a walk I'll bring a hamper from the base.'

Highly amused, she asked, 'Are you prepared to carry it five miles along a hilltop?'

'We'll eat it before we set out. Go without breakfast and you'll be fine.'

They began to walk back, then sat for a rest near a fallen tree. Jenny talked for a while about her work with Molly Guthrie, not only for the Polish refugees, but in arranging cultural visits for foreign servicemen. 'They don't all want just to drink and chase girls.'

'What else is there to do?' he asked innocently, as he lay on the grass with his arms behind his head.

She laughed down at him. 'Walk five miles to eat Brussels sprouts, Captain Benson.'

He made a face. 'Don't remind me. By the way, I spoke to Bucket day before yesterday. He said you and he had met up at some kind of musical gala.'

'It was a charity do, so a number of Americans were invited.' She gave him a mischievous glance. 'They have plenty of money.'

'Mercenary gal!'

'Molly and I arranged a dinner party for six of them with some single girls, prior to the gala. I was delighted to see Bucket there. He looked very tired, but was terribly nice to me. Molly was so charmed she invited him and his friend to the Manor during their next leave. Pat Chance is delighted. She really fell for the big, blond Billy Challoner.'

'No idea what girls see in blonds,' Jim said lazily, enjoying listening to her and indulging in light flirtation on an afternoon when the only additional sounds were those of birdsong and distant tractors in the valley. The sun was still warm, the grass smelt sweet, the sky was empty of gunsmoke and spiralling aircraft.

'I also thought he was rather gorgeous.'

'Is that why your aunt invited him home?'

'My *aunt*?'

Jim glanced up at her. 'Lady Guthrie.'

'She's not my aunt. Whatever made you think that?'

'You live with her.'

'I moved in with her and Charles soon after Rob joined the RAF. They needed our cottage for the new farm manager. I work for her. Well, I suppose I work *with* her now. I seem to have become an unofficial daughter.'

Jim sat up with a frown. 'So Darston Manor isn't your family home?'

'Heavens, no!'

Jim listened to her with mixed feelings, yet her story explained why he had believed Stallard to be a redneck. This girl, intelligent, cultured and self-possessed, seemed so right in her present setting, and he could not imagine her as the daughter of such parents.

'After the tragedy, Rob joined up in the belief that I'd be getting married within a few weeks.' She looked away over the valley. 'That didn't happen, and Molly offered me a room at the Manor. It's become my home now.' After a slight pause, she added, 'I often wonder how my life would be if that bomb hadn't fallen on Gran's house. I know Rob does.'

Jim moved closer, still trying to accept all she had told him. 'I know what my life would be if the Japs hadn't bombed Pearl Harbor. My father would have forced my resignation and entry into the company boardroom. He *would* have,' he insisted, at her look of doubt. 'He stopped at nothing and used anyone and any means to get what he wanted. That's why he's in this mess. I'd have been deep in it, too. As it is, I'm simply feeling the backlash.' Jenny put her hand on his, and he clasped it. 'No sympathy, ma'am.'

'I'm not offering sympathy, Jim.'

He took courage from that. 'The marriage that didn't work out. What happened?'

'I was too young; my parents were too eager for it. Phil went to sea, Mum and Dad were no longer there, Rob sought freedom and I realized I wanted it, too. Phil never found out. His ship went down before he had leave.' She gave a sad smile. 'Who knows, he might also have been regretting the engagement and worrying over how he'd tell me.'

'These things happen. Remember that night at the Savoy? Bucket questioned my motives; asked if I was starting something serious or trying to get at your brother through you.'

'Oh?' Her clear gaze encouraged him further.

'I guess at our first meeting I got a kick from knowing you were entertaining someone he wouldn't have had in the house. Maybe I even relished the thought of his fury when he found out you were dating me.

A lot has happened since then. Today, it seems Bucket might be right on the first count. How do you feel about that?'

Whereas most girls would then have thrown themselves in the handsome J.T. Benson's arms, Jenny Stallard merely said, 'It's quite a relief, because when I began telephoning everyone I could think of, without a shred of pride, to find out where you were, I had to face the fact that *I'd* started something serious with *you*.'

*

Five weeks later, Jim was given command of a new B-17. In that time he had taken part in eight missions over Germany as a second pilot. Although he had not been given the chance to land after an operation, he had done so when flight-testing the various aircraft. None of his landings had been particularly smooth or praiseworthy, and he soon learned that ground crews all came out to watch his descents then turn away wiping their brows in disbelief. This bothered him until he sensed a change in attitudes towards him. Somehow, his *bête noire* had become an idiosyncrasy, and these earned pilots curious respect. Jim discovered he was acquiring a new identity. The go-getting football hero of adolescents had become a figure of the past. There were different heroes now. Captain James Theodore Benson was liable to become one, if he lived long enough.

Along with new aircraft came men to crew them, and nine were assigned to Jim. He met them briefly before supper one evening and recalled the CO's advice to treat them as a family. There was the usual mixture of the brash, the thoughtful, the gauche and the nervous. They were all strangers, unhappy about forming a new team with a new commander, whose attempts at landing had to be seen to be believed. Jim spoke to them the way he had as captain of a football team, but the approach did not appear too popular. Ill at ease, he brought the meeting to an end by asking if there were any questions.

'Yeah, Captain, is that right your old man's heading for the penitentiary?' drawled a gunner who looked as tough as they came.

Unprepared for such outright attack, Jim said, 'That has nothing to do with the team we're going to be.'

'Sure does,' averred the gunner. 'Mine's a jailbird, too. Kinda gives us somethin' in common, don't it?'

Amid laughter, a young blond lad called out, 'How many missions have you done, Captain?'

'Very few, which makes me as new to this game as the rest of you. We'll have to show the other crews who's boss of this squadron.'

A cheer went up, then a voice from the back asked, 'Why did some of the guys suggest I keep a parachute handy when flying with you?'

Jim smiled. 'You might get a softer landing that way.'

'Is it true you wrecked three B-seventeens in a week, sir?'

'No ... but give me time.'

There was more laughter, and Jim knew then they were starting to relax. He had sudden insight to why Brad Halloran was successful. He was a buccaneer of the air, a rascal who kept a bottle of bourbon under his seat, and who knew the weaknesses of those who flew with him. He nevertheless put his trust in them, and they in him. He might be unorthodox and break the rules, but he got them home every time. That was all any crew asked of their pilot.

When they assembled the following morning in the chill, frosty air, it seemed to Jim that he had killed the budding team spirit. Each member of his crew stared sullenly at the painting of a favourite cartoon character on the camouflaged fuselage, and the words *That Goddam Mouse* beneath it. There was utter silence from them as other crews rallied to *Sweet Lulu*, *Bluegrass Baby*, *Mississippi Sue* or *Red Hot Mamie*, all depicting scantily clad beauties.

Just as Jim was about to tell them to climb aboard, the gunner whose father was in prison said loudly enough for passing crews to hear, 'Gee, I just got it. *That Goddam Mouse* will drop deadlier shit on Germany than any rodent they got. Honest-to-God *American* mouse-shit, fellas!'

There was a ripple of laughter, and the team spirit was back. 'Go to it, Mickey,' said the front gunner as he climbed up to his turret.

Philip Robards, the second pilot, raised his eyebrows at Jim. 'Almost blew it, didn't you? What made you do it?'

Jim settled beside him. 'When I thought about a name, there was only one possibility. I have my reasons.'

'Thank the Lord for Clusky. He looks and acts tough, but he's the one who'll keep this crew together.'

'Not me?' queried Jim.

'Uh-uh, you'll just ferry them back and forth. You're stuck up front from start to finish. They have to do everything back there.' After a moment, he added, 'But they'll only do it because they can trust you to keep them airborne.'

Jim smiled. 'I regard us as a team. I'll expect you to work as hard as me, Phil.'

Robards smiled back. 'Thanks. We'll keep this ship flying, even if it does have a God-awful name.'

Jim prepared for the ritual of starting up engines. 'It'll grow on you ... and if you've been reading the newspapers you'll know there'd never be room on the side for the names of all the girls I've known in my life.'

As the days passed, the crew of *That Goddam Mouse* slowly ironed out their differences and settled down. They first went into action at the end of November, and returned relatively unscathed due to heavy cloud over most of France which held off enemy fighters. In strong winds and gathering afternoon gloom, Jim put down on the runway after an approach that had swung like a pendulum. His crew had begun groaning or cheering according to the expertise of each landing but, amazingly, they did not appear to be seriously worried. Jim could only think that after nine or ten hours of danger they were glad to return to earth by any method.

On their second operation over Mannheim they lost one of their waist gunners and part of a wing. Two other crew members were wounded. The first death in their midst affected them badly, and they all made mistakes next time they went out. Jim was glad when they went yet again within three days. It did not do to have long spells of inactivity after a tragedy. On this occasion, they were shot up so badly that Jim had to make an emergency landing at an RAF base on the east coast, and he had every excuse for leaving the runway to cut a deep gouge across the station's makeshift football pitch before coming to a halt. The RAF did not take too kindly to him, however.

Throughout this period, Jim met Jenny whenever it was possible. He thought she must be neglecting her work, because she came each time he telephoned. Her smile, her perfume, her calm, cool voice and her laughter made some sense of his present life. The qualities he had so disliked in her brother were a form of salvation in Jenny. The Stallard determination, the decided opinions, the unshakeable loyalty and that

English reserve provided a rock in the sea of uncertainties Jim's days had become.

As Christmas neared, and winter weather across Europe gave less opportunity for flying, Jim managed to get hold of a Jeep on several occasions and drove to Darston Manor. An invitation to spend Christmas there prompted him to tackle Jenny about it when they rode across the hills backing Thoresby on the two remaining horses in the Guthries' stables.

'Surely your brother will be here for the holiday.'

'Would it matter?' she challenged.

'Naturally. He has the greater right.'

She cast him a troubled glance. 'He's never regarded the Manor as home; refuses the offer of a room here for his leave. Deep down he feels it's the house owned by his former employers. I think that's partly why he never comes to Thoresby now.'

'And I'm the other reason.'

'He's never liked quarrels. He either clams up or walks away from them. We haven't been in touch for weeks. I only know he's all right because there's been no telegram with the dread words.' She forced a smile. 'Here we are talking about him again. Come on, I'll race you to the spinney.'

The gallop was exhilarating and they pulled up laughing and breathless. Jim gazed around at the bare trees against a grey sky, and at the wet hillside dotted with rabbit holes. 'I never thought I could look at such a desolate scene and think it beautiful.'

'Everything's beautiful when you're in love,' she said quietly. 'We are, aren't we?'

He turned and saw a rosy-cheeked girl in a thick cream sweater, a brown jacket that had a patch on one elbow, and breeches that had been new before the war. He saw a face full of character and clear green eyes that always mirrored her feelings. Eyes now filled with tenderness.

'I think we should come down to earth and talk about that,' he suggested, swinging his leg over the saddle and going to where she sat on the roan mare.

Once she was beside him they began to lead their horses round the edge of the spinney, their breath clouding in the chill December air and their boots growing shiny from the moist grass.

'I was a rich, privileged kid with everything going for me. I used it all without a second thought. When my mother died, I played even harder. I joined the Air Corps because flying was fast and exciting. Then your brother got under my skin and began beating me at the game. Only then did I see that here was something I really wanted, and begin working at it.' He paused in the long run-up to what he had to say, and studied the cold, leaden sky as they sauntered on. 'When my father went under I thought I'd gone with him, but I sure as hell know I'm a darn sight more important to the world right now than Theo Benson ever was.'

She squeezed his hand. 'You don't have to justify yourself to me.'

'I have to justify myself to me.' He halted and faced her. 'The future's cloudy, and living has become the most precious commodity around. When you come across something wonderful the instinct is to snatch it before it vanishes.' He touched her hair with a light caress. 'In my time, I've taken numerous women to bed, but that's only a part of what I want from you. I can't offer much in return. It's crazy to consider marrying, but it's a crazy world right now. We both know it might be for a very short time, but let's snatch it before it vanishes; have happiness for however long it lasts.'

'We'll *make* it last,' she said fervently, then caught his other hand to hold on to it very tightly. 'I don't want any fuss. I had a wedding dress in my wardrobe for months and never used it. Phil's parents were incredibly upset when someone else wore it. Let's just go off and get married on the quiet.'

He drew her close. 'Are you quite sure that's what you want?'

'Very sure ... and make it as soon as possible, please. I don't want to waste any of that precious time together.'

He sighed with relief. 'Anything you say, ma'am.'

*

Christmas was only ten days away. Those fortunate enough to be granted leave were counting the hours. The rest were busily putting up decorations and organizing dances or parties to make the most of the festive season on duty. There had been no operations for some days, due to an unusually early snowfall over south-east England and blizzards over France. This aerial inactivity prompted a prolonged bout of what Dennis Averell described to his wife as essential mischief-making. Whether residents in areas surrounding the station would have agreed is debatable, but they had grown used to the noisy pranks of restless young men over the past four years. They seemed likely to continue. The hoped-for invasion of France had not taken place, and there was little hope of an end to the war until it did. Everyone prayed that the coming spring of 1944 would bring landings in Europe, especially the restless young men engaged in noisy pranks.

Rob awoke to the luminous whiteness produced by snow outside the windows. Oh God, another day on the ground! Beneath the blankets he was wearing his shirt and underpants. The boys must have brought him home and put him to bed. His head ached and his mouth felt like sandpaper. They had gone to the Wheatsheaf to celebrate his promotion to flight lieutenant, and the devils must have slipped something in his drinks. He had no doubt Donald had been the instigator. He sighed. They were all bored and jaded by too many days on the ground.

As he stumbled to the bathroom, Rob wondered what on earth he was going to do all day. Being grounded gave him too much time to think, and hijinks in the Mess provided little relief from his thoughts. He knew he had been moody and irritable lately, and during the last few operations he had been over-careful, had hesitated where he usually made snap decisions. For the first time in his career, he had difficulty keeping his mind on the job.

Returning to his room to dress, he instead sank on to the bed with his head in his hands. He had been an almighty fool. His salary would increase with this promotion, but a flight lieutenant's pay would not give Rebecca the things she was used to. It would have been bad enough if she had declared she would gladly live in a garret and eat bread and cheese so long as they were together, but she fully intended to live as she always had, by paying for whatever her husband could not afford. He could not let her do that, but how was he to deal with it?

The engagement ring had set him back so much he had had to borrow ten pounds from Donald to see him through the month. Repaying the debt had left him short the following month, and he had no idea how he would rent a place to live in and support a wife in any comfort. Thankfully, they now knew he had not made Rebecca pregnant on the night of the gala. On the two occasions they had made love since then, he had taken the right precautions. She was eager for a child, but in that respect Rob felt totally in charge.

Getting to his feet, he dressed with a heavy heart, then stood by the window gazing across the snowbound airfield. Rebecca had reluctantly agreed to wait until he finished his tour before getting married. After three more operations he would be grounded for three months. He sighed again. He had made a mess of everything. He should have stuck to what he had written in his letter of farewell. He was normally so decisive, so well in command, but Rebecca undermined his defences with disastrous ease. If only she had not caught him off balance straight from a raid, with kisses in front of the CO and her father! If only she had not been there to offer comfort after Johnny's death! He should instead have gone to the Wheatsheaf and got paralytic. Yet he knew in his heart that those days at Romney Marsh had started something that could only be satisfied when he was with her, loving her.

Rob's eyes narrowed as he watched one of his fitters tramping through the snow to the cookhouse. Had he also made a mess of the tests on Lambourne's beam system? Why else had he been passed by in favour of Yanks? Lambourne was deeply upset over the decision. The Wingco was genuinely sorry and had explained that the Eighth Air Force had taken a great interest in the invention, and the Americans were better able to fund extensive tests. They had borrowed two Mosquitoes and were getting encouraging results, but Rob yearned to be in their place.

Down in the dining room, the officers were eating breakfast and discussing their plans for the day. Rob felt the usual sharp pang on scanning the faces and not seeing Johnny's there. He missed like hell that perky 'Wotcher!' Making his way to a seat almost opposite Donald, he was instead greeted with an energetic 'Hi there!'

'Morning,' he returned heavily. 'What are you so breezy about?'

'Had a letter from my folks. They've posted me a parcel for Christmas. Oh boy, are you guys going to be envious.'

'Hope it makes you sick,' said Johnny's replacement cheerfully.

'Hey, Rob, shouldn't you be sitting nearer the Wingco now you're a flight lieutenant?' asked Donald, then added with a grin, 'you do recall that's what we were celebrating last night.'

'I don't even remember last night, much less what it was in aid of,' he returned, 'but I shall expect much more respect from you in the cockpit.'

'Okay,' replied the Canadian deliberately.

'Get stuffed.' Rob eyed his eggs and bacon without enthusiasm.

'How about taking the train to Town, catching a show and following it with a slap-up dinner?' suggested Rob's neighbour. 'The six of us. Split everything six ways.'

'We're on,' said Donald, also speaking for his pilot.

A WAAF orderly approached to tell Rob he had a telephone call, and his head was still throbbing as he walked to the lobby to pick up the receiver. 'Stallard here.'

'Rob, dear, it's Lucy. I wanted you to be the first to know. He's a boy, and he looks exactly like Johnny, only more wrinkled. I can't tell you how thrilled I am. Of course, when they laid him in my arms I wished with all my heart Johnny was here. But I know that wherever he is he can see his son. He'll feel so proud. You'll still be his godfather, won't you?'

'Of course. Congratulations, Lucy. How much d'you bet me his first word will be "Wotcher"?'

She gave a wobbly laugh. 'You've been so good to me, Rob. Mummy and Daddy are too emotional over it all, but you've been a tower of strength.' She ran on in her usual bubbly fashion about the birth, while Rob thought wildly that Rebecca might one day tearfully confide to another man that she was sure wherever Rob was he could see his son and feel proud.

When he eventually hung up he felt heavier of heart than ever, so he decided not to finish his breakfast. As he walked to the stairs he noticed there was a letter in his pigeon hole. The handwriting was Jenny's. If she was hoping he would go to Thoresby for Christmas she would be disappointed. He and Donald had offered to swap with a crew who were both newly married and anxious for their first Christmas with their brides. He took the letter to his room and read the single page.

Dear Rob,

I know this will come as something of a shock, but please be happy for me. Jim and I were married at the weekend in a Cornish village. We told nobody, not even Molly and Charles. I wanted it that way. Jim's now flying B-17s so we felt we must grab every moment together. I'm still at the Manor because he's at a nearby base. It would be so special to see you at Christmas. Please come if you can. Take care.

My love,

Jenny.

Folding the letter with hands that shook, Rob put on his greatcoat and went out. The snow had frozen overnight so that it crunched beneath his shoes, but he saw nothing of the sparkling beauty around him, for his vision was from the past. J.T. Benson leaning nonchalantly against his fancy blue convertible, saying, 'I think it's clear enough she's with me. She's in my car,' before driving off and sending up a shower of grit and dust. What he had done now was far worse.

The bastard! A hole-in-the-corner wedding without telling anyone. The sly, despicable *bastard*! It was clearly the only way he could get what he wanted from Jenny. How *could* she be so taken in? Whatever had possessed her to succumb to such madness? He would leave her high and dry when he tired of her, and go back to America leaving no forwarding address. Why had she not trusted her own brother when he warned her? Why had she ruined her life in response to charm and a handsome face?

He stopped to lean on a sandbagged gun post and stare blindly at the aircraft lined up at Dispersal. He had made a complete mess of this, too. He should have gone to Thoresby long ago and put her straight on Benson. He should have made a greater effort to prevent the bastard from doing this to the one remaining member of his family but he had left it too late. All he could do now was stand by to pick up the pieces when Jenny learned the truth.

*

Halfway through January Rob took part in the penultimate operation of his tour, as a flight commander in place of the crew who had spent Christmas with their new wives then been killed while testing their aircraft. The cause of the crash had not yet been discovered. Rob could not get the tragedy out of his mind. Two more squadron widows!

The flight returned during mid-afternoon as the sun was fast sinking in an ice-blue sky. There was already a frosty bloom on the roofs of hangars and huts, denoting a cold, crisp evening ahead. It had been a brilliantly clear day. They had raced in, struck home and left again, having smashed the marshalling-yard to kingdom come. All six crews were cock-a-hoop with success and urging each other to celebrate in style after dinner.

Rob sat in silence at the controls hearing their enthusiastic interchange. Today had been flying at its most thrilling. None of his team had been harmed, and everything had gone smoothly. The target had shown up clearly and they had all hit it with satisfying accuracy. It had been a piece of cake. The Mosquito was surely the perfect aircraft. She responded to his touch with complete obedience. There could be nothing more wonderful than hurtling along a few hundred feet above the ground on a day when the sky went on for ever and everything below it stood out as if freshly painted. He used to feel so elated at times like this. Today, all he wanted was to clean up, eat dinner, then turn in early. He was in no mood for a rowdy evening. He had been like that ever since receiving Jenny's letter. Then there was Rebecca. God knew he wanted her desperately, but she seemed unable to understand that he wanted to give, not only to take from her.

'You coming to the Wheatsheaf?' asked Donald, adding on seeing Rob shake his head, 'It's the ideal thing for wedding jitters. As your best man I advise getting plastered as often as possible, while you can. Once you're a sober married man you won't be able to afford things like that. It'll be pipe and slippers in front of the fire every night.'

Suddenly, getting drunk sounded immensely attractive. He would become insensible very quickly and would know nothing more until morning. 'All right,' he said. 'As best man you can buy the first round.'

'Attaboy!'

While Rob was dressing in fresh clothes for dinner he received a message that the CO wanted to see him. Thinking it would be news of his posting, he put on his tunic and cap to walk over to the office. He shivered in the chill of dusk; the moon had already risen to put cold light on the faint glitter of frost over every flat surface. Where was he going to be sent as a grounded dogsbody for three months?

It was immediately apparent to Rob that the matter was more serious than news of a posting. The CO's expression was grave and he seemed ill at ease as he invited Rob to sit down.

'I hear it went well today,' he said as heavily as if it had been a shambles.

'Yes, sir. They didn't know we'd arrived until we'd gone.'

'Good, good.' He studied Rob for so long it made him equally ill at ease. 'I've had some rather shocking news, Stallard. You know the Americans have been testing the beam system since it was modified. They've been so successful they went ahead with live rockets this morning.' He sighed. 'Something went wrong. It seems likely that one of them malfunctioned and exploded the moment it was activated. The

Mosquito blew apart at a hundred and fifty feet. One of the engines hit the observers' boat. I'm afraid Professor Lambourne and two naval officers were killed. Your fiancée is on the danger list in Folkestone Hospital. It's a terrible tragedy. I'm so very sorry.'

'Yes ... thank you, sir.' Rob got up hastily, saluted and left without waiting to be dismissed. He walked blindly through the sparkling evening, his footsteps ringing on the frost-covered tarmac, until he came up hard against a shape he recognized. He leaned back against the fuselage, staring up at the engine clear-cut in the moonlight, as tears slid down his cheeks. He had tried to protect her from being bereft at his passing. It had never once occurred to him that he might be the one left bereft by hers, and the pain of it was too much to bear.

Chapter Sixteen

The sister smiled when Rob gave his name. 'I'm so glad you've managed to get here. Medical skill is all very well, but love often works the miracles we can't always achieve.'

Flushing slightly, Rob asked, 'She is going to be all right, isn't she?'

'As you've been told on the telephone, Miss Lambourne is critically ill and it's too soon to know how her injuries will respond to treatment. She has been through a terrible ordeal in which she saw her remaining parent killed along with several others. This happens frequently nowadays, and much depends on the personality of the patient and the help given by those still able to. Shock and mental stress are additional reasons for our concern.' She led the way to a side ward where she paused to say, 'She asks for you constantly. There are no close relatives, so it falls on you to instil in her the will to recover. She needs you now as she never has before, Mr Stallard. Don't fail her.'

Rob was shocked when he entered. Rebecca's face was so pale that her eyes seemed enormous and much darker than before, as they stared at the wall facing her bed. She was being given blood through a drip, and the bedclothes covered a frame to keep the weight from her body. She looked so ill he was almost afraid to approach.

'Here's a handsome young man to see you,' said the sister quietly. 'I can only allow him to stay for ten minutes, but he can come again this evening.' She turned to Rob. 'I'll send a nurse when your time's up.'

Left alone with the girl who usually swept him along with her indomitable self-possession, Rob felt unequal to the situation. His facial muscles seemed frozen as he gazed at her beloved face, which resembled almost a death-mask wet with tears, and he had a swift mental vision of blanket-covered corpses in a hall where rain dripped through a hole in the roof. Oh God, he could not face losing *her*. He might as well be lost himself!

'I brought these,' he said with difficulty, holding up a large bunch of yellow chrysanthemums. 'I hope they're what you like. I haven't had much experience at buying flowers for girls.'

Rebecca began to sob as she gazed back at him, and the sound was so heartbreaking Rob dropped the flowers and knelt beside her to cup her face with his hands. 'Don't, please don't,' he begged. 'I'm here with you. Everything's going to be all right, I promise.' Struggling to tug his handkerchief from his pocket, he then wiped her drenched cheeks. 'I can't hold you because of this flaming cage, but once they take it away I'll bruise you black and blue with my arms.' He took one of her hands, but was afraid to grip it too tightly. 'You'll have to make do with this for now.'

Worried that he might do more harm than good with his visit, Rob said whatever came into his head in his desire to calm her, and the sobbing gradually subsided. 'I know what it's like to feel terribly alone,' he added softly, 'but it's rarely so. There's usually someone who cares. *I* do. I always will.' He stroked her hand. 'On the night of the gala you were there when I desperately needed you. I'm here for you. Remember that. I'll *always* be here for you.'

A nurse opened the door and said he should leave now.

He thought it was far too soon but he got to his feet, still holding Rebecca's hand. 'Can't I stay a little longer?'

'You can come back later,' she said, adding in the brisk, lighthearted manner of those used to dealing with pain and distress, 'a dashing young pilot bringing flowers and kneeling by the bedside is best in short doses. It can cause havoc to a girl's pulse-rate, can't it, Miss Lambourne?' She grinned at Rob. 'You can kiss her goodbye so long as you don't make a meal of it.'

Feeling his colour rise at her banter, Rob bent to touch Rebecca's dry lips with his own. 'I'll be back soon, I promise. We need to talk about this wedding we're going to have as soon as you're better. It's not going to be a hole-in-the-corner affair. You'll have a white dress, flowers, bridesmaids — the whole works. Think about that until I come back this evening.'

She spoke for the first time, and it was through more tears. 'Haven't you forgotten something?'

He shook his head. 'I was leaving the best bit until last.' Leaning closer, he whispered, 'I love you, Rebecca Lambourne, and I will until my dying day.'

Only as he made his way to a cafe for something to eat did Rob reflect that his choice of words had not been ideal.

*

For the second time in a week, Dennis Averell wished he was again just one of the boys. He did not relish what he was about to do, but Air Commodore Griffin had insisted: 'He won a DFC for destroying that train, didn't he, and I've seldom seen anyone steadier when clipping the waves as he was during the tests of Lambourne's beam system. That's what's needed here.'

'Stallard has only one more op. to complete his second tour, sir, and I'm reluctant to send him on something like this when he's overdue for a rest. He's had rather a tough time lately, and he's recently got engaged to Lambourne's daughter, who's critically ill in hospital.'

'We're supposed to be fighting a war, not acting as agony aunts.' Then the senior man had relented somewhat. 'Dennis, none of us wants to send boys out to do things like this. They've all had a tough time, and most of the bloody young fools are getting engaged or married. Stallard's the ideal chap for this kind of job, so we have to send him. The Met. report is good. He should have every chance of pulling it off.'

*

Rob knew it must be something special when he and Donald were sent for two days after his brief visits to Rebecca. They listened in silence as they were told that news had been received of a conference of German military chiefs reviewing defences along the French coast in expectation of an invasion.

'We've got them worried,' said the Wing Commander. 'They know that when we make our move they'll be unable to withstand the combined might of us and the Americans. However, anything that further lowers their morale will hasten the end. All I've been told is that at this conference will be one of the men at the very top — you can draw your own conclusions from that. It's being held this afternoon' — he tapped the map on the wall behind his desk — 'in this remote spot along the coast. There's an old lading-station no longer in use because the sea bed has built up too much to allow large ships in. It stands at the end of a long causeway of rocks, which makes it easy enough to defend from land or sea. Our only hope is to attack from the air. That's why you're here.'

'There can't be any permanent gun emplacements,' observed Rob, all his thoughts now on the job.

'A report we received early this morning says mobile light ack-ack has been moved overnight into the woods bordering the shoreline, two machine-guns have been installed inside the building, guards at the landward end of the causeway are dressed as fishermen, and two gunboats are hanging around the vicinity trying to look innocent.'

'For a "secret" meeting they've made it pretty darn obvious something's going on!' Donald exclaimed.

The CO gave a grim smile. 'They know the French Underground has spies everywhere. They can't keep anything secret. All they can do is to make the place as secure as possible. They're grasping at straws, Winkie, and praying a Mosquito doesn't come a-visiting. I've given you some idea of what you'll be up against by way of defences. Your best approach will be over the trees and out of the sun. There's a seventy-five per cent chance of some just when you need it. You'll get the full details at briefing. Take off at fourteen hundred. Test-fly your aircraft and stand ready.' When they reached the door, he said, 'I almost forgot. Your posting came through about half an hour ago, Stallard. You're to report to Sixty-Two OTU as an instructor. I've heard your views on "grounded dogsbodies", so I imagine you'll be pleased over this chance to continue flying.'

'Yes, sir,' mumbled Rob, wondering when he had mentioned grounded dogsbodies within the Wingco's hearing.

'Following the new policy of trying to keep successful crews together, you have been given the option of staying with your pilot, Winkie. How do you both feel about that?'

Rob and Donald exchanged a long look. Then Rob said, 'If they teach him to speak proper English, it's all right by me.'

'If he picks up the fact that it's possible to fly higher than thirty feet, I'll tag along,' Donald offered.

'Right, I'll indicate your agreement with official brevity. Good luck, gentlemen.'

Although Rob was pleased that he could continue flying, he knew the Operational Training Unit was way up near Sunderland. It would be impossible to see Rebecca except during long leave, and she needed his constant support right now if she was to have any hope of recovering. He would have to tackle that problem when he got back; see if he could have her moved to a hospital near the OTU.

*

They took off in pale sunshine after a brief wintry shower. 'Take a look at that!' Rob exclaimed, causing Donald to glance up from his chart. 'First time I've ever flown under a rainbow. That's luckier than a four-leafed clover.'

'Never knew that,' murmured Donald, gazing at the great arch of colour ahead, 'but if you do fly under it we'll be somewhere over Java by then, pal.'

'You have no soul! While I appreciate the beauties of nature, get your head down and work out a course for the spot where fishermen have Lugers in their creels, and several clumps of trees are not all they seem.'

They crossed the Kent coast at speed. It was not a long flight, and Rob wanted to be back before dark. At this time of year the weather could change very fast and, despite the weak sun, it was already growing colder. He almost felt sorry for the bogus fishermen and skulking gunboat crews as Donald gave him the course. He set it and settled back to await their landfall.

'I'm only going to make one run at it, Don.'

'Good. I don't like the sound of those guns in the trees.'

'They won't bother us. We'll be so low they'll never know we were there.'

'Can I have an assurance from you that you're not planning to fly in through one window of this goddam place and out through the other?'

Rob frowned in concentration. 'The lading-station is fifty feet high. I plan to approach over the waves, then climb to about a hundred and fifty feet when we're about a thousand yards from the target.'

'I'll have to be quick ... and bloody accurate,' protested Donald.

'You are, that's why I can get away with something like that. Soon as you release them, I'll make a steep climb over the sea, and hop it.'

'Okay.'

'I might chuck you out as I leave if you say that again.'

Donald laughed. 'You'll be saying it by the end of the war. I've got a bet on it with Shunter Raleman.'

Rob glanced upwards — he was constantly gazing around for other aircraft — and saw an awesome sight. 'Look up there.' Far above was a veritable armada of giants returning home. 'Flying Fortresses,' he said. 'They must have been over Germany again. See those gaps in their ranks? Poor devils!'

'They're Yanks. I thought you hated their guts.'

'Only one, and he might be up there with them ... or maybe he should be filling one of those gaps.'

'He'd be out from under your skin.'

'And my sister would be a widow.'

'Ah, I see it all now.'

Rob hardly heard him because at that moment the starboard engine cut out, refired, then cut out again. 'Trouble,' he said, glancing swiftly at the oil-pressure gauge. The reading had dropped dramatically. 'The bloody thing was all right when we tested it.'

Coughing and spluttering, the engine made a valiant attempt to keep going. Rob knew the signs well enough. He would have to shut it down within a matter of minutes. A Mosquito could fly quite steadily on one engine, and if it had happened on the way home he would not be worried. They were now in a more tricky situation. There was no question in his mind of turning back, but the attack plan had to be revised.

'We'll have to climb, Don. Our approach will be slower. The only good thing is that you'll have longer to ensure you plonk them right on target. I'll do what I can with the guns, but at five hundred feet they won't be as effective as I'd want. You'd better work out a course that'll take us to the nearest home runway on the way back, just in case.'

'Okay.'

Rob began his climb. It was a sign of the special relationship they had built up that Donald made no protest, and Rob did not expect him to. After cutting the engine Rob flew on, searching for the first sign of the French coast.

'Looks like we've struck the twenty-five per cent chance of *not* getting any sun,' he murmured. 'That puts paid to my hope of flying out of it at them.'

'You should be seeing the mouth of a river by now,' Donald told him. 'Make a hundred-and-eighty-degree turn over it, then you'll be right on the button for the causeway six miles due south.'

Rob gazed at the hazy outline of the coast, searching for a ribbon of water. When the sun was out rivers usually glistened with giveaway brightness. Today, the approaching land mass looked universally dull.

'Got it!' he said suddenly. 'I'll do as tight a turn as possible, but make allowances for this lady of ours. Good thing we can see where we're going. I'll stick to visual until we turn for home.'

Fretting over his lack of speed, and aware of the adjustments he must make with their engine-power halved, Rob took the aircraft round until he lined up with the coastal fringe. The sky was a uniform grey, without even a solar glare that might aid their approach by dazzling observers.

'You'd better stand by,' said Rob, as he pulled the handle to open the bomb doors. 'You're only getting one chance, then I'm hotfooting it over the sea.'

They watched, silent and tense, for the first glimpse of the causeway as the Mosquito droned onwards.

'Okay, there it is,' said Donald calmly. 'A couple of degrees starboard should do it. Keep her as steady as you can while I line up with that black and white building.'

They had been spotted. The light ack-ack in the woods opened fire. Seconds after that, Rob became aware of the gunboats racing inshore leaving converging white wakes in the pewter sea. Secrecy, surprise and all hope of hit-and-run had been lost the moment the engine packed up, so the pair were not thrown by the fierce attack. They had known it would come. Doing his utmost to concentrate on making it as easy as possible for Donald, Rob struggled to hold the aircraft steady and level while shells came at them from the woods and the sea.

'Just a little longer,' Donald yelled as the Mosquito lurched violently on being hit somewhere near the tail.

The noise was deafening as they neared the target. It seemed to Rob that they were crawling along, after the speed he was used to. A hundred yards from the building he spotted shutters over upper windows opening to reveal machine-guns. It was almost impossible to fly with any accuracy. They must have sustained serious damage at the rear. Rob recalled the struggle he had had on returning from the train-busting in Holland. He had thought all lost then, but had survived. He would do so again. Straining every muscle, he flew at the target as the guns in the upper storey added their fire to the hail of deadly metal coming from all directions.

'Left a bit. Hold her steady,' yelled Donald, as they closed on the lading-station. Then the sweetest words to any pilot: 'Bombs away!'

They had dropped them in the nick of time. Another shell put an end to all hopes of continuing, and there was only one course for Rob to take. 'I'll try to guide her as far from these woods as she'll go,' he shouted above the thunder of the bombardment. 'We might stand a chance on open ground. How'd we do?'

'Nothing left but a smoking ruin, pal. Serve 'em right!'

Putting all his strength and skill into an attempt to make a survivable crash-landing, Rob watched the ground approaching too fast, despite his hauling back on the column with his feet braced against the floor. He could not overshoot the woods, but he spotted a clearing ahead and prayed he could reach it.

'Stand by,' he yelled hoarsely, as the Mosquito lurched sideways, righted itself, then surged forward in a pancake landing that ended in a splintering crash in an area where trees had thinned to form a natural dell. The aircraft slewed violently, but was brought to a standstill within feet of the far side by the marshy ground within the clearing.

Rob was thrown sideways and cracked his head on the metal windscreen frame. He heard a cry behind him, and it penetrated his stunned senses to tell him they must get out before she blew. Badly winded, and bleeding from his forehead, he followed the well-taught crash procedure. Unstrapping himself, he struggled to open the top hatch. A task that had always been easy enough now turned into a mammoth effort, but he eventually succeeded and turned to Donald. 'Let's get far away from here.'

The Canadian looked white and in pain. 'I think I've broken my arm. My legs don't feel too hot, either.'

'Can't help that. You've got to get out before she explodes. Stand up, and I'll help you.'

The moment Donald moved he gave a sharp cry. 'I can't bear weight on my right leg.'

'Stand on the left one,' Rob ordered. 'I'll get out and give you a hand up. I'm not leaving you here, so you'd better make the effort.'

Outside on the wing, Rob bent to grab hold of Donald's battledress and tug with every remaining ounce of strength he could summon. A strong smell of fuel added urgency to his actions, but Donald was in severe pain and cried out with every movement. Rob somehow managed to get the other man free of the cockpit and on to the wing, then he jumped to the ground and took Donald over his shoulder. Although Rob had the greater weight and muscle, it was nevertheless a job for a Hercules to carry the unconscious Canadian over marshy ground into which his boots sank at every step.

The line of trees that had looked dangerously close on landing now seemed a league away, but Rob eventually reached their cover and entered the gloomy wood, coughing and panting. His whirling thoughts told him safety was still far away — when the aircraft burst into flames the trees would be set ablaze all round them — but his body was reluctant to obey his mind. Just a short rest; just a chance to get his breath back.

The doggedness often cursed by those who knew Rob rose above all else to drive him to further effort. He was not going to be roasted in a French forest; neither was his friend. Gripping Donald tighter, he set off deeper into the dark interior. He had no idea how much time had passed before it dawned on him that the Mosquito was not going to explode.

'You gorgeous girl,' he breathed, as he sank to the soggy earth and dropped his burden beside him. 'You still love me after all I've just done to you.'

Sitting in a daze, Rob eventually grew aware of movement to his left. Struggling to his feet in alarm he saw a most welcome sight. Coming through the trees was an old man pushing a light handcart. Small and hunched, dressed in shabby clothes with a dirty grey blanket looped over his shoulders, he was far from the idea of a knight in shining armour, but Rob saw him as such.

'Ici, monsieur,' he called in schoolboy French. 'Mon ami est ...' He thought feverishly and the word came to him. 'Blessé. Beaucoup blessé,' he added urgently.

The Frenchman arrived unsmiling and uttering a torrent of words Rob could not understand. Yet he appeared ready to help, so Rob stammered the few simple phrases he could muster from his unhappy years at Darston Grammar, and made descriptive gestures to back them up. The

Frenchman waved his arms and continued talking non-stop. They eventually both fell silent and squatted beside Donald, who showed signs of coming round.

'Don, this man has a handcart,' Rob explained. 'We'll get you on it and wheel you to safety. At least, I think that's what he's proposing. I can't understand him.'

Donald's pale eyes swivelled to look at their saviour. Then he began speaking rapidly to the man, who leaned nearer to hear the faint voice. Nodding energetically, and holding an animated conversation with Donald, the Frenchman stood and wheeled the handcart alongside the Canadian, spreading his stained 'cloak' over the hard surface.

Donald gave Rob a faint smile. 'I forgot to tell you I speak French better than I speak English.'

At that point, they heard voices in the direction from which the Frenchman had come. Rob saw a group of grey-uniformed troops approaching, and his heart sank. 'The game's up, Don. I hope you also speak German, because they're going to be bloody furious over what we've just done.'

The enemy soldiers had no need of words; their guns made their intentions perfectly clear. Donald was thrown on the handcart, where he passed out again. Then Rob was prodded forward by a rifle in his back. When a shot rang out he turned in hot protest, disregarding the gun barrel at his spine, but Donald was still being wheeled forward a few feet to his rear. The Frenchman was now an inert heap at the foot of a tree.

Rob glared at the soldier who had taken revenge in the most cowardly way. 'You great bully. *He* didn't do it; *I* did. And I'm bloody glad, if it finished off a dozen or more like you.'

He was pushed so hard he fell on the muddy ground. When he looked up he encountered a gaze as cold as any he had seen, and he knew the war would be vastly different for him from now on.

Twelve hours later, after non-stop fruitless interrogation by a German officer hoping to exhaust his prisoners into telling more than their name, rank and service number, Rob was locked in a cell of the local prison and given a bowl of thin turnip soup. Donald was being treated by the military surgeon after Rob's repeated insistence, although he was unhappy about their separation.

Sitting in the windowless cell on a hard bench, Rob fully realized the implications of his situation and put his head in his hands. He was to be sent to a prisoner-of-war camp tomorrow — a place surrounded by wire and armed guards, where he would be treated with contempt and locked up each night. He would be posted as missing until the Red Cross were given details of his capture, which could take up to three months. Within that time he could get no word to Rebecca. Believing him lost, she would have no reason to hold on to life. In that cold dawn, Rob found no reason to hold on to his own.

*

That Goddam Mouse came in on three engines, but was otherwise reasonably undamaged. On her fuselage were four tiny mice, painted by the ground crew to symbolize four 'kills' by the gunners. Jim made a surprisingly soft landing, which led to a voice from the rear suggesting they always cut one engine before their approach.

Jim grinned at the man on his right. 'You go along with that?'

Robards shook his head. 'If this ship needs four, that's the number that makes me feel happiest.' He flexed his shoulders, and eased his back. 'That was a long one today. I feel I've been sitting here all week.'

'We all need a rest, but I guess we'll only get it if the weather worsens again.'

'D'you think we'll land in France when spring comes?'

'If we don't, there'll be nothing left of Germany to capture,' Jim murmured, taxiing to the space assigned to him. 'We've been hammering at them for months now. If they won't sue for peace, we have no alternative but to invade and break them that way.'

Jim felt he could sleep for several days, but he must ring Jenny before he could get his head down for the few hours he would be allowed. She always heard them come back, and counted them in. Then she waited for the call that would end her fears. It was the one disadvantage of living near the base. Despite that, neither of them regretted what they had done. Jenny declared she would still worry if they were not married, and being his wife was the most wonderful gift she could have. For Jim, having someone to return to made his present life bearable. The snatched hours together sustained his sanity.

The CO was present at debriefing, which suggested that a significant event had occurred. As his expression was not one of delight or excitement, the men guessed he was not about to announce Hitler's surrender. After congratulating them on the success of their mission (the loss of fifty men's lives did not constitute failure), he gave the news that the squadron was about to be split. Half the crews were to remain and be augmented by men who had not yet seen action.

'This squadron has built up a tough reputation, men. Your success and battle experience are needed to show the way to greenhorns; give them confidence. Flying in formation with crews that have returned time after time gives them a sense of invulnerability. As you all know, that's of utmost importance.'

'What about the other crews, Colonel?' called a senior captain.

'They will join a squadron in Lincolnshire, with much the same duty. The boys up there have had a run of very bad luck. Their losses have been unusually heavy. Like you, they've seen their buddies go down on every trip. Morale is rock bottom after the death of their commander in a Jeep accident on icy roads. They have this feeling they're jinxed. Useless to send greenhorns to that situation.' Colonel Hoyght read from a list the names of the captains whose crews should pack up ready to fly to their new base on the following afternoon. Jim's was one of them.

On his way to a telephone, he thought swiftly. He would find an apartment or a small house near the base, so that Jenny could join him as soon as possible. She would not be happy about giving up her work with Molly, but they had discussed this possibility and both agreed that to be together was their first priority. Knowing his resourceful young wife, Jim guessed she would not be idle for long.

When he dialled the number of Darston Manor, Jenny greeted him with a catch in her voice. 'Darling, thank God! I counted five missing and was certain one was the *Mouse*.'

'Hey, take it easy. I'm still in one piece.' He frowned. 'What is it, honey? You're not usually like this.'

'This morning I had a call from Rob's CO. The telegram has since arrived. He's officially listed as missing over occupied France.'

Jim cursed the fact that he could not be with her tonight, or for some time. 'There's every chance he'll ...'

'I know. *I know*. After three months it'll change to "Missing, believed killed in action", unless he's turned up.'

'Did anyone see it happen?'

'No. Wing Commander Averell said he was on a lone raid for which he'll almost certainly get a bar to his DFC. What use will it be to him if ...? I can't believe he's gone, Jim.'

'That's good, because knowing him he'll defy every goddam rule and get back here somehow. You know he will.'

She appeared not to have heard him. 'I've been so caught up with my own life these past few years. Now I've been made aware of how far apart we have drifted.'

'Honey, it takes two to quarrel and he made no effort to meet you halfway. Don't shoulder his blame with yours.'

'I should have made an effort to see him. All I was doing was working for Molly in perfect safety, while he was risking his life day after day. I should have tried to put things right.'

Jim sighed. 'When he gets back you can, if it's possible.'

Her voice grew shaky again. 'There's something else that has made me realize the width of the rift between us. The CO wanted my advice on what he should do about Rob's *fiancée*, who's seriously ill in hospital. Jim, how could he have got engaged without telling me? It was such a shock to be told by an outsider.'

'Same way you got married and told him later. Maybe he was intending to write you about it.'

'But he's never even mentioned a girlfriend. Besides, he doesn't believe in wartime love affairs.'

'Everyone says that until it happens to them. How ill is she?'

'She's the daughter of a professor who was killed at her side in a tragic accident at sea. She's on the danger list.'

'Poor kid! It's going to be a lot for her to handle,' Jim murmured, amazed at the news. How could Stallard have interested a professor's daughter? 'What did you say to this wing commander?'

'We agreed to leave the nursing staff to decide when she should be told. I feel I should visit her, but it's rather a long way to travel, so I'll check with the nurses then write to her.'

'I think you should leave it well alone, honey.'

'I don't,' came the characteristic retort. 'It's the least I can do for Rob. We were once very close, you know.'

'Until I came on the scene?'

She was immediately upset. 'I didn't say that, darling. I'm so *very* glad you did. I love you very much, Captain Benson.'

'You better had, Mrs Benson. I wish I could get over to the Manor, but it's out of the question. Just know I'm holding you in my arms and pouring my strength into you. Keep that pretty chin high. He'll be back.'

'When am I going to see you? A telephone embrace isn't anywhere near enough.'

Jim broke the news about his posting, and the subsequent discussion of their plans appeared to settle Jenny somewhat. When he rang off he returned to his quarters feeling drained. He had no doubts Stallard was dead. Trust him to go out doing something heroic, and individual. He had always been a determined loner!

*

1944 was slipping past. It was already April, and still there had been no Allied landing on French soil. The men of all three fighting services were angry and dispirited, despite the fact that soldiers had been practising landings on beaches along England's south coast, and curious floating concrete platforms had been seen there. Everyone knew it must come, but when, when, *when*?

Jim returned to his first base, along with the other crews who had moved north with him. There were three fewer than before. For two months they had worked hard to revive morale in a hard-hit squadron, but it had plunged again a week ago when *Bluegrass Baby* had been blown apart over Mannheim. The death of Brad Halloran, buccaneer of the air, had made everyone feel vulnerable. They needed a fillip such as the invasion of France.

The pilot of *That Goddam Mouse* had a personal fillip. Jenny was pregnant and back at Darston Manor. Jim was reassured by that. He knew the Guthries would look after Jenny and treat the baby as their grandchild if anything happened to him. The real grandfather was not to be told of the child's existence. That was the way Jim wanted it. Bucket was back in America as a flying instructor, but he had agreed to be the baby's godfather by proxy and threatened to give it a set of drums on its first birthday.

Although Jim was growing to love England in all her colourful seasons, he also longed to go home. He daydreamed about the rosy future the Benson family would have there, while he sat at the controls during the hours they were over safe territory. This extended further and further as time passed. The Germans were running low on fuel, so their fighters were held back to defend vital targets and no longer ranged far afield to attack. With their own long-distance fighters in escort, the American bombers were finally gaining dominance. Once the Allies landed on European soil, the war would be over in no time. The people of occupied countries would rise up, and victory would be swift. Then they could go back to the good life: to steaks and frankfurters, ice-cream and cookies, Cadillacs and the Brooklyn Dodgers, cocktail bars and roadside diners, swimming-pools and tennis courts, Manhattan and Palm Beach.

There was an additional reason for Jim's longing to return home. In a ridiculous campaign of atonement, his wife had taken on responsibility for her brother's fiancée. In vain had Jim insisted that she had no obligation to the girl. The affair between her and Stallard sounded more like a professional link, anyway.

Jim tried to allow for Jenny's natural grief, and for the equally natural emotional effects of early pregnancy, but the whole business was getting out of hand. The Lambourne girl had fought back to health because she tearfully claimed she owed her 'poor lamb' an apology and would not be broken by what had happened. Although Jim had been reasonable over his wife's visits to Folkestone Hospital, he had voiced his dissent when she revealed that she had arranged to have the girl transferred to Darston Cottage Hospital for convalescence. That had sparked the first row of their marriage.

After a passionate reconciliation, Jenny had had her way. She had even talked Jim into visiting the girl there. It had been an uncomfortable surprise because not only was Rebecca an absolute dish but she eulogized over Stallard and confided that he had tested a new invention for the RAF. The same one that had killed her father, two naval officers and the two Americans who had continued the tests.

The substance of Jim's ongoing discord with Jenny was that she had convinced herself she was fully responsible for the rift between herself and her brother. Molly said Jenny cried a lot when Jim was not around, and he guessed it was for Stallard, not for him. All in all, he felt he was being slowly pushed out of her affections by her brother and that damned redhead. He was sick of hearing Jenny say their parents would never forgive her for treating Rob as she had, because he had always done whatever he could for her. When she said it again as they walked across the fields an hour before Jim was due back at the base after a weekend at the Manor, he reminded her sharply that her brother had joined the RAF and left her to cope alone in war-torn Britain while he enjoyed the good life in the US.

'If it was so good, why was he so touchy about it even after two years?' she challenged.

'Don't bring up that Carlstrom business again, for Pete's sake!' he cried. 'That's dead and buried.'

Jenny halted, growing pale. 'Like Rob.'

Cursing his heedless choice of words, Jim took hold of her arms. 'Honey, I'm sorry ... but you've got to get yourself together over this. The past is gone. We have a future to think of.'

'It's as well to put *your* past behind you, but I can't. We were once a close happy family.'

He followed as she walked on, trying not to lose his temper. When he reported back this evening he would almost certainly be told there was a mission tomorrow. The weather was good, and they were making continuous concentrated attacks deep into Germany. He needed Jenny's love and tenderness; surely deserved a loving antidote to the danger of those days when they were not together.

They walked for a while through the April pre-dusk hour, and the sweet smell of sun-warmed grass hung in the still air. A few young rabbits had ventured out to eat, and birds were going to roost in dark echelons against the pale sky. It was so peaceful. Jim slung his arm across her shoulders, needing the physical contact. They had shared two loving nights, and he thought of the hard military bed he would occupy alone for the next exhausting period. He was about to tell her how much he would miss her warm, pliant body next to his, when Jenny shattered the mood.

'Rebecca's doing so well they'll discharge her soon. I've suggested that she comes here until she's strong enough to sort out her future.'

Halting and turning his wife to face him, Jim said, 'You've done more than enough for her already. If she can leave medical care she's strong enough to sort out her future. The longer you continue to fuss over her she'll never stand on her own feet.'

'How can she, after what she's been through?'

'Jenny, you'd suffered a *triple* loss when Rob joined up and you had no choice but to stand on your own feet. You made it through without help.'

Her eyes glittered in the way he knew well. 'You can't drop that subject, can you?'

He sighed. 'I'm trying to make you see you have no obligation to Rebecca, but all I know is my wife is growing neurotic over a brother she had lost touch with, and over a girl who claims he was going to marry her. Where does your husband fit into all this?'

'You're deliberately keeping out of it,' she accused him.

'Because I'm the one with some sense.' They confronted each other for a few moments; a large, tense man in khaki, and a young, confused woman in last year's skirt and sweater. Then Jim said heavily, 'He did his damnedest to stop us from getting together, and you resisted. Now he's gone, you're letting him come between us.'

'That's a terrible thing to say!' she cried.

'It's true. All you think and talk about is how you should have mended your quarrel with him, and the person you're most concerned about is a girl he apparently refused to marry until he was in some kind of trouble.'

Spinning on her heel, Jenny walked swiftly towards the house.

'Oh *hell!*' muttered Jim explosively, as he looked at his watch and saw that he must be on his way. He nursed his resentment as he crossed the field and reached the stables. Jenny was standing by the front steps, where the wisteria was already in bloom.

'I'll call tomorrow evening, as usual.' She just nodded, which refuelled his anger. 'That's if you can spare the time to speak to me.' He went to his car, hating what he was doing yet too angry to stop. Slamming the door, he started the engine with excessive acceleration so that it roared in the silent dusk.

Jenny ran across the gravel to him, her face still pale. 'Jim ... take care.'

'Yeah,' he said savagely, and let in the clutch.

*

They rendezvoused with two other squadrons over the North Sea at 0830 hours to form yet another huge aerial armada. Phil Robards had been given his own ship. His replacement was a twenty-year-old named Cliff Witty, who sat beside Jim in moody silence. That makes two of us, he thought heavily. As he had snapped at the boy during the flight prelims, he made an attempt to recreate the family atmosphere so necessary for success.

'You got a girl waiting at home, Cliff?'

'Did have,' he mumbled, gazing ahead. 'All that crap about Yanks stealing sweethearts and wives over here! I got a letter from Myra Mae — she's the girl next door. Seems she fallen for a British pilot cadet up at the airfield. Just *lervs* the way he talks, and how he treats her like a lady. Even asks permission to kiss her, she says.'

It was hardly conducive to lifting Jim's mood. 'There's plenty more fish in the sea. Believe me, I know.'

'I've given up women.'

'What are you going to do the rest of your life?'

'No problem. It won't last much longer.'

Jim fell silent again. So much for the CO's advice about families! He kept to formalities while the flight proceeded smoothly until they reached Germany. This was usually when German fighters appeared, and today was no different. The raid went ahead with familiar relentless precision, as if the terrible pattern of death and destruction were not taking place all round the wave of Fortresses. Jim concentrated on remaining steady over the target while shells burst dangerously close to them, and he heard the young second pilot sigh with relief when they felt the stick of bombs leave the belly of the aircraft. Then it changed to a cry as a loud clatter of bullets on the fuselage told them they were under attack.

The oaths and shouts from crewmen to whom this had become a way of life rang in Jim's ears as he demanded a course to take them in a wide loop towards the coast and home. He received in reply a toneless voice reporting that the lieutenant was lying across the table with blood all over his head.

Jim turned to his second pilot. 'Get back there and give me a course.'

The boy gazed back at him in fear. 'I haven't done any navigating since —'

'*Get back there!*'

'Yes, Captain.' He unstrapped himself and scrambled from his seat to disappear within the fuselage.

Hardly had Jim time to feel lonely in the cockpit than the enemy fighters attacked again. 'Got him! I got one, guys!' came the triumphant cry from the gunner, Clusky, only to be followed by a scream, then silence. 'Clusky, you okay? Oh God, that other bastard got Clusky. Look out, he's coming in again!'

Again the clatter of bullets, then the brightness of fire around the outer starboard engine. Jim could tell they had been badly damaged elsewhere, and fire was a hazard he always dreaded, but it was his job to keep them in the air whatever happened.

Their plight attracted the attention of one of their own fighters, which chased off the Junkers. Jim veered away in pursuit of the rest of his squadron as an exploding fireball to port signified the end of their attacker.

Offering silent thanks to the pilot of the P-51, Jim set about assessing the cost of concentrated attacks on them. Garth Ritchie, the navigator, was unconscious with serious head wounds. Clusky had been hit in both arms, but was still determinedly operational. The top turret gunner had been hit in the neck and was fighting for breath. Cliff Witty was shaking so much he could not plot a course. All this was reported to Jim by Lieutenant George Gilman, the bombardier, whose father, a stretcher-bearer in 1918, had taught his son first aid.

'Can you do anything for them?' Jim asked, as George perched on the right-hand seat.

'Sure, something, but they all need a doctor soon as possible. I'm not sure about Garth. Head wounds are tricky. Can't promise he'll make it. Top gunner'll be better when I've knocked him out. Panic hampers his breathing. Clusky's tough. He'll keep going until we get home.' He took a breath. 'Is that a possibility?'

'Providing I get a course from Cliff.'

'I've given him something to steady him, and I had basic navigation way back. You'll get a course.'

'To the nearest airstrip on the home side of the Channel.'

'You want to know the score?'

'Some of it's obvious. We're down to three engines and fuel's leaking from one of the tanks. The rudder's playing up badly. Has it been shot up?' At the other's nod, Jim asked, 'What else?'

'Radio's smashed to pieces, and the wings are peppered. Still want that course for England?'

Jim forced a smile. 'I don't aim to join the losing team because some jerk jumped us. Thanks, George.'

Jim then concentrated on fulfilling his vow, knowing it had been a rash one in view of their circumstances. He had flown in on three engines before, although not all the way home as he would today. Fuel could be transferred to another tank. Wings peppered with holes were unwelcome but could hold out if he was careful. The major problems were the damaged rudder and useless radio. They would have no contact with the ground on the way home. When they reached the landing strip they would have to fire flares to indicate that they needed emergency facilities. Jim was already aware that guiding the aircraft was difficult, heavy work. Their one hope was to set a course as the crow flew, and pray everyone left them alone until they were over the home stretch.

'Have we a course yet?' he demanded.

'Almost there, Captain,' came Witty's voice.

'Speed it up. We're drifting.'

George Gilman returned next minute with a slip of paper. 'There's a fighter station right on the coast, and another ten miles inland. There's a heavy bomber squadron sited there, which means the runway will be much longer than the other. Give us more room to put down. It's up to you.'

It was a difficult decision, but Jim decided that if they reached the coast another ten miles would not present too much of a problem, and they would have a greater chance of getting down safely. He set the latter course.

Staying low, Jim nursed his bomber every mile of the way during the next two hours. Cliff Witty came up to give him a break once or twice, but the boy did not have Jim's strength and *That Goddam Mouse* needed firm handling. By some miraculous chance their lone presence went unnoticed by ground batteries over France.

Then they were approaching the English coast, and Jim wondered briefly if he should have elected to head for the nearest fighter station. Would they make another ten miles? Too late to question his own judgement, although she was beginning to shudder alarmingly. Being cut off from ground controls was a nasty sensation. Thank God they were not coming in at night. Visibility right now was perfect.

They crossed the coast losing height inexorably. The greenness of England was a welcome sight. As Jim took in the vista of patchwork fields, tiny clustering villages, market towns filled with red-roofed houses, and low hills covered with long-tailed lambs, the truth of their situation hit him. This was Jenny's homeland, the scene of her childhood years with beloved parents and a brother. She had lost them all, and was prepared also to surrender her heritage to live with him across the Atlantic. If he did not make it during the next thirty minutes, he would leave her with the memory of his bitter words, and a belief that she had lost his love. All because of her brother, who had bugged him from their first meeting and had never stopped.

'Where the hell is this bomber station?' he demanded, as he desperately scanned the terrain ahead. They were going down with every mile, and there looked to be a large town dead ahead. A crash-landing there would be fatal.

Gilman's voice came over the intercom. 'Should be in view.'

'It isn't.' He turned to Witty, now seated beside him ready for the landing. 'Can you see an RAF station?'

'Not yet. Must be the other side of that town.'

'If it is, we won't make it.'

'Oh God, I told you life wouldn't last much longer.'

At that moment, Jim spotted an open stretch of several fields with infant crops, separated only by wide earth tracks. It offered their only chance, provided the rudder held out long enough to make a wide sweep to port.

'Captain to crew. Stand by for a crash-landing. Secure all wounded and be ready to evacuate them soon as we stop. Good luck, guys. I guarantee the *Mouse* won't run out on us now.' He cast a swift glance at his second pilot. 'I'll need you. Forget what's outside the window and think of it as a normal landing, except we're going in on our belly instead of wheels. She's going to take some handling. Be prepared for that.' At the white-faced boy's nod, he added, 'I'm renowned for unorthodox landings, so this'll be my best ever. Here we go.'

Holding his breath, Jim struggled to execute a left bank to line him up with the fields. The Fortress responded only sluggishly, so he had to apply greater pressure, putting further demands on a rudder shot almost apart. By this time they were barely fifty feet up, and appeared to be approaching at breakneck speed. Then, as if the bomber sensed home and safety, she dropped to the ground with a shuddering thump before surging forward across tender wheat-stalks in a great scything sweep.

Jim's formidable strength was of no avail to guide their progress, because the rudder finally gave up and they slithered unimpeded towards a brick barn alongside the road bordering the fields.

*

Jim had entered a world of constant pain and shadows, where voices floated above him without making sense. Every so often, clarity lingered long enough to tell him he must do something undefined but urgent, yet he was held back each time he tried to move. Faces began appearing through the shadows. Women's faces that smiled; men's that looked grave. The voices soon attached themselves to the faces, which was more comforting.

Then there was a different face; one that was not adorned by a white cap. A lovely face with green eyes and a smile more intimate than the others. The voice was different, too. Calm, with a soft burr he remembered from somewhere. He could only gaze silently until tears spilled on to her smooth cheeks, and the face was led away by another wearing a white cap. He had not wanted it to go, but felt too tired to do anything about it.

There was bright light, and he opened his eyes to see sunshine streaming through windows each side of him. He was in a room with pale walls and dark curtains, and the bed he was lying in was hung with a curious arrangement of metal arms and cables. He tried to move his head, but it was held immobile by something that felt like a clamp. Panic surged through him when he realized he could not move his arms or legs, either. A light on the wall ahead began flashing red, and a woman appeared. She was a nurse with red hair.

'It's all right,' she said softly. 'No need to be afraid. Just take it easy.'

'What's going on?' he croaked. 'I can't move.'

'You're in traction, that's all. It's nothing to get steamed up about. It ensures you don't injure yourself further while your bones are mending.' She had a sweet smile. 'You've chosen the ideal time to wake up. Your wife has just arrived. She's talking to Major Kitts right now. By the time I smarten you up a little, she'll be here.'

When Jenny came in Jim could only gaze silently at her once more, because recollection was returning and he felt too emotional to speak. Her pregnancy was now fairly obvious, and she looked so lovely he could only convey his feelings by feebly gripping the hand she had slipped into his, which was somewhere out of his sight.

'Hallo, darling, you've come back to me at last.' Her lips brushed his as she smiled into his eyes. 'Kelly — she's your nurse — said you're alarmed by all this machinery attached to you. It looks worse than it is and it's absolutely necessary.'

'I can't move,' he croaked again.

'It must be horrid, but it's only for a while, I promise.' She kissed him lightly again, then pushed his hair back with a caressing hand. 'Do you remember what happened?'

'Some.'

'Would you like me to tell you the rest?'

'I guess.'

She remained standing so that he could see her. 'You landed in a field and hit a barn. In the impact your spine was badly damaged, hence the traction.'

He absorbed that piece of bad news, then asked, 'How did the crew make out?'

'Young Cliff broke both legs, and Garth Ritchie has a long haul ahead of him. The rest are fine.'

'And the *Mouse*?'

She shook her head. 'The farmer's none too pleased about men trampling the rest of his crop to collect the wreckage.' She squeezed his hand. 'Phil Robards says it's just as well, because no one else would fly a ship with such a God-awful name. Jim, they've all been so kind to me over this long month.'

'*Month*?'

'You've been very ill, darling. So many men from the base have been across to the Manor when they could get away. Major Eames maintains that you're the only pilot in the squadron who could land and gather in the harvest at the same time. Others claim you lived up to your reputation in true style.'

Before he could follow up on that, she changed the subject. 'Darling, I had some wonderful news yesterday. Rob's in a prisoner-of-war camp with his navigator.'

Jim was not sure how he felt about that, so said nothing. Jenny did not seem to expect a comment, and added, 'I don't suppose life there is too good, but at least he's alive, and now we've landed in France he has every chance of being freed before long.'

'We've landed?'

She nodded. 'Two days ago. It's tougher than we expected, but we're hanging on and there's no doubt the war is going our way with a vengeance. Rebecca's gone back to Romney Marsh. She needs to sort out her affairs and prepare the house for Rob's return. I thought you'd like to know that.'

He was growing tired. There was so much to take in. Yet he needed an answer to something before he slept. 'Honey, what's the score with me?' At her silence, he asked, 'I'll never play sports again, will I?'

She said frankly, 'You've a long way to go, Jim, and your final limitations will greatly depend on your courage and determination. You have both in huge amounts.'

He gazed at her through sudden moisture in his eyes. 'I'm so sorry. Look what I've done to you. Saddled you with a crock of a husband.'

Her smile was not in the least forced as she patted her swelling stomach. 'The whole world can see what you've done to me, and I'm immensely proud of the fact. Darling, I promised to stay no longer than five minutes, but I wanted to convince you you'll make it. Together, we can do anything.'

After Jenny had left, Jim lay thinking of what she had told him and his mind went back to Carlstrom when they had all taken to the air for the first time. Flying had been the great adventure; the thrill of a lifetime. He and his friends had been so young and eager. Peter Kelsey was crippled for life, Gus was dead, and J.T. faced an unknown future. Of the four, only Bucket had escaped unscathed. So far! Jim prayed the war would end before it claimed the last of the once-merry aviators.

*

Rob arrived back in England at the end of September. As the Dakota descended over trees ablaze with autumn foliage, across patchwork fields golden with stubble, gentle hills dotted with sheep and pretty clustering villages along winding lanes, he gazed down too choked to speak. Freedom was still too new fully to believe. It was a relief to feel clean, to wear fresh clothes, to shave and clean his teeth with a supply of soap and toothpaste. It was a blessing to eat good food, and to sleep in a bed without bugs. It was unbelievably wonderful to be free of harsh voices over loudspeakers, of guards with expressions of contempt, of high wire enclosures and roaming searchlights, of sudden vicious deprivations like the withholding of mail or recreation facilities. Most glorious of all was the sight of the coastline he had flown over so many times knowing he was almost home. He wiped the sudden dampness from his cheeks with his fist, and was not the only man on that aircraft to do so.

Conditions in the camp had been growing dangerously severe as the half-starved guards cut the prisoners' rations to feed themselves, and the spectre of defeat caused the more vicious to take undue revenge on the men who had helped to bring it about.

One morning, the internees had woken to find the guards gone and the gates open. An hour later, American tanks rolled up to where they were debating their best course of action.

Rob thought 'Hi, there!' the sweetest words he had ever heard, and was still smiling when they said 'Okay'. From that moment he had been in a fever to get home to the girl he loved.

Being airborne was still thrilling, but he yearned to be at the controls. After twenty-eight days' leave he was to report to a training wing for assessment. He had prepared his case. As he had been forcibly grounded for eight months, he deserved to be given something to fly. Hitler was allowing Germany to be flattened and her people starved in his crazy refusal to surrender, so there was a chance Rob might again be in combat. He was not keen to join an operational squadron right away. He wanted some months of settled married life to compensate for captivity.

The taxi taking Rob and Donald from the station to the house on the Marsh on the following day was truly ancient. It rattled and jerked over the long, bumpy track, and Rob's impatience became almost uncontainable as dusk settled over the landscape he remembered so vividly. However, when they arrived, he climbed very slowly from his seat. The door stood open and Rebecca was waiting, yet Rob stopped a few feet away, suddenly afraid to touch her in case she was unreal. She had never looked more beautiful.

She came to him, feathering his cheek with her fingers and whispering, 'I've always had to make the first move, darling.'

When they eventually broke apart the car had gone, and Donald was studying the stars intently. Rob introduced him, and they went inside. Rob sighed with delight over the familiar rooms, despite a pang at the absence of the man with whom he had found such rapport. Supper of lamb chops was brought by Mrs Maple, who merely said, 'Glad you're back safe, but don't tramp through in muddy boots after I've cleaned.'

After supper, Rob broached essentials. 'Don's being repatriated as soon as there's a place for him on a ship, so if he's to be my best man I'll have to arrange the wedding soon.'

Rebecca gave her knowing smile. 'I bought the dress and veil weeks ago, so when you cabled that you'd be here today I went into action. The village church is booked for two p.m. on Saturday — dear old Reverend Bates helped me over the special licence — and the reception will be at the Three Pheasants. I invited everyone by telephone and they all accepted. Dennis Averell has agreed to give me away. He's such a sweetie! I've reserved rooms at the inn for Donald and those guests who want to stay overnight. We'll come back here, darling.'

A curious pain sprang up in the pit of Rob's stomach, and he wanted her so badly his voice was unsteady as he said, 'You always were impossibly bossy.'

The Canadian studied the pair, then yawned loudly. 'Gee, I'm tired. If the wedding's already fixed, I think I'll hit the sack. Don't wake me early.'

After Donald had left, Rob drew his girl into his arms. She asked anxiously, 'You're not angry?'

He smiled. 'If we're getting married within three days, I'm starting the honeymoon now. Come on!'

In the early hours, as they lay half-asleep, Rebecca said quietly, 'You've grown awfully thin. Did they ill-treat you?'

Rob did not want to talk about it. 'Not half as much as you do.' He held her more tightly, remembering those early months when he was almost crazy with the belief that she would not survive without him beside her. It had been the blackest period of his life, and he had known some dark ones. After three months, letters from home had eased his fears. Jenny had seen Rebecca through the danger period and back to health. He owed his sister so much. She was now doing the same in America for her husband. Rob was certain their parents would be proud of her. And of him? Perhaps.

'Come back to me, Rob,' Rebecca whispered.

He stroked her bright hair gently. 'I was just thinking that after Saturday I shall be boss.'

'We'll see.' She snuggled closer. 'You're not going to be old-fashioned over money, are you?'

It was a moment before he murmured, 'I've learned that the only things that matter are love and freedom. We'll sort out the rest as we go along.'

Epilogue

The memorial service in Oak Ridge Cemetery, Arcadia, was being held to honour the twenty-three British cadets who had died during their training at Carlstrom Field and at nearby Clewiston, between 1941 and 1945. Along with large contingents from American and British expatriate societies were some relatives of the young men buried in a special plot over which a Union Jack flew. Among those representing the many thousands who had successfully completed their training was Wing Commander R.N. Stallard DFC and bar, AFC, who was accompanied by a red-haired woman in a smart black silk suit.

Fifteen years had passed since Rob's ten-week sojourn at Carlstrom. He had felt a tremendous sensation of travelling back in time on seeing the station where they had tumbled wearily from the train on that first morning, the dance hall where he had accidentally caused a free-for-all, the banks of the Peace River where he, Johnny, Cyril and Patrick had enjoyed barbecues with generous hosts, and the Trinity Church, where they had attended Sunday services before being taken to the beach in a procession of cars filled with laughing girls and their parents.

Memories had begun flooding back when driving along roads flanked by orange groves, on seeing palms outlined against the violent blue of the sky, and on hearing the warm Southern drawl all around him. Although he had spent no more than ten weeks here, they had had a profounder effect on him than the rest of his time in America. As he crossed the grass on that hot, still morning, Rob vividly recalled the day he had first taken a Stearman off the ground and discovered flying was the most thrilling thing he had ever done. He still felt that thrill on taking off.

After six months as an instructor, he had passed the remainder of the war in action over Burma, where he had been shot down and trekked to safety through jungle. He still had bouts of malaria. After Burma had come Palestine and the Berlin Airlift, before a long spell at home during which his two daughters had been born. He had finally bought a country house on the Dorset coast, near the station where he was currently testing a new fighter. Rebecca worked in a laboratory nearby. Eleven years after the end of the war, life was better for him than any man had a right to expect. The recollections Arcadia revived were of another life, a different man.

*

Jim had been in two minds about attending an occasion he saw as exclusively British, but Jenny had talked him into accepting the invitation as a former cadet at Carlstrom and as founder of the Jaytee Flying Academy. She had been so supportive during the bad times, and instrumental in persuading him to get the business off the ground during those rocky years after the war, so he had caved in, believing that she hoped returning to Arcadia might finally lay the ghosts.

In truth, the several years of pain and endeavour in his bid to recover from crippling injuries, followed by several more of uncertainty over the success of his venture had driven them to the furthest recesses of his mind. Coming back had dragged them out again, and he was lost in a past that seemed to concern someone other than himself. Those four merry aviators were no more. Peter Kelsey had taken his own life, unable to face being permanently chairbound. Bucket was a drummer with a dance band. Finding it impossible to settle to civilian life, the constant travelling, the escape from reality in dance halls lit by a circling glass ball, and being part of a masculine group eased his restlessness. There were thousands of men like him across America, who had been snatched up by war then set down again to make what they could of their lives.

Gazing at the hot sky as he sat in the chair provided for him, Jim recalled his frustration over being unable to conquer the landing technique. How long ago the first time he had taken off to first fly solo! 'Even goddam Mickey Mouse could have done it by now.' Theo was living in Hong Kong. Too many men in high places had owed him a favour, so he had survived, if not unscathed at least unbowed. Shelley was now married to the head of a diamond corporation. Jim had no contact with either of them, so Theo had never seen his two grandsons. When James Theodore Benson II broke with someone, it was final. Jim was more than happy with that.

*

Rob happily greeted the Fosters and others he had known during that short but intense period of his life. They appeared untouched by the

305

years, except that the young girls were now married women with children. They all kissed him enthusiastically, and Rebecca whispered teasingly, 'Are they some of all those girls you fell for at first sight?'

'I was a mere callow youth,' he whispered back. Then all amusement fled as he glanced away and saw his sister gazing at him across the plot containing the white headstones.

'Did you know about this?' he demanded of his wife, still looking at Jenny.

'Of course. We planned it together as soon as I knew you were coming here.'

Jenny crossed to him, sun-tanned and smiling. 'Hallo, Rob. Welcome back to America.' She kissed him, then laughed with the delight of her surprise. 'You should see your expression.'

Rob realized that her letter expressing regret that she would be in Alaska during his brief official visit to America had been part of the plan hatched by two scheming women. The truth suddenly dawned. 'Is *he* here?'

'Of course. Rebecca and I thought it was time we got you two together, and what better place than here?' Jenny linked her arm through Rob's. 'Come on, one of you has to make the first move.'

He hesitated, but only momentarily. In this earth lay young men such as he had been, who had crossed the Atlantic to see this land of sunshine and plenty in order to learn to fly in defence of their country and loved ones. Tragically taken too soon, they were to be honoured today. It was time those allies who had survived became friends.

As they approached, Rob saw his brother-in-law rise from his chair, disdaining the walking stick leaning against it. He was probably still every girl's dreamboat despite fine lines etched by pain around his eyes and mouth, and the stiffness of one leg.

They regarded each other warily for a moment or two, then Rob said, 'I suppose we acted like a pair of bloody fools.'

'Well, we were very young.'

He glanced at the two rows of headstones. 'We all were.'

R.N. Stallard offered his hand. J.T. Benson took it, and their grip tightened until bones almost cracked.

Printed in Great Britain
by Amazon

19454085R00180